BRIGHT MORNING STAR

J.R.BIERY

Cover created with Gimp 2, using a background image from NASA and free commercial use licensed image from Bing of a photograph from the Wagon Train Exhibit in National Historic Oregon Trail Interpretative Center in Baker City, Oregon.

ISBN-13: 978-1515148821
ISBN-10: 1515148823

ABOUT THIS BOOK

Claire Wimberley is an adorable blonde, blue-eyed beauty with little in her head, but dreams and a love for the latest fashion. Although she has worked in the mills in Boston, she has been the spoiled only child of a middle class family. Her best friends are poor Irish girls whose families are always struggling. When first one, then the other, face terrible tragedies, Claire is the first to offer a helping hand and her loving support. Soon she is traveling the Oregon Trail with Lynne's little sister and brothers and her other best friend, Bonnie. Along the trail, Claire must face the fact that she is in love with a married man despite his bitter wife. She is able to be strong until Bonnie is captured by Indians and Bella, the man's wife is murdered in another attack. Can a girl who has never worn anything second-hand in her life settle for a second-hand husband?

DISCLAIMER

DEDICATION

Dedicated to Jerry, my darling husband for forty-seven years. Also, thanks to the members of the Cookeville Creative Writers' Association who prodded and nudged me forward. Special thanks to those who have read the previous three books and written to ask for another. Claire's story is dedicated to all of you. Special thanks to early readers JoAnn, Linda, and Vera. Greatly appreciated.

CHAPTER ONE

Boston, MA 1876

Claire Wimberley untied the ribbons from her favorite bonnet and set the tiny spring-flowered confection on the wagon seat. She fluffed at her hair, with the length pulled up into a subdued knot, the ends into her usual ringlets bounced. She shook her head and exchanged a smile with her friend, Bonnie. The tall, serious girl pointed to her Da and brother Clyde. The man was trying to get the little boy to feed grass to one of the giant oxen and the three-year old was having none of it.

"Do you know where Mother is?" Claire asked.

"Inside changing, as you should be," Bonnie answered.

Claire knew she wasn't dressed for someone setting out by wagon from Boston to the wild West. But today, at early mass, was the first time she had worn the lovely green dress and she wanted to enjoy it. Henry and his wife should be here soon. After all, she had purchased the dress from the Lambtons and knew they would want to admire how well it fit and how becoming the color was with her blond hair.

The children were wild with excitement. Bonnie's four younger sisters, and Lynne's one, ran about the yard and street squealing as they wove a bright pattern of color against the muddied lawn. Mary Anne stopped, alternating giggles and tight tearful hugs with her best friend Meara. The two seven year old's were close, like Claire, Lynne, and Bonnie. She and her friends had done everything together, even working in the mill until it closed recently. Now Lynne was married to a rancher in Montana and Claire's family was carrying her younger brothers and sister to join her there.

Claire studied the pretty little girl, her gray eyes stormier than ever as she talked with Meara. Mary Anne had nearly died of Typhoid fever like her mother. Now at first glance, the two girls looked alike. Both wore Claire's remade dresses. Both had long brownish hair, although Meara's was redder and she was blessed with laughing blue eyes.

All the Magee's had blue eyes, but Bonnie, whose eyes were hazel. Gold or green when she was happy, a muddy brown when sad. And the tall woman supervising the children had been terribly sad. Tarn Michaels, the handsome man she married, turned out to be a monster. After beating Bonnie and causing her to lose their child, he had fled. Claire stared, amazed that there was no trace of all Bonnie had suffered.

Luckily Claire had been able to convince her parents to let Bonnie move in with them. After their maid quit, Bonnie had taken over the woman's duties as cook and housekeeper. Claire stared at the little girls and felt a twinge of regret. She watched them hook their fingers to make a 'pinky swear.'

She loved Bonnie as much as ever and she knew Bonnie felt the same about her. But there was a difference. Even though Bonnie lived with Claire, and they continued to work side-by-side at Lambton's shop, their relationship had changed.

"I'll be right back, yell when the Lambton's arrive," Claire called.

"Wipe your feet, I've no time to be redoing floors," Bonnie said.

Claire wandered through the empty house, feeling a lump in her throat for the first time. This was the only home she'd ever known. It seemed smaller without furniture or all the people crowded into it. For the last three months, the three Wimberleys had made room for Bonnie, the twins, and Mary Anne. Now all seven of them would make the trip together.

The last two weeks had flown with all the packing and Bonnie's family helping to take the extra things they didn't want to move. She had not stopped to worry about all she was leaving. From the bathroom, she heard a strange noise. Timidly she knocked at the door and whispered, "Mother?"

Claire heard a choked sob on the other side of the door. She waited, then opened the door as her mother called come in. Her beautiful mother sat on top of the closed box, busy wiping her nose and eyes. Claire flew in to take her into her arms. "Oh Mother, what's wrong?"

Elizabeth Wimberley blew her nose and tried for a watery smile. “Just feeling foolishly sentimental dear. I’m ready. Did you need a minute to change?”

Claire shook her head, irritated that everyone was making the same suggestion. “I decided to wear this. But talk to me Mother, I can tell something is wrong. You never cry.”

“I’ll be all right. I just need a minute to calm down before your Father gets back. He’s so excited about the trip, and has been counting the minutes. You know how he is.”

“I know. I thought you were excited too. Don’t you want to go out west?”

Mother choked on a loud sob and Claire hugged her tighter, shocked for a minute. She had never asked, none of them had asked what her Mother wanted. She tried to imagine what it must be like for her mother. She was leaving friends and neighbors, her church, her home, and her beloved gardens. At least when they reached Utah, Claire would have all her family and dear friends around. With the Lambtons coming along, she would even have her employers there as well.

Rocking her mother in her arms, Claire continued to babble, hugging her close. “It’s the lawn and flowers isn’t it. Because Father laughed about them this morning. I know he is proud to have another unpleasant surprise for that scalawag buyer. Poor Mother, you worked so hard on your roses and flowers. But we can plant some when we reach our new home. There is a lot more sunshine each year out west. You will have the most beautiful flowers for miles around. Father will build you an even bigger and finer house, you'll see. It will be wonderful."

Elizabeth Wimberley hugged her daughter and smiled at Claire for the first time. "Of course, maybe we can even dig some root stock for the new rose garden if we hurry."

Suddenly they heard yelling from outside.

"Come on then, sounds like Father and the Lambtons are here," Claire said, tugging her along.

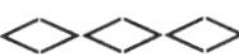

Claire watched the McKinney twins tumble down from the second wagon, running up to look around at the harnessed oxen.

"Aw, you should have waited on us, we could have yoked up the teams," Jim complained.

"I know you could, but Da and the girl's wanted something to do so, they helped me do it," Bonnie explained.

"Did you remember to make the picnic lunch?" his brother Tom asked.

Bonnie smiled, "I packed it, and all the other food in the house. We're all ready to leave."

The little girls had rushed to surround Bella's little boy and Claire wondered again at how strange it was. Little Barney with his tremors and jerks repulsed her, but seemed to fascinate all the children. They seemed to find him beautiful and sweet, perfectly precious in Mary Anne's words.

Bonnie yelled, “We’re all ready to leave.” It galvanized everyone. The Magees left Barney Lambton to crowd against Bonnie.

Father was talking with Mother about the flowers. Claire saw him start to protest before he noticed her mother’s tear- streaked face. Wearily he nodded and took a shovel and burlap sack and walked to dig each one as she gave him directions. He and the lads would have worked hard loading the store stock and household furniture with the Lambtons, yet he still took time to make her mother happy.

Claire stood restlessly, looking from one group to another. She saw Bonnie crying, the first tears she’d seen in her friend’s eyes since the week when they had first brought her home. Heartbroken at losing her baby, racked with pain, Bonnie had been half-out of her mind in a drugged stupor and always sobbing.

Bonnie’s Mum and Da held the tall woman the longest, their voices as watery as her own. “You’ll be careful. You’ll write, like your friend Lynne did?” Mum asked.

“I’ll be fine,” Bonnie said. “I’ll check on the boys when we reach Ohio. Father Wimberley thinks we’ll be there before they ship out. I’ll send mail back from there and remind them to write you too.” Bonnie raised a hand to her throat, watched Mary Anne and Meara embrace beside her. “If you move, how will my letters reach you?”

“Send them to Father Patrick at the rectory. He’ll get them to us,” Da said.

Claire felt her own throat close up and could feel tears threatening to spill. Bless the poor girl. How must it feel to be like Lynne and Bonnie, torn from those you love? She could never leave her parents. She turned to stare at them, saw her mother close to tears again as her father protested digging up bulbs and the peonies. She heard his loud sigh and breathed deeply as she saw him raise her mother's chin with his dirty finger, and then plant a kiss on her lips before moving over to dig the bed of tulips.

Claire sighed at the gestures of love all around her. Quickly, she dared to look over at the Lambtons. Bella was fussing with the boy on the seat of the wagon. Henry Lambton stood at the back, raising the tailgate where he had rearranged a couple of boxes. She dared a glance, noticing the cloth tight across his shoulders in the white shirt. She blushed, afraid to be caught staring at the handsome man. He banged the gate latch home and lifted his jacket to slide back into it. Fastidiously tailored at all times, like her, he had not donned trail clothes yet.

Claire turned back to see Bonnie receiving tender hugs and kisses of farewell from each family member. She saw her father loading the shovel and sack of bulbs and roots, then helping her mother up into the wagon. He called to Claire and she rushed forward past the Lambton's wagon.

"A beautiful day for our trip," she said to Bella, noting she had arranged the little boy in the floor box of the wagon.

"Yes, beautiful, as are you my dear in your new dress."

Claire whirled, hoping the flounces of the pseudo-bustle were still neatly in place. "Yes, it fits perfectly, don't you think?"

Bella's gaze darkened as she nodded, but Claire was afraid to look for approval from Henry Lambton. Dropping a quick curtsy to her employer, she raced forward, surprised when Henry followed to give her a hand up onto the seat in the wagon behind her mother's.

Nervously Claire accepted his steadying hand.

"Most becoming," he whispered.

Claire kept her eyes lowered, but felt a tremble at his touch. She sat breathlessly on the seat of the second tandem wagons. In minutes, they were off.

Claire listened and clucked to the long line of animals in front of her. There were three pairs of oxen pulling each double wagon team. She copied the calls her mother made, and made sure the brake was off as Father had instructed. Behind her, she heard Bella's shrill voice make the same sounds. Claire knew it wasn't the same as driving a team of horses or mules. These dumb plodding animals would move as the person walking beside them directed. But still, she wanted to do her part right.

It was quiet on the empty streets now they had left the noisy Magees behind. Claire had watched the family with another loaded wheelbarrow wave and Bonnie throw a last wave and kisses after them.

With the signing bonuses for Bonnie's brothers, Ian and Shawn, her parents had money for the first time in ages. With the boon of their household belongings that her Mother couldn't pack, the Magees had told Bonnie they were ready to move into a house of their own.

Although they had seemed grateful, Claire was surprised they didn't fuss more about the Wimberley's generosity. Proud Irish indeed. They had accepted the gifts without any insistence from the Wimberleys, much like Bonnie took Claire's old dresses from the charity barrel for her sisters.

What did it matter that they would have had to pay to have someone to cart the extra furniture and clothes to the dump or the church? Worse, they might have left it behind for the new owner. Claire's Father had insisted on taking or removing everything useful. He was still upset at having to take a lower price for the factory and their house from the same southerner who had been driving his business into the ground. Still, there were a lot of good things and she knew she would have acted more grateful than the Magees.

Embarrassed at her pettiness, Claire looked forward at the young woman walking beside the head of her oxen team. Willow they had called the tall, reed slim girl. Bonnie had been Claire's protector from the teasing and jealousy of the other children when she started school. She had adopted Claire and Lynn McKinney as though they were all sisters. Devoted friends, they had been together ever since. Lynne had been the sensible one, Bonnie the protector, and Claire had been called goose.

For something to do, Claire shook the lines over the back of the cattle and one of them mooed in protest. Bonnie looked back at her in surprise and Claire shrugged her shoulders and relaxed. She hated the nickname Goose. She wasn't a fool.

She made an effort not to look behind her. Maybe she was. From the first moment she saw him she had been in love with an unattainable man. All she wanted was a true love. All three girls had wanted the same, a man as good to them as their own fathers. Lynne had found one. Unlike her first letter about the ordeals of her trip, the last one had been full of gushing examples of how wonderful Phillip Gant, her new husband was.

Bonnie certainly hadn't been that smart. Tarn Michaels had been a handsome devil, but he had only shown his devilish side to the poor girl.

Claire looked down at her hands shaking on the reins. Wasn't she in danger of doing the same thing? Risking her heart on a handsome man. Worse, Henry Lambton was married, and to judge by Bella, not the kind of husband she wanted at all. Claire ran a hand over her sides and squirmed on the hard bench. If they ever stopped, the first thing she was going to do was get rid of her corset.

CHAPTER TWO

Father announced at the beginning there would be no stopping until nightfall. At the pace the oxen moved, if someone needed to get down to find a bush or just walk or run around, they could. Claire looked at Bonnie as she hurried around, handing out the cold biscuit sandwiches she had made that morning. Fidgeting, Claire took the biscuit and whispered, "I need to get down, but I don't think I can with the wheel turning."

Bonnie signaled Henry Lambton and yelled to Father Wimberley. "Stopping for a minute." The tall girl then grabbed the lead pairs yoke and yelled "whoa." While waiting for Claire to copy the gesture with the reins.

Minutes later a red-faced Claire clambered down and headed for the bushes. She could hear her Father complaining, but a minute later her Mother and Mary Anne joined her. The little girl had been running alongside as much as she had ridden up on the wagons. Her hair ribbon dangled untied and she was covered with sweat and a light film of dust. It only made her happy smile more charming.

"Sorry, I just was afraid to get my dress caught in the wagon-wheel," Claire said.

“Thank heavens, I was ready to pop. Your father is impossible,” Mother said.

Bella stumbled as she walked over to join the group and Bonnie took over shepherding Barney along. “Men, just because they can stand by a tree and it’s so easy for them,” Bella fumed.

Afterward, the ladies stopped to rinse their hands and walk about. The men looked as grateful for the break as the women and animals. Mary Anne showed each of the women in her favorite tricks for climbing up and down safely. Claire walked with her mother to give her a boost up.

“You’re lucky you have that silly bustle, this seat is killing me,” Mother said.

“Maybe we can make cushions or something,” Claire said.

“Father brought his empty feed sacks, in case we get grain along the way,” Mother said.

Refreshed with her lunch beside her, Claire smiled and lifted her head toward the sunshine all around them. It really was wonderful to be riding along on the covered wagon, after listening to her father and the McKinney boys talk so much about them. So far, the trip had been easy.

The road was the wonderful macadam surface made of finely crushed compacted rock. The few wagons and buggies they met seemed annoyed, but were easily able to work around the train with its three sets of tandem wagons. The big oxen with their amazing horns walked along contentedly as though pulling the joined wagons with their heavy loads was easy. So far on the well-graded roads there had been no large hills to contend with. Occasionally, they could still catch a glimpse of the ocean far off beyond the trees and fields. Claire sighed in contentment and devoured her cold biscuit.

Finally the light was fading. As they passed a farmhouse and empty fields, Father Wimberley left them. He walked out to the house to ask the farmer if he knew a safe place they could stop and camp for the night.

When he came back, he was red-faced and wouldn't answer any of their questions except to nod. A bearded man soon walked down and smiled at them. "I haven't seen this big an outfit in years."

"Oh," Father Wimberley said. At the man's smile he answered. "It's just my family and friends. We plan to join a bigger outfit when we reach Missouri."

The farmer led them over a hill and off the road onto a grassy area. He helped them make the first awkward circle of the wagons in the field of high grass. "First ones through this month, got some good food for your animals, right beside the river here with plenty of sweet water." He walked them down and while the men led the oxen to drink, Bonnie started a fire and began to cook while Mother Wimberley kept her company. Claire walked down to the river and watched the men and boys stand beside the big oxen. The animals waited their turn to wade out into the mud of the bank and drink their fill.

Refusing to feel guilty for not helping, Claire wandered back. When a rabbit jumped across the path she let out a little squeal. She was surprised when Mary Anne was the only one to look her way. Little Barney was busy doing his wheeling, awkward version of walking where he wanted to lean down and grab grass or weeds. The little girl went back to paying attention to him. Off the path, there were daffodils blooming near the small clearing. Claire wondered if there had been a house here once, maybe a modest frontier cabin. As she looked about she found a couple of split rails.

Satisfied that she was right, she looked along the fence row for anything else of value. She was rewarded by a thick clump of weeds that she recognized from their own garden. Thinking to please her mother, she gathered as much as she could carry and rushed back to the fire.

The men were returning and Claire picked her way carefully through the soft fading light. It didn't take long to learn to watch your step where the oxen had been. When her father called to her to be careful, she gave him a smile, aware of another set of blue eyes following her progress.

While the men led the oxen into the circle, they used the oxen yokes between the spread out wagons to make the circle large enough to contain all the animals. Claire dropped the bundle of fragrant herbs at her mother's feet.

"Fresh mint," Mother exclaimed.

Claire smiled. "There are the remains of a cabin closer to the river. There were daffodils growing near the road, so I looked around. I remembered you told me they never grew wild, just where the settlers had planted them."

Claire's mother lifted a single fat leaf and rubbed it between her fingers. The scent of mint filled the night air. But instead of making her happy, it brought tears to her mother's eyes.

"Your father was in such a rush this morning, I didn't dare ask him to dig the daffodils too."

Claire leaned over to hug her mother while Bonnie laid her spoon down by the fire and walked over to smell the mint. "I can brew a good tea with this. Do you want me to braid it while the beans are cooking?"

Mother Wimberley nodded and rose stiffly.

"Come on Mother," Claire said, "We can take the lantern for when it gets dark and I'll show you the place. Maybe there is something good still growing there. I'm sure Father will be happy to dig some for you before we leave in the morning. He has to go past it to water the oxen in the morning anyway.

As though one of the smelly beasts knew they were being talked about, it bellowed loudly. As the women walked past, they could hear the men talking beside the wagons.

"Where are your horses?" the farmer asked.

"Decided we didn't need them," Father said. "The women don't ride."

"Oh, that's a mistake. You need at least two good ones. Save you money in the long run. That way one of you can ride ahead, locate a campsite and the water hole before dark. You just lucked out making it this far before having to stop."

Claire and her mother smiled at each other. The man must think he had a pair of suckers, ready for the plucking. Her father looked the part of a traveler, in his sensible brown woolen clothes. But Henry looked every bit the part of the city slicker, out in the country for the first time.

Claire knew her father would have enough sense to ignore the huckster. She certainly had no intention of climbing onto the back of any smelly old horse. Sidesaddles were treacherous devices, as the victims of the runaway mount in the city could attest. Besides, neither she nor Mother had a riding habit. The idea of riding made her shudder.

Bonnie walked out to join the two women, whispering, "I need to find a bush, might as well go together. Mary Anne promised to watch the fire, and Bella took over braiding the mint since Barney wanted to keep pulling leaves to smell it.

As they passed the talking men, Bonnie stopped to stand with them and waved the women on into the fading light.

"How far out of Boston are we?" Father Wimberley asked.

"About twelve miles. Now, that will be $1.50 for the night."

Claire watched her Father stiffen. That was as much as a week's wages at the mill when she and the girl's had first started. She understood why he looked so angry and was arguing with the man.

"There are only two families here, the spare wagons in tandem are to carry goods we plan to sell in Independence. I thought you said two bits per family."

"I can let you stay, for seventy-five cents, but that's the best I can do. You've got eighteen oxen, that's a lot."

As she and Mother walked on Claire was shocked to hear Bonnie's voice.

"For water and grass growing along the river?" Bonnie asked.

It wasn't dark, but might be by the time they returned. Claire watched her mother use her pocket striker to light the lantern, then look around in satisfaction as she patted Claire's shoulder. Her mother found a rambling rose, the daffodils and a woody herb called rosemary that was growing like a bush. Poor father, Claire didn't want to be the one to tell him, she would leave it to mother.

Back at the camp circle she heard Bonnie's strong voice first. The boys had raced back with a barrow full of dried corn and she was telling them what to do next. Maybe that was the difference. Bonnie had always been the quiet, timid one. Now she was always wanting to tell others what to do.

"Go on, go get a couple more before it's too dark, we girls can take care of that," Bonnie said.

She waved to Claire. "Here, help me spread this out."

Claire stood still, then let her mother take the lantern back toward the fire. "How, what?" she asked.

"Hurry, I've got to get back to the dinner. Just throw a handful of cobs where they can reach it. They'll take care of shelling it."

"Can they eat that much?" Tom asked as the big oxen happily crunched the hard corn. Jim turned back with the empty wheelbarrow.

"We'll throw it on top in the wagon with the tools. No sense letting that farmer skin us. Hurry, but stay together," Bonnie yelled.

She took Claire's arm and helped her throw a handful to one of the giant oxen. "See?"

Claire didn't want to scream, but the big animals suddenly all seemed to be ambling in her direction.

"Just throw a handful out in a lot of directions. Hurry before they get to the big pile and start fighting over it."

"Bonnie, something is burning," Bella called out in her shrill voice.

And Claire was alone.

For a moment she thought about running back to the fire. One of the big oxen mooed loudly, and Claire bent down. She grabbed four or five cobs at a time and tossed them in the direction of whichever ox seemed the closest.

Finally, she was not coming up with any more and she realized the cows were busy swishing their tails and eating. Sighing with relief, Claire stood in the lengthening shadows. Bonnie had believed she could do it and Claire had fed the oxen by herself. Just like at the mill, she could learn to do any job if she put her mind to it. Although, like there, there were still many jobs she had no intention of learning or doing. The first was how to start a fire or cook. Look where that had gotten Bonnie.

It was dark and the women strained to hear the voices of the men and boys as they plodded back to camp. The men were silent but she could hear Tom and Jim giggling. The two men carried burlap totes full of corn while the boys pushed the last overloaded barrow.

Men and boys were all grateful for the river water Bonnie and Claire had carried. Claire stared as her father splashed water greedily while Henry stood there, shaking out his coat first and brushing his pants. She was grateful for the shadows near the end of her wagon. She watched Henry unbutton his shirt sleeves and deliberately shrub his hands and face to remove all the chaff and dust.

Claire joined the women as Mother and Bella set out the stools around the flat boards. Her Father had planned for everything, even made special sanded boards to fit together to serve as a table on the long trip.

"I don't know about the rest of you, but I am so exhausted," Claire said with a sigh. Still, the warm food was wonderful, even if it was just beans, cornbread and pork. "Thank you Bonnie, I'm going to bed," Claire mumbled, as soon as she finished.

Bonnie smiled, looking tired herself. Bonnie collected the tin plates and shooed everyone off to bed. Claire knew she would sleep well tonight.

CHAPTER THREE

Claire climbed over the tailgate, already looking forward to sleeping on her feather mattress. It rested atop all the crates and boxes containing china, linen, and decorative items that her mother could not bear to part with. She unbuttoned her new dress, depressed at the thought that she would have to wear the plain serviceable clothing for the duration of the trip. At least she had been given the chance to look pretty for one day.

She unbuttoned and removed her shoes, unhooked and unfastened the front of her dress while sitting on top of the bed. She felt something move beside her on the mattress. Mary Anne had climbed in and out of every wagon all day. Irritated, Claire was going to tell the child that whatever she had found to play with, she should have put away.

Claire smiled. The girl was outside still, helping Bonnie wash up the metal plates for the next day. There was no way to scold a child who was as sweet as little Mary Anne.

Resigned, Claire stood ready to move whatever was rolling on the bed to put it away. When she put her hand down to reach it in the dark, it moved.

Her scream shattered the darkness, blood-curdling with terror. The others were already in their wagons ready for bed, except for Bonnie and Mary Anne by the fire.

The twins were in the wagon they would share with Bonnie for the trip, looking out toward the fire and trying not to laugh. Claire almost tripped as she fell out of the wagon. Her mother and father were the first to react, but it was Bonnie, who caught the hysterical girl. Claire's dress was down around her waist, her small breasts squeezed high above the tight little corset that she had suffered through wearing all day.

Bonnie caught and sheltered her in her arms drawing her away from the fire where she was clearly on display. Bella yelled at Henry when he started out of the wagon to help the half-dressed girl and he realized himself in time. Father Wimberley climbed down, fastening his shirt. By then, Bonnie had helped Claire back into her dress and the girl was almost coherent enough to tell her father that there was a serpent in her bed.

Robert Wimberley yelled at the top of his lungs. "Tom and Jim McKinney. Out here on the double."

The young boys stood before him, trying to look innocent but looking guiltier by the moment. “I don’t care which one of you did it, but both of you climb in there and don’t come out until you’ve caught that snake. And don’t you dare pretend you don’t know what I’m talking about.”

Bonnie released her friend into her father’s care. “You’re saying those boys think it’s funny to release a poisonous snake into someone’s wagon?”

He turned so he was whispering to both older girls. Mary Anne danced around outside the wagon where she had been planning to go to sleep, afraid and excited to see a real snake.

“The farmer warned us he kept a couple of snakes in his corn crib. Told us to not be afraid. They’re nonpoisonous but deadly to mice, rats, and poisonous snakes that get into the feed. I knew the boys were asking a lot of questions about it at the time. But I thought we were lucky when we didn’t see any.”

Mary Anne squealed and backed up to stand, dancing around next to Claire who was standing in her stocking feet, shivering.

The boys held out the bright red patterned snake and it curled its five foot length up around Jim’s hand. Even Bonnie stepped back behind Mr. Wimberley, who shuddered.

Using his angriest voice, he said. “You little-son-of-a-guns, I ought to tan your hides. If you weren’t sleeping with

Miss Magee, I'd make you try to get some sleep with that monster in your bed."

The boys at least had enough sense to look ashamed.

"But it's late, and it will be morning before you know it. I want you to take that thing up the path toward that fellow's barn. Don't release it anywhere near these wagons or the oxen. You pull a prank like this again, and I'll blister your bottoms good."

The boys were gone in a shot. In the distance, they heard them arguing about who should get to carry the snake.

Bonnie was the first to laugh and Father Wimberley gave a snort and grabbed Claire's shoulder. "You going to be all right, girl?"

"I guess. That was the most terrifying experience of my life. I will pay those two scamps back, if it's the last thing I do."

Bonnie patted her shoulder. "Don't be too mad, they didn't know how scared you would be. Besides, like your father said, they were just trying to have a little fun. Lord knows they have little enough time for it, with all the work they have to do every day."

Claire nodded and started to climb back in the wagon and then stopped. Her eyes were round and her voice trembled. "What if they brought more than one?"

Her father wasn't sure, but he tried to be positive. "They'd still be in there trying to catch it. You heard them arguing about whose turn it was to carry it. With two, they'd be fighting about something else. Go on," he leaned close and gave her a kiss on the cheek. "Get some sleep."

As she still stood there, poised on the step to go in, he lifted Mary Anne up. The little girl slipped past Claire to look around, just in case there was another snake. She wanted to be the one to catch it.

Bonnie went to bed, exhausted but still smiling. When the twins came back minutes later they were whistling in the dark to keep from being afraid. She leaned out of the end of the wagon and shouted, "boo!" As both jumped, she laughed at them.

Only after she had made them wash the snake off their hands would she let them climb into her wagon. Finally the twins settled down, one on either side of her as usual to keep them from fighting. Tom said "We're sorry, Aunt Bonnie, we didn't think it would scare her that bad."

Bonnie reached over and tugged his nose hard. "Stop lying and go to sleep."

Jim sat up and stared at her, determined to ask. "But Aunt Bonnie, what was that thing she had on under her dress? It looked like it was squeezing the life out of her."

Instead of laughing, Bonnie reached out and lightly smacked him on the cheek. "A corset, now get still and go to sleep."

They both were quiet for several minutes before Tom whispered again, “I’m glad you don’t worry about looking pretty, Aunt Bonnie.”

“That’s it.” Bonnie sat up and began pinching both until they were begging for mercy and howling. When she stopped, no one said a word.

Claire pulled on the tan, linsey-woolsey dress over her chemise and bloomers. She had stored the corset and elaborate petticoat away, along with her cute high-tops. The end of the trail seemed ages away. Lord, in six months she would be nearly eighteen. She wedged her small feet into her sensible boots. Hating to, she pulled on the big tan poke bonnet that had been recommended for the trail.

Unlike Bonnie’s loose fitting dark brown dress, Claire’s was tailored. It was very simple except for the carefully sewn smocking at the waist, neck, and sleeves. She had used the same material and design in the ugly, full-brimmed bonnet. For the first time in ages, she didn’t bother to comb any of her curls into ringlets since they would be hidden under the hideous hat.

Mary Anne came back to check on what was taking so long, everyone else was through with breakfast. “Bonnie said you need to hurry.”

Claire almost said what she thought of Bonnie Magee giving her orders, but didn't bother. Looking one last time in her hand mirror, she slid it into the carefully compartmentalized trunk and stopped. She grabbed and tucked the small atomizer into her sleeve and rushed before her breakfast was packed away for lunch.

Bonnie handed her friend a tin plate with gravy and biscuits and the last cup of coffee. She leaned to look down the large brim into her friends' sparkling blue eyes.

"Only you could make a simple traveling dress look so fashionable."

"You don't think it's too plain," Claire leaned closer to whisper. "I've given up the corset until we reach Ogden."

"No one could tell, you've such a tiny waist anyway. I like it, but can you see out of that big funnel?"

"Of course, if I take my time. You know how fair I am, I can't risk burning up under the blazing sun. Besides, Mother and I made them to match."

Claire sat to quickly crumble the first biscuit and spoon it up with the gravy.

Bonnie smiled and shook her head. Today looked to be as fair as the day before. Everywhere one looked, it was green. The oxen lowed as they grazed the lush grass and the three children ran about, the twins teasing Mary Anne for a minute with a pretend snake. Father Wimberley called for the twins to go see Claire, and then help water the stock.

Claire finished the last bite of biscuit and handed her friend her plate. She stood and took a gulp of the strong brew, almost missing her mouth because of the edge of the big bonnet. Irritated, she loosened the string and let it fall to hang down her back.

Mary Anne ran up beside her and copied Claire's stiff pose. Claire took a second swallow, and handed the little girl, her cup to hold, as she dealt with the boys. Almost eleven, the lads were tall and sturdy, with light brown hair and teasing blue eyes. Like their sisters, they were only half-Irish, but that was the half always thinking up mischief.

Claire waited until the pink cheeked boys began to stumble out an apology. "I think you ought to kneel, lads, if you're truly sorry."

They looked at each other and then up into the guileless eyes of Claire. Father Wimberley yelled something in their direction, and both boys dropped to their knees.

Again she heard the words "We're sorry, Aunt Claire."

"For what are you sorry boys?" she let her voice quaver, remembering her fright and embarrassment the night before. "For terrifying me half to death. For putting a serpent into my bed and then laughing at my terror. For making me run screaming into the night half-dressed."

The boys made the mistake of looking at each other, their lips half-curled in memory of their successful prank.

Quickly, before they could spring away, Claire pulled out her bottle and sprayed both with the heavy floral scent.

Tom moved first, falling backward as he did. Claire doused him good. As Jim danced out of reach she yelled for reinforcements. Laughing, Mary Anne clapped and giggled in the background, Claire laughed when Henry Lampton blocked Jim's escape. More carefully, trying to make sure she only got her scent on the boy, she squirted him even more.

Mary Anne teased, "Oh, but boys you do smell pretty."

The twins looked like they were going to take their outrage out on their little sister.

Henry released the boy and just stood staring at Claire as she laughed at both of them. Bonnie moved up to grab each lad by the scruff of the neck before they could reach Mary Anne.

"Aw, gee, you didn't have to soak our clothes, Aunt Claire. Now the oxen will run when we get near."

"Good, we'll make better time." Bonnie said, as she gave each lad a shake and a sound swat before turning them toward the cattle.

Father Wimberley stood laughing, pretending to switch the boys as they herded the oxen down to the river.

He let the lads grumble a little more, then said. "That's a lesson you'd better learn now. You'd best never try to trick or harm a woman."

They started to argue, then both grew quiet. "What do you mean, they'll all gang up on you?" Jim asked.

Tom swatted at some of the gnats lying low on the river bank, Jim was doing the same. They let the first yoked animals step into the water and Father Wimberley knelt and came up with a handful of mud for each of them.

"There, best rub that around on your neck and ears, so the bugs don't eat you alive today. They might think you're some kind of new, two-legged posie."

Each boy smelled the muck and then carefully applied it to their faces and the rest of their exposed skin. Mr. Wimberley yelled and the first pair of oxen splashed back onto the bank to graze while another set took their place.

"Then what did you mean?" Tom asked.

"I mean a woman has hundreds of ways to get you back, and they always will. A sweet girl, like our Claire, she might look like she's going to cry, then spray you with a little perfume. A mean one, might try to hurt you. An angry one, might just nag you to death." He didn't have to say like Bella. "Another might burn all your food, or put starch in your underwear. There's a lot more ways, but you'll learn those when you're a little older. No, the reason you better treat women like ladies and show them respect is it's dangerous not to. Women will always use some of their wily ways against you, if you don't treat them right."

CHAPTER FOUR

There was a lot of arguing from the Lambton's wagon each evening, then a lot of crying and pleading from Bella. Everyone looked uncomfortable around the battling couple, waiting for the storm to pass. Nearly two weeks after leaving Boston, Henry shared what was upsetting his wife.

"Bella wanted to stop in New Rochelle seeing her parents. She's afraid she might never get to see them again if we don't stop now. But it will mean about a four hour delay in our trek across country, and the trip's long enough. I've tried to convince her it's not fair to the group, but Bella doesn't care about inconveniencing everyone else."

The Wimberleys stared at him in disbelief. Claire felt a little tremble in her own heart. What if it were her parents? What if it were her last chance for a kiss or hug from them? Henry was still talking.

"Well, I've agreed to stop. We'll just keep moving when you make camp. And then the next morning, we'll hustle. Try to catch up with you in the next day or two," he said.

Robert Wimberley looked speechless for a moment, then shook his head. “No need for all that. We’ll stick together. Sleeping with the wagons, we can go anywhere. Tell Bella we’re happy to stop. Looking forward to meeting her parents.”

The change in Bella was remarkable. The next day she was all smiles, rushing to help the other women with the cooking, fussing over what she should wear for the visit. Claire could not remember when the woman had looked happier or prettier. Even the first day of their big sale at the old store had not affected her as much.

The happier Bella became, the more attentive and kindly Henry treated her. After seeing nothing but sparring between the couple before, Claire felt strangely betrayed by the sudden peace between them.

Claire sat in her usual position on the wagon, behind the oxen and their smelly tails. She had her magazines on the bench beside her, but flipped through them restlessly.

Henry Lambton emerged from the woods, something held behind his back. Claire swiveled on the padded bench to look as soon as he walked past. When she saw he clutched a fistful of wild Iris, their purple blooms furled like organza over their blade-like leaves, her heart sank. This time she recognized it as jealousy.

By now it was a familiar ache. When she first went to work for the Lambtons, she had found Henry to be the first person who valued the things that she did. When she talked about fashion, everyone else tuned her out. Henry was interested in all things sartorial and fashionable. He appreciated her ideas for marketing their goods and listened when she suggested the store hold a sale. He asked for her advice when placing orders and pricing goods.

She had enjoyed this respect for her intelligence. Growing up being called goose, even by her best friends, it was a welcome change. Other than that, she thought nothing about Henry. He was nice, handsome, and well-mannered. But he was married.

True, Bella Lambton was a cold, angry woman. He deserved someone better, someone who respected and cared for him. Claire remembered the first time she realized she might have feelings for another woman's husband.

As always, it was one of her friend who pointed it out to her. The Lambtons had a terrible row in the store and Bonnie had handed little Barney off to Claire to tend while she went up front to break up the fight.

Later, Bonnie had laughed when Claire looked offended. "I had no choice. I didn't want my bosses to get into a donnybrook in the front of the store. Who would pay us then?"

Claire agreed. "They were having a terrible fight, weren't they?"

"Aye, besides, I knew you worked wonders with children," Bonnie said.

Claire looked surprised. She had thought it was Bonnie, who had the way with children, not her. Slowly she had admitted. "I'm just upset. If they want to argue about traveling west, why do it when we're present? They had all night and morning without us."

"It sounds like he was telling you their plans before he'd talked them over with her. It would make any woman mad, even you."

"Those things she said about me, about Henry wanting to follow me. It's not true, there's nothing between us. He has never shown any interest in me by word or action."

"You sound unsure if that's good or bad? Have you taken a fancy to her husband?"

Claire had stomped off and ignored her friend the rest of the way home, but all night she had gone over her reactions.

The next morning she had decided to skip work and never see him again. Although she loved working in the lovely little boutique, she was determined to quit.

Then Bonnie had once again given her a talk. Bonnie was in a race to go say goodbye to her brothers, Ian and Sean. As usual, she was telling Claire what to do. She had made Claire see she had a duty to her parents. Her father was counting on Henry to buy a pair of wagons and join them on the trek west. Besides, if she stayed home to cry, Bella would know she had been right.

Ever since that day, she had prayed that it was not so, and done all in her power to avoid the man. But on a wagon train headed west, with miles and days to go along together, it was difficult. In a party of ten people, there was no way to ignore or avoid the man entirely.

She was careful. There had been no more long discussions about fashion. Although he would occasionally ask her opinion and she would give it. She made sure they were with the rest of the group when they talked. Claire always sat beside her parents while he sat beside Bella, or on a separate bench with the twins.

At night, she read the Bible to Mary Anne and tried to keep her thoughts pure. It worked, until she would see him the next day, struggling with his team, and he would give her his warm friendly smile. She couldn't help her feelings, she would smile back. Honestly, she smiled at everyone. But then she wondered what it would be like to kiss such a handsome man. Would his mustache tickle? That was when she would worry her beads and pray.

Mary Anne repeated her name. Claire shook her head and looked down, as the nimble girl timed the wheel's turn and scampered up onto the seat beside her. Claire managed to move the magazines in time.

"What is it poppet? Did you finally find a snake of your own?"

Mary Anne shook her head, her eyes suddenly very big. "No, Father Wimberley warned me that the ones from here west are poisonous. There's rattlesnakes, and copperheads, and moccasins, and...cobras, or some more like that, I don't remember them all. I don't dare look any more."

Claire shuddered and extended her arm to pull the shivering little girl closer. "Thank goodness for that. What is it than, that you've got behind your back?"

Mary Anne brought the flower out triumphantly and waved it at Claire. For a moment, Claire felt as pierced as if she had jabbed her with one of the blade-like leaves. Closing her eyes for a second, she managed to transform her reaction. She opened her eyes wide and exclaimed, "My how beautiful."

"I know, Bella gave it to me, and she told me its story."

Claire looked dubious. "Your flower has a story?"

"Yes, the Iris is one of the bravest flowers. It pierces the soil in the spring, and unfurls its banner. That's why many people call it a flag. That way all the other flowers and animals know it's truly spring," Mary Anne parroted Bella's voice. Like all the McKinneys, the little girl could imitate anyone. Like Lynne, she had the same high, sweet voice. Claire could sing, at least a lot better than Bonnie. But she had never been able to sing the lead stanzas in church like Lynne.

Claire rolled her eyes, reached out to touch the flower which was already looking wilted. "I'm not sure the daffodil would agree with Bella."

Mary Anne smiled and sighed, taking a deep scent of the purple petals. "I know, but she was so happy, I pretended to believe it was a real story, not one she just made up. She's good at telling stories."

Claire gave the child another squeeze and brushed her hair back so she could stare into the serious gray eyes. For just a second, she imagined it was Lynne, not her little sister. They were both so much alike, serious, wise, and always kind. Claire gave her a soft kiss on the brow before releasing her. Minutes later, the little girl was gone. Doubtless, to share the flower and tale with Mother, maybe even her brothers.

CHAPTER FIVE

They arrived at the large home of Bella's parents in New Rochelle early in the afternoon. Claire was shocked by the size and grandeur of the federal style brick mansion. There was a small stream across the land that divided the shoreline view from the house. In minutes, the wagons were parked diagonally, each open to the breeze off the water. Claire climbed down, looked across to where Henry was helping his wife down. In amazement she watched him step up on the side of the wagon to retrieve little Barney. He had always shown as much aversion for the boy as Claire felt.

Claire stared, hoping the boy wouldn't drool over Henry's best suit, but he quickly handed the child to his wife. Claire welcomed Mary Anne's small hand in hers as they walked behind their wagon and up to where her father and the boys were unhitching the first team of animals.

An elderly couple appeared at the big door of the house, then ran down the steps and across the lawn to a small footbridge. Bella raced up her side and they met in the center on top over the stream.

All the Wimberleys exchanged a warm glance at the heart-felt embraces. Claire couldn't help it, she snuffled a little as she stepped into her mother's arms. They folded Mary Anne between their full skirts.

Henry walked onto the bridge and the three stopped their tearful hugs. Firmly, but politely Bella's father shook her husband's hand. From where they stood, they heard Bella's mother. Her voice sounded just like Bella's as they welcomed their daughter's husband home.

Nervously, as a last thought, Bella introduced her son, but his grandparents were moving away, talking enthusiastically to her about how glad they were to have company.

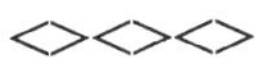

Finally, they were all inside. Bella's parents had insisted that they use the bedrooms instead of the wagons. Father Wimberley and the boys refused the offer, insisting they'd rather be outside near the cattle. One of the maids rushed to show the girls their rooms before rushing back to the kitchen. Claire and Bonnie would share the room beside Bella and Henry. The Wimberleys had a room at the end of the hall. Mary Anne was going to share the bed with Claire and Bonnie.

The children were in awe of all the beautiful things displayed throughout the house. No wonder Bella seemed driven. She was used to a different kind of life. Before, Claire had felt wealthy. Now she saw that they were merely middle-classed people. But Bella's father seemed to have an instant rapport with Robert Wimberley. Perhaps it was that Father had owned a factory, or that he was still willing to set out across the country on an adventure. The two men had immediately disappeared into his library to talk about the western frontier.

There was a little flurry as the cook rushed to prepare food for so many guests. Bonnie and Elizabeth Wimberley volunteered to help in the kitchen, but Mrs. Switzer refused to hear of it. Claire settled in the small parlor with the Lambton's and Bella's mother. She was glad when Bonnie and her Mother joined her, although Bonnie looked as though she were sitting on a pile of nettles instead of the lovely horse-hair stuffed sofa.

Henry looked even more uncomfortable than Bonnie in the room full of women. Claire was disappointed that Father and Bella's father had excluded him. After a few minutes of being ignored by his wife and mother-in-law, he excused himself to go keep an eye on the children. Of course he didn't mean Barney. The small boy was sitting big eyed at the foot of his mother, looking from her to his grandmother and back. It made Claire smile, it was so clear he was working it out for himself.

The two were remarkably similar. Claire knew she looked like her own mother. Well, Mother was a little older and plumper, and didn't worry about her appearance as much, but their eyes, nose, and cheeks were similar. Bella and her mother were both raven haired and dark eyed. If anything, her mother was even darker than Bella, with eyes that were nearly black. Although Bella was a tiny, thin woman, her mother was even thinner. They were both all sharp angles and shrill voices and seemed to have forgotten everything and everyone but each other.

Claire had to contain her sigh of relief when the cook finally had the maid call everyone into the dining room.

Perhaps the most impressive room to Claire was the large dining room. All the furniture was waxed and polished mahogany, highly carved and massive. It gleamed under the lit chandelier. The table was set for twelve with matching, gold rimmed china and gold lipped glassware. Remarkably, the glass-fronted, china cabinet still held more dishes. The food had been set out on a huge sideboard. It all smelled strange and delicious.

After Mrs. Switzer assigned everyone a place, she directed them to carry and fill a plate, with orders for the children to go first.

The same maid who had freshened the beds and shown them to their rooms, stood patiently answering questions and helping the children. There was plain meat, cold mutton, neatly sliced. There were an array of vegetable dishes, stewed or pickled, but all familiar. There was some thin sliced, hard brown bread which the girl offered to spread with soft cheese or butter for the three older children. There was a hot dish of cabbage rolls. Bella managed a small plate and filled it carefully for Barney.

Claire smiled at Bonnie at the strange way of serving guests, but both eagerly took their place in line. The food smelled good and tasted great. Bella's mother had seated her daughter at her right, Mother Wimberley on her left and the girl's and children beside her. The men and boys she seated at the opposite end, flanking her husband.

Claire studied Bella's parents. They did not look old, but they acted older than her own parents. They were cordial to Henry, but it was clear they did not know what to say to him. The same was true for little Barney.

During dinner, Bella whispered to get her mother to look at her grandson. Barney sat listening in his mother's lap, watching Mary Anne sing him a lullaby. When Mary would stop he would make little crooning sounds back to her. His eyes were shining with love and there was always a smile on his face. The women watching sat silently, until Bella's mother reached out to touch him for the first time. Smiling through their tears, mother and daughter hugged.

At the other end of the table, Bella's Father and Henry were smiling at the women when Henry said something that made the man turn to stare at him.

“What do you mean you sold the store? That was not in our agreement.”

Bella’s mother stared at the man, her face as amazed as her husbands. Suddenly there was a loud and noisy argument. It was easy for Claire to see where Bella learned to yell and complain.

The Wimberley’s stood hastily, and made their apologies before withdrawing for the night out to the wagons, leaving the family to work out their disagreements, urging the children outside with them. Claire and Bonnie crept upstairs. The argument was fierce now and little Barney, the only child present, was crying. Bonnie made a face at her, but Claire remained by the door, holding it open a crack so she could continue to listen.

Her parents were furious that Bella sold the store without letting them know. Claire heard Bella’s mother yell. “We could have bought it back. You knew your father was struggling now that the bank has failed.”

Claire felt her own body tremble when Bella didn’t answer. When Bella couldn’t defend herself, Henry took over.

“It was just a matter of time before we lost the business. You don’t understand how difficult it is to run a store when the city’s commerce is shrinking all around you.”

Now there was nothing but silence, which was worse than all the yelling. Slowly, Henry continued.

"We've most of our stock in the wagons, and when we get out West, I expect we'll be able to sell it all for a large profit. Then we can repay you."

For a moment, Claire leaned her head against the door frame. Oh lord, it sounded like… she didn't let herself complete the thought, just turned to where Bonnie was standing in her petticoat, busy washing before bed. She wanted Bonnie to tell her what she thought it meant, but if the tall girl had heard, she didn't react. Maybe it wasn't important to her. As the Switzers continued to scream and yell, she tried not to hear all the mean things they were saying about Henry.

As she heard the Lambtons storming out of the dining room, Claire quietly closed the door. Again, she looked at Bonnie, hoping for reassurance that she had misheard part of the conversation. Bonnie was humming a hymn to herself, in her big, vibrating voice. Claire stood with her hand on the cold glass of the doorknob behind her and prayed.

Claire took her time at getting ready for bed, surprised at how good it felt to have the luxury of a big lamp like the blown painted globe one on the washstand. Bonnie had emptied and rinsed the bowl and the pitcher was still half-full of clean water. Such luxuries. There was also a large mirror and she tilted her head, trying not to feel vain at her own image. She was wringing out her washcloth when she heard the door next door slam. She watched the center of her own eyes grow blacker as for a minute there was silence.

She had just climbed into bed beside her friend when they heard the angry whispers through the surprisingly thin walls.

As soon as Bella joined Henry in their bedroom, their argument began in fierce, deadly whispers. "I just learned you didn't do what you promised. You didn't send my father part of the money we owe them. I insist we at least pay back half. That will leave each of us with the same amount of money, and our debt will be cut in half."

Henry said, "I don't owe them. It wasn't a loan, but your dowry that they gave us. We need that money. It's a long way to Utah, and we've no idea what the expenses will be."

Bella's voice wasn't a whisper. "And if we're robbed, then we won't have the money and we'll still owe all the debt. What will you say then?"

He didn't answer. They even heard the whoosh as he snuffed out the lamp. From the corner of the next room, they heard Barney whine. The angry silence was worse than hearing all the angry words.

Claire trembled and tried to see Bonnie's eyes in the dark. Bonnie must have sensed her staring for she muttered. "At least he didn't hit her, Tarn would have split my lip if I'd raised my voice like that to him."

They heard a soft knock on the door and Bonnie called. "It's open."

Mary Anne slipped in, running across the floor. She already had on her nightgown, and her shoes without socks. Claire heard the thud of the first shoe, waited for the other. Next door, they heard the boy cry and the sound of his mother getting up to tend to him. Claire raised the covers and let the small girl slip between them.

Mary Anne took a few minutes to get settled, sighing with pleasure. "Wow, isn't this heavenly."

Claire tried to relax and fall asleep. The mattress was soft and thick, the support underneath more than a few slats, since it did not sag under all their weight. Even with three in the bed, she didn't feel crowded.

There was only a glimmer of moonlight through the long window and its thick velvet drapes. She couldn't see the furniture, guessed it was dark like the kitchen furniture, large, and heavily carved. Claire focused on a tiny strip of the wall-paper, the trail of vines with morning glories if she remembered right. In the dark, there was only a pattern of grays on white. She thought there were three colors of bloom, blue, violet, and rose. She tried to guess by the depth of gray, which flower was which color.

Even as she heard the deep breathing of the two beside her, she made herself focus on the paper as one tear after another dripped off her cheeks onto the downy pillow. In the silence, she heard a door open and close. She couldn't hear the footsteps, they were so soft.

For one wild minute, she imagined another tap on the door. Bit her lower lip to keep from calling out come in. But the image of the handsome man slipping into the room and into her arms for comfort would not disappear. Claire eased out of the warm bed onto the cold floor. Kneeling, she raised her hands together and bowed her head, but she heard another door open down at the other end of the hall.

Bella had slipped in to talk to her parents. Claire turned her beads and breathed her prayers.

CHAPTER SIX

The next morning they were ready to leave with the first light. They started with a cold breakfast of hard tack and goat cheese and were each glad to leave for their own reasons.

Claire was tired at the beginning, but soon they were finally past the islands and onto the mainland of New York State on the long road west. The next planned stop was in Columbus, Ohio, where Bonnie hoped to catch up with her brothers. Young boys, too young for war, Ian and Shawn, were in basic training for the western war.

Once again on the highway outside of the large town, they stopped while Bonnie rummaged through the food-stuffs to provide another cold meal. The ladies all headed as usual together toward the tree line.

Now wide awake, Claire noticed that all the joy that had lit up Bella's face the last couple of days was gone. She remembered every word she had overheard last night. Although she had tried to defend Henry in her mind, there was much that the woman had told him that she felt was right.

Instinctively she reached out to take the hands of the little boy, while his mother relieved herself. “Your Mother looked so captured by your son last night.” She didn’t add, before the screaming match that followed.

Bella stood and swung the little boy up into her arms to carry out of the trees before setting him down again to walk back to the wagon. “She told me last night that she was sorry. When the doctor’s diagnosed his condition as deteriorating and hopeless, she thought she was doing the right thing in sending him to the asylum.”

Bonnie asked the hard questions, “You didn’t object?”

Bella’s face darkened. Mother Wimberley moved closer to put a supporting arm around the woman. Claire expected Bella to start crying, she looked so hurt. Bella surprised them all when she raised her face and answered. “I was upset at the time. I had been told my son was going to die, there was no cure. In months, my beautiful baby would be twisted by pain and his little muscles would start to weaken,” her voice cracked.

Claire stared at the sharp, bitter lines of the woman’s face, realizing again that Bella was not old. Like Bonnie, she had suffered too much. Bonnie stood behind her, waiting. Claire took another step closer as well. But Bella’s face went from sad to angry again.

"Then my first husband abandoned me. He didn't want to be burdened by either of us anymore. I was so despondent, when I was myself again, my parents had already placed Bernard in hospital. They told me it was so he would have the best of care. I felt so helpless. I believed there was nothing I could do to care for him."

She stared behind her, tears standing in her eyes for real. "Bonnie, I owe you so much."

The tall woman wrapped the small one in a big hug and Barney gave a squeal of alarm at being crushed between them. Laughing, calming the little boy, they separated.

Father Wimberley called to the clutch of women, all surrounding the mother and child. "Everything all right? We need to get going."

All the women looked at the men. Claire didn't see her father, but the man past his shoulder. A man she now resented, even though he wasn't the husband who had forsaken Bella. She tried to think of something in his defense. Remembered Bonnie's words from the night before. At least he never hit her, and they had overheard enough arguments between the couple to know that he was a far better man than most in that respect. He let his wife yell at him and nag without abusing her in return. But wasn't ignoring her, keeping secrets from her, doing only what he wanted as bad? Claire had no answers.

Bonnie rushed to pass out the meal of bread, cheese, and apples. In minutes they were underway.

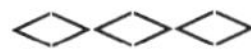

As Claire mounted the wagon, she was aware of Henry, standing and staring at his wife. He leaned forward to give her a hand up with the boy. Bella stared down at him from the seat, still not ready to forgive or forget his behavior of the night before. He looked curious, clearly wondering what the women had been talking about. He didn't ask.

As he turned to walk to the lead animal on their team and goad the animals into motion, Claire saw the sad lines of despair clearly etched on his face.

Did he feel cut out of the group? Seeing others offer Bella sympathy, did he fear no one would speak to him now?

Claire felt her stomach growl as Father began calling to the twins and Henry to move them off the road. To the right was a wooded tree line. As soon as possible, Claire climbed down. Then she reached back under the high bench seat for a bucket and sack.

She might not spend the day walking and gathering wood for the fire, but she tried to help. On her way into the trees anyway, she always tried to find something to add to the fire or for Bonnie to use in cooking. And she didn't want

Bonnie to point out again that at least she could have brought a bucket of fresh water back.

Usually she only found wild onions, strong for eating, but good when added to the pot of beans. As soon as the meal ended every day, Bonnie would move her pot of soaked beans over the cooling fire to give them a chance to cook a little. Claire didn't want to think of another dinner that was mostly beans.

For once, Claire was enjoying just walking about, listening to the birds, and the chattering squirrels in the tall trees. It was beautiful weather, the country peaceful. With luck, her father would find another fat farmer to buy fresh vegetables, eggs, and meat from. Although she had almost stopped minding the beans and bread. By the end of a long day, she was ready to eat her plateful of whatever Bonnie cooked.

His voice startled her, "I don't know why I thought this made sense. This trip will never end."

Claire stood still, staring up into Henry Lambton's face. She was so startled, she couldn't breathe. For the first time in a week, she would need to speak to Bella's husband.

"Are you talking to me?" she asked.

He stared at her, his light eyes probing hers. He shook his head. "What would be the point? I'm invisible to you and everyone else on this trip."

With that, he moved around her into the woods. Standing still, holding her breath, Claire listened. In the distance she could hear his angry muttering. Rushing, she hurried back to the campfire, handing her onions to Bonnie and dropping her bundle of dried brush with what the others had gathered.

"What's wrong goose? You look like you've seen another snake," Bonnie said.

Claire raised her hands to her cheeks, looked around for the others. Her father and the twins were leading the cattle back from the stream. Bella and Mary Anne sat with Barney, who was trying to walk on his own around the two on the bench watching him.

Claire reached out and grabbed Bonnie's hand and drew her back behind the nearest wagon. "It's Henry Lambton. He's wandering around in the woods, talking to himself. He said he was invisible."

Bonnie stared at Claire, reaching out to touch her pale face. "He's been getting stranger, ever since our visit to the Switzer's. He didn't harm you?"

Claire shook her head, "No, he just frightened me." Claire turned and looked back toward the fire. "It's a shame he is so unhappy. Look, Bella now seems happier than him. Isn't that strange."

"Part of married life. Someday you'll understand," Bonnie said.

Claire shook her head. "I don't want a marriage like that. Mother and Father don't play those kinds of games."

Bonnie shrugged, "I never knew how to do it anyway, Tarn was always in charge."

That night Henry Lambton started complaining about Father Wimberley's leadership and the rest of the voices around the campfire grew silent.

Claire watched her Father's face start to glow. Everyone sat up and listened at his sharp voice.

"I realize it will take time, but we are saving the expense of train travel, three to five hundred per person to reach Utah. We are both saving a fortune in shipping costs since we're each hauling a wagon full of goods to sell. Finally, I've put a lot of work and money into building these wagons. This is the most economical way to transport them west," Father said.

He stood up, glaring down at the younger man. "Henry, I explained all of this to you back in Boston. You don't like it, go your own way. Otherwise, shut your yap and don't bring it up again. I don't care if we're the only ones on the road, it makes it safer and faster for us to travel."

Without another word, he stomped off and Claire watched her mother stand up to join him. Claire watched as Henry's eyes looked around at the circle of children and young women. He rose and rushed Bella and the sleeping boy off to their wagon.

As Claire crawled into bed, she managed to smile at the little girl who lay there waiting for her nighttime story. As soon as Claire finished reading, she blew out the candle and stared out through the flapping canvas. She could not remember her Father getting so upset at anyone. He meant it. Maybe she would never see the Lambton's again. Troubled, she wondered if that would be good or bad. Softly she prayed, then relaxed.

Claire was relieved to see Henry the next day walking alongside his wagon, without speaking to anyone, even his wife. The next day, when she saw him at breakfast, he smiled wryly at her. Claire tossed her blonde hair and said "Good morning, Henry."

Looking over, she noticed Bella standing at her wagon. The woman's dark eyes grew brighter, like a hungry raven.

Ignoring her look, Claire sat beside Henry, taking her plate from Bonnie and thanking her. Henry looked at Claire and waited. "Father says it's going to rain."

"Yes, I think he's right." If he hadn't sighed, the conversation would be like the ones they used to have. To keep from starting a fight with Bella, Claire spoke to her next as she sat, trying to position Barney so she could manage her plate and feed him too.

“He looks happy this morning. I thought the rain bothered him,” Claire said in her normal voice.

Bella stared at the girl, then smiled. “Sometimes, I guess he is better today. I’m glad we get to sit in the wagons.”

Claire nodded, “Definitely, but it may just keep things cooled down.” Her Mother stood and walked over to assist Bella. She smiled at her daughter, then spoke to Henry. In minutes, the terrible tension of the last few days was gone. As though the group hadn’t been divided, everyone was back talking to each other.

At the farmer’s market that Saturday in Harrisburg, Pennsylvania, they found the right two horses to buy. The gentle pair of bays were solid animals, well trained, with gentle temperaments. The gelding and mare were named Bob and Sue. Claire thought the matched pair of bays were lovely, like something out of a picture book. They had rich brown coats, black legs and muzzles, and long black manes and tails. Even though they came with saddles, she wasn’t sure she would ever be able to ride one of them, but she followed the children in petting them.

Bonnie loved them on sight. She was already pleading to be the first to ride Sue.

It was the day Henry found the receipt in the Lambton's wagon box. The ensuing argument was loud enough for all to hear.

"I told you we need that money, you stole from me."

"My parents desperately needed the money, money we owed them. We still owe them. I left us half. If it's as easy to sell the clothes out west as you think, we'll have plenty of money."

"You think it's that simple. We have the wagons and now there are no more expenses. What about camping fees, fresh food, or this horse? Don't you trust that I know what is best for my family?"

"I think you would never have paid them anything. I did what I thought was right. What you should have done. What you told me you had done before we left Boston?"

Claire turned away in embarrassment at the public argument. She and her mother led the children into a store to buy candy. Bonnie stayed, clearly waiting to intervene if Henry tried to slap Bella. Claire knew there would be no physical blows. Henry was angry, but he would never hit a woman. It was hard to understand why the couple seemed to like to feud more than live together in harmony.

That night, as soon as everyone retired, the camp became eerily quiet. Even the animals seemed to be holding their breaths and waiting.

CHAPTER SEVEN

The horses changed everything. They had all taken turns learning to ride the wonderful matched pair of bays. The boys claimed to prefer riding their favorite oxen to riding the horses, probably because they were still too short to feel in control even when the saddles were adjusted.

Mother and Claire had been terrified, but taken their turn being led around on the horses and would ride them but only beside one of the men. Mary Anne would only ride seated behind Bonnie or Father Wimberley. Bella had refused to try, using a crying Barney as her excuse. Henry insisted she learn and they had quarreled bitterly for a whole day before she gave in and tried it. Of the women, only Bonnie liked to ride.

The men now posted up and down alongside the wagons, talking to everyone, making sure the oxen moved along by flicking them with new, longer whips. Tom and Jim walked along beside the lead bullocks, and Bonnie walked beside the third. At night, everyone still slept inside under the canopies, the tents neatly stored at the foot of tailgates.

Whenever one of the men needed a rest from riding, Bonnie would mount up and take off. She loved riding ahead to scout and look for food, but with Father Wimberley always fussing, she was never allowed to go very far ahead. He didn't believe in using guns and absolutely refused to let Bonnie try to use one. Henry agreed with him.

One evening at the campfire, Bonnie was complaining about how ignorant and stubborn men could be at times. Claire refused to listen to her friend's complaint about either man. But Claire confessed, "I do envy your boldness."

"I love to ride. If your father would listen to sense, I could find some game to add to the pot each night. We could all use a little more variety."

Claire nodded in agreement, eager as always for her supper, even if it was beans and fried fatback. Bonnie squatted to carefully turn the meat, then moved it out of the way enough to put the pot of coffee on to heat. She stared up at Claire, smiling at her cute friend. Claire, as usual, had the bonnet pushed back to hang from its ribbons around her neck. She had gone back to combing her curly hair into long sausage like curls and letting them spread out from a gathered knot atop her head.

"You surprise me. I thought you'd want to ride. If nothing else, so you could talk fashion again. You two never get to talk in the evenings, do you?"

Claire looked puzzled for a minute, then shook her head. “It upsets Bella if we do, then we all have to listen to them fight.”

“You could be a good rider, if you’d ride astride.”

Claire blushed, scandalized by the idea. “I wouldn’t dare. You’re the one with the split skirt. And don’t offer to loan it to me again. I would be lost in it, dragging it through the dust.”

“I saw a woman in Harrisburg riding astride. She had on a regular dress. Here, step over and I’ll show you.”

Claire followed her around behind the wagons and Bonnie showed her how to sweep her skirt up between her legs and handed her the full skirt hem as she scratched her head. “Well, I guess she was wearing a skirt, because then she just tucked the back skirt into her waistband. Looked a little like Turkish pants, you know those bloomers you told me about before.”

Claire held the skirt tail and turned from side to side. “It might work if I had a belt. You’re right, it does look a little like bloomers, and it doesn’t show the shape of my legs or rear. That would never do.”

“Don’t you have a belt?”

“No, but I will.”

The two women were still laughing when Mother Wimberley yelled at Bonnie. “I smell something burning.”

Claire watched her friend disappear and felt happy for the first time in days.

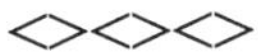

The next day when the two men needed a rest from the saddle, Bonnie and Claire finally got the chance to ride together. Although, still not as confident as Bonnie, the gait of the mare Sue was smooth and she followed everything that the other horse, Bob, did. Claire had no trouble riding, even when Bonnie urged her horse into a trot.

When they returned, laughing, their hair tossed and blowing across their pink faces, the men and boys with the wagon train smiled at the pretty image. Bonnie dismounted and helped Claire down, then began to shorten the stirrups on the gelding. She showed Tom what she was doing and he groaned.

When both horses and saddles were ready, Father Wimberley and Bonnie helped the boys up and into the saddle. The horses walked off with the lighter boys and Bonnie ran alongside, yelling instructions. When it looked like they would be in trouble if the animals decided to run, Bonnie managed to snag both bridles and turned the group back toward the wagon train.

"You need to relax, lads. The horses can sense your fear. Just sit up straight, hold your reins the way I showed you and ride them back to the wagon. When you get there, turn them and ride back."

Claire clapped softly from the back of the wagon as the two boys rode up on the prancing horses. “Now you look like cowboys.”

Determined, the two rode back to Bonnie. When she was satisfied, she took the reins of the pair of animals and handed them back to Father Wimberley.

“Good start for all four of you, I’d say. Another week of practice, and you’ll all be able to outride us, even Claire,” Father Wimberley said.

Claire sniffed at the faint praise, but sat up straighter in her seat. If Bonnie could learn to ride, she could and would.

It was mid-June when they reached Columbus, Ohio. The weather had favored them and it had been a little over five weeks since they left Boston. Bonnie came up beside Claire’s wagon as she approached the riders.

Bonnie spoke first. “According to the farmer last night, we’re close to Columbus. I want to ride to the barracks to see Ian and Shawn.”

Henry Lambton answered, “You want to ride cross country in this. Look at the sky. I vote against it. We’ve not time to pause and detour around to this place. Even if we find it, the boys probably aren’t there. It’s a foolish waste of time.”

Father Wimberley agreed, “You know, Henry and I seldom agree, but darling, we can’t spare the time. We need to keep moving while the roads are good. You see that wall of clouds. It’s going to pour any minute. If we turn off on the road to the fort, we might get mired in mud and lose an entire day.”

Angry, Bonnie didn’t argue, just donned a yellow rain slicker and took her place beside the nervous oxen.

The rain began as soon as they pulled onto the road. The road was macadam with no danger of getting mired down.

Bonnie yelled to Claire. “I can’t bear it. Every step is taking me farther from the arsenal and training center.”

“Fussing won’t do you any good, you heard the men,” Claire answered.

“Why do the men get to decide?” Bonnie snapped.

Claire stared at her angry friend, past her to the boys in their own slickers. The three in yellow were the only discernible shapes in the driving rain. She couldn’t even hear the riders in the pouring rain. Claire sneezed, reached behind her for her shawl and one of the oversized umbrellas to prop in front to keep her dress from getting damp.

Later, after the first shower stopped, they encountered a large cargo wagon headed the opposite direction on the road. It was pulled by a team of four mules. When the men rode up beside the wagon to talk, Bonnie moved up closer as well.

"A fine day for traveling. That's a pretty big load."

The man looked at the oxen and series of wagons strung out along the road. The oxen looked painted, their brown and white spotted hides still wet from the storm. The canvas covered wagons bloomed white, like spring mushrooms behind them. He shook his head. "You folks lost?"

Father smiled tightly. How many times had they been asked the same question, in just that tone, Claire wondered? "On our way to Independence, Missouri."

"Well, this is the road. Not near so pretty once you pass Vandalia, Illinois. Up 'till then, she's a peach to travel. Especially on a day like this one."

"Where are you headed?" Henry asked.

"Just up another six miles. Taking supplies for the Columbus Barracks. They've been ordering a lot, feeding and training a bunch of troops again, getting 'em ready to fight the Indians. Hadn't been so busy since the Civil War ended."

"Is there a shortcut from here?" interrupted Bonnie.

The man looked at the tall woman and grinned. "Well, I might could give you a ride, but the road changes up ahead. Still pretty good. We could talk awhile if these mules get mired," he said, grinning again.

Bonnie blushed and looked off to the right. "I meant riding from here."

"About three miles, if you can fly due North. But they ain't no road that way. It's all farm country. You can't get this bunch through. No way."

Bonnie turned and walked ahead to the Wimberley's wagon. She climbed up into the back of the wagon, took out one of the sandwiches she'd made up for lunch and one of the apples. She shoved one into each pocket. She pulled a canteen from under the end of the oilcloth and shook it. She was filling it from the half-empty barrel on the side of the wagon when Mother Wimberley walked up beside her.

"What's going on, Bonnie?"

"Mother Wimberley, the man says the Columbus Arsenal is three miles across country due north. I've got to go see my brothers."

"Walking alone?"

"I'd rather ride Sue. But walking if I have to."

"Robert!" Mother Wimberley shouted.

Father Wimberley rode up, stared down at both determined women. He dismounted and handed Bonnie the reins. "Henry, you'll need to escort her."

"Nonsense. I'm not riding to hell and back on a whim."

"Get down, then," Father Wimberley said through gritted teeth. "Boys," he bellowed.

"Bonnie, you're not going off alone?" Claire called. "It's raining," she added, even though it had stopped.

Tom and Jim came running and Bonnie turned back to grab a rucksack and add two more sandwiches, then removed the one from her pocket and put two apples in its place. She crossed the long handles over her chest, the strap of the canteen in the opposite direction.

"I don't think you've thought this through," Father Wimberley said.

"I'd feel better if you'd let me take a gun along, or at least your knife with its compass," Bonnie argued.

"And have you shoot yourself or one of the lads. Never," he said as he removed the belt with his special knife from his waist. Bonnie waited until Tom was in the saddle, then adjusted his right stirrup. The angry man adjusted the other.

"Claire," he yelled. Claire leaned forward to stare at them. "Get down, you'll have to manage Bonnie's team until she and the boys return."

Bonnie and the boys turned off the road into the high grass toward the distant hill.

"But Father, what if it rains again." Father had turned his back to her, stood watching bright dots of yellow disappear.

Claire flung the ugly oil-cloth wrap onto the empty wagon seat. Her feet were killing her, even though she wore her trail boots instead of her dress shoes. No one seemed interested that the bottom half of her dress was wet and constantly wanted to tangle in her legs as she walked. At least it had stopped raining again. In front of her, she watched Henry Lambton carefully fold his own cover and pass it up to Bella. She waited, finally saw her Father ahead as they rounded a curve in the highway.

Bonnie and the twins had been gone for hours. She saw her Father pull on the horn of his lead ox to stop them. “Noon stop. Claire, pass out food. You ladies may want to get down.”

Claire’s mouth dropped. What was she? Didn’t she get a break? Instead, she stared at her father as he helped her mother down from the wagon. She had never thought about it before, but he did this every day. Bonnie had done it for weeks, walk along beside these bellowing beasts. Even the young twins did it every day.

Mary Anne appeared beside her. “I can help, Aunt Claire.” The little girl gave her a bright smile and Claire let her arm curve around her. “Thanks, I’ll be back in a minute. Can you pass out the food today?”

But the little girl was already headed to the back of the Wimberley wagon. Why hadn’t she realized how hard it must be for the others?

CHAPTER EIGHT

Hours later, feet numb, back aching, Claire jumped as she heard horses running behind her. She pressed close against the lead ox as she heard someone shout, "Hi-yo, Hi-yah."

Two horses ran past, each carrying a yelling little boy. Claire pushed away from the ox she had been leaning on. A very handsome soldier rode up beside her, something on his lap, his horse prancing as he raised his hat to Claire. She stood wearily beside the ox team, only registering his bright smile. Automatically, she raised a hand to pat her hair. Ahead, still astride their pretty horses, the boys were laughing.

She noticed in front of her, Henry had his coat off. It showed damp circles under his arms as he waved a fist at the boys who'd nearly run him down. "About time you scamps came back. Where is Bonnie?"

Suddenly, Claire remembered her friend. From time to time today, the image of her friend had appeared to remind her to press on. One more step at a time. She tried not to think about her, the way she'd seen her this morning. Bonnie had coiled and pinned her hair out of the way and her eyes had been dancing with green and gold, as she'd complained about men.

Tom was already dismounting to hand his reins over to the man. Claire watched as Henry tried to mount and the horse spun about underneath him. She noticed the army officer smother a laugh before he rode closer and captured the horse's reins. She watched Henry adjust the horse's stirrups before rushing to mount up again.

Calum rode up slowly to capture and calm the horse so the storekeeper could correct his mistake before trying again. Beside him now was a young woman, half-dozing in the sun. With her dark hair and bitter downturned mouth, this would be Bella Lambton. He leaned over and saw the pale little boy on the floor of the wagon beside her and smiled. Again he tipped his hat and said "ma'am," startling her awake.

Now that the woman's husband was seated, Calum rode up to the lead wagon. A tall, handsome man with a worn expression was working the lead team, watching the commotion behind him.

"Hello there, can you give me a hand, Mister Wimberley, I presume?"

"Yes. What's going on, what happened to Bonnie?"

Calum smiled, at least there was one decent human being. "She was stung by a bee, seems to have had a bit of a bad reaction. Is there somewhere I can lay her down?"

Of course," he said as he yelled "whoa" to his team and the two McKinney boys moved to grab a horn of the leader on either side. He clambered into the center of the joined wagons and held out his arms as Calum reluctantly surrendered his burden. Calum stared into the shadowed stillness, not surprised when a little girl climbed over the bench of the wagon with a rag and a gourd of water in her hands.

"You must be their beautiful little sister, Mary Anne." The child looked at him shyly but nodded her head, obviously used to the accurate compliment.

Again he tilted his hat to the woman looking back through the wagon at him. "Mrs. Wimberley?"

"Yes, but how did you know our names?" she asked.

Calum smiled. "The boys did a lot of talking on the ride home, I feel like I know everyone pretty well."

Mrs. Wimberley nodded, confused that he knew her name and she didn't know him. "She'll be fine?" she asked.

He backed his horse, then rode up beside her. "Make her some willow bark tea and give her the rest of the day to rest. She should be good as new by morning."

"Of course, but, who are you?"

Calum doffed his hat and bowed over the hand she offered. "Lieutenant Calum Douglas. I'm in charge of the company of new recruits that includes the Magee boys, Shawn and Ian. Bonnie came to visit them, but I guess you knew that."

"Yes, we've worried about her and the lads all day. We almost stopped at noon to wait for them, but my husband argued she might come across to intercept our train and we would miss her and the boys. I've been angry at him, afraid he just didn't want to waste the day and not make his blasted miles. Are you sure she's all right?"

"He made the right choice. Yes, she'll be fine. I'm going to leave her in your good hands. I've got a lot of men to keep in line, so I can't stay much longer. I'll probably have to ride home in the dark."

Claire stood looking over the tail of the wagon at her friend. "Are you sure she's all right?"

Again Calum rode back and had to smile. They were all handsome women, even this tiny one. He knew a lot of men would faint at her blonde hair, blue eyes, and dainty features. But he preferred a woman of substance.

"With you three ladies to see to her chores and this little lady to nurse her, I'm sure she'll be fine." He stared into blue eyes in a flawless face and understood why the boys had described Claire as pretty as a China doll. Too bad they had added that she had about as much sense. He untied the deer and turned Champ and let him rear. "She shot the deer before she got the bee sting collecting these." He unlooped the knapsack full of blueberries and handed them to Claire.

The girl had wasted no time in running to check on Bonnie. Maybe she was worthy of all the love Bonnie had for this friend and for the mail-order bride, Lynne McKinney.

"Okay lads, your turn to shoot. Have you picked your target?"

Mr. Wimberley rushed up and stood with his hand on the tailgate of the wagon. “Hey, I don’t hold with shooting.”

Calum sat with an elbow on the pommel of his saddle and stared at the solemn face. He motioned away from the others and was relieved when Mr. Wimberley followed. Quietly, pitching his voice so only this man could hear, he told him all he had been thinking as he carried a helpless Bonnie back. No reason he should be the only one losing sleep worrying about her.

“Then you should have stayed in Boston. As I told the lads, the Indians along this way won’t be a problem, at least ‘till you cross the Missouri. But you never know when vagabonds and robbers might attack a lone wagon train. With four helpless children, four beautiful white women, and only two men to defend them, you better start carrying your weapons and know how to use them.”

He turned and saluted the twins as they raised their fingers in a smart salute to him. Father Wimberley nodded, and the boys ran after their new hero. By the time they had fired their rounds, the men had circled the wagons for the night early and quartered the deer. With the women busy cooking the meal, Calum wasn’t surprised to see the two men walk up carrying all their weapons.

Claire stood over the pile of wet wood. She held her mother’s striker and flint and took a deep breath before trying again. The white spark landed on the wet bark and went out. She was so flustered and tired, but so were all the others. She looked at Henry and his mouth curved down in sympathy, but he raised his empty hands and shrugged. She watched where his hands still dripped pink before Mary Anne poured another ladle over his hands for him.

Her Father set the deer haunch down on the bench beside her and patted his daughter's shoulder. "You need dry kindling. Put a pile under your wet logs, then light it." He looked to where the scattered gunfire was coming from.

"Sorry, we promised, we'd be next."

"You and Henry are going to learn to shoot? She asked in surprise.

He stared at his only child, smiled in spite of himself and bent to kiss her cheek. "I'll ask the Lieutenant, he may have some trick of the trade for starting a blaze with wet wood."

She went to the third wagon where her Father had stored all the tools and parts he hoped to sale. A man coughed behind her and Claire stepped down quickly, her hands full of a single dried corned shuck and a bit of straw. She stepped back despite herself.

"Miss, sorry to startle you. Your Father said you could use a little help."

Claire blushed, the man was breathtaking in his bold blue and yellow uniform. There was something familiar about his blue, knowing eyes.

He removed his hat and gave a small bow. “Calum Douglas, at your service.”

Claire smiled, her spirits suddenly bright. He had said it just like a gentleman at a ball. She curtsied and extended her hand for him to help raise her up. “Claire Wimberley, thank you, sir. Do you know how I can start a fire with this wet stuff?”

A minute later he knelt, used his knife to uncap a bullet and dumped it over the small dry kindling she had found. He pocketed the lead shot and took her flint and striker. In a poof the flame shot up, with a sizzle and pop the wood began to burn.

“Is this what you’re cooking for supper?”

Claire nodded, trying to not look as inept as she felt. Tom and Jim had followed him over and were watching in awe. Boys, run cut me a couple of forked trees, about this big around. He held out his finger.

They held up their hands. Calum glowered fiercely. “Right, I guess knives would be too dangerous as well.”

He turned and, using his knife, whacked through the top of a young tree, then he cut the spreading limbs off. In minutes he had the thin slices of the deer skewered over the fire. “After you finish cooking tonight’s supper, just put the other haunch up and leave it over the fire all night.”

“Bonnie usually puts the beans over the fire for the next day.”

“You can put both up.”

He tipped his hat to her and the other two women who were now coming out of the woods. "Good-day, ladies, later."

Calum was glad he had been working with green recruits the last month. He needed every bit of his patience. Robert Wimberley was afraid of guns, a challenge in itself. Henry Lambton was just uninterested in them. Although reluctant, Calum was able to motivate them and train both to at least handle the guns safely, how to load and fire each one. He encouraged them to practice.

The women were a different story. Elizabeth Wimberley didn't hesitate. She was only interested in learning to fire the pistol, but when she sighted down the barrel, she fired as though she had already picked out her target. Bella only took the weapon at his insistence. She seemed horrified at the idea of ever firing it until he asked her what she would do if Indians attacked, and she was the only one left to protect her son.

Instantly, she stiffened. He went through the instructions again and all three women paid close attention. Claire was last. He was not surprised when the little blonde came to practice with a lace collar added to her plain tan dress. She really was pretty, but he could have done without the fresh spray of perfume. Flirting, she pretended she couldn't figure out how to hold the weapon. He willingly pulled her into his arms, supported her arm and held her tiny hand within his own. When she finally fired the gun, he was not surprised when she squealed at the noise and the kick of the shot. It was a relief when he finished and little Mary Anne showed up. She didn't ask, just waited.

He released the annoying blonde and took the little girl with her impish features and big eyes onto his knee. "Don't you think there are enough people to shoot the guns, that you'll be safe now?"

"I can do it if Tom and Jim can, please," she tilted her head, batting her lashes over those lovely gray eyes.

Calum laughed. What was it about women? Were they all born knowing how to work their eyes and voice to get their way?

When they walked back to eat, Calum left the others and walked over to the wagon where Bonnie slept. He was rewarded by the opportunity to see her sitting up, rumpled and still half asleep. Her dress was open a button and a damp cloth was on her neck over the sting.

As she opened her eyes and saw him, her eyes changed from soft, nutmeg brown to a lighter shade with little sparks of yellow. Calum tried not to, but he hoped the lights were for him.

All during the meal, he sat next to Bonnie, attentively cutting her meat, getting up to get her coffee. Claire sat on the bench across from them, trying to catch the Lieutenant's eye or draw him into conversation. Ignored, her father or mother would try to answer her questions when the silence stretched out. It was clear, the officer had eyes only for Bonnie.

As soon as the meal was over, he escorted Bonnie back to her wagon. She watched him lift Bonnie up to sit on the tailgate. Although the wagon was between them and the couple, she could see his tall legs, the blue cloth decorated with bold yellow bands down the sides of each leg.

She tried, but she couldn't hear what they were saying. As the couple talked, she watched Calum lean so his legs were at an angle, then move back straight. After the third time she saw him mount up and ride slowly off into the dark. It wasn't her place, but she was surprised that her father didn't ask him to stay until daylight.

Her parents said Goodnight and retired next, urging the others to sleep well. Bella lifted her son to take him to bed and apologized to Claire for leaving her with the cleanup. Henry gave her the same annoying shrug, he had earlier. Peeved, Claire stood, ready for bed as usual, but tonight she was left with the job of clearing up. Fine, it was a good thing that no eligible man would notice her. She didn't want to be a wife and have to do this every day.

CHAPTER NINE

Claire came out of her wagon last, groaning as she sat on the tailgate, still in her wrapper. Bonnie, had risen early, eager to get the fire stirred to life, coffee made and hoecakes fried. The deer meat hung over the ashes of the fire where it had smoked overnight. Claire inhaled the hot smells and groaned.

Bonnie served her friend a stack of cakes drizzled with molasses.

"Thank goodness you're back with us. Yesterday was a nightmare." Mother Wimberley stepped up and finished frying cakes and serving, scolding Bonnie to sit down and take it easy. The men were soon yoking oxen and saddling horses for the boys to take down to the stream for water.

Claire came down from her wagon when the area was clear, stood in her gown and wrapper and whined. Bonnie was back, washing the dirty dishes and doing the cleanup as she was supposed to do. Claire watched while her mother walked over to fuss over Bonnie again.

Mother turned and looked her way, "The men will be moving the wagons out in a few minutes, hurry darling, get dressed."

Claire shook her head, her untamed curls like a soft yellow cloud around her head. "No, I can't do this today. My feet and legs are killing me," she looked past her mother to where Bonnie hummed and worked.

Whispering, she continued to complain, but leaned closer to her mother. "Why can't we just take one day and rest? I'm not tough like some people, I wasn't built for walking along like a cow day in and day out."

Bonnie's eyes flashed, or Claire would have thought she hadn't heard her. Instead of yelling at her, the tall woman finished the last plate and quickly turned to preparing the food for their lunch. Claire watched, already wanting to eat again, as Bonnie rolled pieces of cooked venison inside hoecakes. She stacked them all inside one metal plate and secured another overtop of it. She made a second package as Claire hobbled up to the cold fire pit.

In all the years they had been friends, Bonnie had only seen the girl this worked up once before. It was when Tarn Michaels turned all of his attention onto Bonnie.

"Can I see your big bite?" Claire demanded.

Bonnie stared at her, wondered why Claire was complaining about her. She turned so the swollen, red, muddy spot on her neck was visible.

"Oh. My goodness. Does it feel better, do you feel okay? The way everyone and your toy soldier were fussing over you, I expected it to be bigger."

Bonnie loaded the prepared food, stood the coffee pot in the corner and wedged everything in place with the bag of fruit. Finally, she turned and answered the angry girl.

“He’s not my soldier, and he’s certainly not a toy. He escorted us back for our safety. Why, don’t you like Lieutenant Douglas?”

Claire considered her next words carefully. She wanted to just blurt it out. ‘He made me feel invisible.’ Instead, she said, “He wouldn’t look at me, couldn’t see me. He was so wrapped up in paying attention to you that he never even spoke to me at dinner.”

Bonnie laughed and reached out to point at Claire’s open robe and bring her finger up to thump the tiny chin and give it a tweak. “You dear, are a little too visible.”

Claire heard the men, saw Bella holding Barney’s little hand as she walked him back from the bushes. Claire wondered if Bella had heard the two friends quarreling. No, it wasn’t a quarrel when one friend just kept smiling like a bear in honey while the other went on scolding and complaining.

In horror, she saw Henry and the twins staring and grinning. ‘Getting an eyeful,’ as Bonnie would say. Embarrassed, Claire tried to run back to the wagons, but her legs and feet refused to cooperate. The most she could manage was an ungraceful waddle.

Claire watched as Bonnie walked alongside the wagon and Mr. Wimberley and the twins led the first team out of the circle. Claire fumbled around inside getting dressed.

"Don't worry goose, no need to be jealous. I told him I'm married and not interested. Today you just take it easy. This dumb ox is back on duty," Bonnie called.

Dressed except for her shoes, Claire climbed out onto the bench to apologize to her friend, her best friend in the world save for Lynne. What had gotten into her? She hadn't meant to be cruel, but she had been.

Finally, she managed to get the shoe onto her sore foot, lowered that aching leg as she struggled with the other and began to explain. "Bonnie, dearest Bonnie, I'm sorry. Yesterday when I saw how hard your work is, I promised myself to thank you and hug your neck. You just do everything so easily, and you never complain." She turned to look beside the wagon but her friend was gone.

Ahead she saw Bonnie walking back to help the boys connect their oxen to the wagon. Mary Anne ran up to her and Bonnie caught the sweet girl in a hug.

"I can drive today, if you need me," Mary Anne said.

Laughing, Bonnie swung the child up onto the wagon seat. "I certainly do."

Claire felt like crying. She had meant to say all those things, to do more for Bonnie. Instead, she had insulted and yelled at her.

If it had changed her mood, Bonnie didn't show it. Singing *Goodbye Liza Jane,* in her strong voice, Bonnie led her team onto the road. Claire smiled as the children joined in the song and the boys took their position beside each of the trailing wagons.

When Father and Henry rode by, they looked different. Each wore pistols on their hips and carried a rifle in a saddle scabbard. Resting in the wagon boxes, ready to pull out if needed, were the loaded shotguns. Claire's hand was still sore from the pistol. She hadn't dared to try the shotgun yesterday. The Lieutenant had told her to have Bonnie show her later, when she felt better. For some reason, that had made her even more jealous.

Claire looked back to the campsite, the only sign that they had been there was the circle of ashes in the center of the trampled and eaten grass. Claire could still see the handsome Lieutenant standing beside her tall friend, excited to lead the still dazed looking girl back into the shadows to say Goodnight. What had he said to Bonnie, and why was he so attentive to her. He had ignored Claire completely? Determined, she climbed carefully over the locked wagon tongue into the other wagon and worked her way through her parents' neat quarters.

Claire emerged onto the wagon seat beside her mother, who patted her daughter's knee and smiled. "It's hard to stay angry isn't it, when the day is so beautiful," Mother said.

As they rode to the top of the little rise, they were surrounded by rolling fields of blue-green grass on one side, a pine thicket on the other.

Bonnie's song changed to *In the Pines*, and the children's sweet voices filled in around her lower, vibrating one.

Suddenly Claire swore and twisted on the seat, trying to see the girl singing. "Switch sides, Mother," she ordered and her Mother shook her head, but obliged by sliding under her impatient daughter. Claire leaned out and stared back up the trail. At the top of the rise, Bonnie stood illuminated by the soft glow of morning. "I knew it," she stomped her foot and turned around, gripping the seat beneath her in anger.

"Darling, what is wrong with you today?"

"Don't you hear her, don't you know what it means?" Claire cried.

Claire's mother looked completely baffled.

Claire sulked, making a fist to prop her chin on. "Bonnie never sings. The last time she was happy all the time, was when she was falling in love with that horrible, Tarn Micheals."

"No, you mean that nice Lieutenant Douglas is another bastard."

"No, but he is handsome. Why would two handsome men fall in love with Bonnie?"

Mother stared at her pretty daughter, heard the unspoken complaint, 'and why not me.'

"Well, Bonnie is loving, sweet, patient, hard-working and smart."

"No, she barely had better marks than me. Lynne was the smart one. How smart can Bonnie be, if she married a bounder like Tarn?"

"Have you forgotten, you were pretty taken with him for a while yourself," her Mother said.

Claire knew it was true, didn't see the point of arguing. "But Bonnie is so tall and plain and her clothes are horrible. What do they see?"

As their wagon wound up the next hill, Mother Wimberley leaned out her side. She saw Bonnie on the last rise. The girl was striding along in step with the team, her mouth open in laughter as she talked with the children. Too long limbed and lean, but with large, high breasts, there was no denying she was a striking woman. Instead of ruining her complexion, all the sun had seemed to polish Bonnie's skin gold and her hair sparkled with copper highlights. For a minute, it looked like she was going to step off the trail into the air, like some winged goddess of old.

Mother Wimberley caught her breath and sat back on her seat. It was her imagination. Bonnie had been through poverty, abuse, and a tragic marriage. She should slink along with bowed head and humility. Instead, Bonnie, who had always been shy and quiet, now was speaking out, offering her opinions, as though they were as good as anyone else's, even the men. She was like the rough ore Robert smelted and turned into shiny steel. The more adversity that was heaped upon her, the stronger and brighter she emerged.

For the first time Mother Wimberley looked at her cherished child and felt sorry for her. Calum Douglas wasn't the only man who might make the comparison between the two girls and choose Bonnie over Claire. A minute later, she had decided on an answer. "Well, she is very tall, and Tarn and the Lieutenant are both exceptionally tall men. Maybe that's why they like her."

Claire smiled for the first time all day. "I think you're right, Mother. And I don't want a tall man. They're too hard to kiss."

Suddenly, Claire reached out for her startled mother's hand.

"All I want is to find someone to love me, someone like Father, who has always loved you. I just don't think I'm going to ever find him."

Mother wrapped her daughter in a reassuring hug. "Love will find you, you just need to make yourself ready."

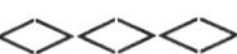

At noon, it was Claire, who walked to thc rear wagon, then walked to each of her fellow travelers, handing out the food Bonnie had prepared. When she reached the mounted riders, it was Henry who gave her a special smile as he accepted his food. Before he could comment, she held out the last sandwich to Bonnie.

Her friend stood surprised, then swept her into a tight embrace. In minutes, Claire was saying all the things she had tried to say earlier. Bonnie let her babble on, then stopped her with another big hug. "Thank you, friend." She raised her hand, extending her small finger. Claire hooked hers around it. "No more jealous fights, okay?"

Claire laughed, "No more, I promise."

As the two walked off to eat together, Claire missed how Henry's face darkened. He watched the two women settle in the shade of some nearby trees to eat and talk. He had no problem with whomever Bonnie chose to love. But the thought of Claire wanting the tall Lieutenant took away his appetite.

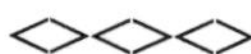

Two weeks later, as they passed through Indiana early in the morning, they stopped at a farm house. In the meadows beyond the farm house, several dairy cows grazed. Someone whistled and three barking English shepherds stopped carrying on. In the barn, they found a farmer pitching hay down. He whistled sharply and the three dogs who had sat down at the farmers, 'quiet,' sprang into action.

By the time he had the feed-boxes full, the dogs had a string of cows headed toward the barn, ready for milking. The Wimberleys were able to buy some of his stored pumpkins and wheat. The boys quickly loaded everything inside Bonnie's wagon on top of the tools.

Father Wimberley watched the boys trying to pet the young dogs whose long coats flashed as they zipped around the herd, and then back toward the boys, temptingly close.

The farmer watched the boys playing with the younger pair of dogs. "Your boys there need those dogs. I can make you a good price. Here Tip and Tyler," he called. The black animals ran low to the ground with lovely splashes of white on their faces and legs. Like the twins, the dogs, were almost identical. The farmer whistled and the dogs ran up and sat at attention, waiting. "Go on boys, they'll let you pet them now."

Tom and Jim sat wistfully petting the silky ears, talking to the friendly dogs. Father Wimberley paid for the animal feed, milk, and eggs and started to shake his head. “Sorry, it’s not a bad price, but I can’t afford to buy them.”

“They’ll earn their feed. They’re already trained herders.”

Father Wimberley stared from the boys blue eyes into the pleading brown eyes of the dogs.

“Good watch dogs, too. Give you plenty of warning when anyone’s around.” When he saw the man start to shake his head again, he said. “Go on, take ‘em for free. You paid up fair for the tucker. Twin pups and twin boys, meant to be.”

The men quickly learned the whistled commands and appreciated the dog’s help in moving the oxen each day.

The three girls all loved the well behaved animals. They were mirror images of each other, but none were sure which was Tip or Tyler. Tom said Tip was the one with white on the left side of his face. Jim argued they were mirror images and the girl’s noticed the other did have white on the right half of his face. Bonnie liked having them sleep under her wagon. Ever since Calum Douglas had planted fear of marauders and thieves in their minds and advised them to keep guns nearby, it had been harder to fall sleep.

Claire loved to have them along whenever she walked away from the wagons. She still had a lasting fear of snakes, but didn't worry with the dogs along. They reminded her of the spaniels in the portraits of royalty, and she enjoyed pretending she was a princess and they were her pampered pets. The boys insisted they were English shepherds, not hunting dogs.

Mary Anne tried to tie a red neckerchief around the one called Tip, and had a blue one beside her for the other dog. But the two animals managed together to pull it off. Mother Wimberley refused to let her try again, insisting it hurt the animal's dignity to be dressed up like a doll.

Barney Lambton was also thrilled with the friendly dogs, and would grab their fur and squeal whenever they came near. In turn, they would lick him and run along to herd him whenever he got up to walk. It gave Bella a little time for herself, and she made a point of slipping them treats to keep them nearby during meals.

CHAPTER TEN

The first week in August they finished the first leg of their journey. Camped beside the big river, Claire stood entranced by the city lights on the other side. Tomorrow they would cross where the Missouri met the Mississippi over the new Eads Bridge into St. Louis, Missouri.

When Bella walked up beside her with Barney in tow, Claire made room for her. "It is frightening, isn't it?" Bella said.

Claire was surprised, usually Bella ignored her, talking to Bonnie or her Mother instead. The warm breeze from the river carried the rich smell of all the life and river traffic far below. "I think it's exciting. After we leave this city, we'll be heading onto the real western wagon trails. We'll join another wagon train, a bigger one. There will be more men and women to help us."

"More men for you to choose from for a husband."

Claire laughed, "That too. They say there are as many as ten men to one woman in some of the towns out west."

"You are a very pretty young woman. I'm sure you will have no trouble finding the perfect man." Bella said, then turned to walk back to the campfire.

Claire was grateful for the darkness. What did the woman mean, that she wanted her to stay completely away from her husband, to find a man of her own? Claire placed her hands on her hips, leaned back as she inhaled deeply of all the promise. That was what she wanted, wasn't it?

In the dark, she heard the children running and squealing as they played tag in the tall grass. Bonnie's strong voice called everyone to come to dinner.

As she walked back, Claire heard the two men talking, arguing as usual. Father didn't trust the new bridge, especially since half of it was taken up by a railway span. He planned to move one tandem wagon across at a time. Of course, Henry argued it was nonsense. It would have been engineered to support a lot more weight than their oxen and wagons. Father won the argument as usual.

Father Wimberley announced he would sell the wheat and pumpkins tomorrow. At sunset, the boys had pointed out a big frame building with sunflowers painted on the roof and the word flour, laughing that someone didn't know how to spell flowers.

"I think St. Louis might be the place to sell the buckets and tools from the foundry too. I'm not sure what we'll find on the trail to come. We've freighted it this far, but I might have an easier time selling the wagons if they're empty," Father Wimberley said.

Bella spoke up, her sharp voice directed at Henry. "We should try to sell some of our goods as well. We have no idea what waits for us along this trail." All the travelers had read the books with their tales of abandoned furniture and treasures along the difficult road. Henry told her, "I've made our plans and I intend to stick to them."

Bonnie smiled at Claire. The women knew the argument would go on through the night. They knew from the past that Bella would not give up the argument until Henry agreed.

The sale of the wheat didn't go as planned. The mill wasn't eager to buy last winter's grain. After testing each bag, they agreed to take it, but at a smaller profit than Father had expected. Surprisingly, the hard-shelled pumpkins sold easily to a store for almost as much as Father had paid for everything.

Next Father drove to the business where he had planned to sell the factory equipment he had hauled from Boston. The man he had corresponded with wasn't there. He tried two other places in the industrial area below the railroad bridge. No one seemed interested. They followed directions from the office secretary to find a room for the night to freshen up. Father tried not to look insulted. The secretary promised to send word if the owner came into work later.

The Southern Hotel faced a grassy area they were told would soon become a town park. Without asking permission, they made a square of the wagons and picketed the cattle and horses in the grassy field. Leaving the women and boys with the wagons, he and Henry checked into two rooms. After bathing and dressing in clean clothes, Father rushed to get the wagons ready before the messenger arrived.

The women, Barney, and Mary Anne went up to the hotel rooms. After their long baths, Bella, Mary Anne, and Barney stayed upstairs to sleep in the soft feather beds. Claire and Bonnie came down. The young women were both giddy with being clean and well-groomed for the first time in weeks. They promenaded up and down in the hotel lobby and received many curious and admiring glances.

Father guided the boys to unhook and form a tandem of the two wagons carrying tools. The twins were excited to be left to guard the rest. They didn't want to sleep in the hotel since the dogs weren't welcome there. Father and Henry went back to visit the barber shop for a shave, haircut and shoe shine.

The pair of girls met the two men outside the barber shop, having a heated discussion as always.

"The men said St. Louis is the fourth largest city in the country. You'll make more money and please your wife if you try to sell some of your merchandise here," Father said.

Before Henry could start his protest, Claire said in her happy, bubbly voice. “Oh, do try Henry, there were some wonderful looking stores on the main street.

The messenger was calling for Robert Wimberley, and Claire gave her father a kiss for good luck as he rushed out.

Bonnie looked at Henry. “Claire and I are at loose ends, since the others are sleeping. We can come along to help.”

When Bonnie volunteered to stay with the wagon while Claire and Henry talked to the store manager, Henry smiled at the pair. Claire said, “I’m confident if a man will come down to see the stock, he will buy it.” It was agreed the three of them would try it.

Henry located the busy manager at the first store, but he refused to even look at what he had to offer. His reason, he already had suppliers he had been using for years. Claire looked around at the store with the full shelves and the clerks, all neat as a pen in white shirts or blouses, black pants or skirts. She liked the uniform they wore, even the black bow tied at the neck of each. It was more flattering on the women than the men, but she doubted if this manager would care what his employees thought.

The manager of the second store at least came down to the street to look inside the wagon. He laughed at what he saw. “No way to tell what you’ve got, the way you have everything stacked and piled.

Henry was ready to give up when Bonnie spoke up. “It’s in the same shape as the other merchandise you get arrives in. You can’t expect it to be shipped across country on hangers or racks, can you?”

“What did you say?” the man demanded.

Bonnie stuck her brogan up on the box frame as he blustered toward the front of the wagon. “You heard me. If you want to loan me an iron, we’ll press any or all of it, and Claire can model it. Then you can decide.”

The man stared at the striking woman with her flashing amber eyes, then at the angelic little blonde beside Henry. He directed them to drive the wagon on into the warehouse.

They used the wagon for Claire to dress in, although there was hardly room to stand in the crowded space. Claire modeled one of her favorites first. It was a light blue gingham dress with soft bows at the neck and a tier of ruffles at the rear, each caught with dark, little blue bows. She even found a pair of blue shoes and small feathered blue hat to compliment it. The warehouse workers seemed more interested in the fashion show than in working. Henry stood guard at the rear of the wagon, Bonnie at the front, while Claire changed.

Ready, Claire raised the ruffled parasol Henry handed her and walked toward the open front door of the warehouse and back, glancing over her shoulder and twirling the tiny umbrella for the manager. He nodded, but looked unimpressed.

The second dress was a rose taffeta ball gown, off the shoulders with lace insets to modify the décolletage that was too old fashioned and bold. It was the skirt that brought the dress into the modern era, again with the fullness pulled toward the back, rather than the sides. This time Claire wore a lovely pink and white lace petticoat beneath, and managed to raise the skirt enough to show the extravagant garment as she climbed in and out of the wagon. This time the manager looked more than impressed.

Bonnie had a deep blue wool dress ready, but the manager waved a hand that he'd seen enough. Claire held the blue garment in her hands, and the buyer shook his head and whistled. "I'm going to hate not seeing you in that, I'm sure, but I think I've seen enough to decide."

An hour later, after hard-haggling, Henry had sold two-thirds of the stock, all at a substantial profit. On the way back to the hotel, Claire back in her own green dress, giggled and squeezed Bonnie's hand in excitement. "We did it. I can't believe it only took two dresses for him to decide."

"You looked so pretty, what choice did he have. There are a lot of women in this town who will snap up those dresses," Henry said.

"He looked only because you spoke up and demanded he let us show him. What happened to my shy friend?" Claire said to Bonnie.

"I think she died with her baby," Bonnie answered quietly. But as she drove back, she didn't miss observing Claire's other hand was firmly clasped in Henry's.

<><><>

Father Wimberley met the buyer in the restaurant in the hotel. The man said he was wanting to buy equipment for his gold mine in the Black Hills. Mr. Wimberley convinced him he would be able to use or convert all of the equipment for that purpose and offered to make him a good price.

As soon as the man saw it, the deal was struck for the equipment. Then the man astonished them all by paying eight hundred for the tandem wagon and team to haul it in.

Returning to the hotel, the trio rode the lift up to the room for the first time, rather than take the stairs. The tall bellboy stood at the pulley and held the door open for the three to enter, then closed the cage door securely. Claire could hardly breathe she was so frightened. Bonnie of course, had insisted they try it since she had seen others pulled up to their rooms and thought it made a lot of sense. The ropes were actually steel cables that passed through the large lipped pair of wheels mounted in the front corner. The cables, then disappeared through the floor and ceiling. As though it were effortless, the man pulled and the car rose with a lurch.

Claire squealed and Bonnie and Henry pressed her between them. She noticed Henry was as nervous as she was as he held onto the top rail of the cage as they were pulled up beside the giant staircase. Claire rolled her eyes at the people carefully climbing the stairs holding onto the handrail. She wasn't surprised to see Bonnie smirking at them. When the cage stopped on their floor with a wire squeal and a lurch, Claire screamed again in surprise.

Laughing nervously, Henry held out a hand and led her to wait impatiently as the gate was swung open. Bonnie remained, staring down through the cage floor and pushing a little against the back of the carriage to make it sway. Claire wasn't surprised when the Bellboy gasped and whispered, "Best not do that, ma'am."

Claire pulled free of Henry and reached out for her foolish friend. "Don't you dare, if the rope should rock off of the wheel, the whole thing could crash down and kill us." The black man in the carriage closed the gate after crossing himself. Claire watched him muttering a prayer as she heard the bell ring downstairs. Gritting his teeth, staring straight ahead, the man lowered the contraption to the first floor.

Claire slapped at Bonnie's arms and scolded her as the two women made their way down the corridor to their hotel room. Henry walked at a distance from them, then turned and knocked on a neighboring door for him.

CHAPTER ELEVEN

Claire couldn't stop talking about selling clothes to the wonderful department store. She told Mother that she had been offered a job at the store to model clothes for customers. Of course she had said no.

Still dressed, Bonnie lay down on the second bed in the room, the one she, Claire, and Mary Anne would share tonight. It was foolish to stand around talking and primping when there was still an hour before dinner time. In a minute, she was relaxed and asleep.

An hour later, when Mother Wimberley urged her to get up and get ready, Father Wimberley was standing in the room, brushing his hair and straightening his tie. Mary Anne was trying to push between him and the mirror as she tried to retie her hair ribbon. Claire put down her powder puff long enough to retie it for the excited little girl.

Bonnie sat up sleepily and yawned. It looked to her that the boys had the right idea. Dressing up for dinner, and all the primping was pointless. Impatiently she combed and recoiled her own heavy brown hair into a neat chignon at the back of her head, smoothed her skirt and blouse and headed for the inside washroom at the end of the hall. The Wimberleys refused to ride down in the 'contraption,' but Mary Anne was eager to ride down with Bonnie.

As Bonnie and the little girl rode down in the open cage, Mary Anne pointed to her parents and Claire, oohing about how pretty they looked. A floor lower and she was calling and waving to Bella and Barney. The little boy started a thin wail of alarm. As soon as they reached the main floor, Bonnie moved to stand at the stairs. As Barney began to struggle and flail about, Bonnie reached out and took him from his mother.

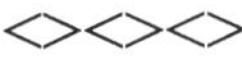

Bella took Henry's arm as soon as she released the boy. Bouncing him on one hip, Bonnie began to talk to him and try to calm him down. When the Wimberleys joined them, they all began the long promenade toward the restaurant near the rear of the hotel lobby. The large marble tile made musical clicks as they all walked briskly down it toward the immense room with its big chandeliers.

"Can we afford to eat here?" Mother whispered.

"Of course, I made a killing on the equipment I sold today." He turned to stare at Henry. "How about you, Lambton? Did it go well?"

The two men loudly discussed their success as they stood waiting to be seated. Barney again squealed loudly.

"What's wrong? Do you want to see the boys? Do you miss Tom and Jim?

Barney put two fingers in his mouth and hesitated in mid-cry. "The pretty horses, do you want to go pet Bob and Sue?

Barney looked around at the crowded dining room, at the well-dressed strangers. He made a low, tentative cry.

"Your doggies, do you want to see Tip and Tyler?"

His eyes widened and he pulled his fingers out with a pop. "Doggies?"

Several people turned to stare. In his red velvet suit, with his black hair and eyes shining against his white skin, the boy was beautiful. Several smiled and pointed to the noisy child. One woman waved at him and he raised his eyebrows in surprise. That brought another wave of appreciative laughter.

It took only a moment to convince Bella and Henry that Bonnie should take care of Barney at the wagons with the twins tonight. Even the Wimberleys barely argued. "I'll order four meals and send them out to you in the park," Father said.

Free at last, Bonnie rushed from the noisy, crowded hotel into the peaceful warm night.

<><><>

Claire called good-night, but was quickly distracted as a small orchestra at the back of the room began to play. Enchanted, she watched the beautifully dressed couples slowly stand and begin to fill the floor to dance. When she looked past her Father's shoulder, she saw Bella staring at the dancers and placing a protective hand on Henry's arm.

When the woman stood to whisper something in his ear, Claire felt a familiar wave of envy. Especially when Henry bent to fold her arm around his to lead them both into the crowded room behind the maître d'.

The excitement remained, through the careful studying of the menu, the detailed description of entrees by the waiter, and the grand meal that followed. Everyone at the table was happy. Mary Anne watched the dancers with such wistful excitement, Father Wimberley finally escorted her onto the floor between the arrival of their salad and main course. The little girl ended up standing on his feet to dance, a position Claire had used in the past. The pair received many smiles and admiring glances as they twirled past.

Without a word, the Lambton's slipped onto the dance floor. For a moment Claire was too shocked to think how it made her feel. She tried to channel Bonnie's emotions, and think how wonderful it was for the pair to have such a pleasurable moment since they usually argued from dawn to dusk. Without Barney to worry over, Bella looked relaxed as she gazed up at her happy husband.

Excited, Claire tried not to show her disappointment at not getting to dance, as the food finally arrived. Father Wimberley and a skipping Mary Anne rejoined the table and Claire made a point of assuring the girl how lovely she had looked and how well they had danced.

The food was so delicious, Claire forgot about the dancers. But as everyone seemed to be finishing up, she again stared longingly at the dance floor. The waiter returned to clear the table and describe the list of desserts. All three women ordered desserts, with Claire and Mother offering to share half with Mary Anne. Father and Henry chose to order an after-dinner brandy.

While they waited, Claire again looked longingly at the dancers. Father rose and escorted his wife onto the floor and the two girls at the table watched and laughed as they moved in a waltz around the floor. As he returned his wife to her seat, Robert Wimberley extended a hand to his daughter. Even though the desserts were arriving, Claire leaped up at the chance to dance on the beautiful lighted dance floor. The tile beneath their feet was black and white marble, laid in a diamond pattern. Claire and her Father laughed as the orchestra started a faster reel, but he gamely danced on.

When the number ended, they had to look around for their table. As they looped arms and spun around, a man taking her arm bowed his head to her. “Good evening, Miss Wimberley.” Father Wimberley stared, trying to puzzle out who the man was. Claire explained, “He’s the manager of the store where Henry sold most of his goods today.”

“Did you consider my offer?” the manager asked as they looped arms again.

Father Wimberley looked between the two in amazement, as he whirled his new partner past. Claire looked up at the smiling man and shook her head. “We are traveling west, I couldn’t abandon my family.

Changing back to her father, she muttered, “I explained to Mother that I was offered a job at the store today, to model the clothes for the customers. I guess she didn’t get a chance to tell you,” Claire blurted, as she was once again whirled away.

“Nonsense, you’re not interested in anything like that,” Father shouted.

The Lambton’s were the next couple in line and Father smiled as he linked arms to whirl around with Bella. Claire still felt miffed at her father’s attitude and so Henry asked what was wrong as he took her arm and twirled her.

“Just explaining who the store manager was that just spoke to me,” she said.

Once again, she linked with her father and danced up and down the rows between all the other dancers, then around to form the arch for the others.

But as her father walked her back to sit down, he breathlessly took his own seat and stared at her, clearly upset. “You did tell the man you weren’t interested, didn’t you.”

Henry and Bella were also returning to their seats, both in high-color from the rapid steps of the dance. Henry leaned forward, clearly anxious to hear her answer.

“Of course I did. I haven’t traveled all this way from Boston just to go back to work in a store. I plan to find and marry a suitable man once we settle, wherever you are taking us. Then my only job will be to supervise the servants and raise a family.”

“Good,” Father said, then lifted and swirled the amber liquid in the balloon shaped glass before taking a sip.

“Really,” Bella said. “It would seem with a little money from your parents and a good job, you could become independently established here. After all, St. Louis is far larger than any city where we’re headed. There will be many more eligible men to choose from here.”

All three of the Wimberleys looked shocked. Claire was the first one to speak. “I plan to settle close to my parents and friends.”

“A young woman alone in this place. Who would ever think that was a reasonable choice,” Father said and Claire noticed her Mother nodded.

“I moved to a city far from my parents to establish my business in Boston,” Bella said.

“But you had a husband,” Claire and Mother said at the same time.

“Yes, I do have Henry. I suppose you are right,” Bella said. “And you do have your friend, Bonnie.”

“She and I have made our plans. They involve visiting out friend Lynne and building homes nearby.” As she talked, Claire’s voice had risen.

Henry raised a hand and made a shushing sound. “Ladies, let’s focus on finishing this delicious meal.” A bell boy with four stacked trays stopped by the table. “Do you think I should go with them,” Henry asked.

Father shook his head. “No need. Bonnie and the lads will have things in order, you can count on that. Here in the city, it’s safe enough. Tonight, you and your lovely wife should enjoy your private room,” Father said, his eyes full of meaning.

Claire looked at Mary Anne. The imp had cherry juice on her lips and Claire raised her napkin to blot it away.

“You told me I could have half of your dessert, I just figured you wouldn’t mind if I ate the first half” Mary Anne said.

Claire stared at the mangled cherry pie, the soft cream almost melted around the plate, surrounding mostly crust. “I guess it is what I said.” Determined to be happy and enjoy the rare evening of fun, Claire took a bite of the pie. Even with melted cream and mostly crust, there was enough of the sweet tart cherries to turn the corners of her mouth up in delight. “Hmm, remind me to not be so generous next time.”

But the little girl was helping Mother eat the brown chess pie she had ordered. When Claire looked across to see what Bella had ordered, she watched Bella hold out a forkful of white layer cake for Henry. He made a moan of delight and the couple shared a secret smile. Flustered, Claire looked around the large room. She laid her napkin down, then determinedly finished what remained of her own dessert.

The waiter returned to serve coffee and clear the table. Somehow they had managed to make all the food and desserts disappear.

Once more in the hotel room, a curtain drawn between the beds, she and Mary Anne lay giggling, too happy to sleep. In between the pauses in their own conversation, they could hear the reassuring murmurs of her parents talking in the next bed. After they had shared their favorite things about the grand dining room, the amazing music and dancing, and the delicious food, her father called. “Good night, girls. Early start tomorrow.”

Lamps blown out, in the dark the small girl quickly fell asleep. Claire could not relax so easily. The conversation with Bella came back to her. Now her mind wanted to come up with clever lines to say. But it wasn’t a play, and there would be no chance to go back and tell her ‘...’ and there

Claire lay. What could she tell her? The woman was right. If she had Bonnie's courage, she would want to live an independent life. But what kind of woman actually did that? Even Bonnie planned to live near her brothers and friends. Maybe her answer was the best one. Bella had been able to leave home because she had a husband and wanted to make a new life with him.

Claire put a hand over her heart. That wasn't what she wanted, to be far away from her parents. She wanted to live a normal, happy life. One surrounded by family and friends who shared her values and faith, who would be there in her hour of need, who would love her. A board outside her door creaked. Claire waited until the door at the far end of the hall closed. A man traveling to the hotel bathroom. There was one at the end of the hall nearer their room for women to use. Such a modern, beautiful building. Feeling safe and happy again, Claire drifted into a deep sleep.

CHAPTER TWELVE

Claire argued all the way down the path from the hotel. "Why do we have to leave in the dark? Can't we stay another day, there is so much more of the city to explore. Henry and Bella still have merchandise they need to sell."

Father was repeating what he had told her while they dressed and packed to leave the room. "Time is money. We don't want to end up on the trail in cold weather, we have to make every day count now."

Bonnie had a fresh pot of coffee brewed when the travelers came down the path from the hotel. She offered the sausage and campfire biscuits and was pleased when all were accepted. "I thought you would be eating fancy again this morning. I'll need to stir up some more for our lunch."

"The restaurant wasn't open yet and Father wouldn't wait. Bonnie, you tell him one more day to rest wouldn't hurt."

Bonnie shook her head. "We can't stay, the police stopped by last night and told us we are camped illegally in a public park. They said if we moved on out this morning, they wouldn't write a complaint and make us pay any fine."

She passed around the last biscuits, telling the boys to just be patient. “I promised we’d be gone.”

“You should have been here,” Tom said.

“A whole crowd of people stood around watching us get in trouble,” Jim said.

“Bonnie made us sing, but the officer let us stay when he learned we were Irish. They were Irish too,” Tom added.

“See,” Father said.

Claire didn’t want to give up. “Aren’t you tired to the bone of all this. We must have walked a thousand miles already, but Father says we’re only now getting started. Isn’t it horrible?”

Claire watched her friend pour the batter into a long pan to shove into the campsite stove. The metal box was another clever invention Father had made.

Bonnie straightened, “It’s not been all that bad. When I get tired, I just climb up on one of the oxen and ride a few miles, just like the boys.”

Bella and Henry picked their way carefully down the path. Then suddenly Bella brushed past Claire and raced to the wagons, calling her son’s name as she ran. Barney sat beside the campfire, happily wedged between the twins on the oilcloth, with the dogs stretched out beside them.

“Hi, Momma,” he called and Bella’s face changed as she turned and smiled. She said good morning to her beloved child with a noisy kiss. The boys sprang up, to give her room, excited to talk about the cattle rustlers who had visited in the night. While they jumped around and talked, Father and Henry asked dozens of questions.

Bonnie was just finishing explaining how she'd heard the oxen's bells and fired the shotgun. "I think they were going to steal whatever they could find in the wagons," Bonnie said.

"I thought the dogs would be some protection, give a warning. Didn't any of you stay awake to guard?" Father asked.

The boys were interrupting again, defending their beloved animals. "We were on watch, but we ate so much food, we fell asleep," Tom admitted.

"Tip and Tyler ate what Barney couldn't, so they fell asleep too. But when Bonnie fired the gun, they took off after the thieves with a vengeance. Tip came back with cloth from one of their jackets or pants," Jim said.

Mother Wimberley stood at the rear of her wagon, shaking out the clean clothes she had picked for each to change into. "Bonnie, Claire, it's your idea. I've convinced Father to make the time, but you have to hurry to change if we're going to make an early mass."

"We'll keep an eye on everything," Henry said to Father. He had taken the shotgun from the front box of his wagon and stood defiantly ready. Claire thought he looked remarkably sweet holding the noisy gun she knew he hated.

Claire came down from the wagon, her spring bonnet in place, her favorite green dress shaken out for another wearing. "It will probably be our last chance to attend church until we reach Utah."

Bella looked up from where she was feeding Barney one of the warm biscuits. “We’re Jewish, darling. You remember that, don’t you?”

Claire blushed, even without Bella saying them, she heard the words, ‘silly goose.’

What was wrong with her? Even if he wasn’t married, he was Jewish. She and her parents were good Catholics and so were all her friends. She looked away from him and hurried to hook her arm with Bonnie. All the way to the church, Bonnie continued to talk about the thieves. It was hard for Claire to get a word in about the grand hotel, the food, music, and dancing, but she tried.

Inside the church, with its high arched ceiling and tall stained glass windows, she felt suddenly humbled. Kneeling and crossing herself, she followed her parents and Mary Anne into a pew near the front, leaving room for Bonnie at the end.

During the long opening prayer, she felt the magnitude of what Bonnie had been telling her. Thieves, worse, they could have hurt the children, or... As the terrible thoughts and images flooded her mind, Claire trembled. She raised her head to stare at her friend. Somehow Bonnie had found the courage to chase them away.

At the priest’s loud amen, the others opened their eyes. Bonnie stared at Claire, looked amused at the rapt look in her large, blue eyes. Bonnie reached over to pinch her, but

Claire caught her hand and held it for a minute, trying to say all she felt without words. Bonnie nodded, put her arm around her shoulders and exchanged a hug.

Minutes later, Bonnie was tugging the stack of folded flyers with a message about repentance from the back of the pew. She leaned across Claire to pantomime to Father Wimberley someone writing on the paper. He patted a pocket, then passed her a pencil.

All through the Latin service and on into the English translation by the priest, Bonnie wrote. Claire looked at the paper, saw Ian and Shawn's names at the top. Curious, she looked over at Mary Anne, who shrugged, then tried to see what had made the girl think of so much to write just now. As she turned on the pew to look behind, she saw the men who had filed in after they arrived, filling the next two rows behind them. Soldiers.

One of the men coughed, another twirled his thin, dark mustache and smiled at her. Claire tried to look shocked and swiveled back to face forward. But she was aware of whispers among the troops behind them. Flattered, she folded her hands in her lap and tried to look pious.

Another reason besides the fact that he was already married, to lose interest in Henry. The west was full of handsome men. Not all would be like Calum Douglas, some would want a short, pretty girl to marry. There were a dozen possible candidates seated behind them. Ten to one, she had read in one article. She would meet the perfect man, then, well then she knew how to win him.

When the priest admonished all present to give thanks and to beg forgiveness, Claire fumbled for her beads. Quickly, she bowed her head and thanked him for protecting and keeping everyone safe last night. She also thanked him for giving her the wisdom to know that one could feel an attraction for someone and not act on it. That a special awareness and fondness for them was not the same as love. She prayed for God to let her know when the right man was present and to guide and protect her heart. Finally, she prayed for each person in their party and murmured, amen.

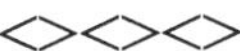

By the time they emerged from the shadows of the entrance, Claire was laughing at the pretty flattery from the two soldiers beside her. She heard Bonnie talking to one of the young troopers, a thin man with red hair and mustache much like her brother Ian.

Claire watched as the young man pulled a letter from inside his shirt, blushing at having the women watch him undo his shirt buttons. He was so young and sweet. Claire had to give him a big smile. Both watched him smooth out the paper, pull a thin, worn pair of sheets from the envelope and offer the empty envelope to Bonnie.

Happily, Bonnie accepted and addressed the back of it to her two brothers, listing Lieutenant Douglas and the fort at the bottom of the envelope before tucking the three sheets of printed paper that she had covered the backs of with her own letter.

"I promise you, Mrs. Michaels, I will try to find and give them this letter as soon as we arrive. If they are not there, I'll personally mail it to wherever they may have been posted."

The boy actually bowed to them and Claire and Bonnie both dropped a curtsy. So old fashioned and sweet. Why couldn't they have all been at the dance last night?

Father Wimberley stepped up to take his daughter's arm, Mary Anne grabbed Bonnie's hand. "Hurry, times wasting," Father said.

Maybe we'll see you on the trail, the officer in charge of the troops called after the girls.

In their absence, Henry had harnessed the oxen. While Barney played with his doggies, Bella had made the lunches. For a while he and Father Wimberley argued about how to run the wagons. With one tandem set of wagons gone with the machinery as well as its three spans of oxen, the choice seemed simple. They put the wagon Bonnie had been in charge of behind their own and ran them in tandem, each still pulled by three pair of oxen. In minutes they were all on their way west.

As they pulled out of the park gate a man ran up to stand in their path. “Please mister, have you a wagon to sell.”

Father Wimberley warily studied the man who was holding his arm close to his body.

“We done had our outfit stolen during the night,” the rough looking man added.

Claire shuddered. There was something very unsavory about the man and his skinny companion. Bonnie climbed down from her seat beside Mary Anne and stared hard at the man. She reached into the wagon for her shotgun and cocked it. The man winced at the loud sound and stepped back.

“I might, but it wouldn’t come cheap,” Father Wimberley answered. Bonnie looked at the still loaded bed of the second wagon and shook her head. Cautiously, she walked back to examine the back of the tandem bed of the Lambton’s wagon. Bella looked through to ask what was holding them up.

“There’s room in my wagon for the rest of your goods, but it would mean the lads and Mr. Wimberley would have to use the tent. A man claims his wagon was stolen during the night and needs to buy a wagon right away. I don’t know if he’s going to make a realistic offer, but it might be a chance for you to make a profit.”

Bella called out to Henry and repeated everything to him. Bonnie watched the other members of the group beside the side of the road. There was something familiar about the dark eyed man. Decided, Bonnie walked up to join the men.

The one holding his arm was arguing, “Three hundred is mighty dear, we’ve just been robbed. We could pay you fifty, then at the end of the road, maybe pay another two hundred.”

Bonnie used the wagon wheel to step up so her mouth was at ear level and hissed to Father Wimberley, mounted on his horse.

Both mounted men turned to look at her. “Don’t look, but the man behind the gate was at the department store yesterday. I’m pretty sure the one talking is the one I shot last night. Be careful.”

Claire made room for her friend to sit on the wagon seat. And Bonnie whispered to her. “Do you recognize the man behind the gate? I’m pretty sure he was at the department store yesterday. Claire stared at him and her mother tried to follow the conversation. “I think you’re right,” Claire said.

“Hey, we’d like to see the wagon up close. Show us all its features, you know, any built-ins or secret boxes, that sort of thing,” the man with the bad arm demanded.

Henry rode up, excited at the prospect of making an easy sell. “Well, Mr. Wimberley has some fine details. The benches fit into interior slots on each side and clamp during the day, but can be taken out and used for seats when you camp.”

Mr. Wimberley angrily moved the rifle from the sleeve of his saddle and angled it across his arm. “Sorry, we don’t do business on credit. Good luck to you,” Father Wimberley looked to the twins. “Move ‘em out lads.”

Claire was aware of how disappointed Henry looked, but at least he had enough sense not to say anything to Father. Bonnie dropped down from the wheel as Henry rode back to manage his wagon. Claire watched Bonnie stalk ahead, the shotgun still cradled in her arms. Even over the creak of the wagons and the plodding and lowing of oxen, Claire heard the man whisper.

"You will be sorry, just you wait mister. You and them women will be real sorry."

CHAPTER THIRTEEN

"You said he was there when you sold the clothes?" Father asked.

"What do you think they were after?" Henry asked.

"I'm sure of it. Remember Henry, when I told you to block one end of the wagon while I guarded the other. There were two men, supposedly working in the warehouse, but both were trying to watch Claire change." Bonnie paused for a minute. "They must have seen the store manager pay Henry. I don't think they were really after the oxen last night, they just couldn't get close enough to get the money without waking the dogs or boys."

"It doesn't make sense," Father said. "What does their trying to catch a glimpse of my daughter in her skimpies have to do with last night? Claire was in our room all night."

Claire blushed at the image, then perversely wondered if Henry had been tempted to peek.

"How were they able to get past the three of you, and the two dogs, to take the bells off the animals in the first place?" Henry asked.

Claire listened closely to the animated explanations. Everyone had an opinion to offer. She racked her brain for something interesting to say.

Bella leaned forward from coaxing Barney to eat. “Maybe someone at the hotel, one of the bell boys or waiters, saw your wallets were thin and thought there was probably a lot more in the wagons. You both were talking about all the profit you made in town.”

Mother nodded. “Remember I warned you about talking about your business in public.”

Henry looked annoyed and the others exchanged glances.

Claire grabbed Bonnie’s hand. “Maybe they drugged you?”

Bonnie made a face at her. “Put something in our food? How, when?

“If they were in cahoots with the waiters,” Mother said.

Father interrupted her, “Where did you learn that word, cahoots?”

Mother looked guilty. Claire knew she didn’t want to admit that she and her daughter had snuck and read the dime store novels he had stashed in his room.

Bonnie saved her from having to answer. “If they searched the wagons and didn’t find what they were looking for, maybe then they tried to take the animals instead,” Bonnie said. “It could be. I ate a little before dinner came and let the boys and dogs finish my meal. That’s why I wasn’t as sound asleep.”

“That’s why they wanted us to show any secret places in the wagon,” Henry said.

“If we had, they might have robbed us there and then,” Father Wimberley said. He looked at the frightened women in front of him, but didn’t need to voice what they were all thinking.

“Thank goodness Calum Douglas taught us all how to use our weapons,” Bonnie said. No one else spoke.

“I think our priority at this point is to keep moving, stay on guard. As soon as we get an opportunity we’ll join up with other wagons,” Father Wimberley said.

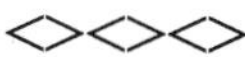

The soldiers they had met at church showed up just before noon on the trail. They were in high spirits, conducting one of the daily patrols that would end with them back in town at one of the red-light saloons near the river.

For a while, they rode along with the party, listening to Father’s tale of the thieves the night before. The sergeant in charge promised to be on the lookout for the men. “If we find them, we will arrest and take them back for questioning. But since you said nothing was taken, we probably won’t be able to hold them.”

“They threatened our women,” he lowered his voice and repeated the threat.

“One of them may have been wounded,” Bonnie said. “I fired to scare them off last night, and this morning, we were stopped by a man who was holding his arm as though it were hurt."

Claire was smiling at the soldiers riding beside her wagon, especially the one who kept twisting the ends of his mustache and rolling his eyes at her. He was so ridiculous, he made her laugh. The soldier on the other side of her wagon couldn't help but try to compete.

"Goodness, Miss Wimberley, you are so gorgeous. With that golden hair and those blue eyes, why you're like a perfect, like a perfect summer day." It was Mother's turn to laugh this time. "I meant no disrespect ma'am. She's just the prettiest girl I ever met."

The mustache roller didn't want to be ignored. "A lovely, English rose, just like her beautiful Mother," he said, raising his hat and bowing from the waist to them both.

Claire smiled at Mother, hoped it was true that she was as beautiful as her mother. Mother was half Irish, on her Mother's side. But she had always been called beautiful, especially by her husband. Up ahead, Claire heard Father raise his voice, knew he and Bonnie were telling the sergeant their exciting story. She was curious, but too busy being flattered to try to listen.

Henry rode past, grumbling as he had to ride his horse off the trail to get past them. He scowled at all of them and Claire tried not to laugh again. Two of the other soldiers moved up after Henry and soon Claire was parrying comments and compliments from all four of the soldiers.

When the sergeant ordered the troops to follow him, Claire felt bereft. It might be wrong, but she loved the flattering attention of the young men. After all these days on the trail, it was nice to be made to feel young and pretty again.

Henry rode back to his wagon, again his face was dark and angry when he looked her way. Claire ducked her head until he was past. The last thing she needed or wanted was to be scolded for flirting with the soldiers. She felt too happy. Instead, she traded places with Mary Anne and hurried to keep pace with Bonnie. She needed someone to talk with.

Bonnie smiled down at the bubbly blonde who was chattering away as she breathlessly tried to keep up. Impetuously, Bonnie lifted the pink faced girl onto the back of Shadrach, Tom's pet oxen.

Claire gasped and teetered. She fastened a hand on the smooth wood of the oxbow to keep from falling. But as the animal plodded along, undisturbed by his unusual rider, she relaxed. Finding her balance on the well-padded shoulders, she took a deep breath and continued to ask Bonnie's opinion of which man would make a better husband. When Bonnie shrugged, Claire pouted in irritation. "Okay, I'm going to tell you about each one again. But now this time, you need to listen, because I'm counting on your advice."

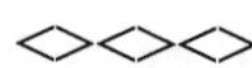

It would be two weeks before they reached Independence, Missouri, where the trail would split and lead them to northern Utah. With each passing day, the men grew more and more irritable. With only two tandem wagons, there were too few, even when separated, to corral the animals at night. More time was spent by the lead rider in finding a suitable camping place. Not only did they need grass and water, they needed suitable terrain or several sizeable trees. Usually they had to create a rope corral, since they couldn't hobble the cattle and there weren't that many hills or valleys.

Although neither man was a weapons expert, they were always armed and ready for trouble. At night, each man stood four hours of guard duty. At first they alternated early and late watches, before realizing they would have better sleep if they kept the same pattern. So Henry stood late watch, Father took the early morning hours. They tried, but the dogs were unwilling to split up. So Tip and Tyler kept, or slept, watch with each man. It was reassuring, because any strange sound or smell would bring the animals instantly awake and bristling in readiness.

The women learned to work quieter. At times, Claire felt they were walking on egg shells. Anything that Bella said, Henry would flare up in anger. Father Wimberley went to bed as soon as he ate supper, or he and Mother would argue.

The women remained by the fire, talking softly each night. Henry and the twins would check the cattle, washing their necks when the yokes were removed, lifting and cleaning their feet. At the beginning of the trip, that chore had seemed foolish nonsense listed in the pioneer handbook. But after so many days on the trail, all knew their safety and success depended on the health and well-being of the oxen and horses.

The days seemed longer and the nights shorter. Claire had taken over the dish washing, just one of the things she now did to help Bonnie. Ever since the girl had chased off the thieves, Claire was determined to treat her better, to help her friend. Tonight was no different.

Claire stood at the edge of the camp's light, emptying the dish pan after washing the last of the plates. She felt a tremendous relief when she saw a large glow near the horizon. When she heard a twig snap nearby, she jerked with surprise, until Henry spoke. "Beautiful, isn't it? First real town since we left St. Louis."

"Independence?" Claire asked. It could only be the rugged frontier town where they hoped to join a larger wagon train. In the dark, she couldn't see him clearly, but knew he nodded. "Father still has a wagon full of mining hand tools, gold pans, and wagon parts to sell. As well as his second wagon. What about you?"

She knew the Lambtons still had a third of one wagon filled with boxes of undergarments, dress shirts, and skirts to sell. The store owner had been uninterested in any of their 'boxed goods.' Patiently, she listened to Henry's cultured voice explain everything to her again.

In the distance, they heard Bella stand, keeping a hold of Barney so the child wouldn't fall. In the night, it was easy to hear her movements. Claire knew she could hear their conversation as well. Guiltily she hurried back to the fire.

Independence was teeming with a hustling population of wagon trains, trappers, and soldiers. Calvary men rode past and Claire eagerly searched for familiar faces. Bonnie searched as well, then yelled out to one of the soldiers. When she learned they were headed to Fort McPherson she was able to hand a letter to one of the soldiers to pass on to her brothers.

Claire had helped her write it, reminding her to tell them about the other soldiers they met in St. Louis, and about the thieves she'd chased off. Mainly it was full of news to reassure them all were well.

Bonnie was walking as usual, holding hands with Mary Anne and carrying Barney. The twins walked like bookends beside the tall woman. All were busy taking in the strange people and sounds. When Barney screamed, Bella and Claire both clambered down from their wagons. Bella reached him first and took him from Bonnie's arms. Mary Anne had her face buried at Bonnie's waist. Together the young women turned to where a handsome man on a wheeled platform saluted before rolling along the boardwalk. He used his knuckles to paddle along because he had no legs.

Bonnie and Claire exchanged a glance. Claire remembered Lynne's words about her mail-order bride ad when she first read it. Phillip Gant had written a simple description, *Tall, well-formed veteran without vices* and Lynne had joked he was *probably an old goat with one leg or one eye*. Claire crossed herself in prayer for her friend. In her last letter, Lynne had assured the girls her husband was perfectly formed and handsome. They had both giggled over that part of the letter.

Although Claire had been tempted by all the ads for brides, she lacked the courage, or desperation, to answer one. She could never marry a stranger. She needed time to find the perfect man, one her family would approve of. She knew he was out there waiting for her somewhere and she was keeping her eyes open. Even if she had to kiss a few frogs to find her prince, she was determined she would find him.

As their party drove down the main street, a man rushed out and asked if either of the men wanted to sell a wagon and team. Henry sold the Lambton's second wagon, along with four of his oxen. He rushed to move his leftover stock to empty the wagon. Father Wimberley moved around them and on to a store ahead that had tools in front. He had no luck there, but then moved on down the street, letting Bonnie and the boys stay with the wagon while he made inquiries inside.

Claire returned with Bella and Barney to the Lambton's wagon. Claire helped Henry move goods and empty the second wagon, then held one team of oxen as he freed the first two pair. Tom and Jim ran up and helped him. She noticed they made sure that the oxen he sold didn't include their pets. As soon as the wagon was ready, Henry dismounted and went in to ask the merchant if he was interested in acquiring any new merchandise.

When he returned, he looked furious. Over Bella's protest, he moved the wagon and pulled back the cover. The quicker he moved the angrier she became. "This is not the way to do business. At least let me straighten and cover our own belongings." Henry ignored his scolding wife. Claire offered to take the boy so that Bella could help him, but the angry woman climbed down and carried the still complaining child onto the boardwalk and into the shade.

Red-faced, Henry tried to call out to a couple of passing pedestrians. Suddenly Claire climbed up onto the front of the wagon, removed her bonnet and fluffed her hair before turning and smiling to the riders and travelers passing on the street. "Come take a look. We have all the latest lovely things from Boston. Delicate, lacy scanties. Wonderful, whale-bone corsets. And incredible petticoats." With each item named, she pulled one from the labeled but jumbled boxes to unfurl and hold up in front of her. In minutes, they had created a traffic jam and Henry turned from the sidewalk to face the street and collect money. Surprisingly, most of the first customers were men. But soon the working girl's from down the street poured up from the saloons to pick through things.

Bella looked horrified, but Claire just smiled and held up another unmentionable for inspection. At the end of the hour, the merchant who had sent Henry fleeing came out. He agreed to purchase all of the remaining undergarments, but passed on the ordinary shirts and skirts. On the condition, that Lambton move on from his business and not sale any more in Independence. Henry agreed.

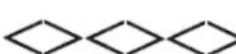

Frustrated, Father Wimberley tried every store without luck. Bonnie pointed to the Lambton wagon and Claire waving a pink petticoat at a cowboy. He turned his wagon around. Bonnie laughingly raced to join her friend. She helped Claire down from the wagon and together they ran to where her father had pulled his wagon to a standstill.

"Here's your sales girl. I don't think those cowhands were buying petticoats for themselves. Just let Claire get their attention, you can explain what you've got for sale and how much you want for it. The twins happily climbed into the second wagon, handing out items or holding them as Claire repeated her antics from the front of the wagon.

It was harder to get a crowd, but many of the passing wagon trains were interested in the spare oxbows and wagon-wheels. A few men on foot or horseback also stopped to inspect the items the smiling blonde was holding aloft. “Looking for gold?” she called. “Then you need the best gold pan, hand-forged in the best foundry in Boston.”

“Goldie Locks, reckon that has to be a lucky pan since you’ve already touched it,” the man who had addressed her so boldly was elbowed by his friend for his brass.

Claire’s father glared at the man and Henry stepped away from settling Bella and Barney back in their wagon, pulling out his shotgun, just in case.

The men lowered his head, removed his hat and grinned sheepishly up at the trio. “Sorry folks, I didn’t mean any insult to you miss. You’re just such a sweet, pretty gal. Reckon you’re the prettiest to come through town in quiet awhile. My apologies if my remark offended.”

Claire relaxed and smiled as she held out the pan. “Apology accepted, if you’re buying a gold pan?”

“For one of your smiles, beauty, we’re both buying,” the man behind him said.

As one item was sold, she took the next. “If you bought that wonderful pan, you probably need this oak-handled shovel to move the dirt into your pan,” she said.

It took a little longer, but a store owner came out and bought half the remaining lot at noon so he could get rid of the competition.

Father Wimberley and the boys shifted the remaining cargo into his wagon, raising the beds higher to rest on top of the remaining stock. He then sold his empty wagon without a team. He sent the twins back with a pair of oxen so Henry's rig again matched his own. Each family now had a single wagon pulled by four oxen.

The fear that had prodded them since St. Louis, again made them rush to find a secure campsite before nightfall. Every man who had admired Claire wouldn't be as gallant as the gold miner. When they were directed to a campsite full of fellow travelers, they felt a little safer. When the soldiers came by, they finally relaxed.

CHAPTER FOURTEEN

It did not take long to figure out where to walk. The trail made by other wagon trains had left a broad muddy path through the center of town to the camping grounds. As usual, there was someone on hand to demand a fee for the delivery of feed for their oxen. Since there wasn't a sign of anything left alive on the muddy ground, Father Wimberley paid up. He asked only that the stable owner deliver to his animals first. The man grunted in answer as he took the money.

Claire and Bonnie went for water together, with Bonnie carrying her usual shotgun. On the way to the city well, they overheard a lot of camp talk. Most was repeated tales of Indian trouble and revised accounts of Custer's defeat on the Little Big Horn.

When they came back, neither girl was surprised to hear the two men in their group arguing again. Henry wanted to leave with the large train that was pulling out in the morning, Father insisted they had no choice but to wait until there was a large enough group of others to form a wagon train pulled by oxen. Their animals, as good as they were, wouldn't last trying to keep up with mules and horses. It was Bella who broke up the argument by calling Henry to bed.

Claire wondered why he argued so fiercely, when the Lambtons could always go their own way at any time. Father had certainly pointed it out to Henry enough times. Even she knew their main priority was to join a wagon train headed west as soon as possible. They needed others for safety against the Indians or any other marauders.

It was the first night for the travelers to not all sleep under the canvas wagon tops. Father Wimberley and the twins were struggling to pitch one of the big tents, leaving his wagon to the four women. Standing around beside the fire, Claire and Bonnie smiled as they heard Henry and Bella arguing as they shuffled things around inside their crowded wagon. Claire saw the couple were merely building a high wall with the boxes to surround their mattress.

Claire and Bonnie offered to help, but were sent on to their beds. The older man's face was gloomy, the boys aglow with excitement. Claire kissed her father Goodnight, then led Bonnie over to the Wimberley wagon. "You can sleep with Mother, since the bed we sleep in is a lot shorter."

As Claire and the young girl shook out the covers and climbed in the small bed wedged near the back of the wagon, Bonnie cautiously removed her dress to prepare to sleep with Mother Wimberley. "Do you think he will be all right, the boys looked excited, but I'm not sure Father was?" Claire asked.

Mother Wimberley looked out the front flap of the wagon to stare at her husband. He looked frustrated, but Tom and Jim were already holding the post in a different position and his face changed into a smile. He turned to wave at his wife and she pulled the center gusset to close the wagon, embarrassed at being caught watching. Robert never complained, but she knew today had exhausted him. She had heard his groan when Henry had asked about the new sleeping arrangements.

"Your father will be fine. At least with us in the center of the camp, our men won't have to keep their usual watch. The fact that troops are camped on the perimeter of the wagons should keep us all safe."

Claire hoped Bonnie wouldn't mention all the talk about the Indians, they had heard on the way to the well. It wouldn't help in any way, and they all did deserve one peaceful night of sleep.

<><><>

Finally, on their second morning in town, the team Henry had sold and nine other ox drawn wagons joined them. As they left town, they felt safer with more rifles and men.

There were several disapproving glances at Claire and Bonnie. Bonnie sent Mother to find out what the issue was. When Mother walked out to where the women were taking care of business, she heard one loud-mouthed woman, Kaye Raglon, objecting to letting the Wimberleys and Lambtons stay with respectable people. Mother Wimberley didn't hesitate. "And just what do you have to object to?"

"Well, it was unseemly, the way you all were selling goods on the square," the pug-faced woman complained.

Mother pointed out they had done only what they came west to do. They had hauled the goods from Boston with plans to sell them along the route, preferably in Independence.

Then the woman nodded at Claire. "It was unseemly, the way your girl held up those things and swished around to get men to buy them. No respectable woman would have. Course I noticed you sold plenty to the undesirable kind."

"It seems you're pretty experienced at judging 'those women.' I won't ask where you gained the experience. But I will remind you that the Bible says, 'judge not, that you be not judged.' I can assure you, Claire is an innocent and was only trying to help friends sell merchandise. She used to be a clerk in their store in Boston. I think you had better stop trying to divide our small group," Mother said.

"Well I never, you can't talk to me that way," the woman protested.

Mother held up her hand to stop the woman. "We're leaving. Just remember, there are a lot of perils along this route. We will all need each other's support in the days to come. I don't want to quarrel with you," she extended a hand to the woman. "May we part as fellow travelers and allies, not enemies?" Mother Wimberley stood poised, her blue eyes and perfect complexion in marked contrast with the other woman's coarse looks.

Finally the woman extended her hand as one of the other women nudged her. Claire stood with her head lowered, her red face hidden by the wide brim of her poke bonnet, biting her tongue.

Mother and Claire walked back toward the wagons. "I'm sorry, Mother, I never thought about making the wrong impression. I just wanted to help Henry and Bella sell their goods." Mother nudged her back and they hurried toward the campfire. "Hush," Mother said, wrapping her arm around her daughter's bent shoulders. "You had no way to know, but from this point on, remember to practice modesty and decorum. The last thing we want is to be left by this party because of an old biddy like that's gossiping."

As they approached the wagons, Bonnie rushed out to the pair, well aware that something was wrong. Claire climbed up into the back of the wagon, pretended to be busy straightening the already straight cover on the beds. When Mother Wimberley wouldn't tell her. Bonnie climbed into the back of the wagon and pulled a tearful Claire into her arms. "Oh little goose, what's wrong now?"

Sniffling, Claire tried for a smile. "The women were gossiping, complaining that the Wimberleys and Lambtons weren't suitable people to be in the same train with them."

"Who, tell me which one and I'll go set them straight?"

Claire let her bonnet fall down behind her, tried to smile at her friend but her mouth crumpled instead. "That ugly Kaye Raglon. She accused me of being one of those women, you know, the kind that bought all the expensive lace undergarments."

When Bonnie looked ready to chase out after them, Claire grabbed her skirt and used the thick wool to pull her back. "Don't, Mother already told her off. Made her shake hands and everything. I just didn't think, I was just trying to catch people's attention in order to sell as much as possible."

"Well, if the women are talking, the men soon will be. You be careful and stay close to the wagon at all times It wouldn't do for one of them to get you cornered."

Claire stood up, reassured enough to go back to sit on the wagon seat to relieve her Mother of the chore or at least keep her company.

The next day, all were working in harmony. If the men had heard the gossip or added to it, no-one gave any sign. It was early in the day when they appointed Father Wimberley to be in charge of the wagon train. One day, and he had convinced all that he was the most qualified and capable to drive the lead wagon. He and his boys seemed to get a good deal more from their oxen than the others could. But like all cattle, when the lead animals moved forward, the rest followed.

That night, Claire was walking back with another pail of water when the thing Bonnie warned her about happened. A leering man stood in her path and dared to speak to her. “I heard about your fancy petticoats and other things. I figure if you showed everyone in town, you could show me if I ask nicely for a peek.”

“I don’t know what you heard, but it wasn’t true. I showed nothing of mine, in town or anywhere else. Please move so I can pass,” Claire said with as much outrage as she could manage. This wasn’t the first man to ever try to corner her. She had pushed away the foreman at the mill a half-dozen times the last week when she was the only woman still on the floor. Of course, then she had the long hat pin that her mother insisted she carry.

The man looked confused for a minute, then shook his head. “Naw, my Ma wouldn’t lie about something like that. Come on now, girlie. I just want to get to know you a little better.”

When he stepped closer, Claire did what Bonnie had taught her, she stepped forward hard on his foot, then pushed him away with great force. The man yelled and grabbed at her and Claire screamed. As she backed quickly out of reach the man started to rise and they both heard the ominous ratcheting of a shotgun.

“You heard the lady. She told you to move out of the way.”

“It’s you, ain’t it? You’re the dandy she was selling her bloomers for. Bet that wasn’t all she was doing for you.”

Henry shocked Claire when she heard him swear.

“Well, I ain’t afraid of no city man, no matter how many women he handles.” The man was lurching to his feet when they heard another voice speak, one as loud and angry as Henry’s.

“You better stand up and apologize now, or you and your mother can just head on to Utah alone. I won’t have any man who is disrespectful to my innocent daughter in this wagon train.”

Again, the man looked confused. The twins moved out of the shadows, as confused by what was being said as the young man. When they looked at Claire, they saw she was frightened and rushed up to stand beside her. "You better stay away from Claire, mister, or we'll…" Tom wasn't sure what the threat should be, but Jim needed to yell too. "We sure will. You ought to be ashamed, acting so mean to someone as sweet as our Claire."

The man stared at the pale face, the enormous blue eyes of the innocent looking girl before him. He took in the threatening stance and glares of the four men who had come to her rescue. Suddenly he felt worse than foolish.

"Miss, I'm sorry. I sure am. My Ma was telling tales, and I…"

But Claire had already turned and stormed off, leaving the confused man to face all her protectors. "I really am sorry, fellows. I promise, I won't get out of line again."

"And you'll tell the other men on the train to leave her alone," Father Wimberley ordered.

"Yes sir, yes sir. I certainly will. I'll try to set Ma straight as well." He lowered his eyes and muttered, but "she probably won't listen."

Henry glared at him, reluctantly lowered and eased the mechanism back on his gun. His eyes pierced the foolish young man, who had the grace to finally meet his gaze before looking down. "I'm sorry Mr. Lambton, I had no right to say what I did…"

Again, his apology faded as the man turned and stalked off back to the wagon train, motioning for the twins to follow him.

Behind the man who was starting to look angry again, Father Wimberley spoke. “That’s her second warning. Next time you’re leaving. There’s too much out there to worry about to have someone on the train stirring trouble between the members. Tell her loudly, and tell her I mean it.”

CHAPTER FIFTEEN

Claire returned to her wagon, searched for and finally found the hat pin in her hat box. Fuming, she carefully stuck it along the inseam of her arm with the big pin head just at the fold of her wrist. When Henry came stomping in, complaining about the Raglons, Bonnie and Mother rushed to the wagon and tried to offer her sympathy. Claire assured them, she was fine, that the men in their group had rescued her. She noticed Bella looked smug rather than upset like her Mother and friend. She knew even after working with her for months, Bella secretly approved of the attacks on her character. Though there was nothing between her and Henry, Bella had always been jealous of them.

Claire swallowed and sank back in the shadows as her Father appeared and told them how the matter had ended. Hopefully the young man and his mother would listen. If not, she knew Father never made threats or postured, the trouble-making pair would be gone.

<><><>

After supper, Father Wimberley groaned as the boys raced to take the tent out of the back of the wagon. Mother Wimberley reached up to rub his lower back in sympathy. Bonnie looked at the older man and shook her head. “Let me take the tent. The boys are used to sleeping with me anyway.”

Father Wimberley shook his head. “You’ve no idea how hard on you it can be.”

Laughing, Bonnie grabbed the bag of tent posts as the twins ran past. “At least let me give it a try tonight. If it’s too much, you can have it back tomorrow.”

Mother Wimberley smiled at the tall girl and looked past her where her daughter stood, quietly rinsing the tin plates as Mary Anne passed the emptied ones to her. The two shepherds stood happily snapping up scraps, with only an occasional lick on a plate if the little girl wasn’t fast enough. “Let her Robert, so I can rub some of these aches away for you in my bed.”

The couple exchanged a secret look and Bonnie walked on to set up her bed for the night. She knew it had been difficult for the older woman to fall asleep last night. Tonight the couple would be together the way they belonged.

When the tarp was unrolled with its blanket bedrolls inside the canvas tent, she sighed as she looked toward the boys busy arguing about which got to sleep next to the tent opening. The boy's black and white dogs, Tip and Tyler, stuck their noses through the tent flap and whined for attention. Bonnie shook her head. "No, you don't. You two can sleep under the wagon or outside to guard the door. Get, she snapped," The two dogs bowed and growled a little, but both backed out as directed. "You two," she turned to look at the twins. "Tom left, Jim right. Get your boots off. The light is going off on the count of ten."

At noon, Bonnie passed out the lunches she had made in the morning. She carried Claire's to her last and sat on the tailgate of the wagon beside her friend while they ate. After Bonnie brought up yesterday's encounter, Claire showed her the hat pin and how quickly she could push it forward if needed. Swinging their feet together, Claire asked Bonnie how difficult it was to sleep on the ground.

Bonnie shook her head, "A piece of heaven. Made me remember sharing our pallets on the floor, me and my four sisters. The lads are no problem, it's those spoiled cow herders that are the problem."

Claire laughed as the pair of matched shepherds appeared as though they knew they were being talked about. Although she wasn't sure which was Tip and which Tyler, she smiled as the pair of dogs managed to gain their balance enough to walk along behind the wagon on two legs. Even

Bonnie laughed at them. Both tossed one of the dogs a bite of crust, and the two disappeared.

Father Wimberley rode up beside the laughing girls, admiring the pretty picture they made. "Did Mother tell you then? I thought you would like the news."

Both looked puzzled, but it was Claire, who asked. When she heard the news, she squealed with delight. For the first time since leaving St. Louis, they would have another chance for music and dancing. The plan to have a meeting of all the wagon teams was a great one.

Bonnie had been complaining about the drawbacks of being in a large group of wagons and worse about the problem of following another train with forty-two wagons. There was little to gather or collect along the trail when so many were covering the same ground ahead of them. She now got to ride more, since there were fewer wagons and animals to keep track of. With less work for the men, they shared the nice bays, Bob and Sue. Usually it was the twins who rode out with her, but Claire had ridden with her once or twice. Still, Bonnie was frustrated, because she saw no chance to shoot game.

Father Wimberley interrupted her thoughts. "The Raglons only emphasized the problem. We are a newly formed caravan and it's time everyone had a chance to meet and get to know each other. I asked the others yesterday, and we decided tonight was a good time. Looks to be good weather, and we are near enough to the troopers to have good protection still."

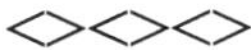

The soldiers passed through just after he left. They talked brusquely with everyone, but they made time to visit and flirt with the Wimberley party. They were pursuing renegade Indians on their way to the next fort, and seemed happy for the diversion. Bonnie dropped off the tail gate to resume her trek beside the Lambton's wagons. The soldiers tried flirting with her, but she was better at ignoring them. Most moved through the caravan, looking for other pretty girls to chat with. She noticed how Claire fairly sparkled like a glittery angel at all the flattery and attention. When Henry rode past his wagon and kept pace with the lead animals, Bonnie could tell from his glower that he had noticed too.

Her friend was a woman of her word. Claire had turned her attentions to finding a husband among the horde of young men moving west as they traveled. She knew it was wrong to even consider another woman's husband. Bonnie knew the girl was honest, there had been nothing untoward to happen between her and Henry Lambton. Still, it was always there, that current of awareness between two people. Everyone in their party sensed it. Bonnie didn't have to look to know Bella was even now staring at Henry's stiff back atop the prancing bay, carefully holding the animal in check so he could keep the girl and her admirers under his gaze.

Only when the troopers raised their caps in salute to the women and moved on did Henry relax in the saddle and ride the horse forward. Bonnie knew it wasn't just coincidence that Claire was working her way through the wagon's crowded interior to join her mother on the wagon seat. Sighing, she fell back a few steps to talk to Bella about the dinner and dance later that evening.

All forty-three people from the eleven wagons of the oxen wagon train met for a shared supper, enjoying dishes made by others. In the midst of the warm conversation, as people tried to learn more about their neighbors, the laughter and bustle of the women preparing the food stopped. Everyone listened to the haunting sound beneath the starlit night of the howl of wolves in the distance. When a second wolf answered, farther away, there was silence followed by a little awkward laughter.

As soon as the delicious meal was over, the men brought out the fiddles and jugs to play a tune. Volunteers were called for to sing or call the dance. When no one came forward, four of the young women whispered together before stepping onto the makeshift platform. While Bonnie and Claire sang with two other young women on the train, the married couples moved out to dance hesitantly in the flickering flames of the campfire. The children danced around amid the older couples.

Claire winced when Bonnie hit one of her flat notes. She tried to sing louder to hide the sound. Lynne and Bonnie both loved to sing. Singing was alright, and Claire had been told she had a lovely voice. But she only sang when at church or in a group like tonight. The other two were as her father joked, Irish song birds.

Claire was aware of the young men standing in a row, whispering among themselves as they looked over the serenading women. Were they really the only single women in the wagon train? When Kaye Raglon's son looked her way, she noticed he bowed to her and said something sharp to the man beside him. Both seemed to regard her again with a little more admiration. It made her feel annoyed and pleased at the same time. She shed her flowered bonnet to reveal her curls and shook her head for a minute. Carefully, she set her fanciest hat at the end of the wagon. As the fiddler changed his tune, the girls all sang a ballad and the line dancing partners twirled around in pairs to the waltz tempo.

There were only seven men available. Two were still boys, one was the Raglon man, and she had no interest in him at all. At the second tune, men came up and shyly asked the singers to dance. One short fellow asked Bonnie, but she shook her head, announcing she was married. He turned to

Claire and held out his hand. Smiling, she gladly accepted. At five feet, the man was just perfect in height for her. As the others danced, Bonnie sang a duet with a sad-eyed old man about the lost love of Barbara Allen.

Claire danced next with a young man named George. He told her of his plans to strike a claim and return home rich to his sweetheart. When she asked him if he had proposed to the woman before leaving, he shook his head. "Did you at least tell her your intentions and ask her to wait?" When he shook his head, Claire shook her own and laughed at his answer. "Well, what will you do if she finds someone who will speak up and ask her? If you return home rich only to find her married?"

He appeared insulted and left her to one of the other three who were traveling west together. This one, James, was considerably taller and Claire was getting a crick in her neck, leaning her head back far enough to talk to him.

James told her all four of them were from the same town. When the news of the gold strike in the Black Hills appeared in their paper they were playing cards. It was the man who had just danced with her who had come up with the scheme. All younger sons, with no chance of inheriting enough land to ever make a go of it, they all knew they needed to move on to find a way to earn more money. It was George, the man who had left mad, who suggested they pool all their assets and head west.

"Of course, it didn't take a lot to convince the rest of us. Cobb there and Gerald, they were ready to leave the moment he said anything. But we all worked another month, so we could stockpile things we needed to make the trip. Then we rode the train to St. Louis."

"Really, isn't that terribly expensive. Where was it you were from, James?"

"Hanover, Pennsylvania. We're all members of the same church and went to school together when we were younger. Well, we all knew we wanted to do it. So we kind of stowed away you might say, in one of the train cars, after we loaded our sheep on it."

"Your sheep?"

"Well, it was the same as ours, so to speak. We kind of each brought a few head from our parents' farms. Planned to sell them with the notion of buying a wagon with the proceeds when we got out west."

When Claire was quiet, he took the chance to move the pretty girl to the other side of the fire not realizing they ended nearer to her parents. Two men were already paying attention and were moving their way, but his maneuver had earned him a few more seconds to converse with her.

"You're not married or engaged are you?" he asked.

Claire again shook her head to answer. At his follow-up question, Claire paused to give a thoughtful answer. "Of course I want to marry. What woman wouldn't want that? I want to wed and have children, maybe even three or four.

Her mother and father stepped up closer to the couple and the tall man bowed over her hand and disappeared into the crowd.

The other two men approaching were elbowing and pushing each other as they converged on the little blonde. Claire sighed and Father chuckled. In minutes, the man named Gerald had swept his prize away. Claire tried to signal Bonnie as he twirled her past. In minutes, the jug blower and a man with a mandolin joined the fiddler and again played a Virginia reel that had everyone changing hands and moving through to the faster dance. There was even a pass when she danced with Henry before he and Bella were swept away down the aisle of dancers.

It was followed by another reel and Claire was actually breathless when the last man, called Cobb of all things, released her to a waiting Bonnie and Mary Anne. The three young women moved to the table where desserts and coffee were being served. With much giggling, the girls discussed the dance and the men who were now wearing out the other two single young women. Claire chided Bonnie for not dancing. Bonnie only gave her a look.

Mary Anne, with all the innocence and enthusiasm of a child, urged Claire back into the dance with her. The two young women exchanged smiles when the darling girl picked Tom and drug him out to be her dance partner. Although he groaned at dancing with his sister, Claire noticed the lad was a good dancer, like all the McKinneys, and was really enjoying himself.

As the camp settled down to sleep, Bonnie teased the pretty girl about dancing with so many handsome men tonight. Claire laughed and Mary Anne interrupted to announce she had danced with two good-looking boys herself.

"Tom and Jim?" Bonnie asked.

"Yes, but I wasn't counting them. The dark-haired boy with the long nose, you know the one that looks like a gypsy."

Bonnie smiled. She had noticed the little boy that looked closer to her sister Reagan's age of five than Mary Anne's seven years.

"Was he a good dancer?" Claire asked.

"Very good, he was a little short but he could move to the music. I also danced with the boy from the last wagon. He was tall, but he wasn't any good at all."

"Why didn't you dance, Bonnie?" Mother asked from the other side of the little girl.

"Well, first, I am married. Second, they were all too, too short for me." The others laughed. "And third," she hid a deep yawn behind her hand, but didn't reveal the third reason. She heard the other women yawning too. In her mind's eye, she imagined swirling about the fire in the arms of a handsome Lieutenant while her brothers stood with the fiddler, singing the tunes.

As Claire settled down to sleep, she tried to bring up images of each of the men she had danced with. She wasn't a writer like Lynne, whose letters had kept them all enthralled with her stories. But she decided she would list each man she met along the journey, the single ones, and after their name, all the particulars she could learn. Sleepily she opened her journal and by candlelight listed the single men at the dance, even the Raglon one. Mary Anne turned away, muttering about the light while Mother and Father quickly began to snore.

When Claire tried to recall their particulars to record on the line beside their names, only one face came to mind. Instead of the suitable young men, all she saw was a handsome man with neatly groomed blonde hair and a trim mustache. His smile flashed briefly, as he hooked her arm with his to spin her in one circle of the reel.

CHAPTER SIXTEEN

Claire flounced down from the wagon, wearing her pink gingham dress and its matching bonnet. Although not as durable as the tan linsey-woolsey or as stylish as her favorite green dress, it was still one of her favorites from home. Last night she had met the other maiden ladies as they discussed what to sing after dinner. Bonnie had offered several tunes but the girls had looked to Claire for a final decision. It had buoyed her self-esteem, and she had immediately taken a liking to the timid cousins from Nauvoo, Illinois.

They had been impressed by her sense of fashion and had invited her to visit as soon as possible. She would meet with the first girl, Faye, as soon as breakfast ended. The other cousin, Dorothy, in the afternoon. Like having a full dance card last night, having other ladies to talk with filled her with pleasure. Although she had Mother, Bonnie, and Bella, after all these weeks together, there was little new left for them to share. Dorothy in particular had asked for news about fashion and Claire planned to take her last Godey's magazine. Of course it was four months old, but she had the stack of duplicate fashion flyers the buyer had given her after modeling for him in St. Louis.

Impatiently, Claire noticed that the men were still not back. They spent longer setting up camp each evening and were slower to roll out of bed each morning. She complained as Bonnie cooked breakfast, and the tall girl pointed out the obvious. “We’re part of a bigger wagon train now, more people and animals to water at the end and start of each day. At least it gives me more time to cook and prepare the meals.”

Although Claire had told herself she would help Bonnie more, it was hard to change her habits. The day Bonnie had ridden off with the twins to visit her brothers, Claire had discovered exactly how much work the woman did. But where it was hard on Claire, Bonnie made everything easily and with a smile. Claire fumbled at everything and took twice as long. One day of walking beside the big oxen had exhausted her for a week. So unless Bonnie complained, Claire wasn’t going to interfere and hurt her friend’s pride.

Besides, sometimes she did the dishes, which seemed generous enough. She also helped to fetch water each evening. All of them had a series of chores, even Mary Anne.

One of Father’s new chores was assigning a position for each wagon in the longer train. The trail dust grew thicker the farther back in the line a wagon rolled. So unlike some, Father forced the group to allemande back and let the tail wagon move to the front each day. Once a group had ridden at the back, they saw the fairness of the system. Since everyone hadn’t, there were a few grumblers like the Raglons.

Grass was becoming scarcer because they were on a part of the trail where wagons had been moving through for nearly a year. The trail was well defined, with clear watering holes and camping sites. But that meant that the land around those sites was pretty closely cropped. Father argued and seemed to have convinced the majority of the men that they would be better off, unhooking their animals and leading them to water, then bringing them back to the uncropped grassland to graze at night. But the plan meant the women would have more steps to walk to carry water and that more men would be needed to guard the animals. Again there were complaints.

The Raglons pointed out that every group didn't have a pair of boys and well-trained dogs to help them take their animals to water and to herd them back to the newer sites. Father insisted they were lucky, so far there had been plenty of water for the stock. They better appreciate the fact and make sure they kept their barrels full for the time when the trail didn't end at a river or stream. So now, the men took the time to top off the barrels first each day. Bonnie no longer had to drive a team and was trying to figure out what to do with her new freedom. She gladly took over that chore for their party and the Lambtons.

Claire didn't care. She was delighted to have other women to talk with on the train, ones who weren't married and tired each day from tending children. Unlike Bonnie, they were eager to talk about potential marriage material. She intended to rate the prospects among the men on the train, the troopers who had ridden through, and have someone else to speculate with her about the miners and ranchers waiting ahead.

Claire stomped back from her visit riding beside Faye Brewer. Father and Henry had both offered their mount so she could ride, but she had laughed at the idea. Instead, she just remained by the trail until the sixth wagon rolled up and let Faye's father help her to climb up beside his daughter. The two girls had sat with Claire's log between them on the seat, giggling as they came up with descriptions and nicknames for each of the eligible bachelors. Cobb of course became corn cob, Gerald, with his long wild hair became Geraldine, George, King George.

Claire was surprised the girl had already taken a liking to one young man. When she learned it was the Raglon boy, she had to bite her tongue to keep from warning her away. If it were Bonnie or Lynne, she would have confided what he had said to her two days before. But since she didn't know if Faye might have formed the same opinion of her character, Claire was afraid to say anything.

When, an hour had passed, she asked help in climbing down from the wagon. Mr. Brewer seemed a little annoyed by the request, but did stop his oxen so she could dismount. The wagon behind him yelled and someone farther back swore. Claire was sure it was the Raglon's voices she heard complaining. Holding her head up and thanking him, she hurried to reach her own wagon. But in the soft churned trail, it was hard to walk fast. It seemed like the wagons and oxen were moving faster than she was.

Annoyed, Claire abandoned the road bed and climbed up onto the shoulder. Here the grass was tall and her gown kept snagging on weeds and brush. It really wasn't any easier to walk fast there. As the Brewer's oxen passed her and she saw Faye looking up at her in surprise, Claire began to panic. She was afraid the Raglon's wagon would pull up beside her and that horrid Raglon man might accost her again, Claire did her best to walk faster without falling or dropping back down into the rough dirt of the road bed.

It didn't help that the people in the wagons that had greeted her before as they passed, now wanted to have conversations about the most trivial things. "Didn't she think the day was lovely? Had she had a nice visit with her new friend? What was that she was carrying in her arms?"

Claire had been taught good manners, so she made small talk with each group as she drew alongside. She could feel the sun pinking her cheeks even with the bonnet on. It didn't have the full brim and dust ruffle in back the way her ugly western poke bonnet did. For the first time she wished she had worn the dreadful thing. At least if she had grabbed her parasol, she would have been able to use it as a cane, or to shield her complexion from the hot sun.

By the time she reached the Lambton's wagon she was breathless and embarrassed. She could feel the perspiration darkening the thin gingham of the dress bodice, knew her face must be ablaze from the heat and her exertions. Bella looked up in surprise as Claire called to her and tried to hurry past. Of course, now Bella wanted to talk to her. Claire tried to rush without panting, held her arms tight against her waist as she answered the same inane questions.

"Did you have a nice visit with your new friend, what was her name, Faye Brewer?" Bella asked.

"Faye Brewer. Yes, we had a lovely visit."

"It's a nice day for a walk isn't it? Not a cloud in the sky."

Claire swallowed, looked up at the blazing sun and almost stumbled when she looked back down. Her skirt snagged again on a tall weed. Claire noticed in disgust it was the horrible plant Bonnie called beggar lice. It would leave tiny little triangular burrs along her petticoat and skirt hem. She flipped the skirt free and looked to see she was right, They ran in a long jagged row across the hem of her best slip.

In horror, Claire looked up to see Henry riding back toward her. Before Tom at the ox's shoulder or Bella in the wagon seat could ask about the book she clutched tightly, Henry called out to her.

"Hold up a minute, you can ride Sue back to your wagon."

Bella made a hissing sound and Claire wondered if her face could look any redder. "No thanks," she murmured. "I'm almost there, and you know I hate to ride."

Ignoring her protest, he extended an arm and swept her onto the horse, sitting in his lap. Claire closed her eyes, prepared to faint dead away with humiliation.

Henry managed to turn the horse on the trail and ignore his wife's protest to trot up beside the Wimberley wagon and hand her off onto the bench as her mother scooted over. "There you go. Next time don't be so pig-headed. Take one of the horses."

He turned around again and pounded back to post along beside his angry wife.

Claire looked across to read horror in her Mother's eyes as well. She couldn't believe Henry Lambton had dared to manhandle her and talk to her in that tone.

That night, James Temple, or bean pole, as she and Faye had named him, came to call with his friend George beside him. Very politely he asked her Father if he might walk around the outside of the wagons with his daughter and her companion. Claire was as surprised as was her father, but Mother seemed pleased with his manners. She invited the two self-conscious young men to join them for coffee and bread pudding, but both were too well-mannered to accept. Instead, they walked off as though they had to inspect the cattle peacefully grazing between the bend of the wagons and the ribbon of the river winding behind them.

Bonnie fussed and Mary Anne volunteered to go instead. Mother laughed and insisted the little girl stay to help her wash up while the big girls went for a walk with their callers. As they left the firelight, George carrying the lantern, he held Claire's elbow. Behind them, Bonnie fell into step beside James. Like the bay horses or the cattle dogs, they were matched pairs in height. As soon as they reached the shadows, James moved up to take Claire's other arm while Bonnie and the dogs trailed along behind.

All three were very proper. The conversation was about the fun they'd all had dancing the night before. James turned to include Bonnie when he thanked the ladies for the wonderful music. Bonnie sniffed in answer. The man turned back to trying to draw Clair's attention. He really had no competition. For whatever reason, the short but handsome George seemed to hold some animosity toward the lovely little Blonde.

They completed the big arc, then turned and started back. Finally, there was a pause in conversation when they were about half-way around the circle. They could hear the men back at their own campfire arguing.

"What did Miss Faye have to say about the dance?" George's question surprised Claire. She looked over into his blue eyes as he lifted the lantern so he could watch her expression as she answered.

For a moment, Claire felt annoyed. How dare this little man prefer someone as plain as Faye Brewer to her? Especially since she was the only woman on the train who was the exact height he was. They even shared the same coloring, pale, fair haired and blue-eyed. Several people had remarked about what a cute couple they made. Then she realized how silly her feelings were and laughed.

"She had a wonderful time dancing, too. I think she found someone she favored," Claire said.

But no matter how the men asked, she refused to betray the other girl's confidences. "You'll just have to call on her tomorrow and ask her for yourselves," Claire told them as they neared their own wagon. "Of course, you'll probably have to walk out with her, with her father or mother as the chaperone."

"No need," James said. We'll walk her and her cousin Dorothy about, same as Gerald and Cobb have done this evening. They'll be coming to pay their respects to you here, you see."

Claire became annoyed and pulled her arm free from James. They could hear voices near the fire. For a moment she wanted to make a big ruckus, demand why the two men assumed she would be home if they called. The nerve of these two, to think that after one meeting she would be pining for their courtship. Instead, she bristled, "How did you decide between you, who would call on whom this evening?" she asked. At least the two men had the grace to look embarrassed.

She blushed as she imagined the answer. Maybe these two were the losers of the argument, the ones who had to call on her first. As to how they decided, did they flip a coin, or as she suspected, for this dishonest foursome, dice or cards would be their answer. She felt delighted to have a reason to scold them for whatever they answered. But she heard Henry yelling and tilted her head to listen, raising her hand to shush their response to her question.

The argument stopped as the young people grew closer. Claire's mother made her own shushing sound in warning.

James stepped back and took Bonnie's arm as they entered the clearing.

Instead of feeling flattered, Claire felt disappointed in the quality of her first suitors. Cheeks pink, she stormed across to bend and kiss her mother's face. Then abruptly, she said good night to all, and turned toward their wagon.

The men bowed like gentlemen and said Goodnight, but clearly they were aware they had insulted the girl, although neither was sure how they had done it. They moved quickly out of the firelight and around inside the temporary corral back to their own campfire and wagon. As soon as they had left the circle, the argument resumed.

"It's wrong for a sheltered young woman to be allowed to parade around in front of God and the rest of the train. It could be bad for her reputation."

Bonnie coughed, "She wasn't alone, or do I look like a bread pudding to you?"

"No, well, I know she wasn't alone. But I just don't think it's seemly, that's all," Henry said.

"Well, when you have your own daughter, you can train her up the way you like. If Claire is to find a suitable man to marry, she needs to have a chance to make her selection from the eligible men she meets. Then, if she finds one she likes, her mother and I will make sure he is worthy." He rose, blustery and stiff.

Bella called from their wagon, "Aren't you coming to bed, Henry?"

He fumed, still wanting to argue. He stomped off, clearly at a loss for what to say next.

"Robert, are you all right," Mother Wimberley asked.

"Still a little stiff from sleeping on the ground," he answered.

"Well, keep your original accommodations. Didn't bother me at all? You ready for bed boys?" Bonnie said as she looked around for the children.

"They've already set up and turned in. So's the little girl," Father said.

"Do you have guard duty early or late tonight?" Mother Wimberley asked.

"Don't have it at all. Me or Henry. Best to bed, all of you. We'll be moving out at the crack of dawn tomorrow."

"Tomorrow and every day," Claire said from inside the wagon.

Bonnie patted the canvas as she walked past, grinning. Claire took a deep breath. The flapping noise was as loud as though she'd said 'Goose.'

Claire should have kept quiet. But the only thrill she'd had was just now. Talking with Faye, she had realized her new friend was far less intelligent and fun than her two real friends, Bonnie and Lynne.

That afternoon she rode back to keep her date with the other girl. Mortified by Henry snatching her up like a child to carry back to her own wagon, Claire had not dared to stand and wait to catch a ride with Dorothy Brewer the way she had Faye.

Instead, with Bonnie beside her, riding between her and the Raglon wagon, Claire had ridden the mare back to the ninth wagon. Bonnie tied Sue to the back of the wagon, then returned to her patrol on Bob.

There was almost no dust and Claire and Dorothy had fun flipping through the women's magazine. This time when the visit was over, Claire had managed to tuck her skirt, mount the way Bonnie had taught her, and ride back to her own wagon without any fuss. This time she had only to nod or wave at people as she passed.

Holding her breath beside the already sleeping Mary Anne, Claire waited for her parents to climb in from the front of the wagon and get ready to sleep together on the mattress that butted up against the one the girls shared. Space was at a premium in the tightly packed wagon, but with Father's invention of the removable benches, each wagon had room for two regular mattresses. Both were elevated on top of cases and boxes from home with an extra stack of boxes between the two mattresses.

Now, exhausted, she needed to sleep. But her only thrill in the long day made her heart pound and her eyes refuse to close. Henry and Father were arguing about her. Henry had been angry because of the two miserable excuses for men who had come to court her. He had argued about what was proper for her to do.

No matter how much they both liked to pretend, she had definitely heard it there in his voice. Henry was jealous.

Her heart beat faster in her chest and she had trouble breathing. He was married. It was wrong to feel this way, a terrible sin. But Claire felt the tears catch on the ends of her lashes and breathed slowly to ease the tightness.

They had done nothing wrong. She had gentlemen calling on her tomorrow night, according to James Temple. Maybe it was good that the men had walked with the Brewer cousins first. She would wear her green dress, make sure she had finger combed her curls into a nest on top of her head. It would be late in the day, no need for a hat or gloves.

She tried to remember again, what either man looked like, but all she could see or remember was Henry's voice, full of emotion, as he argued with Father that she should be sheltered.

CHAPTER SEVENTEEN

Claire woke in a dither of excitement, light headed from her sleepless night. She had decided to put the Lambton's out of mind completely. There were twenty men for every woman on the frontier. She could have her pick. All she had to do was outshine the other women, and although it probably would sound immodest, it was something she knew she already did. So what if the handsome Lieutenant had ignored her and sparked to her tall friend. Mother had pointed out how sensible that was since he was so unusually tall. Claire had no interest in tall men. If James Temple were any taller, she would cross him off as well.

She was determined to shine tonight, just in case one of the four friends, from Hanover had hidden qualities that would make him a worthy mate. It was difficult with her limited wardrobe to choose from. It even meant taking a sponge bath in the moving wagon to freshen up before changing clothes for the evening. Afterward, Mother combed and helped her style her hair, the way Mother loved to do. Claire had babbled about the possibility that one of the men might be the right one this time. She discussed the others with her mother, pointing out their flaws.

Mother's advice was that it took time to find the perfect jewel, one sometimes had to overturn a lot of worthless stones. Father was riding beside the wagon, apparently listening. He teased Mother that she hadn't picked through very many and she had blushed and been flustered the rest of the afternoon. Claire asked again, but her mother told her she would only be bored by the story of how they met.

When Claire insisted, pleaded that a daughter had a right to know how her own parents met, Mother relented.

"Our Father's came over from England together, right before the war. Your Grandfather Wimberley was a watchmaker and Grandfather Howard was an iron worker. America is such a young country, always with some new frontier to explore and conquer." Mother said and paused as Father called out something to Jim ahead.

Mother resumed as soon as the wheels began to turn again on the big wagon. "Well, they planned to become gun makers, or at least prepare ammunition. Americans are always shooting someone or each other."

"Grandfather met grandmother on the boat, right. Like Lynne's parents met."

"Yes, but Lynne's parents met twenty years after your grandparents. Abigail Walsh, well her distant ancestors were Welsh, but she grew up in County Cork in Ireland."

"And she already had all her things embroidered with W's, don't you see." Claire interrupted again, this time with a fairly good imitation of the grandmother who had died when she was young. She lost both grandparents to the same epidemic that took Lynne's baby brothers and her father and older brother, Sean. But for a moment, the laughing, merry little grandmother was alive again.

"You are just like her. All golden curls and sunshine. I hope you never change. I always have some of Mother with me in your smile."

Claire leaned closer and hugged her mother as the woman's voice tightened with emotion.

"Whatever would I change into, a pumpkin?"

Mother laughed and pinched her nose before kissing her on the forehead.

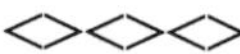

That night had been as disappointing as the first. The men were polite, but very dull, wanting only to talk about how much better mining would be than sheep farming. Claire wondered if they expected to actually just walk around putting nuggets in their pockets. She had heard her Father and Henry talking about how the good ore had been found and claims staked. Now was the time for large scale mining, and an opportunity for merchandising to the new settlers. Besides, weren't any of these young fools worried about the Indians?

Back at the campfire, Claire was relieved to find Henry and Bella had already turned in for the night.

She squeezed in between her parents on the bench, nudging her Father.

"You interrupted the story today, so you have to tell it. How did you and Mother meet?"

Her father laughed and circled her shoulders, reaching out a hand to tickle her mother's neck. "We met in the cradle. Our parents lived next door to each other, worked together at the same factory. Your Grandmother didn't have a cradle so when your mother was born, she put the baby to bed during the day in the cradle beside me. I was a month older. We've practically been sleeping together ever since."

"Oh posh," Mother said, cheeks flaming as she rose abruptly. "You are lucky I chose you Robert Wimberley. I had lots of beaus to pick from. I might not have been as lovely as Claire, but I had my suitors."

Father chuckled and Claire stared up at her beautiful Mother. Was she really prettier than Mother? She looked to her Father, but she could tell in his eyes, her mother was the clear winner.

"Come back, pet, I was only teasing." He gave Claire a squeeze and a kiss on the cheek, then rose to follow his still fussing wife.

Claire knew they would take their time making-up. Frustrated, she sighed.

Bonnie came over and sat down beside her, giving her a rough bump of the shoulder. "So what's all that flurry about?"

Claire shrugged. "Nothing, really. Bonnie do you ever wonder. Will we ever have that? What our Mother's had?"

"Our Mother's?"

"You know, Lynne's parents, my grandparents, my parents, a love so sweet and wonderful nothing else matters."

"Aye, it does seem to be harder. But I don't know why not. You know, my Da and Mum love each other like that. They had a hard patch. It was more than Da losing jobs and drinking. I think it was the last bairn. I wish I hadn't been at the factory and had had a chance to see him. But ever since we met Barney, I've thought a lot about my little lost brother."

"You mean you think he wasn't born dead?" Claire whispered in horror.

"Aye. I've thought and thought about how they were before, and how my Da changed after the boy was lost. I think he wasn't born perfect, had some kind of defect. Well, you know how it is when you're poor."

"They couldn't afford a handicapped child or to house it in an asylum."

"Aye, and me Mum would never have the heart to do for her own bairn that way. It must have been awful hard, but I'm thinking my Da forced himself to do it." Bonnie's voice broke and for a minute it was Claire who held and comforted her.

"You don't know that. Your father loves his children so much."

"Aye, he's a weakness for the little ones, all right. But you see without work, he couldn't see the others starve for a mite that would never be right, could never do anything. I mean I love Bella's little boy. A pure angel, he is."

"I know. When she talks to him or sings and he sings back to her, it's so sweet. I just feel so sorry for him."

"Aye. But he'll never be better and she already knows from the doctors that he will just grow worse and weaker and then die as a wee lad," Bonnie whispered.

"You think that's why your father started drinking."

"Aye, it would have broken something inside him, to have to do that to one of his own bairns. But if he didn't, why didn't they wait until we were home from school to bury him. At least let us see the baby and give the angel a kiss goodbye. Everyone does you know."

Claire's hand shook inside Bonnie's. She had been the one to hold the pan to catch Bonnie's little son when he was born dead. A result of the horrible beating Tarn Michael's had given her. She leaned into her friend, nestled her head on her shoulder. It was Jim who brought the crying girls to their senses.

"Hey, aren't you ever going to put out the fire and come to bed. The dogs won't stay out when you're not in the tent."

Bonnie blew her nose, hugged her friend who laughed and blew her own. Bonnie stood blustering, calling out and snapping her fingers. "Tip, Tyler, here, now."

The guilty dogs shot out of the tent, their coats shimmering like silk in the firelight as they shook before crouching, heads lowered to the woman's big boots. "You two rascals know better than that. What am I going to do to you?"

The dogs looked up, brown eyes pleading at the woman shaking her finger over their head. One whined first, Claire thought Tip, since he seemed to be the leader of the pair's antics, then the other whined an apology as well. Laughing,

Bonnie bent to fondle and tug at the shepherds folded ears until they were upright triangles again. The two followed their mistress to the mouth of the tent and then flopped down at the entrance as she disappeared inside.

Claire woke late, in a grouchy mood. She had gone to bed feeling sad for all Bonnie's troubles, even for poor Bella. No wonder the woman had always been so sharp and bad tempered. At least since Barney came, she had seemed to mellow and grow more human, less witch-like.

Henry emerged from their wagon as though called by Claire's thoughts. When Bonnie handed him a plate of biscuits and gravy, he took it, then waited for his tin cup of coffee. "Where's the rest of your family, this beautiful morning?" Bonnie asked.

Henry looked as gloomy as ever as he took a tentative sip of the steaming brew. "Rough night. Barney has been having trouble with all the dust."

Father handed his empty plate to Claire and held his cup out for her to warm up the coffee that was left. "Sorry, Henry, if I had realized how hard it was on the child, I would have set you two at the front of the train. Maybe I can talk to the other wagoneers, see if they have any objection to giving you the lead every day."

Henry sat down, rested his cup on the bench beside him and dug into his breakfast. After swallowing he said, "Nonsense, you know it would just start a big war. Some people, like the Raglons, are always looking for something to fuss and complain about."

Claire looked across at him in surprise. Some people would say the same of the Lambtons.

"Well, from now on, you can go in front of us. I know it's just one wagon closer, but maybe it will help."

Bella came down the steps without her son. Apparently he was finally asleep. "Then that will mean another day before we are the first wagon. What kind of deal is that?"

"Of course, when I reach the back, I would let you go on to the lead," Father said.

"And all of us have to listen to that screeching cow, Kaye Raglon. No thanks," Bella said.

Henry looked ready to argue, then threw up his hands and stalked off. Claire knew there were the oxen to water and harness, and all the other chores of getting the wagon train in motion. But as she looked at Bella and the sour look she gave him, she doubted it was an eagerness to work that sent him running. The woman was always nagging him about something. Claire closed her eyes and pulled her string of beads from her pocket. While she mindlessly turned the beads through her fingers, she said another prayer.

Bonnie poured coffee and served biscuits and gravy before preparing the food for their noon stop. Claire wondered if she were praying for the miserable couple, too.

Claire lifted both buckets and turned to follow Henry's retreat toward the river. He would pretend to ignore her, as usual. But she knew if she called out, he would rush to help her before Father, or Tom and Jim, could reach her.

For a moment she almost resumed her silly thoughts from the night before. But under the soft light of the new morning, they felt very foolish. She had no idea about love, was determined not to let it lead her toward any rash behavior or wrong decisions. Look at poor Bonnie. She had raved about being in love, about how wonderful, how awesome a man he was. Then, last night, they both recalled the horror she lived through as she learned the man, Tarn Michaels, was really a demon. Claire knew the girl better than anyone. Had Bonnie learned her lesson and given up on true love? No, she had confided in Claire before that she spent each night dreaming about an unattainable man, this one in uniform.

Henry Lambton was married, but they could be friends. Both the Lambtons were her friends. Claire was determined to use her common sense to look elsewhere to find a man to marry. She was not going to covet another woman's husband.

But when Claire moved forward to dip her first bucket in the clear water above where the animals were muddying the stream, she looked to the side to watch Henry. He had his trail clothes on, the bib overalls snapped over a gingham shirt hidden by a denim jacket. In the straw hat he could be any of the men moving along the wagon trail. She raised the full bucket and waited for the water she had stirred to settle before filling the next. In the pool she saw a dreamy, blue-eyed girl, with her loose blonde curly hair floating around her shoulders. For an instant, Claire wasn't sure if it was her reflection.

When she looked up, she saw Henry staring at her. His eyes were troubled as he studied her and Claire's heart began to pound furiously in her chest. When he smiled, she bent down to scoop the second bucket quickly. Someone behind her was complaining, impatient to be next.

Moving too quickly, she sloshed water on the hem of her travel dress. Trembling, she held the buckets out farther and tried to steady her gait. Maybe she wasn't so smart after all.

CHAPTER EIGHTEEN

Mother sat beside Claire as Jim prodded the team forward. It was already warm, another clear, dry day and Claire were happily talking to Bonnie. The tall girl was striding along beside her, keeping pace easily with the slow animals.

"Okay, pretend for a minute. We are at the end of the journey, both happily married to important men," Claire said.

"Rich, important men," Bonnie interrupted.

"Rich, prominent leaders of the town. Of course we are neighbors of the famous Lynne McKinney Gant. We three matrons will be pillars of the community. I will set fashion trends, based of course on the latest fashions from Paris and New York."

"Of course," Bonnie said, with her nose in the air, her skirt held out to the side, as she swished for Claire's amusement.

"Lynne will host the literary community. By then she may well be a published author, famous for her poetry and tales of her journey west," Claire said and when Bonnie snorted, Claire went on.

"Why not, she certainly has written enough pages. Maybe Phillip will have her writings printed and bound. She won't have to have a 'nom de plume' because Lynne can be a male or female name."

"I say Mrs. Gant, I hear the First Lady bought copies of your latest book and shared them with all her friends," Bonnie added.

"Well, at least the Governor's wife will have done that," Claire said. She stared at Bonnie, taking in her straight back and impressive figure. It seemed forever since they had bothered with a nice game of pretend. Claire was enjoying this one immensely. "And you, Bonnie, will lead women to fight for their rights."

Claire's mother laughed, especially as Bonnie started talking about how women in the new western states would have all the same rights as men. "They are already allowed to buy land, at least along the new railroads. I'm sure someday they will have the right to vote," Bonnie protested.

When both laughed at her, Bonnie blushed. "Well, it may be a small club, but I think there will be women interested."

"In being like men?" Claire asked. "Are they all going to wear bloomers in public like Amelia Bloomer did way back in the 50's?"

"I don't know anything about Amelia, but if she thought women should have the same freedoms as a man, then yes," Bonnie answered. "Wait, they will dress just like men, trousers and all." Both women began laughing so hard that

Mary Anne climbed off of Bella's wagon and ran back to see what was so funny.

It was an uneventful day. It had started the same way as all the others. This time they were three wagons farther back in the chain, position eight and nine. Barney Lambton started coughing so hard he looked blue. In a panic, Bella screamed and Tom pulled the oxen to a halt as she scrambled down from the wagon seat to carry the boy clear of the dust. Henry was in front several wagons talking to one of the other married men. When he spotted her, he raced the mare back to them. As soon as he dismounted, he boosted his wife and her sick child onto the saddle.

Mother was able to finally pull their wagon to a halt, mainly because their lead pair were standing with their noses pressed against the tailgate of the Lambton's wagon. Shadrach bellowed loudly. Claire could hear the two wagons behind them yelling as they also brought their teams down. She stared at the three Lambtons, unaware that her hands were shaking so badly it made the cloth in her lap make a flapping sound. Claire swallowed, tears filled her eyes. It had only taken one glimpse to see it all.

Henry was holding the reins of the prancing mare, the horse still excited by the mad dash and change of riders. Henry's face was a perfect image of regret. Everyone in the wagon train who saw him, understood how deeply affected the man was, his sorrow splashing out over all the others.

Claire watched how tenderly he touched the boy's cheek and ruffled his soft dark hair. She felt another dagger as he raised himself up enough to whisper something to Bella, whose body curved protectively around her son. Then Bella placed her hand over Henry's where it supported the child's back.

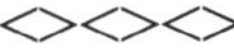

Bonnie turned as she heard a little squeak. She watched Claire raise her hand to her heart and gasp again. Bonnie left her to her mother as she ran forward to climb up onto the abandoned seat of the Lambton's wagon. She snapped the whip out over the oxen to get them to hurry up and join the other wagons. But she had seen the stricken look on the girl's face.

Had Claire been making up lies in her head? Had she assumed Henry didn't have any natural feelings of love for his wife and child? This was the woman he shared a bed with every night. As she snapped the whip in the air over the lead oxen again, she called out giddy-up and the wagon lurched into motion. Bonnie was relieved to see Henry publicly show his feelings. She just felt sorry for Claire that he had kept them hidden so long. Poor Goose.

As merry as Claire had been before, she was now morose, the picture of dejection. It was Bonnie again who came to her rescue. She drew her off to the side with the pretense of taking a walk to look for something they could add to the stew pot.

"Talk to me, Goose, what's going on?" Bonnie asked.

Claire sighed and then stared at her friend. "I think it's possible Barney might die. It's so sad."

Bonnie stared at her friend and then blinked. "It's possible that any of us will die at any time. Bella told us she knew Barney wouldn't live long, nothing has changed about that. I mean, tell me what's really bothering you."

Claire looked at her friend, lowered her eyes, pretended to look around. "I don't see anything edible. This country is so desolate, I hope its greener where we're going."

"From all the descriptions we read, it's even worse. No, I mean you and Henry."

Claire looked up, startled. "There is no me and Henry."

"I know that. Apparently, you don't. Or do you think your sad looks go unnoticed. How hard do you think it is for Bella? Do you think your mooning around after her husband is going to make her feel better?"

For a minute, Claire couldn't speak. "You've no right to talk to me like that. I've done nothing, said nothing, ever, to Henry."

"But you've thought it."

"Bonnie, how do you expect me to control what I think. Don't you think I want to? You don't have any idea how guilty I feel, how hard this is?"

"Well, you'd better. If other people notice it, there will be talk. Once your reputation is ruined, there'll be no more gentleman callers on this wagon train. I know your behavior has been proper, but you have to hide these feelings from others. You know they are wrong or you wouldn't feel guilty."

Claire struggled to hold back tears. "I didn't know I was that transparent. I had no idea anyone else knew what I'm feeling."

"Only for anyone with eyes in their head. You just need to act, pretend like we did earlier when we were playing your game. Act as though none of this exists, that you are searching for the one man who can make you happy."

Claire tried to smile, her mouth trembling a little as she said. "Tomorrow we'll move back to the front, Henry and Bella will be in the lead so Barney will be better…"

Claire froze and stopped arguing when Bonnie raised a hand. In surprise and delight, she watched her friend, hoist her rifle and fire. Together they ran to capture the flopping rabbit.

The two girls returned, laughing and giggling, to the surprise of the twins carrying water to the campsite. Mother was starting the fire and putting the bean kettle over the flames.

Bella sat on the bench from their wagon, with Barney stretched out on it, his head in her lap. Mary Anne stood over Barney, cooling him with her Japanese fan that Claire had given her at the hotel. The boy twisted his head at the sound of the laughing women. Claire rushed in, shouting, “Don’t start the beans yet. Bonnie shot some fresh meat.

Working quickly, Bonnie had the rabbit skinned after cutting off the hind feet. She tossed the two rear feet to the boys for good-luck charms. Then she snipped the tail and handed it to Claire, motioning toward Bella. Claire took a minute to wind a bit of ribbon around the sticky, bloody part and shake all the dust off. Trembling, she walked up to Bella and offered her the furry trophy.

Bella looked as hesitant to take it as Claire had been, but finally she reached out to accept it when Barney kept turning his head to see what the other boys were playing with. She extended the soft white trophy toward her son and Barney touched it, his eyes growing wide. Finally he smiled. Both women smiled at each other in turn.

Claire felt something ease in her heart. She took one of the pails that the boys had set down and dampened her handkerchief to hand to Bella. The woman took the peace offering and ran it over the little boy's face, leaving his thick black hair standing up on his forehead. Without thinking, Claire reached out to smooth it back into place. When finished, Bella returned the handkerchief, gripping Claire’s fingers as she did to fold over it in wordless thanks.

Claire dried the last tin plate, and stopped to stir the beans, before storing the last dishes away. Mary Anne was sharing another of Bella’s stories with one of the twins.

Mother was trying a eucalyptus salve on little Barney's chest and all the men were busy. Claire didn't have the heart to refuse to do the work alone. At least Bonnie had put up the lunch before taking off, this morning, gun in hand. After last night's surprise success in bagging the rabbit and everyone's enthusiastic gratitude for the change in fare, she couldn't blame Bonnie for her excitement.

At the last minute, Father had refused to let the girl take the gun with her. "Not if you're going to be walking alone. You could fall or the gun could accidentally go off. Just wait a while until we're underway, than Henry or I will ride along with you."

Bonnie put her hands on her hips and stood eye to eye with Claire's father. For a moment, Claire wondered what that would be like, to have the courage and conviction to talk to men eye to eye.

Bonnie said, "If I wait, there won't be any game left, or anything edible that hasn't been trampled underfoot."

"Then walk on and pick up anything good you find. Just keep the lead riders in view and make sure they can see and hear you. The Brewer brothers are riding lead today, and they're armed."

Bonnie didn't even bother asking for his compass knife like she had borrowed to ride to the training camp to see her brothers. She just slung a gunny sack over her shoulder and stormed off, calling back. "Lunch is put up, just wash the dishes, girls. I'll be back."

As soon as everything was in order, even the half-cooked beans loaded, the wagon was in motion. Claire relaxed as Father walked beside their wagon, talking a little to Mother and Claire about how fortunate they had been to have such fair weather.

When she looked through the gathered canvas of their wagon she could see Mary Anne singing to Barney as Bella looked forward and then down at her son. At least he seemed a little better today. Maybe Mother's salve would heal him, or at least his breathing trouble.

Minutes later, the fathers of the cousins Faye and Dorothy Brewer pulled up, their conversation about the long-legged woman who had out-paced them forgotten. In the middle of the road, seeming to appear silently out of nowhere, an Indian wearing a feathered bonnet sat mounted on a small pinto horse. He raised his feathered staff in one hand, his open palm in the other.

Although they both had rifles on their saddles, neither thought to use them. The men sat frozen, until the Indian spoke again. "Greetings."

One of the brothers nudged the other and both held their hands in the air to mimic the man's gesture. The long-haired Indian kicked his horse and rode up to them. Using surprisingly correct English, he announced, "I am Washakie, Chief of the Shoshoni, friend to white men, enemy of Sioux and Blackfeet. I am here to collect my toll."

CHAPTER NINETEEN

Jim was the first to spot them, yelling to Claire and Mother to look. Father and Henry rode up. As always, when there was something interesting to see, Mary Anne scrambled down from the Lambton's wagon and raced to climb up to join the Wimberleys. Henry moved his horse to a protective position in front of his wife and her son.

Although all the travelers had been drilled on what they should do if Indians attacked, no one had suggested what they should do if a friendly one just rode up to the wagon train to talk.

At least the Brewers knew to bring the Indian to talk to Father. Claire felt the small hairs stand up on her arms, even though she knew this was one of the friendly Indians. They had seen several when they were doing business in Independence. One had even looked on with interest at what she held aloft when Claire was helping to sell Henry's surplus stock.

As the three men rode back through the wagon train, each family they passed became excited and alarmed. There was a wave of commotion and talking as they wove through. The men riding beside the Indian kept saying, "Make way.

there, we've got a big chief come to pow-wow with our Wagon Master." The man talking, stumbled over the Indian's name.

Each time, the chief repeated what he had told the front riders. When they finally reached the Wimberley's wagon, all were whispering excitedly in anticipation. Annoyed by all the commotion, Henry shushed them. With great dignity, the old chief spoke loudly enough for all to hear.

"I am entitled by treaty with my friends, the white knives, to a toll. A horse or cow will be paid by any party passing through my land. I have been fighting those cowards the Sioux, who passed through the Three Forks after their battle at a place you know as Little Big Horn. These are not good Indians. They kill many whites, many of my people too."

Father Wimberley extended a hand and the chief clasped it at the elbow with surprising strength. Father tried to copy the position, grabbing the Indians elbow so that their arms were pressed together from wrist to elbow in each other's grasp. Looking his visitor dead on, he surprised everyone as he spoke. "We will gladly honor your treaty. Thank you for your friendship. Give us a minute to talk."

He turned around to look for Bonnie, spoke to his daughter instead. "Claire, get some food for our guest while we work this business out."

Shaking, Claire stepped down from the wagon and walked to the rear to find the food Bonnie had packed for lunch. She held onto the side of the wagon, breathing deeply as soon as she passed out of sight of the Indian. Finally, she stilled the shaking long enough to lift the covered tin plate and hold it against her chest as she walked unsteadily over to the strange man and his odd horse. The little mustang was spotted like some of the oxen in big brown and white splotches. Claire said a silent prayer as she stepped closer and closer. She heard Bella gasp behind her. When she looked at them, she saw Bella had grabbed Henry's arm to keep him from drawing his rifle.

Claire continued to step forward. If only Bonnie were here. She would probably be enjoying the chance to speak up to the Indian and tell him what to do like she did everyone else these days. Claire could imagine how happy the girl would be if she were going to offer food to a real live Indian.

Channeling her friend's courage, Claire stepped forward and lifted the plate to Chief Washakie, looking down at the ground as she did so. "Please accept this food. I hope you enjoy it."

As soon as he took the tin plate, she backed away. The old Indians' eyes crinkled as he studied the skittish girl. To the white's she would be pretty. Little nose, big eyes the color of sky, and hair like new corn tassels. He smiled down at the frightened girl. She reminded him of his white horse that had pale eyes and pink nostrils and lips. It could not see or hear very well, but it was easy to ride. He looked from her to the others sitting on the wagon seat. The older one looked much like the same face. He smiled and pulled loose a Spanish coin with a string of beads from the front of his buckskin. He held it out to a pretty little girl with eyes like storm clouds.

She hid behind the older woman until Washakie smiled and shook the present at her again. A boy draped over a big ox yelled at her. "Take it silly, he's trying to give you a present." Another boy repeated the words, "Take it," and he saw the boys were alike, with eyes like grown men. Mary Anne stood up and reached across Mother Wimberley's lap to take the present.

She studied the coin and beads, then looked up into the kind, wrinkled face. "Thank you." Then she gave him a shy smile and the Indian grunted in pleasure.

The Chief stepped his horse closer to the second wagon. The woman on the seat was good, darker with a fine nose. She looked angry when he peeked over the front board of the wagon to see the sick boy she had hidden there. Good woman, more like Indian than white. The man, with wild fair hair and a mustache to match, moved between the woman and the Chief.

Chief Washakie raised his hand again. "Come in peace, collect treaty toll."

Claire stared at Henry, the man's face had turned pale and his jaw shook, whether from fear or anger, she wasn't sure. He hooked his thumb at the sound of the other wagon men moving forward. Claire squeaked as she saw Indian's appear on either side of the trail. She pointed toward them and all the people became quiet.

Chief Washakie stared at the gift being lead toward him. It was the tallest horse he had ever seen. With a strong voice, the leader of the group said. "Here, this is the best horse in our wagon train. You will never find a bigger horse than Bess, or a more willing mount. Take this horse and your men. Leave us in peace," Father Wimberley said.

Balancing the plate on one knee, Chief Washaki took the reins, shook his lance in the other hand. "It is good when the white men honor the treaty of the long knives. We fight the same enemies. Shoshoni and whites live in peace." The Chief turned his pony awkwardly around, the reins pulled behind him as the big mare stood braced flat footed. He looked into the intelligent brown eyes of the big horse and clucked to her, relieved when she snorted, but lowered her tall head to trot along behind.

As soon as the Indians were out of sight, Father Wimberley called out to all the people to get quiet and to get moving. In their panicked flight, no one thought about the missing girl.

As soon as they calmed down, Father Wimberley slowed the train. Claire climbed down, wondering what Bonnie would do for lunch, when the impact of the missing girl hit her. Stumbling at first, she rushed to her Father's arms. "Bonnie's gone."

He looked about, whispered up to Henry. “Did you see Bonnie on the road?” He released Claire to her Mother’s arms as he turned to mount again. Calling men together, he quickly arranged for a search party. He stopped his horse by the frightened women and children. “Don’t worry, we’ll find her. Take care of the animals and go ahead and eat, we’ll be back in minutes.”

Claire looked on the verge of hysterics, the children were all whining. Father Wimberley caught his daughter’s shoulder and turned her back to face him. He leaned forward from his saddle to whisper to her. “Get hold of yourself.” His eyes bored into his daughter’s. “Bonnie’s a strong, fierce woman with a wealth of common sense. You step into her place and take care of everyone. Keep these children calm.” He raised up and stared down at her. “Until we’re back with her, you’re in charge.”

Claire felt his expectations like a heavy weight around her shoulder. She stared around her. Barney was raising his voice into a high keen of fear. Drawing herself up as tall as possible, she forced a smile.

“Finally, a break. Let’s see what Bonnie made for us to eat, ladies. Children, let’s get busy watering the stock.” She stood with her hands on her hips as she looked around at the other travelers who were just now dismounting. Determinedly she went from wagon to wagon, explaining that they were going to rest for a minute, and why. To each of the men who had remained with the wagons she reassured them that the others would be back in minutes. She shared her Father’s orders quickly and was soon back at the wagon.

Mother held out the tray with one last biscuit sandwich. “I don’t know what the men will eat when they get back, this is the last one. We gave that savage half of our …”Hearing herself, she paused and swallowed hard.

“We should have time. We’ll make something as soon as we finish eating.”

When the boys ran up, dropping crumbs to their dogs, they were panting. “We’ve got them all watered and we’ve eaten. Can we take Tip and Tyler and look along this part of the trail, as long as we stay in sight of the wagons.

Claire saw the fear, heard their request for permission, but knew they would be gone to search, whether she gave permission or not. The dogs looked as bright and eager as the two boys. “Of course, but search one side and come back to me to report. Then search the other. Do not go off on your own.” She whispered fiercely. “We need you to stay and protect us.”

She hoped it was what Bonnie would have told them. It seemed to work. Tom reached out to give her a hug and so did Jim on the other side. Both were already nearly her height. “Don’t worry, Claire, we’ll protect you. Do you want us to carry the shotgun?”

Claire knew what her father would have told them. Trying not to pull their strength to her when they needed it the most, she shook her head. “No, I’d better keep and carry it while you’re gone. Go on, be quick about it so you can come right back to us.”

<><><>

The search went on for two hours, but no trace of the girl was found. When Tom's dog Tip gave a yelp, the four came racing back. They had found a scrap of blue shirt with its brass buttons. Claire picked up the big shotgun and hoisted it to her shoulder. Aiming toward the tree line to their right, she fired. In astonishment, she ended up sitting on the ground. Before the boys could pull her up, the search party ran toward the wagons.

Tom held up the clean scrap of blue cloth with a pair of flat brass buttons. Father Wimberley took it, extended a hand to rest on top of the lad's head for a minute. "Good job, son."

He turned away from them, pulled the men away to talk. Only Henry remained with the women. Claire offered him the beef jerky and apples that they had ready for the men. He looked offended, but didn't complain. He took a dry strip and an apple while Claire poured him a cup of cold coffee.

Claire wondered for a moment how he could stand to be here while the men were arguing so fiercely. Henry looked at her as she dusted her skirt, and when she straightened, shrugging his shoulder he whispered. "Are you all right, now?"

The annoyance she felt evaporated. Trying not to smile she nodded her head, held out an arm for Mary Anne to rush beneath. "We're fine, go see what they've decided."

◇◇◇

"I don't see how we can go off and abandon one of our own in this country, especially a woman," Father Wimberley said.

Some nodded, but it was the Raglon boy who said, "She should have had better sense than to go traipsing off in this country. Don't see none of the other women acting like that."

The Brewers looked at each other, and then seemed to come to an agreement. "She ought to be fine, from what we've seen. I mean she walked right past our horses this morning. Shc's probably taken cover somewhere. Our trail only leads in one direction. Woman like that shouldn't have any trouble following it and catching up."

"Is that what you'd want us to do if it was one of your wives or daughters?"

Henry finished his coffee, unaware of those watching him resentfully. All the other men were tired and on edge. Henry asked for and was handed the neatly cut square of uniform. "How many men were in that patrol, do you think? Twenty-five, thirty?"

Father Wimberley stared at the man, his eyes cold with resentment. Others raised their voices, all uncertain what to do next. When the Raglon boy asked the question, "So what are we going to do?"

"We have three choices. Stay here, eat a bite, and then ride out another time to search before dark. Second, conduct a search and send a rider on ahead to Ft. McPherson for help. Third, admit the girl was taken by the Indians today and ride on to the Fort right away."

Henry Lambton raised the winning argument. “If a troop of trained soldiers weren’t safe from Indian attack, who among us has any chance of getting there alive?”

They all agreed they were better off doing as many miles as they could to reach the fort and safety themselves. They were still nearly two weeks away at best.

When Father rode toward them, Claire could see from the droop of his shoulders the news was bad. Mary Anne started to cry and Claire held her, quietly, weeping openly.

The boys wanted to argue, but Father Wimberley shook his head. “Let’s move ‘em out. We’ve got a lot of miles to make before sundown.”

Claire saw Bonnie’s image in her mind’s eye, the way she had looked on the trail after Calum Douglas left. She was shining in the summer air, laughing and singing with the children. For a moment it had looked as though she would take flight, she was so happy.

Smiling, she shook the little girl. “She’s fine, I know it.” She looked to the lads who looked so lost. “We’re going to rush to the fort. Lieutenant Calum Douglas will be there. If anyone can get her back for us, he can.”

For the first time, the boys looked hopeful.

As the train began to move out, Claire didn’t climb back onto the wagon seat. Instead, she determinedly whipped the flank of the lead oxen on the wagon Mother was guiding. “Come on Meshach, hurry up there boys,” she called. But as she walked along, she knew she was a poor imitation of her friend. No one talked about their fears, but each man and woman felt exposed and vulnerable. If the Indians could take a woman as fit as Bonnie, who among them was safe?

Claire swallowed her own fears, tried not to remember when Tarn had struck Bonnie down before her. Tried not to let all the questions, fill her with panic. The Indians had seemed kind. They were the only Indians, they had seen on the trail. If they had Bonnie, she had to believe they would recognize her goodness and be kind to her. But Claire's lip trembled at the thought. 'What would they do to her?'

She coughed on the small clouds of dust that rose with each firm step of her tiny boots. When she wanted to cry, she reached up to touch her bruised shoulder and let the ripple of pain stop her thoughts and the tears. She had to be brave for Bonnie and the children.

The day Bonnie went missing, seemed the longest day in her life. Darkness wasn't far away when they finally made camp, far away from the site on Father's map and thus far away from water. Again the men and children had to carry water to the complaining oxen.

The train had stopped beside the only grass for miles and circled the wagons. Tonight, the men would split guard duty, each one of the four staying on alert guard for two hours before waking the next due to patrol.

Claire used the water from the barrel, moving her head in disgust when something moved in the bucket. It took a while, but she was able to start a fire without having to waste gunpowder. That alone gave her a sense of pride. Carefully, she put the kettle of beans over the fire, letting Mother and Mary Anne show her how Bonnie would have done it.

Just hearing her friend's name, brought tears to her eyes. Claire was too tired and impatient to cry again. She poured the water through a piece of cheesecloth into the coffee pot.

With every motion, she blocked the fear with the single question, 'what would Bonnie do.' With extra tenderness she served each of her fellow travelers their supper with a troubled smile. The food might be terrible, but she knew it would get better. As exhausted as she was, the work kept the fears at bay. Claire dreaded having to face her bed.

CHAPTER TWENTY

Claire struggled to sit up, suddenly aware of one of the horses nickering at something in the dark. Her head ached, and she was surprised that she had finally fallen asleep. She had been reliving the terror of having to serve food to the old Indian Chief.

She recalled how he had studied each member of their party, weighing their attributes as though he might take any of them as his 'toll.' She had somehow felt disappointed when he dismissed her, and turned to Mother, and then to Mary Anne. The little girl had accepted his tribute to her beauty and now wore the Spanish gold piece pinned to her gown. Claire had pinned it there, reassuring the little girl and her brothers that if the Indian Chief had Bonnie, he would not harm her.

They had looked like they might argue, then agreed with her assessment. Still, they were frightened. She noticed the lads accepted Father's orders to sleep under the wagon instead of the tent. She knew he wanted to keep them safe without Bonnie to protect them. But he had told them he wanted them nearer to protect the girls.

When she heard one of the dogs growl from under the wagon, she struggled to her feet and into her wrapper. When she grabbed the edge of the gathered canvas of the opening she held a gun in her shaking hand. The moonlight highlighted an armed figure outside.

In a gush, Claire let out her breath and sank onto the crate behind the raised tailgate. “Henry, you frightened me,” then her face fell as her eyes teared up.

Henry stood still as the guard dog sniffed his shoe, then lowered his hand to let the animal touch his fingers with its cold nose. Satisfied, the dog slunk back under the wagon to the boys.

As the girl lowered her gun onto the mattress, he angled his rifle toward the ground and dared to step closer. “You should be asleep,” he said.

“I was until the animals woke me,” her voice sounded strangled on the whispered words.

Henry stood near, not daring to touch her. He waited, and she raised her head and gave him a pleading look. “For a moment I hoped it was…”

He tried not to move, but his left hand reached out of its own volition to grip her slender wrist and force her hand down from her face.

A deep cough from the front of the wagon, then Robert Wimberley’s rough whisper, “Is that you, Henry, already?”

Henry was staring at the angelic face, the portrait of sorrow with the cold moonlight painting her face and the silver tears glittering on her cheeks.

Henry shook her arm and released her to step back again. They both heard her father climbing out of the front of the wagon. Another four hours until dawn. Trembling, Claire turned back and slipped beneath the covers, each breath sending a silent prayer upward for Bonnie.

Only two hours later, Father began waking all the weary travelers.

Claire tried again to cheer the grumbling children as they woke up. Finally, she convinced all that Chief Washakie had the girl. The men gathering at her Father's summon looked like they believed her too. Boldly she turned to talk them into following the Indians to recover Bonnie. Instantly, they ignored her. For a moment she wished for Bonnie's courage to demand that they listen.

Instead, Father started talking to the group that had gathered. "You need to get the wagons ready early. We're camped where there is no water. How many of you used all your water last night to water your stock? The men looked around in the limited light of the lanterns to the men or woman beside them. Slowly many began to raise hands. "That's why we need to get moving. I want us to be at this watering hole at daylight. These animals, and none of us, can make it without water. Without it we won't last."

There were some half-hearted arguments, but he shook his lantern and pointed ahead to the clear trail in the moonlight. “The trail is marked from all those who’ve gone before us. We’ve got the full-moon to light the way. Stop jawing and get harnessed. Those who are ready, help your neighbor. We need to get to that water.”

Father’s fear pushed the others. The wagon train was underway while it was still dark. Claire felt helpless frustration as she realized they were moving constantly farther away from Bonnie.

There was no time to feel annoyed at having to do all of Bonnie’s work. Her past complaints evaporated as she watched each of the small figures in their group, the women on the wagons hunched under their shawls, the children stumbling along beside the wagon with her. She wondered if any others were still searching the dark and fretting about the missing girl. With each step, her fears increased.

When the sky grew pink ahead, she saw the lazy bend of the river gleam below. She felt a sudden calming of her troubled heart. With every sunrise, there was hope. Hadn’t she been taught that her whole life. She wondered if Bonnie were watching the same sunrise, feeling the same burst of hope. She prayed that she was. To keep from obsessing over it, she handed out dried beef strands and a canned thin biscuit to each of the people in her small group of nine.

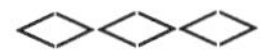

Downstream, Father and Henry lowered each of the wagon's barrels, then rolled them over to the river to fill with the water above the watering cattle. Women and children splashed below the watering hole, men not tending the cattle moving even higher, blending into the cane break along the water's edge.

Most of the travelers were eager to break their fast. Claire wondered if all had as well provisioned a wagon as the Wimberley's. A few started fires to start cooking the beans for the next meal and Claire rushed to do the same. When the young men who had come to call, seemingly so long ago whistled out and stopped by her fire, Claire was delighted. When the first two dropped a string of four fish beside her fire, she clapped her hands in delight.

"Do you know how to clean them?" Cobb, one of the last two, asked.

Claire knew she was dusty and flushed from the night walk and the rush to get something for the group to eat. Nervously she reached up to brush curls escaping from the unwinding night braid. For a moment she felt breathless at the young man's stare. Blushing, she shook her head in answer.

Cobb and Gerald remained beside the fire as the other two men headed toward the Brewer's wagons. Cobb gutted the fish and Gerald scraped the fish scales. Tip and Tyler darted excitedly about near the activity and the men tossed them the guts to snap up. Gerald left the pink glistening fillets spread on the flat rock beside her fire.

Cobb blushed at her effusive thanks, but Gerald spoke up boldly. “Had to do it, Claire, you looked so pretty this morning. Like you better this way, with your hair down.”

Henry and Father were returning with the full water barrels, carefully rolling them in front of them. Father called out, and Claire’s suitors moved over, each to help one of the men put their barrels back in place at the end of their wagon.

“Have you refilled your own?” Father asked after saying thanks.

“Got distracted with the fishing,” Gerald answered.

“Better hurry and fill up. We’ll be leaving as soon as people down their breakfasts. We’ve still got miles to catch up.”

Cobb snorted. “Don’t be silly, we just caught up when we arrived here.”

Father looked at him and shook his head. As usual, Henry was ready to argue. “The animals need a rest,” he said.

“We need to reach Fort McPherson as soon as possible to get help to find Bonnie Michaels. I want to catch up with that large wagon train too, for safety.”

When a coyote howled, in broad daylight, the men stopped arguing. The two would be miners jogged off to get and fill their water barrel and tell the others as they passed. Father turned and walked back along the line of wagons to spread the word in that direction.

Claire stared at the fish that was already curling at the edges where it seared on the hot rock. Rushing, she called Mother and with her help stirred batter for some flapjacks to wrap around it.

Bella came up with Barney held against her hip even though he was struggling, wanting to reach down to get the dogs. “Nice, to have suitors at dawn. I like these kind of edible tributes better than flowers.’

Henry came back. Claire noted his unbuttoned shirt with rolled sleeves, his uncombed hair. She pretended not to notice him observing her.

She grabbed tin plates and cups. In minutes she was sharing the warm fish and bread, laughing with the surprised twins. Both were talking about catching their own fish.

“If we reach another spot beside a river, you can get the men to show you how. Wouldn’t hurt for all of us to learn, like when the Lieutenant showed us how to shoot,” Henry said.

Claire raised her eyes to try to catch him. It was wrong, but she had to wonder if he liked her better dusty and ungroomed as well as she liked the way he looked. She heard Bella snap at one of the dogs. It had tried to take the food from Barney’s hand. Father scolded it and each of the boys pulled their dogs over to them. For the first time in days, Claire felt the tension she had created, spread within the group.

One of the young dogs growled and she heard one of the twins give it a swat. Wearily, Claire rose, trying to swallow her last bite of food past the knot in her throat. She collected plates quickly, rinsed them and handed them to her Mother to dry.

Wearily, Claire made an attempt to raise her arms to pin up her hair, but failed. For a moment she felt as though she could fall asleep on her feet like the plodding animals.

Riding past, Henry called something to Father. Reluctantly, he looked back at her, then noted the boys stretched atop the lead oxen for each team.

Mary Anne was leaning against his wife, already asleep. Bella Lambton's eyes were closed and she seemed to sway with each turn of the wheels. Dismounting, Father stood behind Claire, refused to listen to her arguments. In minutes she was mounted side-saddle and Bob trotted up beside Henry's mare.

"Go on, you two ride up ahead and look for the campsite. We'll try to make another mile, but I'd prefer to camp by water tonight."

Claire opened her eyes wide, trying to wake up. Henry reached over and took her reins to lead the horse with the warning. "Grab hold of the mane and saddle horn before you fall off."

Claire did as instructed. In minutes they were moving ahead of the lowing oxen. Claire was surprised, since it seemed the animals were picking up speed.

The trail dropped over the rise, but there was still no sign of the river. Nervously, Henry rested a hand on the gun at his hip, moved the horses at a fast walk down the rise. It was two miles before they found a thin stream beside a well grazed campground. Henry rode past it, but the stream seemed to disappear completely. Grunting, frustrated at being stuck with the girl, he swore, called Father a name that snapped Claire to attention.

"You've no reason to do that."

"The hell I don't. Here he's stuck me with playing nurse-maid to you, and he expects me to find a reasonable camp site."

Claire leaned forward, tried to tug the reins out of his hand. "I don't need a baby sitter, thank you."

She almost fell forward, but grabbed the horse's neck to keep from falling off. Swearing even louder, Henry gave her a push up right and returned the reins to her hands. "Then wake up and keep your seat. We're riding back toward the wagons, there has to be a better spot than this. Those cattle might not make it without water, but they need full bellies as well after the way he's treated all of them today."

Claire squirmed, trying to adjust her uncomfortable position on the saddle. She had one leg hooked around the pommel as usual, the other leg jammed into the stirrup. If she fell off, it wasn't her fault. Bonnie was right. Men expected the impossible of women. How could one ride in this ridiculous way and keep control of their mount?

When Henry stopped a few hundred feet back to beat through the brush, Claire took the chance to awkwardly dismount. Only when she had the full skirt of her dress tucked between her legs the way Bonnie had showed her how to, did she look at the horse, ready to mount again.

Unable to reach the stirrup, she rode the horse over to a leaning tree and used it to climb up and lean over to mount the gentle horse from the wrong side. It snorted, as impatient with this female as Henry seemed to be. When Claire looked up, she was unable to see the infuriating man.

CHAPTER TWENTY-ONE

Frightened, she screamed for Henry. He rode thundering directly through the cane stand, tearing his shirt to reach her. He was even angrier when he found her mounted astride the horse. She hid her mouth to keep from pointing out his shirt was torn. His arm was exposed, too white for someone who rode in the sun every day. Most of the other men were brown like Bonnie.

He wasn't amused by her laughter. He looked ready to shake her for scaring him so much. In the distance they saw the train moving their way. Henry pulled at the wide swatch of ripped fabric on his sleeve, watched it wave like a white flag as he raised his arm to signal the wagons.

"If we ride back, I can sew and mend your shirt when we reach my wagon," Claire said.

"No need, Bella will take care of it," he answered. "Besides, didn't I hear your other suitors tell you they'd be calling on you tonight? You might want to wash your face and comb your hair before they arrive, the bank of the stream is through that cane break."

Claire stared at the broken reeds, looking dubious. Swearing again, Henry handed her his canteen and ripped the rest of the sleeve to hand her to use as a washcloth. At any other time she would have refused. But there was no way she was riding through that brush, and he had reminded her of two good reasons she should primp.

So what if he had a wife to sew his shirts, adjust his neckties, and scold him, among other things. Claire took the cloth wet it and did a thorough job of cleaning her face, neck and ears. Then she held it out away from her horse, to use more water to rinse the dust from it. She passed both back to Henry, ignoring the rapt way he was watching her.

She struggled with her hair, only managing to repin it enough to stuff beneath her dangling bonnet. Oh dear, if she didn't watch, she would be as boiled red as an Indian.

Riders from the wagon train thundered up to them, looked around and smiled at Claire, who brightened again at the warmth of their looks. If they didn't like what they saw, they didn't shower her with disapproval like Henry. When one of the men offered to help her dismount, she accepted gratefully.

Henry pointed out where the stream was to the other man, and together they rode their horses back and forth, breaking down the barrier of the cane break.

As soon as her feet touched down, Claire was reminded of her pinned skirt and inappropriate position riding astride. Quickly she tugged the hem loose from her waist and stepped away to walk and force the skirt to fall full around her hips and legs.

"Wish you hadn't done that," James Temple said. "Was hoping to get a better look at you in your riding get up. Saw you riding that way once before, the day you called on Dorothy Brewer."

Claire looked around, nervous to be alone with this young man. She had always been properly chaperoned before. He stepped closer and she backed out of reach until she collided with the side of Bob's warm neck. There was something in the way James was grinning at her that made her duck beneath the horses' neck so the man was on the other side from her and the horse was between them. Raising on tiptoe, she continued to talk to him as he leaned boldly on top of the saddle and smiled down at her. Once again, Claire was reminded that she didn't like tall men. At 5'10' he was the same height as Bonnie, two inches taller than her Father or Henry.

She was trying to think of what to say that was appropriate to wipe that look off his face when Henry and George crashed up from the creek. George was talking, something about, "yes, this looks like a great spot. Look at all this grass."

Henry seemed pleased that someone finally respected his opinion, then he saw the way James Temple was ogling a blushing Claire. The fool girl, if someone didn't watch out for her all the time she was going to be bedded and wedded before they reached Utah.

"Claire, do you need a boost up so you can ride back to your parents' wagon?" Henry called.

Claire turned to look at him, annoyed by his tone of voice. She had just been thinking of how to manage that very thing before he arrived, but there was something about his condescending tone that made her determined not to obey.

She stepped back from the patient gelding she had been using for a shield and shook her head. “They will be here in a few minutes. I think I should gather firewood and be ready to start the campfire when they arrive.”

“I can help you,” James offered. At Henry’s glare, she shook her head. “Do you think you and George might catch a few more nice fish for us tonight?”

“This time of day, I doubt it. But we’ll try again in the morning if you like. Those boys with you, Tom and Jim, they made us promise to show them how it’s done.”

She continued to talk as she walked toward the tree line. “They told me about it several times already today. Well, everyone will be here in a short while. Excuse me, gentlemen.”

Claire dropped a curtsy as though she were meeting the men at morning mass. It had the right sobering effect. They nodded and tipped their hats and George even bowed.

She was very much aware of being watched by all three as she walked toward the small growth of brush and carefully scanned it before picking up a few broken branches and making a small pile. They were all talking, although even from a distance she could tell that Henry disliked what they were saying. He seemed to prefer arguing with everyone.

Until the wagons arrived, there was no way to know where their campfire would be. Unlike most of the areas where they circled the wagon train, there would be no marked fire-pits. She called to the men as soon as she thought of it. “Maybe you could find a few flat rocks by the stream. Everyone will need one for their coffee pot beside the fire.”

When she moved back into the open and looked around, she was surprised to see Henry still standing there, holding the reins of the four horses. The others were doing as she requested and looking for stones. She wanted to smile at the curious look on his face. It was as though he was trying to decide something, but all he was doing was staring at her.

In the days that followed, Claire had her hands full, keeping James at a distance. She did it by using teasing chatter about the other girls the boys were calling on, the Brewer cousins. “I thought you and George had made up your minds on who your favorites were.”

He looked confused, but Claire laughed as she said, “Oh come on, James, Bonnie and I watched both of you walking around with Dorothea and Faye.” For the first time in over a week she included Bonnie in the conversation without feeling a pang for her. She realized that like the others, she now believed Bonnie was safe and would return as soon as they let Calum Douglas know to go search for her.

“I’d rather walk out with you, but your chaperone is gone.”

“You know my parent’s agreed to walk with us. They did it once.”

James shuddered and Claire laughed. James had tried to put his arm over her shoulder and whisper something in her ear. Both Father and Mother began talking loudly about the strange weather. James had increased the distance between them again. When James left that night, Mother asked Claire the important question. “Do you like this young man? Is he the one?”

She had been shocked to admit to herself that he was most definitely not the one. The others tried to pretend to be busy, but she knew they were all listening. Bella in particular seemed eager for her to find someone. “I guess I like him, the best of the four who are on the train. He can be amusing, and it is flattering to be pursued. But no, I don’t think he is, although I could change my mind – at least that’s what he keeps telling me.” She said the last with a laugh. The other’s laughed too.

Jim scooted closer to Claire, staring up at the girl with soulful eyes. “If you just wait a couple of years, Tom and I will be old enough to get married.”

Claire stared into the earnest face, saw the emotion in his eyes and didn’t laugh. Instead, she put hands on either side of his face, puckered up, and leaned forward to kiss him. He backed away in terror before her lips connected, managing to slide off the bench into a heap. Claire swallowed her laugh and sighed, as though truly disappointed. Tom jumped over his brother and puckered up with his eyes closed.

This time Claire did laugh before leaning in to give him a quick kiss. Tom flung his arms out and fell on top of his brother. Father had to move in and separate the two boys who had immediately started a grappling brawl. "Claire, be serious. You don't know your own power. A young woman is like a perfect flower." Suddenly he was stuttering, waving his hands, unwilling to finish the analogy.

Henry sat on the bench beside his wife. She had little Barney beside her, feeding him, and Henry was sitting far enough away that the child's sticky hands didn't touch him. In disgust, he watched the boy extend a hand for one of the dogs to lick, before returning it to the bowl.

Father Wimberley dealt with the two boys, shaking them by the collar and threatening to douse both their heads in the water barrel if they didn't stop the constant scraping. His wife just sat clucking her tongue at all three of them.

Henry stared at Claire, the cause of it all. In the firelight, her carefully combed hair fell from her topknot as soft golden curls. One couldn't see what color her eyes were, but he knew they were a bright, clear blue. All one could see was the perfect outline of her small, perfect face and figure.

She had dressed to please her suitors, two of which had showed up again for a short time after dinner. Now both Cobb and James were gone.

Claire rose and moved forward to take Jim to one side. Henry wasn't surprised to see her quickly lean in to kiss the boy. He watched Jim, as embarrassed and thrilled as before, but at least he managed to not fall down. “There, now you’re both even. No more fighting. Promise?” Claire asked.

Jim nodded and Father Wimberley nudged his brother until Tom stuck out his hand and they both shook on it. With relief, Henry watched the boys as they trudged off to take care of whatever chore the man had given them. He watched as Claire obediently turned into her Father’s embrace, giving him a kiss on the cheek as well.

Henry sighed, uncomfortably wondering what those soft, bow-shaped lips would feel like. What should her father have told the girl? That like a flower, every man who saw her would be thinking of plucking such a pretty bloom for his own. Someone needed to explain to the girl what that plucking would involve, probably her mother if the father couldn’t speak up. When Henry turned at Bella’s sharp voice, he wondered how long she had been studying him and how much she had seen on his face.

She held out her son and Henry tried to find a smile for the poor lad. All he could think as he took the child was what foul thing Barney would do to him next. At least he was in his rough trail clothes. A little slime from the boy’s slobbers, plop of food, or worse, wouldn’t matter as much. It still made Henry shudder with disgust as he took him and he heard Barney’s strange little laugh as a reward. He stared at the laughing boy and smiled in return. Barney reached up a damp hand and touched his mouth and mustache, then giggled again.

It started the boy hiccuping and Henry was relieved when Bella returned quickly to take her son back. At least he hadn't made the gagging sound tonight when the boy touched his face. He was trying. A lot of good it did him. Bella already harped about something as she took the boy back and said Goodnight for all of them. Henry had learned long ago to not argue back. Still, he could tell from the shrillness of her voice, this would be one of their long nights.

CHAPTER TWENTY-TWO

Disgusted with being told again and again by Bella that he was making a fool of himself, mooning over that girl, Henry rose and dressed. He knew it was foolish since he would have to stand watch soon anyway, but he couldn't lay in his bed of thorns any longer. In the past, he would tell Bella, she was crazy and to stop worrying. But tonight he couldn't bring the lie to his lips. He was obsessed, but he didn't dare admit it to his wife. But he had heard it in her voice, the hurt she felt when he didn't deny it as usual.

In the dark, he stood and listened, felt his heart contract as he heard the dry sobbing. She was crying. He could slip back into the wagon and comfort her. Kiss and make love to her. How long had it been since they last made love? Days, weeks? Why had he hurt her? It didn't seem enough to tell her he had never acted inappropriately with the girl in any way. It wasn't enough, because that was all he thought about doing these days.

Henry stood outside the next wagon, holding his breath as he listened again. All he could think about was scolding Claire for her behavior. The way she dressed, the way she acted, the way she looked, all were designed to attract the attention of any male. Look at poor Jim's behavior tonight. She was making herself completely irresistible. Before, when Bonnie was here to guide and advise her, she dressed well, but was always prim and proper. Now, he and apparently others, thought she was available to them if they just asked. Her actions were those of a flirt. He needed desperately to warn her where such wanton behavior would lead and the trouble she could end up in.

Under her wagon, he heard one of the boys stir and one of the dogs whine low in answer. Henry was lucky they hadn't charged out to attack him like the other day.

Behind him, he felt the prod of a rifle in his back and a familiar voice asked, "What are you doing here?"

"Robert, it's me, Henry," he whispered.

The rifle tip remained firmly pressed against his spine. "I know. What are you doing outside my daughter's wagon," the soft, husky voice sounded deadly.

In the dark, quiet night, Henry held his breath. He imagined Bella hearing the question, Claire, the twins. He looked over his shoulder at the older man, pointed off toward the far bank of the river. As Robert lowered the rifle, the two men stepped away from the circle of wagons.

Only when they were far enough away, that they couldn't be heard, did Henry dare to explain. "Bella and I had an argument."

"We all heard you."

Henry looked at the familiar face, stared into his angry eyes. Once again, he worried about the gun Wimberley still held. What had they said, what had he told Bella? He swallowed, he had told her nothing. Silence was his new strategy to handle her insane jealousy. For just a second he wondered if it would work for her father. He shook his head. "She is jealous of Claire."

Robert nodded and motioned up and down with the gun as well as his head. When Henry didn't answer, he asked, "Why didn't you tell her she had no reason to be, like you do every night?"

Henry blushed, was grateful for the dark, he turned and walked along the muddy bank, his feet sliding in spots where the cows had climbed up the bank.

"Well," Robert demanded.

Henry turned and spun up to him, his voice soft, his hands held out to his side. "Go ahead and shoot me, damn you. I couldn't lie to my wife, all right."

Robert stood silently, wondered how he could protect his daughter from this new danger. He stomped past the tormented man in front of him, thumping into his shoulder as hard as he could.

He was almost into the circle again when he turned and walked back up to the younger man.

"What were you doing outside her wagon?" this time, through gritted teeth.

"I wanted to warn her. Now that Bonnie is gone, she seems to spend all her time flirting. Her behavior is more and more reckless every day. Hell, you saw the twins tonight. They're not quite eleven yet and they feel it. Look at what she's doing to that group of four want-to-be-miners.

They are fighting with each other over whose turn it is to visit, who can help her with her chores."

Robert nodded, rubbed his face as he lowered the gun. "Yeah, I see what she's doing to you." He sighed and looked at Henry with a look of pity. "Leave her to me and her mother, we'll talk to her tomorrow."

Henry looked like he had something else to say, then turned back toward his wagon, suddenly exhausted.

"Where do you think you're going?"

Henry pointed to his wagon and the old man shook his head. As he walked past him, he handed Henry the gun. "Keep your eyes peeled, there's something out there, I can feel it."

Henry took the gun, ran a hand along the collar of his own coat to smooth the hair down on his neck. "Good night, Mr. Wimberley."

"Good night, Henry."

Henry woke the man in the wagon in front of the Wimberley's to take his turn, with a warning to keep lively. Something was out there bothering the cattle and horses. He turned back to his own wagon without pausing outside Claire's.

It was even darker inside, but Bella kept things orderly. In minutes he had propped his rifle near to hand, safety on, and hung the handgun out of reach of the boy. Carefully, so as not to shake any dust out to disturb the sleeping child, Henry stripped down into his underwear.

Bella lay facing away from him. Normally she would have turned over to at least whisper a few minutes. From her breathing, he knew she wasn't asleep. If there were more light, he would have been able to see her hair move over her ears as she tilted them in his direction to follow his movements. He had once teased her that Tip and Tyler had nothing on her for listening. He had meant it as a compliment, but as always, she took it as an insult.

Slipping into bed with her, he pretended to be adjusting the covers as though he were cold. Instead, he managed to lift it enough from where she had it tucked around her so that he could touch her. When he placed his hand on her back, she sat upright and turned to glare at him. He knew with the boy finally asleep, she wouldn't dare to yell at him. Insistently he reached up and pulled her back down beside him, so their faces were together, their lips almost touching.

Henry felt her tremble with fury, with hurt, with all the words she would have poured over him like hot lava at any other time of the day. Gathering himself for her struggle, he whispered into her mouth. "Bella, I'm sorry. I was worried that the way Claire has been acting, she might get hurt. I wanted to warn her."

His eyes had adjusted to the dim light enough to see the oval of her face, divided into perfect halves by her long, lean nose. Her eyes were so dark, he could not tell if she were listening and understanding him. Her breaths were like little hot puffs of steam against his mouth. Barney still slept.

"I talked to Robert Wimberley instead. I shared our concerns. He promised to talk to her tomorrow, and to have her mother do the same."

He felt it, the relaxing in her slower breathing, in the way her body sagged against the mattress. It was now or never if he were to save himself from the temptation that was driving him mad. Softly he leaned forward an inch and they kissed.

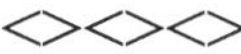

Claire woke, groggy from her long sleepless night. She had managed to brush her hair from her face, but felt too weary to bother putting it up. Struggling into her wrapper and slippers, she climbed out of the wagon and set about the morning chores. For a moment, anger swept over her at the unfairness of it all. Why, when Bonnie disappeared, had all her jobs fallen to Claire? There were nine in their party, not just one. Then she dropped the lid of the barrel down on the water and turned to lean against the side of the wagon.

Struggling to hold back tears, she set the full bucket by her feet and clasped her hands together in prayer. What kind of friend was she? When was the last time she had even tried to imagine what Bonnie must be going through? She had made up a story about a kind Indian Chief taking her hostage, but what if it had been one of the murderous band who killed the young soldier. Claire felt shaken by the thought and covered her mouth to keep from crying out.

The reason she didn't think about those alternatives, was she couldn't. For a moment, images of her dear friend flooded her mind. She could hear Bonnie's strong voice, see her hazel eyes and serene face. For a second she imagined her strong arm reaching around her and clucking over her like a mother hen. She would be nagging at her now to go get dressed and put her hair up before the children woke and saw her looking like this. She had a job to do to keep everyone's spirits up.

Claire started the fire, put on the coffee and beans, which she would finish at the end of the day. She didn't bother to slice the bacon or start the porridge or bread. She knew the smell would draw Tip and Tyler to sniff around and beg. If she wasn't there, they might steal all the morning's meat.

When Claire saw her mother emerge from the wagon beside her father, she breathed a sigh of relief. She made quick work of putting the meat in the skillet and added oats to the boiling water, handing the spoon to her mother. "I'll hurry and dress, I just didn't sleep well last night and got a late start."

Mother smiled, reached out to take the spoon but held onto her empty hand. "Sit, please, before the others get up. I want to talk to you about something important."

Claire was surprised, but looked around to pull up the wagon bench to sit on closer to the fire. "What's wrong, aren't you feeling well?" Claire asked, talking as softly as her mother.

Elizabeth Wimberley stared at her daughter, took in the disheveled appearance and smiled. She had told Robert that it was ridiculous. Claire wasn't a temptress. But Robert had insisted if she wouldn't set the girl straight he would.

"He's worried that I haven't explained the facts of life to you. All the business between a man and a woman."

Claire watched her mother duck her head and blush. She giggled at her mother's modesty. "I know all about that, about… well, Bonnie told us, me and Lynne." Blushing, she leaned forward to hug her.

For a moment her mother looked scandalized, then she relaxed. "She shouldn't have. There are things a married woman knows, but a young girl shouldn't learn until her wedding night."

Claire sat back, hands on hips before leaning forward to whisper. "Did Grandmother tell you on your wedding night?"

Mother snorted, awkwardly using the wooden spoon to flip a piece of the thick slabs of bacon. The oats at the end of the spoon stuck to the meat and skillet, browning with a nice nutty smell. "I had a friend who had already told me. Grandmother did warn me it might not be pleasant, but it never lasted long, and it was a woman's duty if she was to have children."

Claire sat back, hands on her knees for a minute. “That’s what Bonnie told us too.”

Elizabeth sat staring at her child. Did she dare tell her the truth? That it was more than pleasant, not every time, but there were times when it was rapturous. She gave a scowl and finished turning the meat. No, Robert had been emphatic, that she warn her daughter about smiling at the men, at being too exciting – wasn’t that the word he had used.

Claire started to stand up as one of the twins crawled out from under the wagon, scratching in just the way Robert did each morning. She scowled at the boy and he had the grace to look guilty before turning to look for the quickest way to a bush. She hissed at Claire, motioned for her to sit back down, but waited in silence until the other boy, Jim climbed out from the other side.

“He and Henry are worried that you are flirting too much with all the men. That they might misinterpret your friendliness as an invitation. Well, he doesn’t want you to smile at them so much, or look so pretty.”

Now Claire did rise, her eyes full of hurt. “Which one of them said it, which one thought I was acting like a floozy?”

Before Mother could answer, she was gone.

CHAPTER TWENTY-THREE

Today, they were back at the front of the wagon train. Claire had taken the time to comb her hair into a neat chignon and again wore the tan Lindsey-Woolsey to walk in. She made sure the bonnet was on snug to hide her face and she walked along beside the wagon, shoulders hunched and head bowed. With each step she felt the tears floating at the edge of her eyes threaten to spill.

It had taken all her courage to crawl out of the back of the wagon to join the others for breakfast. That people were talking about her, thinking that of her. It still hurt to think that her mother had come to talk to her, warn her to be more, be less attractive.

It hadn't helped that Bella and Henry had come to breakfast, happy and fussing over little Barney. There was something about the way they stood so close together. The way they were looking at each other cut yet another wound for her.

Dawn was breaking over the horizon and without other animals to spoil the view, she could see the vast beauty of the horizon. She didn't want to settle for the third and fourth, or heaven help them, 10th and 11th again. At least, leading off, Barney would be able to breathe easier today. At least, there was that to be thankful for.

Suddenly Father and Henry were racing back, screaming. "Circle the wagons. Women and children secure. Indians."

It was not until she heard the last word that Claire raised her head. Eyes flaring, she was shocked when Henry leaned down to circle her waist and sweep her up. As soon as he released her over the tailgate, she scrambled inside screaming for Mother and Mary Anne. All three worked frantically together to move the boxes. Father had described so many times how to make a wall of crates.

The jostling wagon made it hard, but in minutes, they crowded into the square hole, Mary Anne squeezed between them. Claire jerked to pull the mattress down over their heads, then shoved one of the boxes that shifted back into place. She heard panicked animals, screaming and bellowing as men shouted and swore outside. Again, she braced the shifting crates as the wagon jostled and wheeled onto the weed choked land on the other side of the rutted trail.

Even before the wagons were fully stopped, they heard the whiz of arrows and the patter of bullets cutting through the canvas overhead. The women clasped hands and curled lower over Mary Anne. The sheets still on the mattress flapped in the light filtering through the canvas as they tried to crouch there, knees burning, hearts pounding. Now they heard the fire of their own guns, the noise and smoke quickly filling the small space, taking the breath from their lungs.

In minutes, it was over.

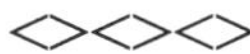

It seemed an hour that they lay, cramped there, before Claire raised the end of the mattress and dared to look out. The sun was still shining, the cattle calmly reached down to eat the grass at their feet. “What’s happening, she called?”

Her father answered from near the front of the wagon. “We saw Indians on the plain, circling a large wagon train. A couple saw us, broke away toward us.”

“We were lucky, the terrain was flat. We’d just passed a big hill where they could have fired down on us,” Henry added.

“As soon as we got the first wagons started circling, we turned and fired at the Indians. There were a half-dozen or so by then,” Father Wimberley said.

“Did they look like that chief that stole Bonnie?” Claire asked.

“I don’t believe they were,” Henry answered from nearby.

“These were nearly naked, with painted faces and bodies, even their horses were painted,” Tom said, his voice still full of excitement.

Mary Anne pushed out from under the mattress to stick her head out through the back of the wagon. “No fair, why didn’t you take shelter in the Lambton’s wagon? You heard Father Wimberley yell all women and children secured,” she shouted.

As the boys began to argue why they weren’t children, the women in other wagons could be heard talking to their husbands, fathers, and brothers.

“Can we come out now,” Mother asked, “it’s sweltering under here.”

“We shot at them,” the boys were telling Mary Anne. The little girl looked in awe as Jim held up the Lambton’s shotgun, Tom held the Wimberley’s overhead and shook it.

“We shot two and they fell,” Henry said.

“I shot one of their horses and blew its leg off,” Tom said without excitement. Claire climbed down and started to move to the horrified boy, but Father shook his head and restrained her.

Your wagon was in the lead,” Henry. “How are Bella and Barney?” Mother asked.

The man raced away. When they heard his gasp of horror, both women rushed forward and Father held the three children beside him.

Claire pushed past the other two to see Bella first. “Take Barney, she heard Bella’s whisper. Trembling, Claire looked into the box and sighed when she saw Barney’s white face and heard his soft little whine. She took the boy as gently as possible as Mother and Henry moved Bella back to her bed.

Claire held the boy, softly patting his back, listening to the gurgle of his labored breath. She felt overwhelmed with guilt. She had done this. If Henry had rushed to his own wagon first, Bella would be safe now.

Claire stayed in the tight circle as other women and children poured out from cramped shelter, families checking to see who else might be hurt. Men still waited, armed at the gaps between the wagons, ready to fight back against the next wave of death. In the distance they heard the firing between the other wagon train and the Indians there.

Suddenly, Father strode into the middle of the circle. "Men, get your guns and be ready. We're moving down there to join the other wagons."

"Are you crazy, we chased them off here," Kaye Raglon yelled. "Let them see to themselves."

Father stood there, his gun clenched in his hand and Claire imagined it was Kaye Raglon's throat. The woman must have read the same warning in his face because she backed up against her son.

"Men, if we don't go and they break through to kill those travelers, we're next. The only hope we have is to join forces, not sit here and wait to see which side wins. You men mount up or take control of your wagons. Women and children back into the wagon beds again. Any shot you have at an Indian, take it."

Ignoring the protests, Father mounted on Bob and motioned to the lads to climb into the wagon with Mary Anne. He yelled and a white-faced Henry emerged from the Lambton's wagon, blood on his hand. Claire raced to climb over the tailgate, carrying Bella's son to her.

Horses might race and a wagon train have speed, but it was as hard to get the oxen turned and into motion onto the trail as it had been circling them in the first place. Once in motion, the big lead oxen set a good pace and the others followed along so that the wagons stayed together.

Claire saw her mother bounce against the side of the wagon. Frantically, she climbed onto the bench to hold the reins, unable to avoid the blood on the seat. Her bonnet was flung back by the wind. It was choking her, but she didn't dare move a hand to untie it.

The men on horseback sped ahead, firing in a single volley at the clump of Indians regrouping below. The effect was instantaneous. An Indian sagged in the saddle as riders from the wagon train charged out as well, firing into the mass of Indians. Like a heat devil, the outnumbered Indians boiled away into the haze.

Claire stood outside the Lambton's wagon, her hands red from the sawing of the reins and from the blood on the bench. There was a brown sticky patch of it on her skirt and she felt nauseous every time the fabric swung against her. Her mother had walked off with Barney to try some salve on his throat and a little mint tea to try to clear his breathing.

Their eleven wagons had been moved, the bed of the wagons blocking any gaps between the wagons of the larger train. Their forty-plus wagons had left Independence two days before they did. It said a lot for her father's ability as a leader, that the slower oxen had gained a day on the faster group with their horses and mules.

The train had been attacked before first light the previous day with a barrage of flaming arrows. Four of their party were wounded, as they poured out of their wagons that morning in a panic. None of those wounds had been critical. Then the Indians had raced at them, guns blazing as they seemed to disappear from sight on the opposite side of their horses. There had been four waves of attacks. The last had taken the life of a four year old child.

They didn't know if they had hit a single Indian but they were now low on ammunition, so many shots had been fired. They were out of water and desperate. Two wounded mules had been shot last night, and both were now being eaten by the exhausted travelers.

Luckily, their animals had been in the center of the wagons or the Indians would have taken all of them. Today, the Indians had returned with more braves.

In the bright sunlight, one of the wagons still burned. The stench of the burning goods lingered, or maybe that was the smell of cooked mule. Claire shuddered at the thought of eating one of their own horses or cattle. On a journey like this, people who were dependent on their animals for their life, became suddenly fond of them.

She stepped closer to see the burning wagon, but all that remained was the charred wooden frame. She heard one of the men tell Father, “This is our second day, Although the Indians had not made much progress, firing into the circle as they rode around the circle of frightened people, screaming the whole time they rode, the Indians had worn out their nerves. The wagon master confided they were almost out of water and were relieved to have the oxen train join them.

Father listened sympathetically, then announced to his own men that they were leaving. “If you’ve got any sense you’ll move out with us. Like you said, they can go home and get more braves. There were enough of them to wipe out Custer’s cavalry. I don’t want to see how many men they’ve got this time.”

“Don’t you want to stay, share our food, share your water?”

“Let’s share on the move,” he turned to look for the twins who came running. “Move our wagon ahead of that burned one. We’ll fasten it on behind and pull it to the fort for them.”

“Mister, we lost two of our mules,” one of the travelers protested.

“We’ve got this wagon, use those mules, but I’m making dust.”

With that Claire scrambled up into the back of Bella's wagon, relieved to see the twins now prodding their teams into motion.

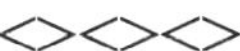

Claire sat holding Bella's hand as the woman moaned in pain. She knew Henry would prefer to be here than riding out to fight Indians or move the wagons. Again, Claire wished she were Bonnie instead. The tall woman was a crack shot and Father would probably prefer her to Henry. Father would want to be here beside his own wife.

Claire rocked at the pain of the word. Guilt again filled her. She had convinced the Lambton's to take their turn at the front of the train three nights ago. Barney was slowly choking to death on the cloud of trail dust stirred up by the oxen. She had been trying to help. Both had been too proud to ask any favors of Father, and he had given up arguing with Henry. It was part of Claire's atonement for causing problems for the troubled couple.

Claire felt tears drop on their clasped hands, sniffled and raised her free hand to cover her mouth so she didn't sob out loud. This woman was dying in agony and there was nothing she could do to ease her pain or stop it. Guilt continued to stab through her. Suddenly, she reached into her pocket, touched the familiar comfort of her beads and drew a deep, slow breath. In minutes, Bella's ragged breathing slowed and her moaning changed to a soft whimper as she slept despite the pain.

Henry left the men as soon as the wagons all settled into an easy pace, galloping back toward his own wagon. Fear for what he might find goaded him. Whatever happened, he would have to face it. At least he and Bella had last night. Without the peace of their new understanding, now would be unbearable.

As he drew up on the outside of the wagon, he peeked inside the billowing canvas. Claire sat, eyes closed in prayer, holding Bella's hand. Quickly Henry dismounted and tied the lathered horse to the back of the wagon before climbing inside. Despite his noisy entrance, neither woman looked his way, although he did see Bella's eyelids flutter.

For a minute he paused there, wishing it was last night and he was still making-up for the fight over the girl across from her, with Bella. Did Claire even remember that Bella was Jewish? He watched the girl, so like his wife in size and structure, so different in every other way. Where Bella was dark and severe, Claire was light and gay. This was the stillest and quietest he had ever seen the girl. Her mouth always twitched with the hint of a smile and her eyes seemed to dance in merriment. She lived for fashion and beauty, loved a good joke, and danced like a butterfly.

He swore under his breath as Bella's eyes opened and she seemed to nail him with one last look. Henry knelt beside the bed, taking her free hand, pressing his lips to her small, cold fingers." Bar.."

Henry looked around as Claire pointed to the small boy who lay in his usual place near the bed. Henry freed his hands from both women to reach out to lift Bella's son.

Each day the child felt lighter, but his small stomach was distended like a little drum full of air. Today, he smelled sweet like Christmas candy. Carefully, he laid the child down on Bella, making sure his small white gown didn't touch the bloodstained bodice of her dress.

"Re-," She began and Henry leaned forward to hear her last words. "Remember the promise."

He shuddered as he breathed in the words with her last breath as much as heard them. Eyes shining with unshed tears he leaned enough to kiss her still warm lips. Groaning, he placed his hand tightly over the mouth and nose of the little boy. At the child's weak struggle he withdrew his hand and staggered back in horror.

Henry swore at death, Indians, and God as he fumbled his way back from the bed and out into the blazing heat of the sun cursed day. Still, he screamed and swore.

Minutes after he mounted to ride back to the front, Claire sat trembling. What kind of monster was this? He stayed for one last kiss, then calmly began to kill the helpless little boy. As she started to stand, Claire gasped and then fell back against the hard side of the wagon. The canvas billowed over her as the world went mercifully black.

<><><>

Mother and the twins raced toward the wagon as Henry turned his tired horse to run toward the line of defenders.

Inside, they moved Claire to the front on a clean blanket. Mother sat Mary Anne beside Claire and moved Barney to her lap. The little boy stared up at the girl and smiled. While she sang to the child, Mother began the sad labor of preparing the body for burial. In this hot weather, it would need to be soon.

CHAPTER TWENTY-FOUR

The troop of eighteen men led by Lieutenant Calum Douglas arrived two days later. He had sent six of his best men back to escort the larger wagon train back on to the Fort, and to protect some peaceful reservation Indians from any more attacks by a new Lieutenant. When he heard the lowing oxen of the smaller train, he spurred his animal forward, intent on seeing Bonnie again.

He smiled as he watched the three McKinney children rush toward Ian and Shawn Magee. While Bonnie's brothers, dismounted and hoisted the children up, Calum welcomed Robert Wimberley riding up to shake his hand. For endless minutes they talked about the other wagon train, he had passed yesterday, how they had both been traveling together, but the oxen moved slower.

Calum tuned the words out as he noted the two Wimberley women. There was something somber about the way they sat that brought his heart into his throat. When he saw an arrow sticking out of the Lambton's wagon, he raised a hand to hurry Wimberley. With the troops help, they quickly had the caravan circled and ready for the night.

<><><>

Claire stirred the beans, grateful that the last of the mule was in this pot. She had hated the thought of including it, but now she had grown numb to what she ate. It seemed the others were too. She looked up at the man who was going to bring Bonnie back to them.

He was dusty, a dark line across his forehead where his hat had rested. She had watched the tall man, his bright blue and yellow uniform no longer spotless, as he helped and directed the actions of all the others. Bonnie was right, he was more than a toy soldier.

She listened as the children described their encounter with the Indian Chief the morning before Bonnie disappeared, Tom and Jim interrupting each other with different information, all overridden by Father Wimberley's more precise recall of what the old Indian had told them. Mary Anne quietly moved forward until she had Calum's attention. She lifted the strange coin that she always wore pinned to her chest these days.

Calum looked from the little girl's face to the coin and then back again. As soon as she finished explaining about it, Calum pulled her over to sit beside him and continued to interrogate the others. Claire watched, noticing the man's intensity as he listened, his gaze on each of the speakers, constantly moving over their features before turning to study the next.

She looked past the tall, handsome cavalry officer to Henry Lambton. It was the first time she had looked at him since the Indian attack. Since the time when they watched Bella die. Without meaning to, Claire shuddered again. Henry sat holding the little boy in his arms, the child lifted so his head rested on his shoulder, Henry's arm under the boy's bottom. He looked so exhausted. Claire wondered if he had slept since they buried his wife. He had been so distraught. Her Father had walked him back to his wagon, listened to Henry's cries of despair.

She heard Calum keep asking, "After he attacked, that's when you noticed Bonnie was gone?"

The boys were explaining, again Father interrupted to describe every minute of their exchange with the old Indian, Chief Washakie. Claire could only remember how frightened she had been at having to serve the strange man their food since Bonnie wasn't there. He had looked at her as though he could tell everything she had ever felt, thought, or done.

"We realized Bonnie was gone when we stopped to eat," Claire said from over the fire. He gave her a hard look and she could almost hear him saying 'because you had to do some work for a change.' She accepted his judgement of her, because it was true. She had never realized how much Bonnie did for all of them. Claire smiled, held out a plate of food as a peace offering. She asked if the others were hungry and began serving food.

Only her Mother and Mary Anne came forward to take plates, but Claire watched as each served one of the arguing men. She continued to fill plates and pass them, grateful that none refused the food except Henry. For the first time she realized he had not eaten since Bella's death. Not a bite.

Now, Ian and Shawn, who had been listening, roared to life, demanding in outrage to know why they had abandoned their sister Bonnie.

Claire's head hurt, she wanted to run and cry, escape all the uproar and the terrible debate. Calum's loud voice pulled her back in as he groaned the words, "So Bonnie has been gone a week?"

She could see in his eyes and face, the torture he was imagining for wonderful, brave Bonnie. Claire wanted to howl in pain at the images, instead she muttered in a dead voice, "Over twelve days."

It was Mother who began to talk, telling the Lieutenant about Bella. Henry interrupted as he made a barking sound. Claire rose, shivering, wondering if he were laughing or crying. "What, Henry? Do you want me to put Barney to bed?" Mother asked.

Claire watched him shake his head violently. It looked as if he was crushing the small boy in his arms. She stepped closer, ready to pull the boy to safety.

"I couldn't protect them, I couldn't protect either of them," Henry screamed.

When Claire reached out to touch him, he stood and moved away. Calum rose and stood beside the man.

"When?" Calum asked.

"I'm not sure, two days ago. They wouldn't let me keep her with me. She's buried on the side of a hill, all alone. There is no marker, no sign for anyone to ever find her."

Father Wimberley's voice sounded depressed, "It was over ninety in the shade." Calum raised a hand. He had been on battlefields during the Civil War. One never forgot the stench of the dead and dying.

"We all are buried alone, Henry," Father said. But before he could finish offering more words of comfort, Henry was muttering again.

"She made me promise to take care of Barney, to take care of him the way we had agreed if anything happened to her. I couldn't do it. She wanted him buried with her, but I couldn't do it."

Claire sank beside him, leaned to wrap an arm around the sobbing man. "I thought, I heard you promise her to take care of him, then I saw you put your hand over his face." She leaned against him. "Oh Henry, I thought you wanted to kill him."

He shot up as though scalded by her touch. "I resented him..."he began and Claire closed her eyes in comprehension. She had misjudged him, thought she no longer loved him, could never love such a man. "I never wanted to hurt him, to ..." the words faded into a gasp. "You thought I wanted to kill him?"

Onto the lap of the shocked girl he let Barney's lifeless body fall. "Now he's dead and we are days and miles from her grave. They will both be buried alone." When he said the last words, she heard the horror, heard how lost and alone he sounded. Helplessly she watched him storm off.

Claire touched the lifeless face, held her fingers over the boy's lips. When there was no movement, she screamed.

Alarmed, Calum whistled to call his Indian scouts, and quickly sent them after the crazed man.

Claire felt emotionally overwhelmed. How could she think Henry wanted to kill this boy? She knew he resented him, remembered all the arguments he and Bella had at the store. Now she had betrayed him again, embarrassed them both by making all of this public. She closed her eyes as though in a faint as her parents rushed forward. Father swept her up and after Mother took the child, he carried Claire to her wagon.

In the dark she heard a thud, tried not to react. As her father gently placed her on her bed, she heard Calum's orders.

"Tie him up and put him in his wagon." She knew the Lieutenant was staring at four angry boys when she heard Calum explain. "Guilt and grief have killed many a man."

As her Father brushed a kiss against her forehead, Claire let her head roll as though already asleep. *You thought I wanted to kill him?* Henry had accused. This time she couldn't even cry or pray. She would always see his face and remember those words.

◇◇◇

At dawn, Claire woke to the sound of the troopers bugle. Amazingly, she had slept through the night. Sometimes the soul can feel as exhausted as the body. But this morning she felt renewed. She took the time to change the blood stained dress and to take a quick spit bath with washcloth and bowl of water, rushing to pull on clean clothes and work her hair into order. Satisfied, she hurried out of the wagon to start breakfast.

She almost collided with Jim, who had stumbled out of the Lambton's wagon, rubbing his eyes. "Hey, those soldiers are nuts. They get up even before your father, and he gets up earlier than anyone from the city."

"Apparently not," Claire said with a laugh. Jim stared at her and smiled too, shaking his head as he backed away. "Got to see the Lieutenant about something." He almost fell as he collided with her father, climbing out of the front of the wagon. Righted, he ran toward the trooper's tents.

Claire was already striking the flint that she now carried in her pocket, quickly starting the fire. She shook the pot and poured the small amount of coffee into a nearby tin cup, setting it on the fire to warm as well. She grabbed the bucket and headed to the water keg to fill both. She paused to return her father's stare. "What?"

Father shook his head, smiled at her, "I'll go fetch some fresh water, give me a minute. You sure you want to cook, Mother and I can do it?"

"I'm fine, guess it will be more porridge and fat back. I wish we had eggs, the shells always brighten the coffee."

Humming, she walked to the food cabinet and began to grind coffee beans. Her mother peered out of the wagon, her hair uncombed and dress still unbuttoned. “I’m hurrying Claire. I can do all that.”

Claire stood on tiptoe to kiss her Mother, dusted her hand before reaching up to cup her face. Her hand smelled of coffee grounds and both women inhaled at the same time. Her mother smiled and nodded before disappearing back inside to dress.

Jim ran past, almost colliding again. She heard him breathlessly shout as he climbed into the wagon. “Yeah, he said to let him loose so he can do it, but we’re both to go along and keep an eye on him.”

She heard Henry swear, “… does he want you to hold it for me too.”

Giggling, Claire could hear the sounds of Henry struggling and the grunt as Tom helped him to stand. Carefully, she looked at the meat as she sliced the side of bacon standing in the skillet. When she had a dozen short slices, she wrapped the pork with the greasy cheesecloth covering and set it aside while she spread out the meat in the skillet and put it on to cook.

Mother appeared and returned the pork and carried the pot of soaked beans with her. “I’m pleased to see you back on your feet. You’ve had us worried you know.”

Claire titled her head to smile and then whispered, “I know, but for some reason, this morning I woke and my heart felt light again. Like some terrible burden had been lifted.” She added the oats to the boiling water, carefully tilted the lid as she covered the pot and moved it back from the flame a little to add the beans. "I know you and Father disapproved of my behavior. That hurt, then Bella died. I've felt guilty and unhappy for too long. I just can't do it. Now Calum has arrived and is going after her, I know we'll have Bonnie back soon. I have to live as myself Mother, not pretend to be someone else, even for you," she whispered.

Mother leaned over and gave her a brief hug. "Good, I knew Robert was wrong. You are like your Grandmother Wimberley. You never knew him, but your grandfather used to tease her. He would say she was 'half-fairy,' because she was so bright and bubbly. I'm glad to have the real Claire back."

By the time the three men returned, Claire had the porridge bubbling. She added hot coffee to the mug with yesterday's cold, and when Henry extended his hand she placed it there. If he noticed she looked better today, he gave no indication.

The troop rode past, Calum pulling his horse up to talk. The Magee brother's dismounted and Claire was surprised to hear them arguing about which would carry the body of Barney Lambton.

"We'll find the grave, make sure the boy is buried with his mother." Calum barked "enough" as Ian emerged with the child, but looked surprised as were the others when he handed the body up to Shawn.

Claire handed the washed plate to Mary Anne to dry and exchanged a smile with the little girl as the soldiers paraded by, looking their way. "Lieutenant Douglas won't come back without her. Bonnie will soon be back," Claire said.

"Won't you be glad to never have to wash another dish or cook another meal?"

Claire surprised herself as she shook her head. "I like the idea of not having to do any unpleasant jobs again, but in a way I'll miss it. Time passes quicker when you're working."

"Idle hands are the devil's workshop," Mary Anne said.

"Work and your heart grows happy," Claire say.

"Whistle or sing to work faster," Mary Anne said.

Father interrupted the cheerful girls. "Get everything on board, we're moving out."

CHAPTER TWENTY-FIVE

Claire trudged alongside her parent's wagons, relieved to see Henry walking beside his own. She noticed he moved, head-bowed, steps slow. Mary Anne sat on the seat guiding the team and Tim took care of prodding Henry's lead oxen.

She still felt sad when she looked at him, still felt the guilt. But like she told Mother, she refused to let it weigh her down any longer. They cleared two hills, saw the ten soldiers that had been left behind by Calum to escort the two wagon trains into the next fort. Father Wimberley rode up beside the lead wagon, four teams in front of their own, but the man refused to push his oxen any faster. For the first time today, Claire felt her father's disappointment.

The other wagon train was just getting harnessed and ready to pull out. If they had pushed, they could have taken the lead. In most places on the trail, there was no passing. She could tell from the motion of her father's shoulders how much passing the other train had meant to him.

By the time they reached the pass, the other train was filing onto the trail and they had to halt and wait. Father rode back to them. “Let’s use the time folks. Wash and refill the water barrels, look for firewood. Any men who want to try it, this would be a good time to fish or hunt. Ladies, chance to wash out some of the clothes. Let’s just not sit here and wait.”

He turned, rode up to Henry. “I need you to be on guard duty while the women are near the river.”

Claire sat in the morning sunlight, her skirt hiked to show her petticoat but not reveal her legs. She had the hem caught twice at her waist to secure it and keep it from getting muddy. Mother had her dress fixed the same way. Mary Anne was barefoot, her dress and petticoat caught like Claire’s when she was riding. As quick as a water sprite, the little girl was laughing as she chased silvery minnows in the shallow water. Tip and Tyler barked and raced along the bank, mirroring the little girl’s actions.

The twins stood next to two of the would-be miners, all four were mid-river with pants rolled and shoes sitting on the bank as they cast lines into the water. None had had a bite.

When father rode up, he looked at the angry Henry and smiled. Good, at least the man was back among the living.

"Okay, load 'em up, let's keep up," he said. As he rode up the bank, he saw a couple of soldiers watching the women as they stood to struggle with the basket of wet clothes. He wasn't surprised to see Henry sigh, but stand to carry the clothes before the suitors or soldiers could make the offer. It would take time, but he was confident Claire would reel in her fish.

It was the next day that the Wimberley wagon train entered the fort. Father was upset when he had to wait at the gates as the larger mule train departed. There would be two days between them again, since many of the wagons that had joined him and the Lamptons needed to restock. Impatient to be gone, Father rushed to restock what they had consumed and did a little bit of business with his tools and wagon parts in trade. Claire and Mother kept Mary Anne with them as they explored the store and the main street.

The boys took off and Father Wimberley sent Henry Lambton after them. The man grumbled, but quickly pursued the route of the boys. When he found them trying to peek over the saloon doors, they backed into him and he grabbed them by the shoulder. "Father Wimberley wants you to stay with us." The boys fell into step with him before one of the boys said. "There are women in their underwear back there, but the men are all dressed."

Henry stopped, released them. “Stay here.” The boys stood there, giggling as Henry walked back and peered over the door. There were two women visible, one about three hundred pounds, the other maybe one hundred. They wore soiled white petticoats and torn chemises. None of the men drinking and playing cards seemed to pay any attention to them. Disgusted, he turned back to see the giggling twins and smiled as he caught up to them. “You had to make me look, didn’t you?”

As he listened to their chatter he saw the Wimberley women leave the little grocery store and take the time to store their new purchases. Despite the dirt and bustle of the army base, they looked clean and wholesome. Mary Anne was jumping around, pointing to the Indians and the animals wandering in the street. Claire caught her little finger and hushed her. Annoyed, he looked the other way. He tried to call up all the hurt and rage he felt the day Barney died, but all the hurt was already healing over.

That evening a small wagon train pulled by oxen entered the fort. There were five wagons left, one had been taken, another burned and the oxen stolen from both wagons.

When one of the members of his own party laughed at the unfortunates, making fun of them for dragging the half-destroyed wagon along, Father Wimberley reprimanded him. “The Indians would have done the same to us, if we didn't have the troopers riding along." The Raglon boy looked as though he was reconsidering.

Father Wimberley was already gone, walking over to meet the members of the other train. Minutes later he had made a deal for them to join his party and sent the remaining wagons over to join the camped wagons. Sixteen would make a lot of difference, since every gun and able man helped to protect the others. He called the twins away from a game of horseshoes and together, they moved the half-burned wagon down to the stables where he could use the blacksmith's tools.

He sent the owner of the wagon to search for lumber while he and the boys dismantled and removed the burned part of the wagon. He sent Tom back to his wife with the burned canvas and orders to use the spare tents. Using two of the four tents that had been stocked with the wagons Father and Henry had sold, she and Claire cut away the burned half and were able to piece out and begin to sew a replacement top. When the wife of the wagon owner came by, Mother and Claire put her to work sewing beside Mary Anne.

Tom carried back his carpenter's tools. By nightfall, the wagon had been repaired. There were only the black boards on one side and the front box to show it had been attacked. One of the officers from the fort came by to observe the work and talk, if not, they would have finished even sooner.

The boys reloaded the goods that hadn't been burned and the man thanked him profusely.

There was no palisade to separate the fort from the rest of the town, but there was a row of decks along the railroad line in front, a rock wall behind and sentry posts along each end. There were the usual 'tame' Indians with teepees along the edge of the fort between those posts. At the other side, the two merged wagon trains circled up. The saloons and red light district were beyond the fort on the wild, or Indian side.

Like the first night outside Independence, Father ordered a joint meal and dance to celebrate their safe arrival and to allow everyone to meet and make friends with their new traveling companions.

The dinner began with a long prayer of thanks for their safe arrival and a memorial for those precious lives lost already on the journey to their new homes. "None of us knows what really awaits us out west. We've sold our homes, uprooted our lives from all we've known, in the hope for a brighter future. It takes a special kind of courage, a desire for adventure and a richer life than the one we've left behind. Let us ask God to protect and guide us on our journey, amen." The last word was echoed by all those in the crowd.

Claire stood, head still bowed. The prayer had brought tears to her eyes. The way Father had described Bella and Barney brought their image back to her. Then there had been the special prayer for Bonnie and to protect Lieutenant Douglas and his men in their search. For the first time she realized how much danger Bonnie's younger brothers, Shawn and Ian were in. Both were boys, only a few years older than Lynne's twin brothers. Claire had Mother and Father, but she always thought of her dear friends Lynne and Bonnie as sisters. Their siblings always called her Aunt Claire. They were as near and dear to her as family.

Someone nudged her shoulder and Claire looked up, embarrassed to be caught crying in public. It was the Brewer cousins, Dorothy and Faye, who she had visited with and shared suitors with before Bonnie disappeared and her life became one of endless chores. "Are you ready, come on, don't you hear the fiddler sawing? It's time to sing for our supper."

Claire straightened, pulling her hankie from her sleeve to blow her nose and wipe her tears. When she looked around, she saw Henry, his pale blue eyes wet as well. Her mother made a waving motion at her and Mary Anne was already on her feet doing strange little hops into the air. The leprechauns were pulling the girl's shoes Bonnie would have said.

Well, this might be the last time for celebration. Father was right, they had no idea what waited ahead of them on the long trail to Utah. Smiling, Claire stood and let the girls pull her forward to be lifted onto the flat wagon bed first, followed by the other two. The memory of Bonnie's brassy voice singing with them clouded her eyes for a second. How she wished she could hear her friend's loud, strong voice once again? Had she really thought it sounded like a braying mule at one time?

Tom and Jim looked up at her, Tom passed her up a cup of water and yelled, "Sing the song from the other night, the one about the dreamer." Jim asked for *Buffalo Gals*, and other people called out requests. When the man with the banjo looked to them, she whispered, *Beautiful Dreamers*. It was a slow, sweet song and some shook their heads, wanting more pep, but Claire stiffened her spine and cued the girls beside her. In harmony, they sang the song together and the fiddlers both tried not to hide the girl's sweet melody.

After a rousing round of applause there were calls for faster tunes and she picked *The Yellow Rose of Texas*, and all the couples began to dance. The men playing the instruments joined in singing the next songs as one by one the girls were lifted down from the wagon. Claire's first partner was the Lieutenant who had pestered Father all afternoon, asking silly questions about how he knew what to do to repair the wagon. The man was polite and was from Connecticut. Claire easily talked with him about the bustle and activity back in the civilized part of the world. She wondered why he was here if he missed it so badly.

Next, she danced with each of the would-be miners who had been on the wagon train since Missouri. Although she had talked and walked with each before, always with a chaperone, none had seemed promising to her in any way. When she looked up as the players were joined by a harmonica player and changed the song to a Virginia reel, she saw Henry Lambton being drug onto the rough dance floor by Faye Brewer.

He had seemed sad minutes ago, now he was actually blushing as the two girls seemed to fight over which would get to dance with him. Mother and Father had already joined the dancers. Mary Anne had danced with her brothers and the young boys on the wagon train. Claire noticed there was a little redheaded boy who seemed the same age, about seven or eight, who was trying to catch her eye. He was one of the new members of the wagon train and she planned to tease the little girl later if she danced with him. She could see the lovely child looking his way as she got ready to dance with her brother Tom.

Claire's new partner was a tall man with sergeant's stripes on his uniform who was gushing about how she was the prettiest little thing he had ever seen. She gave the man a bright smile and together they led off the swirling reel. During the wild dance, she seemed to dance with each of the suitors again, as well as the Connecticut Lieutenant and her own Father. It was the Sergeant who led her through the arched arms and back to the beginning while others danced through.

As soon as the dance ended, the sergeant lifted her back onto the wagon bed. “Sing the *Rose of Killarney*, darling, just for me.

She would have refused, but the harmonica man played the opening bars and one or two in the crowd clapped. As sweetly as though she had sung solo her whole life, Claire sang the lilting Irish song. When she stumbled over some of the words, the fiddler player beside her would call out the next line. Somehow she managed to finish it without too much embarrassment, but she certainly had no gift for memorizing music the way her Irish friends did.

On the last words, “Sure I love you,” she was lifted roughly from the stage by Leray Raglon. She could smell whiskey on his breath and it was clear he had been down at the other end of town.

“Come on, you’ve danced with everyone else. Now it’s my turn. Play us a good one boys,” he yelled at the men on the wagon.

Claire pushed at his hands on her waist and shook her head. “I don’t dance with drunken fools, let go of me.”

Instead he leaned in, trying to force her head up to kiss her. She screamed at him and the soldiers in the group rushed up to take him in hand. Claire stepped back between her parents, struggling to keep from crying. The girls who had sung with her at the beginning crowded in and Claire suddenly shook her head and smiled.

"It's alright, I'm all right now. Come on girls, let's sing another song for these nice people."

This time it was Dorothy who called the tune and the girls sang, *Shall We Gather At The River*. They closed with *Goodnight Ladies* as Father reminded everyone they would be leaving early in the morning.

Claire walked back to her wagon surrounded by the children and her parents. After giving each a hug Goodnight, she accepted a boost up over the tailgate by her father.

In the dark, she could see Henry walking back beside both the Brewer girls. They were talking to him and if she wasn't mistaken, giving him an invitation to call on them. Her father watched her eyes narrow and when the girls left Henry at his wagon, he waited until the man disappeared inside to warn his daughter.

"Henry's a man of property. They will all be pursuing him now he's a rich widower. Best make up your mind what you want girl, before he's taken again."

Claire's jaw dropped, ready to protest, but her Father was gone. Had he just given Henry his blessing? Was he right, if she didn't say anything, Henry would be married again and out of reach mere weeks after his wife died? Did she want to say something to him?

"Come to bed, Claire, I'm tired," Mary Anne called.

Claire scrambled in and shed her dress, corset, and voluminous petticoats. Sitting on the edge of the bed in her shift, she worked her dancing shoes off with a groan, then pulled off her stockings. "I'm sure you are. You danced every dance," Claire said around a yawn.

"Um-hum, all of them. Why are some boys so shy?" Mary Anne complained.

Not bothering with a gown, Claire climbed beneath the quilt and reached out to tickle the sleepy child. "Some little redheaded boy in particular."

Mary Anne giggled and flipped over to catch her hands and stare at her. "It's always the good ones that get away, isn't it?"

Claire snuggled the sighing child against her as she sighed herself. Was he really about to slip away again?

CHAPTER TWENTY-SIX

It was worse than she had imagined, the last weeks of the trek toward Utah. Every morning, she was disappointed that another day had come and gone without any sign of Bonnie. She tried not to notice, but Henry seemed changed since the dance. The terrible melancholy which had him moping about, ignoring his food and everyone's efforts to talk to him, were over.

The first thing she noticed was how he was arguing with Father again. Then she noticed he looked different. She tried to figure out what it was, but it was such a small change she wasn't sure. Finally, one day Mary Anne asked him at the breakfast campfire. "Why did you trim your mustache, Uncle Henry?"

The twins elbowed each other and smirked. Claire stood paralyzed as she realized that was it. Always a handsome man, she had admired him from the first time she saw him. He had a full head of sandy hair, a manly square face with twinkling blue eyes and an adorable mustache. Of course he was married to Bella, her boss, so she had tried to ignore all that. She told herself it was only because she favored a tailored man of fashion. Henry was a dapper man, and that was why she found him nearly impossible to ignore.

On the trail, she had watched him change. At first, he seemed to hate the trail life as much as Claire. At the beginning, it was one of those things they shared, a willingness to listen to each other complain. Bonnie had told her he was a whiner like her, and that was what Claire liked about him. But during the trek, she had noticed him grow leaner, more muscular than before, and less likely to grumble. It was a good thing for a husband and she felt Bella was lucky. Now Bella was gone.

Henry looked handsomer than ever, hair blonder, his eyes bluer in comparison with his browner skin. But these days she had noticed his face was always smooth shaven again, like it had been in Boston, except for his mustache. Staring at him, she saw it. He had snipped his mustache close, so the hair didn't hide his upper lip like before. It made his mouth look even more, more kissable, than before.

Claire felt her stomach sink. Ever since the fight they had in front of Calum Douglas, where she accused Henry of planning to kill the boy as soon as Bella was gone, he had acted like she was poison. Claire had tried to apologize several times, but Henry always had somewhere else he needed to be, something else he needed to do. He never had time to talk to her. What hurt most was he never wanted to make eye contact. In the same brown dress every day, her face and hair covered by the long-brimmed bonnet, maybe she had disappeared. The dress was the same pale color as the cloud of dust she walked through. She felt invisible to Henry.

As she stirred the beans, Claire rubbed her fingers over the back of her hand. They used to be the softest hands at the mill. Now they were rough and dry. She was glad there wasn't a mirror handy.

She looked up in time to see Faye Brewer beside the Lambton wagon. "I know you've probably had breakfast, but I just made donuts and thought you might like to eat them later."

Henry smiled at the girl and Claire sank onto the abandoned bench. The boys and Mary Anne were already rushing, Mary Anne to drive the wagon for Henry, the twins to help him and Father with the two wagons. Mother smiled at her, "You need to hurry making lunch. I'll put away these dishes."

Claire pointed to Henry Lambton, still standing and talking to the awkward girl who had brought him food. "I don't even know what a doughnut is, let alone how to make it. It sounds awful."

"Not sure, but I think it's some kind of fried sweet. I'm sure if you asked, Faye would share her recipe."

Claire rolled her eyes as she stood in a rush. Father scooped up the empty bench to load on the wagon and stared at Claire's peeved expression. He shook his head, then called over his shoulder. "Get a move on girl, we're heading out."

Claire started to sit down and realized too late the seat was gone. As she sank to the hard ground, she heard Faye laughing as she walked away. For a moment, Claire felt like she might cry in frustration. Henry stared at her, shook his head and put the doughnuts beneath the bench, he had just secured to his wagon. Mary Anne sat there primly, watching as the boys moved the yoked oxen into position to chain to the wagon.

Awkwardly Claire rose, accidentally putting her hand down on one of the blackened stones in the cold fire pit. Worse, she stepped on the hem as she stood and heard a tearing sound. She wiped her cheek and stepped back to free the hem. Carefully, she raised the skirt of the dress she had grown so weary of anyway. There was just a dusty footprint on the hem and as she tried to look behind her, she hoped there was no stain on the skirt. Satisfied, she released the full skirt and looked up to see Henry standing there, grinning at her.

"What, you never saw anyone fall before?" From a distance, Claire saw her father already mounted and directing the wagons into position. Today they would be wagons seven and eight, but still, she didn't have time for all this nonsense.

She looked back at Henry, ready to snap at him again, when she saw his hand covering his mouth and a tear leaking from his eye. Surprised, she instinctively raised a hand as though to touch him and he caught her wrist. He turned it so she was looking at her black palm. She stared at him in horror, then looked down to see the black handprint on the side of her skirt.

Before she could touch it, he raised her wrist again. Taking the dirty tea towel she had used to grip the skillet, he poured the last of the cold coffee over it. Nudging her bonnet back, he barked. “Stand still, hands out to your side. I’ve got this.”

Quickly he scrubbed at her face while she rolled her eyes, trying to see what he was doing. Satisfied, he took her hand, her rough, dry hand, and carefully wiped the greasy black soot from her palm. He was rough and impatient. Claire heard the Raglon’s quarreling as they moved their wagon into line. When he finished, he studied her small face, noting the red area where he had scrubbed it so hard. He released her. “Worry about the smudge later. Have you loaded everything?”

Claire grabbed the empty coffee pot, the filthy towel and her fire-dried skillet. Henry took the skillet, but kept a firm hand on her elbow as they rushed to the back of her wagon.

As soon as he released her, Claire raised the stained skirt onto the tailgate and frantically scrubbed with the reverse side of the dirty cloth. All it did was smear. Henry moved quickly to block anyone's view of her, but still when the gold-miners wagon drew abreast, James and George both hooted at them. Cheeks flaming, Claire dropped the damaged skirt and made sure her bonnet was secure to hide her flaming face before walking around to the side of the wagon to take her position.

The wagon gave a lurch and she almost fell again. Looking heavenward, trying not to swear. Claire rushed to follow along beside her own wagon.

Humiliated, Claire knew she would probably never be able to get the soot from the wood and the buffalo chip fire out of the fine woven cloth of the dress. Then there would be gossip. Faye had laughed when she saw her fall. What would she have to say if she knew Henry had washed her blackened face like some mother cat cleaning her kitten? Finally, the four men who had courted her unsuccessfully had clearly seen her with her skirt raised and her petticoat showing. Worse, she had been standing in broad daylight beside Henry Lambton, even though his back was turned to her.

James or Cobb might never say anything to the others, but George would race to tell Faye. He still wanted the other girl for himself. Worrying, Claire was unaware of her mother's voice until she grew irritated. "Claire, stop being a goose and answer me. Get up here beside me right now."

Claire would have argued that she had a job to do, but when she looked, she was walking along the outside edge of the trail, far from the oxen she thought she was switching.

When James Temple rode back to check on her, Claire was once again sitting with her skirt raised and her petticoat exposed. Claire tugged at it, but Mother was so focused, she never released it. Claire blushed, but spoke as James raised his hat and then gave another of his hoots. Her mother jumped at the loud noise beside her and quickly lowered Claire's skirt hem.

Claire swiveled and leaned to look back through the wagon. Sure enough, James was now riding beside Faye. Whatever one cousin knew, the other knew almost immediately.

Mother saw her face and asked with disgust. "Now what?"

Claire described everything, from the fall, to the smeared blacking on her hands, face, and dress. She even described how when the four miners rode past, she had been trying to clean the smudge on her dress.

"Whatever could be wrong with that?"

Claire stared at her mother and then asked her if she knew why James had hooted at them as he rode past.

"I don't know, I was trying to clean your dress," Mother's voice faded away as she realized what she had been doing. "Oh, oh dear."

Claire smiled for the first time all day. "Well, at least I'm not the only goose. You did the same thing Mother. We were both so focused on saving my dress we forgot about my reputation."

"Surely people will understand. My goodness, if one doesn't realize it in time, you can always be looking at someone exposed in some way or other. There is just no privacy with everyone out in the open all day, or inside a lamp-lit tent at night. Why, you can see the outline of everything at night if you look. People know not to look, and they certainly know not to talk about what they see if they do look."

She tilted her head to stare at her Mother's puffed cheeks and eyes sparkling with outrage. "I saw James ride over to talk to Faye Brewer as soon as he passed our wagon. She saw me fall and laughed at me this morning. But no, she wouldn't gossip, not her."

"Well, who cares if they do? You did nothing wrong…," she hesitated and stared at Claire, "… did you?"

"No, Mother, I did nothing wrong except act like an idiot. May I get down and do my job? Are you satisfied?"

"Yes, but be careful darling. It might be the vapors, they do leave one addled when it's that time," she whispered.

Claire climbed down carefully and took the whip Mother handed back to her. She would have reminded her that her monthly was last week, but James was trotting past again. He tilted his hat as he passed, his mouth smirking in satisfaction. Claire shouldn't have, but she let the ox whip drift just enough to land on his horse's flank with a bright snap that sent the animal bucking for a second. This time she hid her own smile as he looked back at her with suspicion.

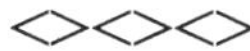

The lead wagons were filing into the campsite for the night when they heard the first shouts. Each wagon behind them cheered as the troopers appeared, running at a trot toward the head of the wagon train. Claire stopped, careful to not move into their path, straining to recognize any of them. It was Ian and Shawn, who rode back to greet her as the other troopers helped the wagon form up a circle for the night. Calum Douglas pranced by on his big chestnut stallion, stopping when he reached their wagons to ask. "Has Bonnie arrived, she was headed this way?"

Claire raised a hand to cover her mouth. "I thought you were bringing her back to us. Oh Calum, haven't you found her?"

The soldier removed his hat, sat restlessly on the big horse, and tried to find a smile. "She's fine, wonderful. We rescued her from Chief Washakie's camp a week ago. We've been at Fort McPherson together, it's well, you know Bonnie. She heard there was a wagon train heading out, coming your way, and she wanted to rejoin this party. I couldn't convince her that I needed her back at the Fort more than you people did on the wagon trail." His voice faded away and he coughed to clear it before Mary Anne held up a dipper of water to him.

He smiled down at the pretty, gray-eyed girl and sipped the warm water slowly. While he drank, he studied Claire. The little blonde was covered in dust from head to toe, her curls hidden by her bonnet. There was a rough red patch on her cheek, a big black stain on her dust colored dress. He noticed there was a gap where the dress had been torn near her waist. She certainly didn't look like a porcelain doll. There was a worried frown on her face now, with the news about her friend.

"I'll leave the men to help you get set-up. We passed a train coming up, but none of them knew anything about her. I'm going back to check again."

"If she's not in danger, why did you bring so many soldiers to find her?" Father Wimberley asked beyond his daughter's shoulder.

This time it was a real smile. "Our mission isn't to keep rescuing Bonnie. We had some criminals, a couple of gunrunners and thieves, to escape the fort. They were scheduled for execution in the morning, but killed some men to escape. We're prepared to shoot them on sight. I just started to worry, with her somewhere on the trail between those men and your wagon train."

Claire could see in his face that taking time to explain this to them was killing him. He might have other reasons, but he was clearly in hot pursuit of Bonnie.

While Claire tended to the cooking as quickly as possible, she kept her eyes and ears open listening for the soldier's return. She heard a shout, but it was her cries that drowned out all the rest. Sitting in the lap of the lead rider was a woman, a tall, brown haired woman, who could only be Bonnie Magee Michaels.

Claire noticed Bonnie was sitting stiffly erect, not clinging tightly to the tall soldier. Calum Douglas looked grim as well. Claire ran to grab Bonnie as soon as the soldier released the woman. Bonnie wrapped the little blonde in a bear hug, then opened her arms wider as Mary Anne and the twins flew up to crowd against her. Mother and Father Wimberley waited until Claire released her. Then they hugged Bonnie as though she was a long lost child.

Claire turned to study Bonnie's tall Lieutenant. Calum stood back and watched Bonnie's every motion. As her light brown eyes filled with tears and started to overflow, Claire saw the same emotion reflected in the soldier's eyes. Henry Lambton was the only one to seem withdrawn from all the emotion.

Claire sighed, wishing for a minute that Henry and she could share their feelings as easily. When her parents released the big girl, laughing happily, Bonnie stepped back so she was again beside her Lieutenant. The man seemed to stretch on his toes so he was briefly pressed against her back. Claire saw an invisible change, as for a moment, Bonnie seemed to relax.

Then the Lieutenant lifted his hat once again, and bade them all Goodnight. He spoke to Henry and she heard Henry answer, but noticed all the questions in Bonnie's eyes. She must have known that Henry was a widower and fair game now. Had Bonnie expected them to be wed by this time? She was the only one to know how Claire really felt about the man. Well, if she was disappointed it was no greater than the disappointment Claire felt.

Claire turned back to finish the dinner, wishing she had some meat or a special treat to serve her friend. Mother stepped up to tell her she could manage if Claire wanted to talk with Bonnie but Bonnie turned back and joined her. "Nonsense, we can talk while we cook." As the children and the men left to water the cattle, Claire relaxed, instantly back to where they had been when she left.

Claire watched Bonnie staring after Calum, wondered what had changed between the two. She couldn't wait to talk to her best friend and find out what she had experienced in all this time they had been apart. Whatever they were saying with those looks of longing, it ended when he turned away from her and mounted to ride out to oversee settling his own men.

CHAPTER TWENTY-SEVEN

Bonnie talked, keeping Mother and Claire locked on every word. The way she talked about her time of captivity, you would have thought Indians were as or more civilized than many of the people they were traveling with. Claire could tell she didn't share everything about her rescue. She would try to get all those details later, when the two were alone. As Bonnie had told her before, Calum Douglas wasn't a toy soldier. Claire doubted he had just talked to the Indians and they released Bonnie to his care. Then, there was the trip back to the fort with all those men.

The story was just getting interesting when the men came back from tending to the oxen. Mary Anne and the boys had caught some crayfish, but the boys told Bonnie that Gerald had promised they were good eating. You just had to boil them till their shells changed color and they floated to the top. Claire backed away from the things that looked like monster bugs. Bonnie put the small pan over the fire with water in it and waited.

"Aren't you going to throw them in to cook?" Bonnie said, rubbing her tummy.

"You'll eat one, won't you Bonnie?" Tom asked.

Bonnie shook her head, "No, go on the water's boiling?"

Mother shook her head and moved behind Claire. Mary Anne stepped forward and said, "Silly, boys." And she dropped her crawdad in the boiling skillet. Amazingly it started to climb back out. Claire knocked it back in with the wooden spoon and they all watched it curl and twist in agony.

Jim shook his head and handed both of his bugs to Tom.

"Baby boys," Mary Anne teased.

Father told her to stop. "Go on, Tom," Father said, "I'll eat one if you will."

Henry smiled at the boys' faces and said, "Me too, Jim, you eat one and I'll eat one."

Tom pitched them into the pan with the dead crawdad, squealing when one pinched his finger. The children danced about the fire in ghoulish delight as the crayfish, squirmed and twisted before dying.

Claire shuddered as she passed out the plates to the men and boys, each with a big pink crawdad in the center.

She ladled Mary Anne's beans and started to put the last one on top and she shook her head. "No, I don't want it. It looks too much like a scorpion."

The boys had found and killed one of the small desert pests their first day outside the last fort. They had carried it around on a stick to tease their little sister until Father told them it could still make them sick or even kill them if its tail stung them. The boys flung it far away into the bushes. Now every morning, everyone went through the new ritual of shaking out boots and shoes before putting them on.

"Nonsense," said Father. "These have wide flat tails instead of stingers. Here," he held out his hand. "If you're sure you don't want to try it. It probably tastes like shrimp or lobster, looks the same only a lot smaller."

Mary Anne didn't answer, just scrunched up a little to stare at the bugged eyes and the waving tentacles. Decided she shook her head and passed it to Father.

"Did this friend of yours tell you how to eat it?" Father asked.

Jim was staring at his crawdad, the same way Mary Anne had looked at hers. Claire felt her stomach swirl at the thought of eating the horrible thing.

Tom looked as reluctant as the other two as he said, "He said you pull it apart, and eat the meat out of the tail, then put it in your mouth and suck out the green stuff in the head. He said that's the really good part."

"Ooh, bug brains," said Mary Anne.

Tom didn't want to, but with everyone watching he pulled his apart. The meat in the tail half stuck out a little.

Father and Henry copied his action with their first crawfish. Father sucked on the white meat and pulled it into his mouth to chew. Henry did the same, and finally Tom chewed his.

"What does it taste like?" Bonnie asked.

"Nothing. I've had lobster, which is delicious. This tastes like nothing. What do you think Henry?"

Henry managed to swallow his bite, then toss the tail down for the dogs to nose around. When Tyler barked in complaint, Henry tossed him the head as well. "Here, if one of you ladies want to try it, you can have my other one."

Father leaned forward with his plate at the same time.

All of them motioned them away. Jim reached out and took one and copied Tom's actions, forcing himself to eat the meat. He smiled when he finished, shrugging. "One's all you need of something like this."

"Are you going to eat its green brain?" asked Mary Anne with a squeal. Both boy's sat holding the ugly heads.

"I will if you will," said Father. He pulled his last one in half and ate the other tail, then turned to wave the tentacle half at them. Both boys suddenly tossed the heads to the eager dogs and Father did the same with a laugh. Soon they were all laughing.

Claire relaxed, pressing her hand into Bonnie's to squeeze her fingers. "I'm so happy now you're back."

Bonnie smiled at her, wondered why she wasn't. For a minute, she wished there were another of the horrible crawdads. She wondered if Calum would have eaten it, even the head.

"Thank the Lord you still have a little good sense. Now finish your plates. Next time, let those gentlemen have your catch as well," Father said.

Mary Anne and Mother cleaned and put away the dishes.

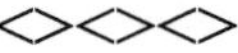

Bonnie and Claire were still talking, long after the others gave up and left the fire. Dark clouds suddenly hid the moon and stars. "Thank heavens you are back. That's the first decent meal we've had all month."

Bonnie laughed. "You two had everything going when I arrived. Besides, the little I know about cooking I learned from my Mum and yours."

"Yes, but you cooked the crawfish."

Both shook their heads, still repulsed.

Bonnie stared at her and said. "Now tell me what's really wrong. Where's my sunny little canary, chirping about fashion, and what everybody's doing?"

Claire's lower lip began to tremble and she blurted out, "Oh Bonnie, I've done everything wrong."

Bonnie's laugh was hollow as she rolled the young woman in for a tight hug. "You're not the only one. I've finally found the perfect man. Calum is big, strong, honest, and a terrific kisser."

Claire bumped shoulders with her. "What's wrong with all that?"

"I'm afraid to accept what he's offering because of my past with Tarn, and the fear that I'm not worthy of his love."

Claire said pooh and stared at her friend. "You are more than worthy. Besides, this is the wild West. People make their own laws. You don't intend to take Tarn back, do you?"

Bonnie shook her head, "Never, but I'm not worried so much about what people will say, but what's right in God's eyes." They sat there beside the dying fire and Bonnie sighed, "But Lord, he is a temptation."

Claire giggled and Bonnie looked at her in the firelight, studying the small red mark on her cheek. She reached out to touch it. "What about Henry?"

Bumbling, crying, Claire told her everything. She explained the miserable morning, then said, "And that's not the worst. Now Bella is gone, all the single women on the train, even the widow Raglon, are pursuing him. Nearly every day they bring him some sweet treat. A fried pie, a lump of fried dough, or a dish of cobbler. I don't know how they do it, they have no more sugar or lard than we packed along. But he accepts all their gifts, then calls on them at the end of the day to help them with any chores that need a man to do. I don't even dare think what that means."

Bonnie sat there looking at the tearful girl until Claire said.

"It's too late, I've hurt him and destroyed any chance we'd have to ever be happy."

Bonnie knew not to laugh this time, the words had rung with truth. As she listened to Claire confess her sins, Bonnie stared into the dying flames. Had she done the same thing? Turned aside the man she wanted and admired for a moral obligation to one she hated?

"Oh Bonnie, what can I do? Some days I feel as though my chest has been hollowed out and filled with jagged rocks. Henry never even looks at me. If I'm standing in front of him, he looks through me like he is still seeing Bella and Barney. Oh Bonnie, he really loved her. I don't think he ever noticed me the way I did him. And after she died, I accused him of trying to smother Barney."

Suddenly Bonnie raised the blubbering girl from her arms to look at her. "You what?"

Claire trembled at the horror in Bonnie's eyes. Even her best friend couldn't understand how she'd said it. Slowly, carefully she tried to justify it by what she saw and heard and how she had misinterpreted things. "I was cruel and cold to Henry when he was at his lowest. When I heard him explain it to Calum, I told him I was sorry. But I could tell I hurt him and it was too late. Now, I've lost him forever. Bonnie, I don't know what I'm going to do?"

Bonnie shook Claire until her head wobbled and then she hugged her. “Stop crying. If you’ve given up, there’s no reason to cry. If you want to change things, then you’d better start. I was shocked when I saw you. Your hair is dirty and uncombed. Your dress is stained and torn. I’ve never seen you look so terrible. Don’t you care at all how you look?”

Claire sniffed, but sat up a little straighter. “I’ve been broken-hearted,” her lip began to tremble again.

“Pooh. Stop thinking about your own problems. Clean up and straighten up. If you think about what you can do to help Henry, the man will notice you.”

Claire interrupted. “No, I offered to mend his shirt, and he said Bella would do it.” She ended with a howl and her eyes filled with tears, “It was before she was killed. Oh, Bonnie, I didn’t want her to die.”

Bonnie looked at her, ready to shake her again. “First, we will get you clean and looking pretty again. Then you can work on the rest. Once he’s looking at you, if you apologize and ask for forgiveness, he’ll hear you.”

For the first time in a week, Claire looked hopeful. As usual, her mood changed instantly. “All right, now tell me what you’ve done wrong, lately?”

Smiling, Bonnie hugged the sweet blonde beside her, holding back nothing. She told about her rescue and each of the heated kisses. “I just don’t know if I can continue to resist him.” She described the temptation and her fears of surrendering. At her protest that she was still a married woman, Claire scolded her. “To that animal, Tarn.”

“Right, I guess I can change my religion and do it, divorce him. But I don’t know how my family will view my abandoning my faith and going to hell. Besides, Calum is Catholic too.”

“Did you ever just want to shoot him?” Claire asked.

“Tarn?” Bonnie laughed. “Only a thousand times. Each time I feel so guilty. I mean, who can I confess to or do penance. I haven’t been in a church since St. Louis. You can’t imagine all the guilt.”

“Oh, I understand the guilt. All the times I’ve imagined…” her voice broke. “I haven’t even had one tempting kiss, but oh, how I’ve wanted them.”

She laughed as Claire again howled in pain. Bonnie stared around at the deserted campfire. “Everyone is asleep. Hurry and get your soap and things and we’ll go down to the river to clean up before it rains.”

CHAPTER TWENTY-EIGHT

Claire climbed over the tailgate and quickly pulled off the dirty, ugly dress. Mary Anne turned over and moaned a little, and Claire froze. Quietly she lifted her pillow and lifted out the gown and wrapper. She hesitated, then went ahead and changed into them and shoved her feet into her slippers. She stood still, the soap and brush in her hand, trying to remember what she had been hunting. Bonnie was waiting.

On the far end of the wagon was a single box. Inside were all Bonnie's abandoned clothes. She had given Claire trouble, but Bonnie had been wearing clothes that fit even worse than her trail dress. She found the girl's single flannel gown and the old robe of father's that Bonnie used for a wrapper now. She felt sad when she realized there were no slippers. Poor Bonnie, she wore those heavy men's brogans all the time. Once they were settled, she intended to get a nice gown, robe, and really big slippers for her friend.

As Claire started out, she froze half-way over the tailgate. In the shadows, she saw Bonnie. She was wrapped in the arms of a tall man, and they were kissing. Not a soft playful buss like the kisses Claire had known. The girl was so tightly wrapped against the man that the curve of their bodies was one. Claire stared at where the giant had a hand on her friend's hip, pressing her closer. Claire felt her own stomach tighten and she grabbed at the tailgate to keep from falling out.

They separated and Calum smiled at the little blonde. Blushing Claire pulled her wrapper closer around her.

Calum cleared his throat. "I must remind you ladies that we're here pursuing two dangerous men. With your permission I will escort you both to and from the river. On my honor, I will only look for intruders."

"Where's your father's rifle?" Bonnie whispered to Claire. She stared up at Calum. "I trust you Lieutenant, but two guns are better than one."

"Here, is this it?" Claire asked.

Bonnie accepted the heavy shotgun and said, "It will do."

The trio walked past the guards on duty on the outside circle of the oxen wagon train. Calum responded to each challenge, asked and was directed to a shallow area that other bathers had been using.

Claire stumbled along, trying to keep up with the tall, long legged couple. Calum carried the lantern. Because he was so tall, the light spread out around them, but Claire still felt breathless and frightened crashing along behind them over the uneven ground. At one point she bent to retrieve her slipper that got pulled off as she stepped through some weeds. Calum handed the light to Bonnie by a dammed-in pool beside the river, upstream from where the cattle had been watered.

Holding onto her friends' arm, Claire managed to keep up. Grateful that she had blown out the lamp, both shed their outer clothing. Unlike Claire, Bonnie quickly shed her dress, slip, and moccasins and unpinned her hair. Eagerly she dove out into the pool of water.

After a little coaxing, Claire waded out into the stream to join her friend, squealing as her feet sank into the mud and then yelping about the cold. After a minute, she was standing as deep as she dared, the water over her waist and lapping coolly against the curve of her breasts. "Bonnie, where are you?" she whispered, "I can't see a thing."

Bonnie splashed up beside her, giving a deep laugh. "That's the whole idea. You wouldn't want all those pesky suitors of yours down here to sneak a free peek."

Claire raised her hands to cover her breasts and looked back toward the brush. "How would we know if they were there?"

"Well, if you'll stay quiet, they won't know to come looking. Lord, I miss taking a bath every day. Did you know almost every one of the Indians bathed every day? At least most of the women did, and I'm not talking a basin and cloth little spit bath. They take everything off and dive in."

"Oh Bonnie, every one swam nude together."

"Just the women and little children would swim together. The men bathed in the river. The women had a little man-made pool like this under a bank of willows for cover. Wouldn't doubt this was made by Indians. They move camp often, but always set up by rivers. The men were forbidden to look at the bathers. It's a big taboo. But of course, at least one of the skunks did, I know."

"One of the braves, looked at you?"

"I never saw him doing it, but from what he told Calum and the others, he was a sneaky skunk and peeked plenty." Bonnie stood up and whispered the details into the short girl's ear, just in case Calum was still close enough to hear.

Claire splashed the water as soon as Bonnie finished. "They should have punished him, put out his eyes or some other Indian atrocity," Claire said.

Bonnie snorted. "No such luck. But Calum did give him a good tussle because of it." A wispy cloud trailed over the full moon and Bonnie looked around. "Let's just get all this dust off and our hair washed before the moon comes out to see us."

Claire took the soap Bonnie handed her and began to lather her arms and legs. Scrunching under the water to move the soap under her chemise and bloomers, just in case the men could see. She relaxed for a minute, enjoying the motion of the water, which now seemed pleasantly warm compared to the night air. When something brushed against her bare leg, she yelped and stood up, jumping. "Oh lordie, lordie, there's something in the water. What if it's a poisonous snake or one of those pinching crawdads?"

Bonnie caught her and held her still, mischievously giving her a little pinch. "Turn around, I'll wash your hair. There are no crawdads in here, the boys caught theirs in the little creek that feeds into the river. There's too much activity. What with all the wagons stopping at this spot all the time, no snake is going to make a home here. If it was anything, it might be a fish that got in over the wall between here and the river. Now stand still and be quiet." Bonnie whispered.

In minutes she had the wet soap worked into a lather between her hands. "It would work better if your hair were wet, dunk under."

Claire looked confused and then yelled, "Oh no." Bonnie laughed as she pushed the smaller girl under water. Claire came up, shaking her head and gasping for breath. "I think I swallowed some of this water, and maybe that fish."

Bonnie laughed and Claire tried to get close enough to pinch her too, but almost slipped and went under again. A minute later, Bonnie was busy shampooing Claire's hair.

<><><>

Two men on the shore strained, listening to all the noise. Calum heard a branch snap and whirled to face an angry Henry Lambton.

"What are you doing out here," Henry hissed.

Calum whispered, "I'm standing guard so the ladies can bathe."

"Guard against what, and do you have to look at them to stand guard, I thought you told Bonnie you wouldn't look," Henry said.

"You can't see anything," Calum said. But suddenly the clouds swept past and in the pale moonlight the two men were transfixed as they saw the girl's revealed. Each saw only one woman, although Bonnie was standing behind Claire and shampooing the giggling girl's hair. Calum studied every line of the heavy, bouncing breasts as Bonnie worked diligently to clean the blonde's oily hair. Henry felt faint from staring at the thin, wet chemise that was all that stood between his eyes and the little beauty's perfect body.

"Quiet, did you hear that," Bonnie said. All four strained to listen. In the distance they heard the second pop of a rifle, waited but heard no more shots and relaxed. When the men looked back, dark clouds had hidden the moon and the women again.

"Go on, hurry up," Calum called from the bank.

Both girls crouched a little lower in the water. "Don't look," Claire yelled in a high pitched squeak. It was again so dark, Bonnie could barely see the gleam from Claire's eyes, nothing of the man on the bank. Placing a hand on the back of Claire's neck, she whispered, "Lean back, I've got you." In the quiet night, the only sound was the gentle lap of the water as she rinsed the dirty suds from the blonde hair. A minute later, Bonnie released her and Claire barely righted herself as they both heard the sound of galloping horses.

"What was that?" Henry said. Henry raised his rifle and Calum moved the end of the barrel so it was aimed away from the girls. Calum shouted, "Hurry girls, get out of there."

Claire sputtered and shook her finger at the men now visible on the bank. "You said you wouldn't… and is that Henry watching too."

There were other shouts as the moon shown brightly above them, from men galloping toward them.

"Fan out and keep low to the ground, you go right," Calum ordered then hissed to the women. "Stay down girls, hold her down Bonnie"

Monroe and Tiller, the escaped gun runners, sped along the river between the two camps leaning close to their stolen mounts as shots rang out behind them. So far, nothing they had tried had brought them luck. As they ran parallel to the river looking for a more sheltered spot to cross, they blinked in amazement. In front of them were two barely dressed females and as Monroe recognized the taller one he yelled to his partner. “Now’s our time to get even. You grab the little one, I’ve got special plans for that tall, bossy woman.”

Claire screamed in terror and tried to run. Bonnie heard the voice and recognized the man she had first encountered in St. Louis. He had been trying to buy their oxen after she had chased him off the night before when he tried to steal them. Now he was planning to catch and rape them.

As the galloping horses splashed into the river behind them, she saw a gun on the bank flash. Impatiently she grabbed Claire and gave the hysterical girl a heave toward the bank, relieved to see her sputtering and finally struggling toward shore. Diving, she swam quickly over and drug Claire through the weeds and mud onto the bank beside her.

On the muddy shore, Bonnie turned and picked up the gun. She pumped the heavy shotgun as she turned. But before she could fire, one of the riders fired at one of the men on shore and she heard him gasp. Bonnie raised the shotgun and fired and the second rider disappeared.

Seconds later, when she was sure both men were down, Bonnie waded farther up the bank, dragging the semi-conscious Claire to drop beside their discarded clothes.

Standing, she heard a voice call. “Are you all right?”

“Henry, is that you?” Bonnie set the shotgun down and then struggled into her slip, fighting it down over her wet body, then she repeated the struggle with the ugly black dress. All the time, she was stuffing her feet into her shoes as she stumbled forward.

"Calum, I'm fine now. Was that Tiller and the oxen thief?" Bonnie yelled.

Instead of an answer, she heard a groan to the left and rushed forward. "Calum, Calum, are you hurt?"

As she dropped beside him, she felt the sticky, wet patch on his chest and screamed for help. In the dark, men were coming. She looked past where she knelt beside the man she loved to where another voice moaned. "Who's there?" she demanded.

"I killed a man."

"Henry, thank God. Run and cover Claire before the others arrive. Hurry."

"Claire, my beautiful Claire," he whispered, then ran toward the girl.

Awkwardly Henry picked up her gown and wrapper. At least in the bright moonlight he could see it and the girl. As he tried to raise Claire up to slide it over her, Claire pushed his hands away.

"Darling, let me do this, hurry, the others are coming and you're practically nude."

"No, Henry, don't look at me. I wanted to get clean for you, but now I'm all muddy again."

Despite her protest, Henry was forcing the gown over her head.

For the first time Henry laughed and crushed her to him. “You goose, you beautiful goose, thank God you are all right.” With more energy, he covered her with the gown, then reached over her for the wrapper. Half-lifting, half-holding her pressed against him, he helped her stand and slid one arm through as he heard Robert Wimberley shouting. “Claire, Henry, what’s going on here?’

Henry held the sobbing girl, holding and rocking her as an angry Robert Wimberley stepped forward to take possession of his daughter.

“She’s fine sir,” Henry said.

“The devil you say, she’s barely dressed and all wet and muddy. If you’ve done anything to harm my girl, I’ll…”

Claire pushed from Henry’s arms into her fathers. “I’m fine Father, Henry saved me. Bonnie and I were bathing while the others were asleep. Henry and Calum Douglas stood sentry to keep the others away.”

Father didn’t look convinced, but started to sweep his daughter up to carry back to the wagons. Henry reached out for her at the same time. “Let me, sir, I’ve got her.”

“Nonsense,” Father said and swept the girl up to stomp back to their wagon with Henry in pursuit. When he started breathing hard and almost stumbled. Henry said softer, “Please sir, you carry the rifle for a while.”

Glaring at each other, Robert Wimberley surrendered his daughter as she turned to wrap an arm around the younger man's neck. Silently the transfer was made and they hurried back to camp.

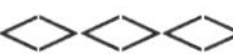

As soon as they reached the wagon, Henry lifted Claire over the tailgate to where Mother and Mary Anne waited. "I think she's alright, just still a little frightened. It was awful," Henry said as he almost collapsed against the end of the wagon.

Grumbling, standing the gun against the wagon wheel, Father answered the two boys. Tom and Jim were running about, jumping and asking questions, the dogs barking beside them. "We've got Claire, I think Calum has been shot. You'd better go see about Bonnie."

Claire looked up at her Mother and the little girl. "Don't just look at me, don't let me get this mud all over the bed."

Mary Anne disappeared to fetch water and towels while Elizabeth Wimberley touched the clump of mud and weeds that were stuck to her daughter's hair. "This should be an interesting story. Stand up, let's get you out of all this, then we'll see what we can do about your hands and hair."

As she threw a clump of mud out of the back of the wagon, she heard Robert's stern voice asking Henry to repeat his explanation.

Bonnie pressed against the wound, heard Calum moan again. The bullet had struck high on his shoulder near the top left button. In horror, she realized how lucky he was to have the two rows of brass buttons. She spread her fingers across to touch the one beside his heart and closed her eyes in prayer.

The men were there, urging her back to examine the fallen soldier. As they pulled him from her, one man ordered the others. "Bring a light, I'm a doctor."

Bonnie pushed her heavy wet hair back from her face and moved forward to lift the shotgun and stare where the renegades had been pulled and plopped onto the bank.

"Are they dead?" she hollered.

"This one is, he pointed to the one in blue. Think the other is still alive."

Finally, Bonnie stared down at Tiller, the one who had threatened and insulted her so many times. His body looked unmarked, until one man held a lantern down and she saw the hole through his neck.

The other man was still unconscious, but Bonnie noted the ragged rise and fall of his chest. His shirt was splattered with small holes and both arms were bleeding. "Best tie his hands and feet. If he doesn't die, the army plans to take him home to execute," she said.

One of the men laughed. "Are you kidding?"

Suddenly two soldiers were standing beside her. "No, do as she says. Then we'll take him."

Bonnie reached out a hand to either side of her and clutched her brother's hands. "Calum was shot."

"Is he going to be all right?" Shawn asked.

With a deep, indrawn breath she whispered, "He has to be."

CHAPTER TWENTY-NINE

Claire told her mother how she and Bonnie was talking long after everyone went to bed.

"I know how it is, trying to catch us with old friends," Mother said.

"Then she told me how the Indians bathe every day and how she couldn't believe how lax I had become about my appearance. At any rate, we decided while all the men were asleep, we would go down to the little pool they have marked off for bathing beside the river."

"What little pool?" Mother sounded curious and Claire would have gone into more detail, but the little pitcher with big ears was sitting there listening.

"Calum Douglas knew where it was, and offered to escort us there since he's in pursuit of a couple of real scoundrels and he said we ladies would need protection from any peeping Toms."

"Tom wouldn't do anything like that," Mary Anne said, but then she looked a little unsure.

"It's an expression, dear. For the man who watched when Lady Godiva made her ride nude through the streets to argue against some law."

"I don't know that story, can I read it somewhere?" Mary Anne asked, but Mother had turned her attention fully back to her daughter. Claire was using the soap and vigorously washing her hands, arms, knees, and feet. She couldn't help but wonder how anyone could bathe in a mud hole and come out clean. She would have to ask Bonnie for the secret.

"Claire," Mother snapped. "I thought you said you and Bonnie were alone. How did the Lieutenant know you were going to bathe?"

Claire looked up, wrinkling her brow with suspicion. "He did show up rather quickly." She shook her head decisively. "No, he was on patrol and saw us getting ready to leave the campsite. When Bonnie told him where we were going he insisted on going along to keep us safe."

Mother seemed to accept her explanation and after Claire rinsed, she ordered. "Lean over, we'll do what we can with that hair. Then I want you two," she looked over her shoulder at a sleepy Mary Anne and smiled. "I want you three girls to get some sleep. You know how your Father feels about getting an early start."

Claire leaned forward so her hair hung over her face into the bowl and very patiently sat still while her mother poured cup after cup of water over it. Finally the water was too dirty to do any good. She emptied the pan out and handed the bowl to the sleepy child. “Careful, don’t drop or chip my basin. Fetch another and then you can go to bed while we finish up.”

Mother straightened and stretched, twisting from side to side. Claire sat with the towel over her shoulders and brown water dripping onto it.

Later, as Claire tried to fall asleep with Mary Anne beside her, she heard her father and mother talking in whispers. The stacked boxes between them was no sound barrier.

“Well, what did he have to say for himself? You saw how she looked when he carried her back to us,” Mother said.

“It was plausible. The Lieutenant is wounded and in Henry’s wagon now. I’ll try to talk to him tomorrow, get his confirmation. But Henry says they were never alone together, that it was a dark night and the escapees the army were hunting were in the area, not to mention a lot of men from the two wagon trains. Well, he’s right, the girls needed someone on guard to protect them.”

“I can’t understand wanting to take a bath in the middle of the night. It’s nearly ten o’clock, now.”

"That part made sense too. They were up anyway and it was a moonless night. Well, even you were wishing Claire would pay more attention to her grooming."

There was a pause and Claire swallowed. Even Mother had been embarrassed by how she looked.

"She doesn't know, has no idea of how cruel the world can be to a girl without a good reputation. You and I may believe him, but what are other people going to say?" Mother said.

"I didn't want to corner him on that just yet. He looked upset, and they were getting the Lieutenant settled and moving the boys out. Bonnie will be with the twins sleeping in the tent again."

Claire twisted in the bed, so that her back was to the whispering voices. She had heard enough. Mother was wrong if she thought Claire didn't know about losing one's reputation. She had seen it happen to girls in the factory before. Hadn't it almost happened to Bonnie? That was why she married Tarn Michaels. Other girls weren't so lucky. They lost their jobs and often ended up on the streets when their names were compromised.

She had done nothing wrong. Nothing intimate had happened between them. Well, he had come to her rescue, covered her nearly naked body from the eyes of all the other men who arrived minutes later. Claire could still feel Henry's arms around her, hear the softly whispered words,

"Little goose." Ordinarily it would have made her angry, but from him, in those moments, it had made her feel cherished.

Smiling, relaxing, Claire slipped into blissful sleep.

It was stuffy and warm as Claire woke to the voices of men outside the Lambton wagon talking to Bonnie. When her mother started to say something, she whispered, "Shh." Together, they sat, shamelessly listening.

The corporal told Bonnie. "I don't think we should be moving him just yet. The Doctor removed the bullet and a partially embedded brass button from his shoulder, said he lost a lot of blood."

Claire had heard two men speak, but for some reason Bonnie wasn't answering. She could tell from the way the men were talking that they knew she was distracted.

"Figure he would want me to get the men back to headquarters, now we've captured that gun runner and done for Tiller. That was our mission, you know?"

Bonnie must have nodded, because an older voice said. "Monroe wasn't as bad hurt as we thought. He's the one you filled with buckshot. Know the General wants to personally see him shot by firing squad. He could take a turn for the worst or maybe even escape again, lest we head on back."

Claire heard the stomp and snicker of horses just outside her wagon. Quickly she stood to dress. Mary Anne was already gone. Mother turned back from her listening post and began to get ready as well.

Dressed, Claire climbed out of the wagon and looked up in surprise at the mounted troopers behind them. Several tipped their hats and smiled at her and Claire brushed her frizzy blonde hair back from her face. She was torn between going back to brush and braid it and finding her friend.

The other wagons of the larger train were going to clear out first. She waved good morning to the twins walking back with the oxen and she watched Father Wimberley and Henry Lambton yoking the teams.

Claire sidled around the wagon and up behind Bonnie. Somehow the tall girl knew she was there and held her hand behind her back for Claire to grab her fingers.

"Figure if the Lieutenant is going to make it, he'll need some nursing," the sergeant said.

"Don't worry, we'll assign a couple of men to stay behind so he doesn't have to return to camp alone. Figure maybe if they follow your wagons on in, they can take the train back to Fort McPherson. Only going to be another week or so," the corporal added.

"Three weeks," Bonnie said.

"Really, that long," the corporal said as he scratched his head. The sergeant elbowed him.

"Probably take about that long for them cattle to make it at that. Reckon the Lieutenant there ought to be fit as a fiddle time he gets back to headquarters, what with all that rest and recreation," the corporal said with a grin.

The sergeant was scowling and shaking his head and Bonnie wondered what the two men were up to. But Calum moaned and she forgot everyone else as she climbed back into the wagon and bent to wipe his face with a cool cloth.

Claire watched as the two men grinned at each other. The sergeant turned to the mounted men and their moaning prisoner. "Hey, you two pups fall out," he jabbed a thumb at them, but the Magee boys already spurred their horses out of line.

"Boys, your orders are to keep an eye on the Lieutenant. When you see he's fit enough, you're to bring him back to headquarters. Just ride up to the track and signal the train. They know to stop for military. They'll bring you all three back to the Fort."

Shawn started to argue, but Ian shot him a look and Shawn swallowed the words. "Yes, sir, Sergeant. You can count on us, sir, I mean Sergeant."

The corporal rode to the head of the line, the two scouts grinned and waved and soon the whole platoon was out of sight.

Bonnie looked out at her puzzled brothers. "Well, if you're to stay with us, best earn your keep. Help Tom and Jim with the oxen. I'd ask you to keep your eyes peeled for something to shoot for the dinner pot, but following all that ruckus ahead of us, it will be no use today and probably the next. Go on with you."

Claire boosted herself up to look inside at where the tall Lieutenant was stretched out under Bonnie's watchful gaze. "Do you two need anything?" Claire asked.

Bonnie shrugged, "If you were to drive this wagon, then I could tell you when we need water or food. He's too hot and feverish right now. I've been trying to keep him sponged and cooled off." Claire looked indecisive. Bonnie said, "Well, that would make it easier for me." She stared at her friend's clean cheerful face. Took in the wild, unbound hair.

Claire blushed as she tried to squeeze it in her hands to stay down. "At least Mother got the mud out of it. I was rushing, in case you needed me and I thought I needed to make breakfast.

"Mary Anne passed out tinned biscuits and jerky earlier. There was time, but your Father didn't want us to wake you or your mother," Bonnie said.

Henry Lambton appeared in front of her and Claire looked down at the ground, too embarrassed to speak after last night. Henry looked equally unsure as he stored the tent pegs and poles and made room for the canvas whenever the boys and their dogs finished pulling and folding it. The Magee brothers stepped in and she heard them giving directions to the younger boys on how to fold and store a tent correctly. Henry looked in their direction and smiled.

He looked into the wagon at the unconscious soldier. “Still no change?”

Bonnie shook her head. “No, but Claire said she would drive this wagon to be on hand to help me.”

Henry turned to acknowledge her presence for the first time. He saw her wild head of hair and smiled instead.

Minutes later he was handing her up onto the wagon seat as Ian and Shawn Magee galloped back to peek into the wagon. Claire wasn’t surprised when the boys stopped beside Henry. “Bonnie said we’re to drive the oxen while you and Claire ride and help keep an eye on the Lieutenant. Not sure what that means, but we’re ready.”

Claire smiled at the two boys, recognizing Bonnie in their features despite their blue eyes. “The twins can show you,” Henry and Claire said at the same time. The boys each had soft red mustaches and she smiled as they finger combed them until Tom and Jim ran up. Each was excited to have the job of training the older boys and soon they were pulling into their place in line.

Claire felt twitchy with energy. After the last few weeks where she had taken Bonnie’s job, she was used to being busy. She hadn’t cooked this morning and she wouldn’t have to walk along beside the oxen trying to keep up. For a minute, she couldn’t tell where to put her hands and her feet kept moving inside the wagon box with each turn of the wheel like imaginary strides beside the wagon.

"I guess I need to get my comb and mirror and do something with my dreadful hair. Everyone is staring at it and trying not to laugh."

"No need," Henry reached behind the bench to fumble around before dropping a small wooden box on her lap. Claire felt a chill sweep up her spine, but then curiosity won and she pushed the little enameled star on the clasp and it opened. Inside, as she had feared, was something of Bella's. A small, beautiful vanity set rested against a molded red velvet lining, each piece carefully secured in its own snug little space.

She should have handed it back immediately. Didn't he realize how personal something like this was? Bella would have opened and used it each morning and evening. Silver, with beautiful inlays of blue enamel bands and a bold yellow star in the center, it was obvious it was an expensive gift from her parents. Like Claire's own had been when she was ten. Mother had given her a set for her birthday. From that day on, she was expected to comb and arrange her own hair, and she had. Unless she were sick or had a bad day, then her mother would use Claire's comb and brush and mirror to groom her hair for her.

Claire lifted the brush, removed one strand of raven black hair that was long enough to have reached Bella's waist. The woman had always worn her hair in a severe bun, or like the night at the St. Louis hotel, in a braided chignon. Instead of dropping it, Claire wound the dark hair in a tight circle around the base of the silver handle. Shivering, forcing herself to smile, she brushed at her own wild tangle of hair.

When she had one side smooth, she brushed the other. She had just lowered the brush when James Temple trotted up beside the wagon. Claire tried to pretend to be unaware of his presence or of Henry's beside her as she carefully and deliberately used the small silver comb to part off six sections. Winding the first, she used one of the pins she'd found in a round silver box to secure it, then wound the next section.

James spoke. "Never watched a woman do up her hair before. That's quite a chore, ain't it?"

Claire finished the third section and lifted the fourth to wind and pin. "Not really. Good morning, James."

"Morning," Henry said.

"Yeah, reckon it's going to be another scorcher. At least them Army fellows caught those felons, heard they killed one of them," James said.

Claire waited, she had heard Henry tell Bonnie last night that he had killed a man. Henry remained silent.

"See the army left a couple of the young ones behind. Don't see what kind of help they will be for us, if we're attacked by Indians again," James said.

Claire looked past Henry to see Ian looking coldly at their visitor. Claire coughed as she closed the case and handed it to Henry to return to its hiding place. As he turned around, he brushed against her. Claire felt more annoyed than before, but she used Bonnie's trick of acting charming to conceal it. Smiling, she introduced Ian to James and vice-a-versa. "Ian and Shawn are Bonnie's brothers.

"Yeah, well, I rode up to make sure you were safe. We heard a lot of rumors and, well those were desperate men."

"I'm fine, Bonnie is fine, the Lieutenant is unconscious from his gunshot wound. We were lucky that the Lieutenant was standing guard." She shivered. "It was a terrifying experience."

"Kind of odd, that's all. You and your friend out skinny dipping late at night, with two men just keeping watch, don't you see. Now I told Leray, Mrs. Raglon and the other ladies…,"

Claire's cheeks flamed red. Henry noticed even her neck was pink. He also noticed there were soft little blonde curls forming at the edges of her hair already. Henry tried not to smile, just felt grateful to not be James Temple.

CHAPTER THIRTY

Claire stood and Henry reached up to pull her back down, but she gave him such a look that he merely held his breath and hoped that the gentle motion of the oxen would continue. Without touching her, he sat ready to catch her if necessary.

“James Temple, you and all the nasty minded gossips can stop spreading rumors. First, we were not bathing nude but in our undergarments. Second, during a cloudy night when all the ne’er do wells are asleep is the only safe time for a woman to bathe on the trail. Third, if it were not for these gentlemen running to rescue us, there is no telling what horrors would have befallen us.”

“Well, never heard of anyone doing it before, and we’ve been on the trail for three months with you.”

Claire hesitated, unsure how to counter his argument without lying. As the wagon hit a rut she swayed and quickly sat back down so that she was eye level again with her accuser. “It was the first opportunity I had, where there was a private pool, a cloudless night, and my good friend back to chaperone me. Also, we knew with the soldiers on guard near the wagons, we would not have to worry about the Indians, but could focus on just getting clean."

"Just seems hard to believe that those two men just happened to be standing nearby, that's all. And Leray Raglon told me he saw Henry Lambton carrying you in his arms, and what you were wearing barely covered anything."

"Leray Raglon has been telling tales ever since he and his mother joined the train. None of it has been true and these lies about last night are the same. I had on my gown and wrapper. My father and Henry took turns carrying me back while Bonnie walked along with the doctor and soldiers carrying Lieutenant Douglas."

"Well, folks want to know what kind of people would let their daughter carry on like this with a widowed man."

Claire let out a squeal and stood upright again. Suddenly three riders approached and surrounded James. Henry rose, trying to balance as well as Claire had and pushed her gently down onto the bench beside him.

"If they want to know that, they'd better ask me," Father said.

Tom and Jim ran back toward the argument and all the following wagons began to slow to a stop as their drivers strained to listen to the shouting match.

"There has been nothing improper between myself and Miss Wimberley," Henry said.

"Neither will there be," said Father Wimberley.

Both men ignored the wagon master, too busy glaring at each other to pay attention to anything else.

"Well, I know you've been sparking every eligible woman on this train, already looking for a replacement for your wife. People heard you and your wife fighting plenty of times, so don't make out that you're spending all your time grieving," James said.

The angry men who were mounted pushed even closer. "What are you all crowding me for?" James yelled.

"We don't like our friend's name bandied about by low-life's and scoundrels. Smells like you might need to take a bath more than once a year, yourself." Ian said as he let his horse bump against the gray of James.

"Stop crowding me. I've got friends too, you know."

Bonnie stood behind Claire and put a hand on her other shoulder. She could not remember ever seeing her friend look angrier. "I doubt it," Bonnie muttered. "You won't have many if you go spreading lies about an innocent girl.

James backed his horse into the clear and started back toward his wagon when he stopped and gave one last yell. "Well, it still seems funny, those two being on hand like that."

Henry jumped down from the wagon and ran down his side of the wagon to catch the bridle of the gray horse. "Not that it's any of your business, but I heard a shot fired. I haven't slept well since my wife died and the noise woke me. I climbed out of bed to answer a call of nature when I heard horses running, it sounded like toward the river. I heard a woman scream and thought it sounded like Claire so I ran down to the noise. You'll have to wait until he's well enough to answer your impertinent questions, but I'm sure since he was on patrol, Lieutenant Douglas responded to the sounds the same way I did."

"You just happened to have a gun with you?"

"Since the Indian raid when my wife was killed, yes, I always have a gun with me."

James snorted with contempt and stared at Henry.

Henry turned bright pink. "And another thing, I am not pursuing all of the women on this wagon train. Several have called on me, letting me know they would welcome my attentions. They came with baked goods and inquired as to my health and invited me to call on them. I think I've visited two, but merely to be polite."

All of Claire's defenders had followed Henry and now Bonnie spoke. "Maybe if you understood the difference between a decent woman and a trollop, you might interest them yourself. Maybe, some of those women would make you a pie. Maybe, if you pleased them, they might offer you more."

Kaye Raglon scowled at Bonnie and Claire, who was now standing beside her. "Not going to beard the she-dog if she's got her whole pack about her."

"I always have my family and friends with me. They were there last night too." Claire answered, advancing toward the instigator of the rumors. "I know they are always prepared to defend me and my honor. If you had paid attention, you would have noticed they were there last night as well."

The woman had the decency to back down and Claire walked back toward the wagon, still flushed. She stood trembling between Bonnie and Mother while the men and boys who had rushed to her defense stood watching. For a moment, there was silence as her lips mirrored the war of her emotions. Finally, she raised her chin, eyes sparkling with unshed tears. She clutched the hands of the women beside her, accepted a hug from Mary Anne, and then smiling, stepped back.

"I'm good. I just need to walk for a minute. Thank you all. It is overwhelming to have your love and support. These ignorant people, they don't really matter. But your respect is very important to me."

"Good." Father stepped behind her and Mother, and extended his arms to hug both women. "But we've got to get this wagon train in motion. Everybody ready?"

The Magee brothers rode back into position, Mary Anne was lifted back up beside Mother Wimberley and Father rode up to the front of the wagon train. Bonnie gave her a last hug and returned to her duty watching over Calum.

Henry called Ian over. In minutes he rode off on his bay, Sue, and Ian's horse ran behind the wagon beside Calum's stallion.

Henry rode after Father Wimberley, leaving the young soldier riding in the front of the wagon. The last thing Claire needed was to share a seat with a Don Juan widower. Although the idea of being seen as a Casanova of any kind made him laugh. He knew it would have amused Bella. She had finally given up on the shy man and asked him out to dinner. The thought of her, her constant jealousy made him slow his horse.

He paced beside the wagon of Faye Brewer, receiving glowers from her Father as well. Was it because he was seen as some sort of a lecher, or was it because he had publicly revealed it was the women who were the pursuers? After tipping his hat to the girl, he finally posted on ahead past two more wagons.

At least Father Wimberley had the wagon train once again moving at a good pace. He tried not to, but as they approached a bend in the road, Henry looked back toward the girl who was on his mind. Claire strode along, not as easily as Bonnie had always walked, but rapidly enough with her short little strides to keep up with the oxen.

Ian must have said something, because the girl turned in surprise to see him riding on the bench. As Henry watched, she dipped her head and accepted the soldiers help in mounting the moving wagon. Relieved, Henry tried to put her out of his mind. The young man was no threat to her, the Magee brothers had been raised to consider Claire as another sister. But the Irish lad would soon have her mood lifted with his silly stories and maybe a song

Grimly, Henry faced forward, saw Claire's father check his horse on the trail to wait for him. This was a conversation he didn't look forward to having.

"You did great, even Lynne couldn't have faced down that bounder and that old harridan better. What happened to my timid little princess?" Bonnie asked.

Claire laughed as she helped turn the meat in the skillet. Ahead she watched the Wimberleys sharing the seat with Mary Anne wedged between them, busily working on making lace. Of all the members in the party, including Henry, the little girl seemed to miss Bella and Barney the most. Did she work so hard at her tatting to remember or to forget?

"Princess, I don't think I was ever…," Claire protested. But Bonnie shrugged, then nodded. Claire laughed, then grew quiet again. "I think I finally had to grow up when you were kidnapped and then we lost Bella and Barney. One can't be precious and spoiled when other people are depending on you to help with the work."

"I like the change in you. But don't let the old Claire disappear, I loved my cheerful little goose, too." Bonnie said as she ladled a cup of broth off the boiling mutton. "I'm going to see if the smell of this might wake that lazy soldier. I'm getting tired of hearing his stomach growl."

"Aren't you going to stay and eat? You know how rare it is to have fresh meat." Claire lifted a piece of the meat she was trying to fry. They, like three other wagons, had bought sheep from the strange Indian boy who had walked up near their camp. Father had shot their small sheep and butchered it quickly. Tonight they would eat the meat they could slice off that she was cooking in the skillet. Tomorrow, they would eat the boiled mutton from the leg bones. In this weather, she had no choice but to cook it all at once. Luckily, most was buried in a pit they had dug under the fire. It was like the one Bonnie had watched the cavalry soldiers use to cook an ox.

Bonnie's stomach growled in answer.

"Go on," Claire said, "I'll bring you a plate as soon as I get a chance."

As the tall woman left her, her Mother came forward to keep her company at the fire. In minutes, Mother had spoon bread mixed and baking in the firebox oven. Claire left her to tend the awful meat and the usual pot of beans as she went to get water and grind beans to make coffee. She had the pot filled and ready, looking at the somber men at the fire. At least the boys seemed happy. The Magee lads were showing Tom and Jim some trick to use with a forked stick and part of the sheep's intestine.

Claire shuddered at the thought of handling the disgusting innards. The sheep's wool had been so packed with dirt and burrs, she still couldn't believe Father bought it. Instead of looking like the wooly pillow with little black legs that had been in her nursery rhyme book, this animal had looked thin and nasty. She raised the lid and turned the braising meat before setting the coffee pot on top of the flat lid. Claire turned her head and held her breath until the air moved the stench away. She had never liked mutton.

She was aware that the angry pair of men, Father and Henry, were both watching her. She knew Henry had ridden off to talk with Father. The question of what they had talked about was clear from their faces every time they looked at each other, then at her.

Claire couldn't think about that now. She tried to focus on the sheep again. Tonight's meal would be a treat compared to what she was supposed to cook for breakfast. Father had saved the organ meat for the morning and it, the brain, and the spongy lungs were soaking in a deep bowl of salted water. The dogs, Tip and Tyler, had shared the thrill of gnawing on the unshorn head with its bulging yellow eyes after Father had split it in half to remove the brain. At least someone enjoyed mutton. Before he had dripped the blood of the butchered animal onto a rock and had laughed as the excited dogs eagerly lapped up the blood. Claire shuddered again.

Claire looked at Henry Lambton where he sat all alone. Other than the angry looks Father kept giving him, no one seemed to be interested in talking to him. She felt the same strange flutter she had felt when she first saw him inside the shop in Boston. Then Bella had appeared.

CHAPTER THIRTY-ONE

Henry stared at the pretty girl cooking supper beside her Mother. It had been difficult, facing her father. But he had been trapped into one marriage on the demands of an outraged father. If and when he married again, it would be to a woman he could not live without, one that he had asked to be his wife.

When Claire finally called “all come and get it,” he had lost his appetite. Somehow he needed to make up his mind. The last thing he wanted was to ruin another woman’s life.

Bonnie set aside the smelly cup of broth. He still seemed asleep. She looked down at Calum and ran her fingers across his warm brow. The Sargent had told her he had lost a lot of blood, but she couldn’t remember it, just the sticky place where she had touched his chest in the dark.

The thought of losing him crowded her mind, but she pushed it aside. Determinedly she dampened the cloth and squeezed the extra water away before wiping his face. This time she unbuttoned his uniform shirt, but he moaned when she started to free his arm from one sleeve. Carefully, she settled for lifting the uniform open enough to stare at his bandaged wound. There was a large pad on his shoulder and a winding cloth wrapped around his shoulder and back to hold it in place. The cloth had rusty looking stains where the blood had seeped through before. Since the doctor was with the other wagon train, she would need to change it soon.

Bonnie held the damp cloth, then reminded herself that she had volunteered to nurse him. She held the cloth over him, then turned to rinse and wring it out again. Ready, she stared at the swirls of dark hair on his chest over the heavy wall of muscles. She reminded herself that she was his nurse and this was her duty. Trembling, she traced the strong column of his throat, watched his Adam's apple bob. Gently, she leaned down to carefully wipe away the dried blood, careful to not disturb the bandage or the binding holding it in place.

When he was clean, she bent to rinse the cloth again. This time she was poised to trail the cloth down over his ribs and flat stomach, when her gaze was captured by the dark line of hair disappearing beneath his waist band. It was suddenly so hot beneath the canvas that she could barely breathe. When she heard Claire's loud voice, she jumped.

Calum moaned in pain and Bonnie folded her hands to pray, feeling guilty for all her impure thoughts. When she looked down again, she saw his hand was over the same area where she had been looking. He groaned and Bonnie dropped the rag into the basin and fled to find help.

Henry stood over the wounded man, uncertain how to proceed. Bonnie had rushed to the camp side, not looking at the line getting their dinner, but clutching Henry's arm to whisper into his ear.

He had been happy for an excuse to leave where he wasn't wanted. Although Father Wimberley was the only one who seemed angry now, he had no doubt when the others learned what had been said, he would be getting dirty looks from the rest. For now, he only felt sad about how it would make Claire feel. She was so sweet and innocent – she didn't deserve to go through all this gossip and hurt.

"Hey, are you going to hold the bedpan or not?"

Henry jumped.

Minutes later, emergency over, he passed the wounded man the cup of broth. "Do you think you can hold this to drink, or do you need me to feed it to you?"

"I don't know. You did empty the bedpan outside didn't you? This smells about the same."

"Claire's boiling mutton. I think it has some wild onions and carrot weed in it too," Henry answered, agreeing with Calum's opinion of the smell. He still held the mug of broth over the soldier.

Calum tried to reach for it, but collapsed against the mattress instead. Sighing, he rolled his eyes. "My head and shoulder are throbbing. Where's Bonnie?"

Henry set the mug down, reached out to feel the feverish brow. "Told her to go ahead and eat, I'd take care of everything. You're hot all right. I better ride to get the doctor."

"That quack. He got the bullet, and my brass button, but he didn't clean the wound. Have you got any whiskey?"

"It's for medicinal purposes only. Right." Minutes later he poured a shot and held it to the sleeping soldier's mouth. "Swallow." Henry said.

Calum brushed at it and it sloshed onto his chest. Bonnie walked slowly toward the tailgate and called, "safe to return?" Henry answered and she peered over at the two men inside.

Henry explained to her and she was quickly inside, squeezing beneath Calum's head on the bed to raise him up despite his protest. With her holding his head, Henry was able to get him to drink. Calum moaned, but swallowed. "Clean the wound with it. A new bandage. Kill infection." Then he was out again.

This time with Henry's help, Bonnie was able to remove the shirt completely. Henry brought Bella's sewing basket up onto the bed.

"What have you got to use for bandages?" she asked.

For just a minute, Henry looked sad. "There are Barney's little shirts, or Bella's cotton slips."

Bonnie touched his hand, then said. "A slip would be fine."

When she removed the bandage, there was a smell, only a little less terrible than the soup's. Remembering watching her mother clean a wound on her Da's leg, Bonnie stared at Henry. "We need a flame and a sharp knife. Bring Father Wimberley to help."

Henry nodded before disappearing. Once again, Bonnie spread her fingers from the shoulder where he was wounded to the center of his chest. God had spared him with that shot. Now, all they had to do was get him to survive his doctor.

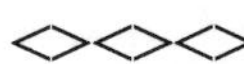

When he approached the fire, the last thing Henry wanted was to ask Robert Wimberley for a favor. But he had been in this position before and would be again. Sometimes a man had to ignore his own pride to do what was right for others. They were still three weeks from Junction City, Utah and he would have to work with this man every day. He needed to make a new beginning.

Walking on the edge of the fire, avoiding the target practice the boys were having with the new slingshot Ian had made, he watched each lad take a turn trying to flip over their empty coffee cups. When the last lad fired and one of the tin cups actually fell, Henry bent to set it back into place before walking up to Claire's Father.

"Sir, I need a sharp knife and your help for a minute," he whispered.

Father stared at him with contempt, then nodded. Without a word to anyone the two men slipped into the darkness. Claire took the last clean metal plate from Mary Anne. Relieved to see Henry and her Father leave together, Claire smiled and relaxed again. Whatever they had said to each other before, was now over. She knew Father was unhappy about all the gossip, but at least Henry had come to talk to him again. It had to be a good sign.

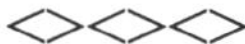

Bonnie stood over Calum holding the hot knife, the compass in its handle spinning to taunt her as she leaned closer. This would hurt, but it would be less if she did it quickly and carefully. Using the knife edge, she ran it over the red part of his shoulder, slicing the hair away. She put the blade back in the flame, then a minute later, she motioned to the men on either side of the big man, holding him down. Calmly she ran the sharp edge over his left breast again, this time pulling as she went. The crusted scab pulled away and Calum moved in a reflect action. The trio repeated the process, this time provoking a yell.

Before he could become even more agitated, Bonnie leaned forward to pour the good bonded whiskey into the bleeding wound. She waited until the men had recovered control of the thrashing soldier, and she poured it again.

Finally, she soaked the thick square of clean cotton in whiskey, before pressing it onto the wound. Calum screamed and Bonnie leaned to push him back down as she pressed against the festering wound. Tears standing in the corners of her eyes, she poured more alcohol onto the back of another new bandage and replaced the soiled one. When Calum relaxed back into the black unconscious state, she sighed. Together the three quickly secured the bandage into place.

“I should have noticed, I was sitting beside him all day,” Bonnie cried. Claire stood, leaning against the seated girl to turn her head onto her shoulder. Father had stayed with Calum this time as Henry had walked the crying woman back to the deserted fire. Like Bonnie had done for her in the past, Claire patted the taller girl’s back and made shushing sounds. “It will be all right. You did what had to be done. You are so brave, Bonnie.”

Bonnie leaned her head back to cry again. “You don’t understand. Mum had to do it to Da’s leg, again and again, before it finally started to heal. I can’t do it, I can’t hurt him again.”

Claire laughed and hugged her even tighter. “Now who is being a silly goose? You don’t trust anyone else to do it, so if it needs doing again, you will do it. Besides, maybe this is the only time it will take. Calum is so big and strong. I wouldn’t be surprised to see him on his feet tomorrow.”

Bonnie snuffled and Henry passed her his handkerchief, grateful that it had nothing more than a little sweat from the back of his neck. Folded and dry, it would do for her purpose. Claire took the printed cloth and held it out to her friend, “Now blow, and get to bed. Henry and Father will take turns sitting up with him tonight, but you need your rest to do it all day tomorrow.”

Bonnie rose, gave them each a weak smile. “I’m good, you’re right.” But Claire held onto her as she walked her toward the tent. The girls took a discrete turn behind the Wimberley wagon and Henry stood with his back to the wagon. The fire was banked over the hot coals. Beneath, he could smell the roasting lamb. Carefully, he lifted the lid on the pot of boiled mutton. Cautiously he cut a small piece of the meat which had grown more appetizing as it boiled for three hours. He ate one small bite, then opened the lid again and took a larger one.

When Claire returned from seeing her friend settled in the tent with the twins, she came back to watch Henry taking another bite from the kettle of mutton. He looked like a little boy, the way he was standing, sneaking food. She had put a plate aside for him, but this had to be better than the hard, chewy meat they had eaten with more beans. Someday she would be a rich married lady. Then she would never cook another meal, especially not dried soup beans.

She cleared her throat and Henry stood, backing away from the kettle. The look in her eyes, so tender, and what, what did he see in her face? What did it matter? He had promised Robert Wimberley that he would not talk to her or do anything else to confuse her about his intentions. There were over ninety people on this train, all of them watching him and Claire, waiting for just one more slip. Now, instead of apologizing or explaining about helping himself to the meat, he merely bowed and backed to his own wagon without a single word.

He didn't have the courage to look back and see if she now looked hurt or sad instead. He wanted to talk to her, to explain what he had told her father before the man or worse, one of the others in their group, took the time to explain it and the look became one of hate.

Sighing, Henry climbed into his wagon from the front. He looked back at Robert Wimberley, who sat grimly keeping watch over the wounded soldier. Henry looked at the impossible arrangement and spent a minute making up another bed. When he lay down on the thin, narrow cot that had been Barneys, thoughts of the poor boy brought even more guilt. Henry felt the weight of all his crimes, but finally slipped into sleep while the older man sat watching, glaring back at him.

CHAPTER THIRTY-TWO

Claire sat on the padded bench, her hands on the reins and the big handled driving whip beside her. She had never used it, with one of the twins always walking beside to prod the team into motion, there was no need to whip the lumbering beasts. As soon as the lead oxen in that day's wagon train started walking, the others moved along at the same grinding pace. If an ox wanted to turn off the road to graze or balked and slowed down, then the boys would switch it or more often, just pelt the reluctant oxen back into motion with small pebbles.

It really was nice for Bonnie to have her brothers here. Regardless of what she said, being kidnapped and forced to wait on a very sick woman hadn't been easy. Claire knew she would have been in hysterics all the time. The few Indians she had seen were frightening. Although the old Indian chief who had taken Bonnie had looked at her with such wisdom and then smiled at her as though he had read her mind and heart. Maybe the ordeal was the exciting adventure Bonnie had said.

Claire wished she could just get down and run along beside the oxen again. A month ago, she would have laughed at the ridiculous idea. But now that she had tried being someone else, she found she liked being busier even more than sitting and reading her fashion magazines. She knew she could never go back to being so idle again.

Behind her, she heard Bonnie's happy voice. Yesterday, when Henry had helped the man to sit up and actually get up to walk into the bushes with a little help, Claire and Bonnie had moved onto the wagon bed and rearranged the mattresses on top of the storage boxes. Now Calum's big mattress was near the front so Bonnie could take a break to visit with Claire whenever he slept. The small cot-size mattress was near the tailgate, so when the man on night duty needed to rest, he could but he was also handy to check outside and leave when he needed.

Curious, Claire looked through the canvas to where Bonnie was attentively bent over the sleeping soldier. When she sat back, she was smiling. Claire knew that meant he was better. This morning Bonnie had told her how relieved she was that his fever was almost gone, but more importantly, the shoulder wasn't red and sore. Claire was as relieved as her friend seemed to be. She had seldom seen her friend cry, the girl always seemed invincible to her.

Less than a year ago, the abusive Tarn Michaels had made her cry. Then the loss of the unborn child had nearly broken her. But Bonnie had risen out of the ashes to be stronger than ever.

As she watched, Bonnie removed the man's hand from her breast. Shocked, Claire turned to look the other way, but she sat up straight so it was easier to listen.

"You sir, are incorrigible."

"Please, kiss me, I'm dying."

Claire had no trouble hearing what Bonnie said, but Calum's voice was low and rumbling. Claire knew it was wrong to listen, but she couldn't move away. This was probably as close as she would ever get to hearing sweet love words. Henry hadn't even spoken to her the last two days. Whenever she drew near, he moved away. She prayed that it was just his way of guarding her reputation. But oh what it must be like to have a man look at you the way Calum looked at Bonnie. Her friend was just as bad, mooning over the tall soldier as though he was the most wonderful. Claire stopped musing and almost dropped the reins as she heard.

"Dying, you faker," but the words died in a gasp.

Claire's mind raced with all the possibilities of what the man had done now. She tried to tilt her head, but it would have been impossible to see what he was doing without turning around and staring. This time she heard the words he said and felt dizzy for Bonnie. If only Henry would ever say anything so wonderful to her.

"I love watching the shamrocks bloom in your eyes. I love you. I want to make you my wife."

Claire held her breath in happiness for her friend. She waited to hear her say yes. Instead, she looked back and saw Bonnie leaning forward to kiss him.

She had heard all her friend's arguments before, but the woman had also told her how tempted she was to ignore the scandal and just have an affair with the man. When Claire had looked at her in disbelief, Bonnie had admitted she would never do it, but lord she was tempted.

When Bonnie raised her head from the kiss, both his hands had fallen away and she knew he had passed out again. The wagon wheel hit a rut and his head rolled against the wagon bed. As though it was what she had been made to do, Bonnie curved into the space between his head and the wagon seat ahead and cushioned his body with the curves of her own.

Claire felt her friend move, knew it meant the soldier had slipped back into his dreams again. With Bonnie so close, Claire dared to whisper. "I see what you mean, the man could be a poet. What I wouldn't give to have a man talk to me so passionately."

"You didn't see what he was doing with his hands?"

At Claire's no, Bonnie raised up to whisper. "If he's like this now, as weak as a kitten and sick to boot, how will I ever be able to handle him when he's well? The situation is impossible. He has his enlistment to serve out, and the Indians are on the warpath everywhere. He could be shot or killed at any time."

"That's no argument. Any of us could die at any time. God doesn't promise us anything in this life, only in the next," Claire whispered.

"Which I'll never have if I surrender to sin in this one. But even if Calum were free, the boys would still be in the army and I don't worry about them when he is in charge to protect them. It's all impossible. If I ever see Tarn, I'm liable to shoot him on sight."

Calum moaned restlessly and Bonnie lowered her voice. "Besides, I want to buy property, set up my own claim, build a house to bring the rest of my family west to join me. That all takes time and work. Maybe by the time his enlistment is ended, and I am free from Tarn, then maybe we can work it out."

Claire heard her friend sigh and sighed as well. As difficult as it was, as many obstacles as Bonnie had between her and marriage to Calum Douglas, Claire was jealous. At least Bonnie knew what she wanted. She loved a man and he loved and wanted her.

But for Claire, every day was torture. She loved Henry Lambton, knew in her heart that she had loved him from the moment she walked into his store. Now his wife was gone, there should be no obstacle between them. Instead, Henry barely acknowledged her, avoided her like the plague, and had never in word her action shown her that he loved her as well. It was hopeless.

As the wagon rolled forward, slow mile by mile, Claire studied the couple behind her. Claire again felt a wave of jealousy. Bonnie dozed with the man she loved rolling softly against her breasts with each bounce. She had everything within her grasp and still she stubbornly refused to take it.

In little more than a week they would be in Utah. Brigham Young argued there was no such thing as bigamy, that God himself had ordained polygamy as the natural state for a man.

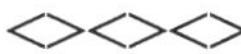

Claire was surprised when she realized Bonnie's light brown eyes were open, staring into her blue ones. Carefully the tall woman eased the sleeping man's head back onto the pillow and extricated herself from the narrow space. It took a minute for her to rise, not wanting to make a misstep in the jolting wagon onto her patient. Finally, she climbed over the seat and sat in the open air beside her friend. Bonnie stretched her arms overhead to take a deep breath and pushed the sweat dampened hair back from her cheek.

The two girls shared a smile as Bonnie flapped her skirts and Claire copied the motions. “Maybe we can shed our petticoats without anyone noticing,” Claire whispered.

“All those noisy thoughts of yours woke me up. How long was I asleep?” Bonnie asked.

“I’m not sure, not very long.

“So tell me what had you fuming?”

“Well, if a man like Young can have multiple wives, Father said the last paper he read claimed fifty-five, surely a woman can have two husbands.”

“Sounds too logical. That would only be true if Brigham Young didn’t regard women as lower than his cattle. He probably walks through his house and snaps his fingers, ‘you there, fetch my slippers, you, put down that silverware and come rub my back, and you…’” Bonnie waggled her eyebrows and pretended to pull on her long bushy beard. Both girls laughed, then looked guiltily behind them, and laughed softer.

“I’ve told myself the same thing. Why can’t I have two? One a devil and brute, the other a loving, kind man,” Bonnie said with a sigh. Behind them Calum wiped the smile from his face and struggled to keep his eyes closed.

“Even without a husband already, I’m not sure would be fair to marry him. We talked about the possibility of my being barren. A woman who was held captive longer than I had just given birth to a half-breed. I had to talk her out of drowning him, told her she was being silly. But you know how people treat those at home who are mixed race. It's bound to be a harder life for her and those little boys."

"Your children wouldn't be mixed race," Claire protested.

"No, but we'll have to talk again about the children. It's not fair to deny a handsome man from having his own sons and daughters."

Claire started to protest, but Bonnie shook her head. "You should have seen his face the first time I told him. It's not a little thing." Bonnie put both feet up on the front board of the wagon, pushing against it. She turned to stare at Claire's little pout of disappointment.

"What's your sad song? Nobody loves me, everybody is telling lies about me, or is it there's not a man alive on this wagon train that would make a suitable husband – that isn't already married."

Claire nodded and Bonnie bumped shoulders with her on the bouncing seat. "Don't worry, old Willow's got a plan, trust me. We'll get you a husband and married, just like that." She snapped her fingers for emphasis and Calum grunted.

CHAPTER THIRTY-THREE

The air was cool after the smothering heat of the day. Claire pulled on her lace shawl, secured her gloves and bonnet, and stepped down into the waiting company. Bonnie wore the same as every day, her brown Lindsey-woolsey dress, although she had added a lace shawl as well. Of course the Lieutenant wore his blue and gold uniform, the children wore hats and the twins had added the dark coats they had nearly outgrown.

Calum Douglas had asked the Wimberley's, who were her guardians on the trail, for permission to walk out with Bonnie. Courting permission had been granted, with the understanding that until she became a widow or the bonds were severed by the Bishop in Boston, the couple were to remain strictly chaperoned.

"It's like the first day of communion," Claire whispered to Bonnie. Bonnie gave her a hug, then Bonnie looped her arm in Calum's and with the parents leading the way, the giggling younger children ran behind. As the parents passed each campfire, they spoke to the campers, introduced both couples as walking out and accepted the customary congratulations and teasing. For the first time, Claire realized that she and Henry were not along merely as chaperones.

Ignoring everyone else, she stared at the handsome man beside her, noted the fine tailored suit, the way his hair and mustache had both been washed, trimmed and brushed. As her eyes dropped to the ground, she saw he wore his highly polished black leather shoes. They were only ankle high and had tied laces. Shoes so stylish had to be Italian.

When she looked up this time, he held out his arm, giving her a knowing smile. "Shall we begin our walk together, Miss Wimberley?"

Her stomach fluttered like she had swallowed a swarm of butterflies. Shaking, she took the arm that was so gallantly offered and straightened her back. Head held high so that the lace on the tiny bonnet barely fluttered, she began the most exciting evening of her life.

After the first promenade around the campground, her parents and the children left the silent couples to meander around on their own. All were aware of the curious campers glancing their way, probably looking for any improprieties.

Claire laughed nervously. "My goodness, no wonder Mother fussed over my preparations. And even loaned me her hat. That was something. They never did that for any of my other suitors."

“Perhaps,” Henry whispered, “none of your other callers had announced their intentions.”

Intentions, was he proposing? Had he made up his mind without even a word to her about his feelings, without a single kiss? Didn’t she have anything to say about things?

Suddenly Claire was having trouble breathing. She had insisted Mother help her lace her corset. After all the walking and activity of the last few weeks, she had lost weight and the corset was almost too big. Mother had protested that she didn’t need it, she was tiny enough, but Claire had insisted. Until she felt the bone of the corset pressed into her skin, she didn’t think it was working. The reward had been her perfect hourglass shape in the dark purple wool dress. She knew she looked glamorous, but her spring dress, bonnet was wrong. Hence Mother’s dark one with its lace trim provided by Mary Anne.

As she gasped and looked pale, Henry called to the others that they were stopping. He helped Claire to the outer edge of the circle, held her gloved hand as she sank onto a low rock. The raised arm worked. Claire gulped in a deep breath and then another.

Now she was so low she realized she had noticed these shoes before. He was dancing at the Grand Hotel in St. Louis, with Bella. The thought made her dizzy. Had everyone known, but her?

Henry squatted down in front of her. His face in shadows, but only his kind blue eyes were locked on hers. “I thought you would be happy.”

“Tell me,” she gulped for air. “Tell me what you told them your intentions are.” Claire was surprised that her breathless voice carried enough force to be heard.

“I told them I’d decided to remarry. That I would like to court you, to find out if you might be the one.”

“And Father said yes,” Claire demanded.

“They both gave me their blessing, on the one condition that I do nothing to hurt you. That if I decided you were not the right girl, that I make it clear and not do anything to encourage your feelings. I promised I would be respectful of you, always.”

Claire took another ragged gulp of breath. “Good enough, as long as you haven’t presumed too much.”

She stood up quickly, leaving a confused Henry below her.

When he rose and took her arm, he tried to be as nonchalant. “We’ll need to catch up to the others.”

Claire shook her head and he saw the curls bounce against her shoulder. “No need, they are there.”

Henry looked ahead and saw the tall couple, wrapped in each other’s arms as they shared a passionate kiss. Henry shook his head and blushed. When he turned to look at Claire he was shocked by the wistful look in her blue eyes. Suddenly he wasn’t so sure he had agreed to the right thing.

All week, as Calum lay recovering, he talked most nights about how he needed help to woo Bonnie. The man had been amazingly forthright with his feelings, his desperate need for the tall athletic girl. Finally, Henry had agreed to his plan to each court one of the friends. He stared from Claire's rapturous face to the couple still kissing. The soldier had moved one of his hands to press the woman tightly against his groin.

Henry was shocked when he heard Bonnie groan. Red-faced and confused, he wrapped Claire's hand around his arm and coughed loudly. "Lieutenant, the Wimberley's will be waiting for us to pass."

Before he could say more, Calum released the girl. Henry was not surprised when the Lieutenant's knees sagged a little. He rushed forward to support his other side as Bonnie kept Calum's arm wrapped around her shoulder to support it. Claire rushed along beside her friend, taking out a fan from her drawstring bag to flutter at the soldier.

When they reached the Wimberley's, Ian and Shawn rushed forward to collect the Lieutenant and help carry him back to Henry's wagon. "Sorry sir, apparently, a third walk around was too much for Lieutenant Douglas. We stopped to let him rest," Henry said. Bonnie excused herself and followed the boys to check on her 'patient.'

Claire looked breathless herself and made her excuses and disappeared to her parents' wagon. With the children already in bed, the campsite appeared deserted. One of the black and white dogs stood in the opening of the boy's tent and gave a condemning bark to Henry before disappearing.

"And so the whirlwind courtship begins," Henry muttered as he tugged at the tight knot of his tie on the way to the wagon. He coughed loudly and the Magee girl had the good grace to come flying out of the wagon.

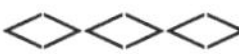

Henry stood, still fuming. He carefully removed the tie and folded it. He brushed his jacket and pants and hung them between the pressing boards inside his trunk. He removed the shirt, sniffed it, and then carefully hung it inside before closing the trunk.

Calum rolled over on the full-size bed and grinned at him. "Thanks, fast thinking."

Henry glared at him as he sat on the narrow cot and unhappily surveyed the arrangement. "I think, sir, if you are well enough to make love, you are well enough to let me have my bed back."

Calum smiled, clearly amused at the angry young man. "I did all this for you, and besides, I barely fit in this bed."

Henry stood, clearly furious. He shook his finger at the soldier who tried very hard to keep a straight face. "Claire had no idea I had spoken to her parents. She nearly fainted when I told her. But then she looked angry about it. I'm not sure she even likes me. All evening, she barely kept hold of my arm."

Calum did laugh. “Man, do you have a lot to learn about women. Come over here and sit down so Bonnie’s brothers or those McKinney twins don’t hear.”

“Have you been married?” Henry fired back. Calum shook his head, raised his hands. “Well, I was married for over two years. Perhaps I should explain what I know about women.”

Calum tried to keep a straight face as he nodded, “Perhaps you should. But come over closer, again, we don’t want the lads to eavesdrop.”

Henry looked distrustful of the larger man, especially since he was now shirtless and probably pantless. Henry had been shocked the first time he saw the soldier without the blue uniform. He did wear the customary knitted underwear issued by the army, but only the bottom, not the top. He claimed it was too hot in the summer for them, so he left them at home.

Had Bonnie, had that young woman, helped him to remove them?

Henry realized he’d said the question out loud when Calum gave up the battle and laughed, “Hell no, she skedaddled out of here when I started unbuttoning my blouse.”

The truth was he had been able to maneuver her close enough to steal another kiss after her brother’s left by pretending to be in pain. Then Henry had coughed and she had fled, without the kiss.

“Well, I know she is a married woman, unlike Claire, but I was shocked at the liberties she permitted you to take.”

This time it was Calum's turn to look outraged. He swung his legs over the side of the bed and started to stand up. Henry stepped back onto his side of the wagon.

"I'm sorry, I was just shocked when you kissed her with me and Claire present to witness it. You must have forgotten that Claire has been a sheltered girl, and..."

Calum did rise and now loomed over him. "I took no liberties that weren't permitted. I love Bonnie and intend to marry her, even if I have to track down this brute Tarn Michaels and make her a widow."

"Well, excuse me, I didn't know murder was part of your courtship plan," Henry said, without backing down this time.

"Hey, quieten down in there. We're trying to get some sleep." Both men froze, realizing for the first time that they had been yelling

"Trust me, Henry, she more than likes you. Bonnie told me she," he sank down, lowering his voice even more. If it had been Robert Wimberley yelling at them, he didn't want him to hear this. "She has been tortured with guilt ever since she met you. Since you were married, she knew she had no right, but she still had feelings for you," Calum whispered.

Henry sank onto the cot behind him. "Don't, don't tell me things to dupe me, just so I continue helping you seduce Bonnie. She's too good a woman for that kind of game. And Claire, Claire..." his voice faded away as he stretched out on the cot.

"That's right, get some sleep, Henry. Whatever you think, you're wrong. I would never do anything to harm

Bonnie. What I said about Claire is true, she has deep feelings for you. That's why she nearly swooned when she learned you had talked to her father." As he talked, he spread the thin blanket over the shocked young man.

Calum stepped back and sat on his own bed, then swung his legs up again. Neither man had used a light to undress so there was none to blow out. In the distance, Calum heard two men exchange words as they passed in the night. For a minute, he thought he heard a sob or cough from Henry's bunk. The man turned away and Calum spread his own blanket, wincing as he used his stiff shoulder.

Somehow, he had made Henry cry. The possible reasons raced through his mind. But the last made the most sense. The fool loved the girl too, but had never had the courage to admit it to himself. For an old married man, Henry seemed to know very little about love.

CHAPTER THIRTY-FOUR

All week Henry had been lectured and coached by Calum Douglas. Now that the Lieutenant was back in good health, hc seemed to have adopted the approach that Henry was another of his raw recruits, and his mission was to prepare him for battle.

It was partly his own fault, in a moment of despair, Henry had confessed that he had never made Bella happy. He had performed his husbandly duty every Saturday night after his bath. But if it was any more satisfactory for his wife than for him, she never showed it. "We quarreled all the time. One reason I have hesitated to pursue any of the other women on the train, but especially Claire, is that I found marriage to be the most miserable state of life."

For a single man, Calum Douglas seemed to have an encyclopedic knowledge of women, their anatomy, and what it took to please them. Although their conversations took place at night, after the promenade with the ladies, it was full of such detail that Henry found his ears burning in shame just to hear it.

"I'm not sure whether to believe you or not. I've never heard that a woman's passion is as great as or greater than a man's. Quite the opposite. My father explained that women didn't care for the business at all. They wanted children, so they tolerated a man's attention. When I pointed out that the upstairs maid seemed quite enthusiastic, he laughed at me. 'Of course, common, vulgar girls like that pretend pleasure, but merely to trap a young fool like yourself.' He told me to avoid trollops and I always have."

Calum had stared at the man as though he had two heads. "Have you taken any of my advice at all?"

Henry blushed again. Claire left her gloves and hat behind at Bonnie's advice. We've been holding hands. She has the softest, smallest little hand. It gives me a remarkable feeling when…"

Calum grinned at him, and Henry grew irritated, "Well, if you're only going to make fun of me."

"No, not at all, go on. And you've kissed?"

"Certainly. Not on the first night, but each night since. Last night she kissed me hello and goodbye. Then we talked, she really is a lively and charming girl. I've always admired her beauty and grace, her cheerfulness and her ability to talk to anyone about anything. She is a phenomenal salesgirl."

"You should get along fine then, but you're going to have to be bolder tonight. I'm leaving tomorrow back to the post. Tonight I'm going to propose one last time to Bonnie. If you ask Claire, then we can have a double wedding. I'm sure the girls will want to make plans and if Bonnie says yes, I'll stay another two days, ride into Ogden with you."

"Ogden?"

"The official name of Junction City, the town where the road forks, one branch to California, the other toward Indian Territory." In the distance they heard Bonnie's clarion yell to come eat. "Henry, your only hope is to kiss her with passion, use your tongue if you can, make her excited by your proposal."

"Easy for you to say. Bonnie kisses you like she's about to eat a big piece of layer cake. Claire kisses me like I'm family already."

Calum slapped his back so hard that Henry almost fell out of the wagon. "How did you ever get a woman like Bella to begin with?"

"I had just arrived in New York from Liverpool. I had the money I inherited from my Father's estate and I planned to start a business. But the property was more expensive than I had expected and I needed to raise more. I took a job as a teller at the bank where I deposited my funds."

"Bella's Father's bank?"

"Yes, well we got along, he saw me as an up and coming young man with excellent prospects. So he invited me home to dinner,"

"And introduced you to his daughter? How old were you?"

They had stopped at the edge of the wagon, watching the other's fill plates and settle in their usual places. Henry finished the story in whispers. "Twenty, but my Father was a haberdasher on Seville Row, so I had a great deal of skill and experience in the business already."

"I suppose there was a lot of hand-holding and kissing preceding the proposal."

Henry realized the man was teasing him and smiled. "Her father told me he would be happy for his daughter to settle down with such a dependable young man and offered me a sizeable dowry. He also had a friend who had a wonderful property for sale in Boston and he helped to arrange a favorable price."

"You were quickly married by a priest," Calum said.

"By a rabbi. Then our honeymoon was on the boat ride to Boston."

"Paid for by your father-in-law?" Calum whispered, tilting his head to whisper into the ear of the young man.

"A gift from my mother-in-law, using her personal funds. They both were keen for us to wed," Henry whispered over his shoulder.

The men moved up to receive their plate of beans and cornbread. The girls serving them giggled and then filled their own plates. It was not until they returned to the wagon without their excited sweethearts, that Calum put a hand on Henry's back. "When did you figure out you had been bamboozled?"

Henry's mouth twisted in disgust. "I knew a little, had read about it and heard men talking in the shop. When we finished the act she looked at my face and could tell I knew. Then she told me she had been married, had a son who was in hospital, and that she was now divorced.

The men lifted up to sit on the tailgate. "It's not as though it were a love match." Henry added. "We barely knew each other. If I were honest, I had been bought for her by her parents. They set me up in business and I served to repair her reputation and standing. But there is something distasteful about that sort of arrangement, which we suddenly had to face."

"Marriages have taken place for far worse reasons. Many of them are happy."

"Ours wasn't. I mean I continued to fulfill my part of the obligation. I treated her with courtesy and kindness. We made love once a week." Henry stared at Calum, trying to read condemnation in his eyes. "She would fly at me, like a harpy, nagging about this and that, always belittling me. Then when Claire and Bonnie came to work for us, she would have jealous fits.

Henry swung his legs back and forth underneath the gate, so that they tapped rhythmically against the wagon. "Then her father went broke and started nagging us to repay the loan. It wasn't a loan. I mean, he gave me the amount as her dowry. Then he sent her Barney. They couldn't afford to pay the hospital for his continued care. You met the boy?"

"When I brought Bonnie back from the training garrison."

"I miss him. He really brought out a different side of Bella. She was a new person, kinder, more human. I thought maybe our marriage would last. Then when we visited her parents, she gave them half the money from the sale of the business in Boston. To be honest, most of the time, I hated her." Henry rolled his eyes and Calum nodded.

"I didn't want her to die. That was horrible. Then the boy died. He placed his hands over his eyes, then rubbed his hand across his face. "I probably never thanked you for taking him back to bury with her. That meant so much to me, knowing they are always together."

Calum cleared his throat. "Enough of the past. The Wimberley's have given us their blessing. Are you ready for tonight? Do you remember all I've told you to do?"

Henry swung down and stood to look up at him. "You weren't kidding about all that?"

Calum dropped down and grinned at him. "You sir, are about to get your first education about love. You may know about marriage, and the mechanics, but holding, kissing, touching someone you love who loves you, it's a whole new experience. Are you ready?"

Henry ran his fingers through his hair as he pushed it back from his face. He rubbed his clean-shaven face and brushed his mustache smooth, making blowing noises through his lips to blow the hairs back into place. “No, but let’s go.”

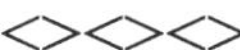

It had taken forever for the other suitors to leave. There was something about two women who were looking their best and bubbling with excitement. They were lucky every man in the wagon trains didn’t show up.

The men’s excuse was that they had been practicing and wanted to play a tune for Claire. Annoyed, Calum and Henry had left to finish their talk while the others listened to James and George tuning a fiddle and blowing a wet harmonica. As they played, both dogs set up a howl.

Mother Wimberley raised her hands over her ears and Bonnie laughed. Ian and Shawn stood up and challenged the pair to play *Barbara Allen.* Vexed, the displaced suitors had to listen while the soldiers sang the sweetest song in their lilting tenors. Even the cattle mooed in satisfaction and the travelers in the circled wagons stopped their children playing so all could listen.

Bonnie smiled as she heard Claire loudly protest to Mary Anne. “I’ve never worn hand-me-down clothes or shoes. I certainly don’t want to begin my life in the west with a hand-me-down husband.”

Claire looked over to the wagon to watch Henry puffing angrily on his pipe as he turned to complain some more to Calum. She watched the handsome soldier lean forward and lift his hat for a moment to shield his face as he rolled his eyes in horror.

Bonnie covered her mouth and laughed as she stared at them too. Calum put his hat back into place and grinned at her. Suddenly she blushed and looked at the Wimberleys to see if they had noticed.

Claire was just as excited. She left the little girl with her brothers and crossed over to sit beside Bonnie. “Tell me again about tonight,” she whispered. She knew Calum had talked to her parents and they had given the tall Lieutenant special permission to meet with Bonnie, while she and Henry sat out in the dark with them. Anticipation and dread were making her tremble.

“Calum said it was the way his people courted in the old country. They had a special couch where the man and woman faced in opposite directions with a barrier between them. They would be left alone in the room with the understanding that both pairs of feet had to remain flat on the floor at all times. The chaperone remained outside, listening and peeking beneath the door at the pair of feet.”

“Oh Bonnie, do you think we dare. What if they change their minds about marriage? Won’t we be compromised?”

Bonnie stared at her, made sure where the children were, before whispering. “I’ve been married, trust me, there is no way.”

CHAPTER THIRTY-FIVE

As soon as the children were in bed, the campfire dead and all the visitors long gone, Calum had Henry help him roll his wagon. Now the two wagons were parked side-by-side. In the dark they had trouble arranging things. The benches were placed between the two wagons at different ends, but sheltered from the eyes of those in the tents or in the distant wagons. Claire knew her parents were awake inside, listening.

The men stood beside them. Claire knew once they were seated between the wagons there would be no turning back. Henry had better propose. Carefully Henry helped Claire climb over the bench and waited while she arranged her skirts before sitting down beside her facing out. Claire giggled nervously and stared into the dark. She could sense the other couple settling into the same arrangement. Both girls were on the inside of the benches completely hidden from anyone, even if there had been more than a sliver of moon in a dark sky.

Claire tried to relax. It was too dark for anyone to see what they were doing. In Bonnie's brown dress, she could not make her out at all. For a minute, Claire wished she had worn the purple wool, not the mint green. Bonnie would probably be able to watch her all evening.

Calum walked around and whispered something to Henry before passing him a full cup of wine. Humming, he walked back around and took his place beside Bonnie. Claire heard Bonnie's startled breath and knew her friend would probably be too busy to watch anything. Calum spoke loud enough for the other couple to hear. "We will share a toast to the old country and to the women we love. Drink."

Claire smelled the sweet wine as Henry raised it to take a timid sip. He held it and repeated, "Drink." Claire leaned back a little and extended her hand to find the cup. Instead she touched his leg, then the soft wool of his coat. Bolder, hidden by the dark and with the excuse of finding the cup, she raised her hand until she touched his chin. She heard the sharp intake of breath and knew it was Henry. He was just as frightened as she was.

When her fingers found his lip and brushed the soft edge of that little mustache, she wanted to pound her feet quickly on the dirt. Only knowing her parents were listening and could come pouring out of the wagon at any instant kept her still.

Henry captured her hand and brought it to the tin cup. Claire trembled as she let her cool fingers touch his on the handle and let him raise it to her lips. She took a slow sip, savoring it as if she had never tasted wine before.

She moved the cup just a little and he bent to drink again. His face was close to her and Claire leaned toward him like a cat that needed petting, letting her cheek glide against his as he swallowed.

They exchanged lips on the rim and when it was empty, Henry carefully set it on the ground beside the bench. This time when he turned toward her, his mouth found hers. Claire sighed into the kiss. The past week he had kissed her, soft, sweet kisses of hello and goodbye. They were nothing like this. As he opened his mouth on hers, her tongue touched his and the rich taste of the wine and the sweet wild kiss flooded her senses.

Suddenly, she felt light headed. Tightly corseted, she found it more than a little hard to breathe. As she leaned back to gather more air into her lungs, Henry's strong arms supported her curved back. He turned her across his own body and one of her legs rose to balance her. "No," she gasped, "I have to keep my feet down."

"Shh," he whispered, raising her up just enough to accomplish both feet on the ground. "Let me loosen that demon corset for you. Sit upright."

"But how…" but he was already undoing buttons down the back of her dress.

Henry sighed, trying to go slow enough not to frighten her. How often the last few weeks had he stared at that long line of tiny buttons and imagined doing just this? Only fantasy he warned himself, but it had not kept him from imagining it. Now, thanks to the bold Lieutenant on the other bench, he was daring to do it. When he was halfway down, Claire managed to reach behind her to still his fingers. In the dark, all he could see were the whites of her eyes as she nodded toward her wagon.

Henry paused and leaned close enough so his lips brushed the tiny shell of her ear. “Three more, please.”

Her hand still held him in its upside down embrace. Swallowing and closing her eyes, she nodded and released him.

As soon as they were undone, he used his open hand to carefully move the fabric apart. Her eyes were wild again, glistening in terror as her heart pounded beneath his hand. Henry stopped the motion, pressed his lips even closer and traced kisses along from her ear to the base of her throat. He felt her chest heave, her breath escape as in a dying sigh.

Moving her so her chest was pressed against his, he managed to use both his hands to pull the dress down to her waist. He was tempted to just settle for touching her breasts through the thin cotton, but her ragged breaths spurred him on. When he finally found the ribbon lacing the front of her corset, he carefully pulled one end and felt the bow escape as trailing ribbons in his hand.

Before she could protest, he resumed their passionate kiss. With each nibble, or a flick of his tongue over hers, he tugged at the corset until it gaped open about her rib cage. He released her mouth, let her take a couple of deep gasping breaths. Pressing her face beneath his chin, he whispered again. “I’m going to remove it.”

Once when he was a boy, he ran to pick up a hummingbird that had flown into the front glass of their store. The rapid beat of Claire’s heart reminded him of holding that tiny living thing in his palm. He had held it there, waiting, until the tiny creature fluttered, struggled, and broke free.

She moved her face, straightened to use both of her hands to tug the last ribbon free and removed it. While he waited, she folded the whale bone reinforced linen and satin garment and held it on her lap, her chin down, her breath growing even.

Henry reached out and took it from her and laid it on the bench beside him. This time when she returned to his embrace, she lifted her face up to his for more of the mind-numbing kisses. He waited until she pressed her lips to his. Gently he stroked her back, more than aware of the silky skin beneath the thin cotton. With each stroke, he grew bolder, hungrier for the need to caress her. He let his fingers trail wider until they flew up and down the bare skin of her arms.

Intoxicated, unwilling to stop, he pulled his mouth away from her lips to trail kisses down one silky arm to her wrist. He kissed the pulse there and felt her hand rest against his cheek. She lifted the other arm so that the inside flesh pressed his other cheek as she held her arm in the air. He repeated the trail of kisses as she lowered her arm to bring the wrist point to his mouth. When he kissed it and moaned, she cupped his lips moved to lift his head so they were face to face, foreheads touching, nose tips crushed and her lips temptingly out of reach.

Softly she whispered the words to him alone. “More, I need more kisses.”

Henry smiled, drunk with happiness at the foolish words. “Where?” he asked, not surprised to hear the quaver in his own voice. Claire lifted his hand to her neck, to touch the pulse below her ear. Henry obliged, only to have her bend her head and capture him there as she giggled.

“It’s not the right spot,” he growled in her ear.

“Your mustache tickles.”

Henry caught her mouth beneath his own, kissed her fiercely, and then whispered. “Quiet, you don’t want to be caught like this, do you?”

Her silence was answer enough, then her hand pointed to the same spot below the other ear. Next was the little hollow at the base of her throat, which brought a reward of a gasp of pleasure. Collar bones, shoulders, and then Henry shocked them both by slipping his hand inside her chemise to cup her breast.

The quiver was back. This time she pressed tight against him, as though she would bury herself in him. He waited, the bold hand trapped with its warm treasure.

“I’m small, I know, nothing like Bonnie,” she spoke, clearly embarrassed.

He kissed her, excited by the idea of where to kiss her next. She leaned back, granting him space.

“You’re perfect,” he breathed into her ear as he slipped the other hand to join the first. “All I can hold.” Gently, so as not to terrify her, he followed Calum’s advice and teased both until her nipples were screaming for more attention. “Claire, darling, please don’t stop me.”

She leaned back, her body twisted so that her face was turned up to him. If she bent anymore, he knew she would break Calum's rules.

Softly, as gently as he could, he raised her back upright, bending so his face pressed against her, then his mouth found and claimed one nipple. Claire sighed, then when he raised up, she brought his head back to kiss the other. He drew the nipple into his mouth and suckled.

She seemed to collapse like a rag-doll. From the other side, Henry heard voices. He pulled the cotton over the damp breasts, waited to be caught.

"Now that we are betrothed, let us take one last stroll together, my beloved Bonnie," Calum said.

Henry waited, straining to listen as he heard an exultant Calum pull the other woman to her feet and help her step over the bench. As they moved away, he sighed in relief. Other than being more aroused than at any other time in his life, with a half nude girl in his lap, he knew it was going to be all right.

A tiny voice whispered. "Is it all over then?"

Henry put a hand over his mouth to keep from laughing out loud at the sound of disappointment in her voice. Firmly he helped her sit upright, threaded one limp arm into its sleeve, then worked on the other. As soon as he finished, she twisted on the bench so he could secure all the buttons. Without warning, she collapsed against him, just as Henry realized he had buttoned crookedly.

"No," he muttered. "Sit still so I can undo and redo these buttons right.

“Good,” she whispered, complying. When he reached the last button she shocked him when she pulled the dress and undergarment down just low enough to expose the small left breast. “This side wants it to.”

Unable to deny her, he quickly bent to suckle it, felt her fingers tug at the ends of his mustache mischievously. He released her, covered the other treasure and this time buttoned her right. Like Calum, he helped to swing her up and over the bench. Henry reached down to lift the folded corset and press it into her hands. He could tell from the way she moved that she was blushing. He hated not being able to see her skin change from porcelain white to rosy pink. She stowed it in the back of her wagon hastily.

As they passed his empty wagon, Claire brushed against him and suddenly she was in his arms, her body pressed against him. Henry kissed her as though he would devour her, used his hands to press her against his arousal. Claire’s knees buckled and she dug her hands into his shoulders to stay upright. Henry had all he could do, not to lift her into the back of the wagon. Instead, he raised his head, and whispered against her mouth.

“We will marry in Ogden, as soon as possible.” Claire pushed back against him and he released her. For a minute, they both stood breathing heavily into the calm night.

“Isn’t that what you want?” Henry asked.

“I expected words of love and...”

He extended his hands, but she shrugged free. When they heard the voices of the other couple, both swallowed. Henry held his arm and Claire took his elbow so they could fall in step behind the others as they passed in the night. He watched the shadowy, long-legged couple leaning together, heard Bonnie's happy voice and Calum's grunt in answer.

For several minutes, they walked in silence before Henry stopped and faced her. Slowly he lifted her hands to kiss one, and then the other. "Lovely Claire, will you be my wife?"

As she stood, not answering, Henry wished the moon would appear. He could tell nothing in the dark about what she was thinking. Was she afraid, or was she going to refuse him. He recalled the teasing words earlier to Mary Anne about having no use for anything second-hand. Then it had annoyed him, but he realized when she giggled that she had been teasing. Henry waited, afraid that she had been serious.

"Although, I had no right to, I think I loved you from the first time I saw you," she finally said.

"Oh Claire," he let out his breath in a single swoosh and pulled her into his arms for another blazing kiss. "I love you. So you're saying yes."

"Yes."

He stopped again to kiss her and heard her laugh and break free to jump around. Henry wanted to shout as well. He settled for capturing her to lift into the air and swing around.

In minutes they were on their own excited stroll around the silent camp.

◇◇◇

The men were almost back to where they had left their sweethearts to go to bed. They began to talk in hushed voices. Henry asked, “How did your campaign go?”

“She now wants to wait until her Da builds a boat and sails from Boston to here. Although a minute ago, she told me not to go. That we could wed in Ogden next week.”

“Well, there you go,” Henry whispered excitedly. “We can have a double wedding.”

“She really wants to wait, until she is sure Tarn Michaels is dead or they are divorced, until she buys her land and builds a cabin, and maybe for the rest of the clan to arrive.”

“But you proposed, what did she say?”

Calum looked miserable, “That she loves me and wants to be my wife, nothing more but nothing less. I’m going back to the Fort tomorrow and taking her brothers with me.”

“I can’t believe you’re going to let her get by with that. The way she loves you, you could force her to go back with you,” Henry said.

Calum sighed and stared, but could only see Henry’s outline. “It’s Bonnie. She’s so damned sensible, so practical. If we don’t wait, if she doesn’t get her divorce and land, she’ll always blame me. She has to want me more than all the rest.”

“You’re going to wait a year?”

“Or until she decides I’m the only thing she wants.” Calum smiled at his companion. “And you, not waiting for a proper year of mourning.”

Henry laughed and Calum was certain it was the first time he had heard him laugh.

"I had to insist she go to bed with her parents and promise to wait until we reached Ogden and a priest."

Calum grabbed him in a bear hug and Henry laughed and tried to muffle the sound. "She loves me and has said yes. I think asking her father's permission in the morning is just a formality."

He stared up at the taller man and said. "I wish you didn't have to go. Bonnie will miss you."

Calum smiled wryly. "I hope so. I tried to leave her reason to."

As they climbed into the Lambton wagon, Henry whispered. "I was wondering if you had any more secrets about women to share."

CHAPTER THIRTY-SIX

When Claire finally woke, it was to the smell of coffee, bacon, and biscuits. She saw Bonnie and Mother at the fire and waved to Bonnie. They ran into the bushes together, laughing, and whispering. “He asked me too, well first he told me we were going to wed in Ogden.”

“Sounds like you straightened him out.” She twirled Claire again, then said, “That soon, we’ll be there in less than a week?”

Claire laughed and lifted Bonnie’s hands. Dust blew up from the dried earth as they danced back toward the campfire.

Bonnie stopped after a few steps. “Calum has gone back to the fort, and he took my brothers. I would have laid there in my warm bed, dreaming, if I hadn’t heard your Mother swearing at the fire. None of the three bothered to come and say goodbye.”

“Hurry, help break the news to Mother and Father.” Bonnie laughed as they both came to the campfire and heard cries of ‘Congratulations.’ Henry was beaming and the twins were jumping up and down. Mother stood with her arms open for Claire.

For a moment, Claire resented Henry for sharing the news without her. He must have read her disapproval because he stepped up and took her hand to kiss in front of the others. “Mary Anne guessed, I was going to deny it, then your Mother looked at me, and I could not lie.”

As her Father walked up to the gathering, Claire broke away and ran to hug him, shouting, “Henry asked me to marry him.”

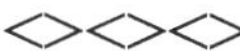

The day they were to enter Ogden was busy. Claire and Bonnie had complained about what to wear for the wedding. Mary Anne volunteered to decorate their best dresses for the occasion. She added lace collars and cuffs to the white blouse and attached a little lace trim to the skirt pockets and along the hem to Bonnie’s black skirt.

Claire looked radiant in her own lace adorned gown, the light-weight purple flowered wool she had purchased in Boston. Her hair had been restored to its old style of golden ringlets and Mary Anne had created a lace scarf to tie beneath the curls but not hide their beauty.

They spent a long time dressing and styling each other’s hair, even after the wagon train was ready to finish the last two miles into the town of Ogden. It was called Junction City by most people because the Union and Pacific railroads met here as well as the Virginia City-Corinne Road. Bonnie was glad to be at the end of the journey, but heartsick still at missing Calum.

Both added their big brimmed bonnets to protect their hair from the dusty trail. Claire pointed out the golden leaved aspens, stark against the dark evergreens. Mary Anne ran about as usual, gathering flowers near the trail.

They were fourth in line today and they watched town people already stopping their business to stare at this group of new pilgrims into the western wilderness. Up ahead one of the wagons stopped, and Tom and Jim stopped their own team, Jim ran up to the outside to take the other end of the oxen yoke from his brother. Bonnie and Claire stepped closer, clasping hands and looking around for the Catholic Church as they strode down the dusty street. Tyler and Tip were racing about eager to get the team back in motion as all heard a woman scream.

Bonnie stared as a young woman in lavender screamed again. As she recognized Lynne, she heard Claire scream her name as well. Before either of them could move a tiny blur ran and leaped into her arms. Bonnie let go of Claire's hands as they both started running for their friend. Tom and Jim left the oxen and bolted for her.

Lynne was laughing and crying, kissing first Mary Anne, then Tom and Jim. Claire was still squealing in delight and Henry dismounted to move protectively beside his bride to be. Bonnie laughed as she heard her friend's happy voice saying over and over again how much they had changed. In six months, their smart friend had been transformed as well.

Lynne released her family, and the children stood back a step to let the three women embrace. Behind her short friend they saw a tall man dressed in black let his hands drop down from his guns. As his face softened with a smile, he started toward them. Claire looked at Lynne. “My, my, that little ad undersold him, he’s breathtaking.” Behind them, Father called to Henry as he dismounted to steady the oxen.

“You look so beautiful,” all three said at the same time as they stepped back enough to see each other. Lynne laughed and whispered, “Pinch me. I can’t believe you’re here. Safe and strong and healthy just as I’ve dreamed it.”

“It's wonderful, isn’t it,” Claire said. “Oh Lynne, Bonnie and I are engaged. She pointed to the handsome blonde man beside the gigantic oxen. Henry brushed his trimmed mustache and smiled shyly. “This is Henry Lambton, my betrothed. We’re going to get married today. Isn’t it wonderful?”

Claire spun and looked around, “Where’s the church?”

Lynne and Bonnie exchanged glances and all three hugged again.

“There are just two in town, the Episcopal and Mormon. Phillip called on each one and this one’s minister is in town. We were married in the claims office in Helena,” Lynne said.

"My goodness, Lynne, you were so brave. We've read your letters over and over. But I've never heard of an Episcopalian?" Claire said.

"Be glad they're not Mormons," Bonnie said. "You don't want to compete with other wives."

"It's hard enough competing with Bella's ghost," the nervous bride said.

"Episcopalians call themselves the Protestant Catholics. But they do have priests and a Bishop," Lynne said. "Who is Bella?"

"She was Henry's wife, but she was killed by Indians between here and North Platte," Bonnie answered. "It happened while I was living with the Indians who had captured me."

"You were captured by Indians? Good grief, Willow, are you okay, did they…?"

"They treated me like a guest. The chief captured me so I could tend his white wife while she died of cancer. The army sent men to rescue me."

"If she were an Indian, they would have just set her off somewhere to die and let the wolves eat her," Claire interrupted again. "This handsome soldier, Lieutenant Calum Douglas rode in to save her. He traded his favorite horse and all his guns for her," Claire said while raising her eyebrows suggestively and giggling.

Bonnie yelled "Goose," and reached out to pinch Claire's waist as though peeved. "If you weren't the bride today." She turned and stared at Lynne. "It's a long story, I'll tell you everything later."

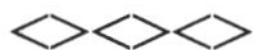

"Am I doing the right thing girls? His wife has been dead less than a month. Maybe I should wait," Claire whined.

Bonnie shook her head and laughed before leaning over to tell Lynne in a whisper, "She told me she couldn't stand the suspense of waiting. If it took any longer to get here, she was going to climb into his wagon and become a sinner."

Lynne laughed out loud and Claire blushed and then giggled herself. "Well, you've both been married. Now, I'm not sure I can." Claire looked nervously around the simple church, nothing like any of the Catholic churches she had ever been in. Luckily, there was no confessional box. The middle aged man staring impatiently at the three giggling girls looked like an ordinary priest in his black suit and stiff white collar.

He stepped closer to Henry, and then held out a hand toward Claire. Nervously, she whirled around, but couldn't see Father. Henry motioned and she stepped forward.

"He just needs to talk to us before the ceremony," Henry reassured her. In a small room at the back of the church, Claire felt better as the priest donned a white cassock and placed a gold stole around his neck. She waited, but didn't see the large ceremonial cross her own priest always wore for weddings.

"A few formalities. Names, birthdates, religious affiliations, etc." Claire gave her name and birth date, then whispered, Catholic. When Henry stated his name and Birthdate, Claire closed her eyes to try to help her remember the date. January 14, 1854 meant he was only twenty-two, just four years older than her. She expected him to say Jewish, but he said, none. “Do either of you wish to make a confession before the ceremony?”

Claire blushed and stared at Henry. He smiled and shook his head. Claire shook hers too.

“Now children, is this an arranged marriage, or a marriage based on love?”

“Love,” they answered together.

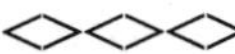

In minutes they were back inside the church near the front, watching the children squirm beside her mother while her friends stood in the back beside her, trying to calm her nerves. All three had shed the cumbersome bonnets and Lynne stood fussing with Claire’s hair while Bonnie repeated, “you look beautiful.”

As the doors of the church opened, Claire turned and sagged in relief as Father entered. He looked a little flustered and she noticed Lynne’s tall gunman escorting him. Phillip Gant left him at the back of the church, and then moved to take his place on the left side for Henry. Claire knew he had been arranging a safe place for their wagons. Did Father have the heavy belt with their money on beneath his coat? What about Henry’s money?”

Lynne and Bonnie were still talking. “Bonnie, really. Is this gallant Lieutenant your intended?” He gave up his favorite horse for you?”

“He’d had the stallion for years and told the chief it had saved his life dozens of times. The chief gave me the horses back when he released me. You should see my horse, Brown Bess, she has the cutest colt.” Bonnie raised her hand in the air to indicate the size of the strange animal.

Claire stood frozen to the spot as Robert Wimberley dusted himself enough to move forward to the end of the aisle.

Lynne whispered as they pushed Claire in front of them to where her father waited to hold her arm. “Good luck, goose.”

Claire slipped her icy fingers into her father’s warm hands and immediately relaxed as he smiled down at her.

“Frightened? You sure you want to do this. You always have a home with Mother and me.”

Claire smiled and felt joy flood through her. “He is what I want, Father.”

The girls walked sedately in front of her. On the Bride’s side of the aisle sat Mother Wimberley with the McKinney children. The boys wore their tight coats over their dusted trail clothes. Mary Anne wore her best dress proudly, knowing she looked pretty today. She moved to the end of the aisle and reached out to hand Claire the bouquet of

Hyssop and Pye weed she had picked on the way into town. The wilting purple and pink blooms made Claire smile and her eyes water at all the love in them.

Three dusky Indians and a couple of strange looking trail drivers, one tall and thin, the other short and round, sat on the left side of the church. She realized Lynne's husband Phillip had brought people to fill in the groom's side of the church. He seemed even more wonderful than Lynne had written. Now he stood by Henry at the altar. Henry was nervously waiting for her.

Everyone was trying to make the hasty ceremony what she had dreamed her wedding would be. In front of her she heard her friends still whispering.

"I love him, Lynne. He is tall and handsome and all that is kind. But since I'm married, he returned to the Fort and his duties while I look for land and a house. I hope to find something off the railroad right of way so I can move my family out here to join me. In a year…" Bonnie was saying.

The priest hissed in annoyance at the whispering women as Claire's father gave her a last kiss and placed her hand in Henry's. The two girls, one tall and the other petite looked guiltily at each other and held hands silently while Claire and Henry exchanged their vows.

All she heard was Henry as he stared into her eyes and said, "I promise to love, honor, and protect."

CHAPTER THIRTY-SEVEN

Afterwards, they shared their first kiss as man and wife. The public kiss was embarrassing for Claire, although they had shared a week of them along the trail. The day after Calum left Bonnie behind, she and Henry had been escorted on their promenade around the wagon by her parents. Nearly around, Henry had pointed out the big mare and her playful colt and while her parents looked, he had swept Claire into his arms to kiss her. When he finally released her, she turned in shock to see her parents kissing just as passionately.

All the way back to the wagon she had to listen to the older couple talking about their first time alone in the parlor of her grandmother's house and her mother's giggles. Angry at their teasing and hand-holding, she had been relieved when they stopped at the wagon and sent the three children along on the next circle. Even though she and Henry had behaved, the children still teased them all the way around about holding hands, and 'ooh, kissing.'

She had made a point of saying Goodnight to Henry without a kiss as she checked on Bonnie with Mary Anne in tow. The twins had volunteered to take the dogs around one more time to check the cattle. Bonnie was so blue, it was hard to console her. Claire was glad she didn't have to make such a hard decision in regard to loving Henry.

Now she and her husband stood at the altar, both accepting kisses from the wedding party. Phillip's Indians faded away as he herded the family and friends toward the hotel and the large dining room he had reserved for an early supper.

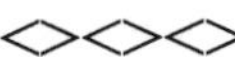

Phillip was holding Lynne's arm and Claire was shocked when he leaned over to kiss her in the brightly lit lobby. "Did you tell your friends, your big news, darling?"

Lynne looked up at her handsome husband and blushed. Bonnie clapped her hands and looked at Mary Anne, who jumped at the sound. "She's expecting. Your sister is going to have a baby. Right?"

Lynne laughed and blushed even redder as all the guests in the hotel turned to stare at the laughing, teasing wedding party. For a moment, Claire and Bonnie exchanged a look. Then they were both pushing in to hug Lynne again.

As the children crowded around their sister, Henry took the opportunity to pull Claire away and kiss his bride. Father kept clearing his throat and finally tutted to break up the kiss.

The happy, exuberant group followed the bell boy into the dining room. Lynne stared at Bonnie's muddy brown eyes and quickly assigned everyone seats like a gracious hostess. She told Claire and Bonnie to sit on either side of her, sending her dark- eyed husband and the children to the other end.

Phillip Gant hesitated, then took his seat at the other end between his two mining buddies, Shorty and Banes, and the three McKinney children. The rough men kept smiling as they watched the excited, pretty young girls at one end of the table, then turned to look at the handsome boys and pretty little girl as they gushed about how wonderful everything was. Henry Lambton sat beside his new bride and the Wimberleys sat across from them, watching their happy daughter and her new husband.

"Bonnie, why so gloomy? Lynne asked. "Did you just hear the news?"

Bonnie looked up, tried to smile as she shook her head.

Claire turned from Henry to focus on her friends, saw Lynne's eyes turn gray and sad too. "Tarn Michaels is dead." She looked to the end of the table to draw support from her husband. "It was horrible."

Phillip spoke from his end of the table. "The blackheart got what he deserved. The inquest acquitted Lynne of all charges for shooting him."

All eyes moved back to stare at Lynne. "You see, I had to shoot him. He had attacked Phillip before and injured him severely and since I was the only one armed."

After all their questions, and her explanation of making Phillip leave his gun behind, but carrying one in her purse, Lynne said. "

"If you don't want to sit next to me, I'll understand. But with the way things were between you and Tarn…," Lynne said.

Claire watched as Bonnie's eyes suddenly turned lighter with sparks of yellow excitement as Lynne finished. "Tarn is actually dead. I'm free. I'm a widow and can marry Calum."

Claire squeezed Henry's hand, waiting until Bonnie finished hugging and kissing Lynne, and then she stood as well. Bonnie was nearly shouting, "Oh Lynne, oh you beautiful smart friend. I owe you so much, so very much. But before you tell me more, where is the telegraph office?"

Claire stood confused as Lynne listened to her husband's request that she order the food as he left to escort Bonnie out of the room.

Lynne kissed her friend, "Thank you, I didn't want either of you to hate me when you found out. But I had to do it."

Claire placed her arms around Lynne's neck and whispered, "Thank you, thank you. She's free isn't she, our Bonnie is finally free of that rotter."

Lynne continued to make conversation with the deliriously happy couple beside her as the other's tried to figure out what to order.

<><><>

Bonnie and Phillip returned just as the food arrived. Bonnie sat down and Claire asked, "What did you write him?"

"Widowed, Tarn Michaels dead. Ready to wed." Claire laughed and Lynne clutched Bonnie's arm.

"Phillip said your marriage started in a telegraph office too. He said you'd written all the details down," Bonnie said.

"He teases me that I've written a book, but I couldn't mail the pages since you've been on the move. It kills me not to see you two every day and be able to share all the wonderful things that happen," Lynne said.

Phillip said from his end of the table, "Not everything is wonderful. Did you tell them how you shot the Indian, too?"

Henry smiled at his bride while she talked nonstop with her two friends.

"There wasn't time to bake a cake, but the chef is making a unique dessert for you tonight, it's called Cherries jubilee," Lynne said. "Don't be alarmed for the children to eat this dessert. The fire will burn off the liquor."

The children were yelling and clapping in delight as the waiter stood over a chafing dish talking about the burning dessert. Everyone stopped paying attention as the messenger arrived with the telegram.

Claire had never seen Bonnie look so excited. Bonnie's hands shook so much that she had trouble opening the yellow paper without tearing it. Lynne and Carrie rushed to brace her arms as she gently tore the edge of the envelope and opened the message. The room was so silent, they could all hear the paper rattle.

Silently Bonnie scanned the telegram. “Reply was requested,” the messenger who still stood there said.

Claire was the one to insist, “Read it out loud, please Bonnie.”

Bonnie’s voice vibrated and grew louder with every word. “Will send ticket tonight. Return to me, Fort McPherson. Leave with General Miles two weeks, Major at Fort Keogh. Bringing cubs. Officer’s quarters ready for wife.”

Phillip and Henry joined their wives.

Claire asked, “What are you going to do. You’ve got so many plans, so many things you have to do. You don’t want to leave us now.”

“I know. I’ve talked about my plans to buy land and make a new home, to wait until Calum and the lads served their enlistment time, and wait until the rest of my family could save enough money and finish the boat to come and join me. And wait, and wait, and wait…”

Bonnie’s whole body shook as she realized. “It doesn’t matter. I love Calum and tomorrow I can be his wife. I don’t have to wait.”

She stared around, saw the messenger. “Yes, yes.” Bonnie yelled.

Phillip paid the man and repeated the message. “She said, ‘Yes, Yes.’” When the man started to protest, Phillip grinned, “He’ll want that extra word.”

As soon as he left, the waiter resumed and poured brandy over the fancy dessert, and then lit the surface. The children's eyes grew bigger and everyone applauded.

Phillip stared at the young bridegroom who seemed just as thrilled as the children by the flaming desert. "You need to be careful. You don't want to set your brush pile on fire." He touched his own upper lip as Henry stared at him and laughed. But the bridegroom waited while the children dove into the wonderful dessert. The girls and Claire's parents were talking loudly at their end of the table.

"Do you know anything about horse breaking?" Phillip whispered in a low, insistent voice.

Henry looked surprised by the question and shook his head. Nervously, he took his pipe out of his pocket, and sat cleaning out the bowl while the last flames died out on the dessert.

"You have to be very gentle when you work with a young horse. Show them the bridle, the blanket and saddle. Add them one at a time."

The boys looked interested and Henry wondered what brought up the conversation. At the other end, he watched the three girls with their heads close together and heard Claire giggle.

Phillip nodded and smiled knowingly at him and Henry realized they weren't talking about horses. "Calum Douglas advised the same, and I've been doing some of those things."

Phillip smiled, looked at the protective parents who were staring at their excited daughter. “That must have been a challenge.”

Henry blushed up to his ears and the boys looked suddenly interested. Phillip leaned down and took a bite of the lush, sweet cherries and smiled, “Tastes wonderful. Should be safe now, Henry.”

Henry put aside his pipe and ate his dessert in minutes. Only when the children were up and running about the table did Phillip pick up his conversation.

“Key thing with a young unbroken horse, is to make the first ride short and gentle. Some people make the mistake of trying to ride the animal to death. Makes them reluctant to let you back in the saddle.”

Henry sat back and stared at the other man. “I hadn’t heard that. Are you sure that’s the best way?”

Bonnie reached out to capture one of the boys as they raced about and Claire grabbed the squealing little girl. The other boy, Jim, stepped back out of range and giggled and hiccupped. Lynne looked uninterested but as he moved she reached out and captured him too. The adults laughed as each girl pelted her prisoner with kisses until they yelled ‘uncle.’

Mother stood and motioned for the children. “I’m going to take them up to get settled. I’ll be in to help the girl’s get you settled darling,” and she bent to kiss Claire. Suddenly

Claire looked as young and sweet as Mary Anne, who was holding Mother Wimberley's hand. "Children kiss your Aunt Bonnie. She'll be back at the Fort and married to the Lieutenant when you wake up."

"I want to watch you get married too," said Mary Anne wistfully.

Bonnie walked over, hugged each and kissed them solemnly. "You'll come to visit us next year. I'll need your help in raising my cabin. Ian and Shawn will be there for the wedding so I won't be alone. Love you all," she stared at them, her eyes tearing up as they whined and fussed at having to say goodbye.

In minutes they were gone, and the friends were standing on either side of Claire. "Come on, I haven't got long before I have to catch the midnight train," Bonnie said.

The waiters stepped forward to clear the table, but the men remained and ordered a brandy. While the women escorted the blushing bride upstairs, Robert and Phillip sat beside the nervous Henry, who looked nearly as frightened as Claire had.

Claire was talking nervously as her friends helped her out of the dress Bonnie had helped her don that morning. "Tomorrow you'll be married too," Claire stared at Bonnie, then at Lynne. "We will all have traveled west and wed. If you had told me a year ago we would be here tonight, I would have laughed at you for being crazy."

Claire let them slide the thin cotton gown over her head, then ducked behind the screen to the commode chair. When she emerged, Lynne had brought the basin and washcloth to her and they took turns, washing her face and hands, even her small feet as she sat on the edge of the bed. Bonnie carried the basin away as Lynne stood over her nervous friend to undo her hair.

"There wasn't a church or priest at the fort," Claire said. "How will you get married? Do they have a claims office like Butte?"

Again, the friends took turns brushing out the elaborate loops and braids of Claire's wedding hairdo. Bonnie shook her head, "There's an army Chaplin for the men. I'm not sure if he'll perform the ceremony or General Crook will marry us. It doesn't matter, as long as I have witnesses when Calum and I say I do."

Claire's nerves started to fade, as each brushed the hair smooth, then pushed it behind her ear. Then the other girl took the brush and finished the other side. Mother Wimberley knocked on the door and came in to sit behind her daughter and hug her. "I hope you experienced women haven't been frightening her," she scolded. Then she looked at her daughter. "It's really not such a terrible ordeal. Henry loves you, I'm sure he will…,"

"Oh Mother, please, I know about all that. I'm not a baby."

Mother stared at her young daughter, saw the edge of uncertainty in her face and just leaned over and kissed her. "All right." She stood and pushed the spread and top sheet back and motioned to Claire. "Come sit here." Claire moved and she covered her lap.

"Goodnight, darling." She bent and kissed Claire's mouth and then left. Each of the girl's lingered after she left, then both laughed as Claire stared up at them. "Phillip and I are going to walk Bonnie to the station and wait with her for the train. We'll send your bridegroom up. Don't bother screaming for help, no one will hear you," Lynne said and Bonnie scolded her.

"Just relax and let him do what he wants. It will be over in a minute. See you and Henry next year for the cabin raising. Don't forget," Bonnie said. Claire fought the urge to grab at them and hold them back. Instead, she sat smiling bravely, the long full sleeves fluttering over her hands. Henry loved her, she was not going to be afraid. But as soon as the door closed over her laughing friends, Claire began to pray.

CHAPTER THIRTY-EIGHT

Henry watched his father-in-law leave, then nervously downed the second brandy. He gulped and it made him cough and his eyes water. Phillip slapped him on the back and rose as Bonnie and Lynne descended the staircase.

A little tipsy, and with great trepidation Henry climbed the stairs and entered the room. On her knees in the middle of the bed, a pale and trembling Claire sat praying. Henry closed and locked the door, and watched her jump as he turned the key. He felt a little guilty, realizing the women must have treated her to the same routine the men had given him. He sank onto the edge of the bed and gave her a timid smile. Instantly she relaxed and moved into his arms. Tenderly Henry kissed her before blowing out the light.

He stood and removed his clothes in the dark, then slipped between the covers to gather her into his arms. She made a little squeak as she put out a hand and touched his smooth warm skin. Exercising infinite patience, Henry began with light kisses to her face, but when he reached for the buttons on her gown, she backed fearfully away.

He relaxed back onto his half of the bed, let his tired head sink into the pillow. Maybe it would be wiser to wait until dawn when he was sober.

Claire heard his soft snore and relaxed on her side of the bed too. Then she realized if he fell deeply asleep, Father would be knocking on the door, telling them to rise and shine and pack up to hit the trail. She would still be a virgin and not a wife. Because of her silly fears, she would be the only one of the three girls to not know what marriage meant. Irritated at herself and at Henry, she scooted closer to the relaxed man in her bed.

Curious, she pushed back the covers enough to see his bare chest, slowly rising as he slipped deeper into sleep. She reached out a hand, felt the rounded mound of his chest, the tiny flat button of his nipple. As she moved her hand across his warm body, she wished Henry hadn't turned out the light. Her finger caught in one of the few swirls of hair on his chest before she touched his other nipple. Curious, she leaned down and put her tongue on his left nipple as he had on her that night on the benches. If it changed, she couldn't tell. Emboldened, she pushed the covers lower.

Henry's breath caught, his world clashing around him. His shy Claire was no longer terrified. He had to struggle to keep his eyes closed and not move before she grew frightened again and drew back. The air in the room had cooled down with the breeze through the bottom of both opened windows. He wondered what would happen if there were some magical way to turn the lights back on. Would she be pleased, or frightened by what she saw?

Claire trailed her curious hand lower across the flat plane of his stomach. One wayward finger led the way, tangling through more hair until she touched him. His body's reaction betrayed him and he let out his breath in a whoosh as she flung herself back on the bed, eyes wide, chest heaving. Fully awake, Henry turned to stare into her wild eyes.

"Hello, dear wife. Are you ready to try this again?" Henry asked, his voice warm with laughter.

Claire smiled back at him and then giggled. "Yes, dear husband."

Phillip escorted the two pretty women across to the rail station and sat on the bench beside them. He was surprised that Bonnie had only one small worn leather bag at her feet. She wore the same brown dress, the lace trims starkly white in the dark shadows. She and Lynne both wore their bonnets again, hiding their faces and hair.

"Well, that should be an interesting wedding night. Did you ever see two more frightened lambs?" He said as he sat down on the other side of his wife.

The women laughed and Bonnie spoke first. “We did try to put the fear of God into Claire. But Henry was married for two years, he should be fine.”

“It’s always your first time when you actually love the woman,” Phillip said and Lynne wrapped his arm around her.

“See, I told you I had the most romantic husband in the world.”

“Claire’s not the same silly goose, we knew in Boston. After Tarn beat me and I lost the baby, Claire took care of me. She forced her parents to take me in, and helped me regain my strength and courage. She found us new jobs after the mill closed. Talked Henry and his wife into believing they needed her help. We were clerks at Lambton’s Clothiers.”

“I can see Claire doing that and loving it, but you were a clerk Bonnie?” Lynne said.

Bonnie raised her legs straight out in front of her on the bench as she laughed. “Wore a ruffled burgundy smock with my name embroidered on it in white.”

They laughed together for a minute, then Bonnie continued to talk. “I think she’s been in love with Henry since the first day they met. But she never did anything to tempt him away from his wife.”

“What was she like, Henry’s first wife?” Lynne asked.

“Bella, well Bella was bitter. I once watched them working side by side at the shop. Both were similar in height and build, but Claire was all golden hair and laughter, and Bella was black eyes and hair, and frowns. She had a son who had some kind of wasting disease. He grew weaker and more helpless all the time, but I'm sure Barney lived longer than the Doctor's predicted.

Bella's first husband divorced her because of the child and her parents put her son in an asylum for care. Calum probably shouldn't have, but he told me what Henry shared about his marriage. He married her because he wanted to start a business and her parents paid for it; bought her another husband. It wasn't a love match. But Bella was terribly jealous of him."

"They both died on the trip?" Lynne asked.

Bonnie nodded, "Bella was shot with an arrow, Barney died two days later. Ian and Shawn, my brothers, fought for who would carry his body back to his Mother's grave for burial. They came with Calum to rescue me from the Indians."

Lynne turned to look at her, "Good, I've always thought of her as our little sister, the one we have to protect. I like thinking of her as grown up."

"Well, it's not her fault her parents spoiled her. She's their only child. But when I was stolen by the Indians, she stepped up and learned to make a fire and cook for all our party. She took care of the children and walked beside the oxen, something she swore she would never do."

"Were you carried off in the same attack?" Phillip asked.

Bonnie shook her head. "No, I was taken earlier, by a different tribe of Indians."

"I didn't realize that," Lynne said. "Do you want to talk about your captivity?"

Bonnie sighed, "I don't know when I've talked so much." She coughed to clear her throat and Phillip apologized and started across the street to the saloon. "Soda pop," he called.

"Beer," both girls said together.

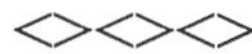

It was almost one before the train pulled out. Lynne had enjoyed all Bonnie's stories, especially the ones about Calum Douglas. She had no doubt her friend and the handsome Lieutenant would be a happily married couple, like she and Phillip.

When Phillip started to sweep her into his arms like a tired child, Lynne protested. "I'm fine, or were you already wanting to carry your baby to bed?"

He let her feet down carefully and held her protectively in his arms.

When Bonnie looked out the window to wave she saw the silhouette of the lover's kissing under the gaslight of the station.

She settled back on the hard bench to rest as much as she could, lulled by the clack of the train. Tonight it seemed all of their dreams had come true. Lynne had found a perfect husband in Phillip. Claire had found and finally won her perfect husband in Henry. And in the morning, Bonnie would finally find her own true love and be able to call him husband dearest. The train wheels seemed to be calling two names as she drifted into her dreams. Calum and Bonnie, Calum and Bonnie, Calum and…

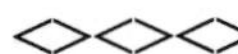

Claire woke to the sound of a train whistle. She smiled, still satisfied, and stretched between the rumpled sheets to reach out and touch Henry.

The bed was empty. Sitting up, she pulled the discarded gown with its endless row of buttons back on and tried to button it without calling out to Henry. In the silent room, she heard a noise behind the screen. She stopped buttoning the gown.

Of course, a private moment. But as she lay there anticipating his return, Claire heard a bark like noise then a clear sob.

She scrambled up and padded barefoot toward the screen. Before she could touch it, she heard Henry groan. "Oh, Bella, poor Bella and Barney."

In horror, she stood there, then as she heard him blow his nose, she turned back to slip into bed. Working frantically, she wormed out of the half-buttoned gown and pushed it off and onto the floor before trying to fake sleep. With her eyes squeezed tight, the tears began to leak from her eye, dripping across her nose and onto the pillow. What a fool she had been. He stilled loved Bella and felt guilty, as though he had betrayed her in loving Claire. Why had she been such a fool? She had been right when she told Mary Anne that she didn't want a second-hand-husband. If only she had steeled her heart against him.

When Henry returned to bed, he slipped under the covers and listened, hoping that Claire was still asleep. When he heard no sound, he relaxed, then turned so he could put a hand on her soft shoulder. He would follow Phillip's advice. But he had never dreamed love-making could be so wonderful. Afraid to move closer, aware of how much he needed the sweet woman again, he settled for leaving his hand on her shoulder.

With Bella, he had only made love to her out of duty. Every Saturday night, he had taken a bath and made love to his wife. It was what his father told him a good husband did for his wife. But he was unsure if he could control himself around Claire. He wanted her now, had thought of nothing but possessing her from that ridiculous night on the bench when she had been so responsive to him. Tonight, she had been as receptive, more, she had initiated the sweetest night of love-making he had ever known.

He felt emotionally raw, as though this night had opened his chest and all his feelings were spilling out. He had cried, for heaven's sake, just like a woman. Loving Claire had done that to him.

When he heard her make a small sound, Henry sighed and trailed his hand down the sweet curve of her back, then lower to rest on the round curve of her sweet bottom. Claire rolled over and in the dawn light, he could see tears in her blue eyes. "Oh, Claire, my love. Are you all right? Did I hurt or frighten you, darling?"

For a moment, Claire wanted to cling to her hurt pride and anger. She could rail at him, the way Bella had always done. Maybe Bella had felt the same sense of betrayal. Was it Henry's fault his wife was so unhappy? Hadn't he been angry, furious, when Bella's son arrived? He was a man who had no interest in emotional ties.

But there was such tenderness in his voice, and an aching need. It called to her own need and desire. She released the anger and moved into his arms, wriggling closer until her flesh was pressed against his own. She needed to touch him in order to keep her fears and jealousy at bay. When Henry moaned in delight, she wiggled even closer. He might still love Bella and feel guilt, but he was her husband now. Claire was determined to make him think only of her when they shared a bed.

CHAPTER THIRTY-NINE

In the morning light, Henry stood beside the bed. The curtains hung limp without a breeze, and he could hear noise from the dusty street below. He was full of doubt. He had tried to follow Phillip's advice, but when Claire turned into his arms again last night he had been unable to resist. Slowly, as gently as he could, he had made love to her. Now awake, he wondered if he had deluded himself. How could an innocent know just how to touch him, what to do to arouse and satisfy him so completely?

Claire stretched, suddenly aware of Henry standing there, staring at her. She wiped at the corner of her mouth, worried that she might have drooled in her sleep. Then she sat up, raising and tucking the sheet beneath her arms, uncomfortably aware that he was dressed in his wedding suit and she was still naked.

Henry felt his heart thump in his chest. Claire sat cross legged, rubbing at her eyes and face like a little kitten. She was staring up at him with her big blue eyes under a wild cloud of yellow hair. He finally found his voice.

"Hurry, darling. We'll be leaving soon," Henry said.

Claire couldn't help it, her lower lip extended in a pout. Everything felt suddenly wrong, like it had last night when she had heard Henry crying about Bella.

"I need my gown," she said.

Henry looked around, found it on the floor and shook it out before handing it to her.

Again, Claire felt her lip betray her. Why didn't he hold it and help her into it, instead of throwing it to her.

"I'm going down to get breakfast and see what the plans are for the day," he started for the door and Claire called out.

"Wait, wait," she was flapping her way into the gown.

He stopped and stared at her.

"I don't want to face everyone alone. They'll know what we were doing last night," she said in a strangled voice as her head emerged through the top of the gown.

Henry stopped, realized she was right. He didn't want to face them alone, either. Lynne and Phillip would both tease them if not the others. Then there were those silly friends of the rancher, Shorty and Banes. Those two would be full of eye rolls and chuckles this morning.

"Hurry, then," Henry snapped as he walked back to sit on the corner of the rumpled bed.

Claire slid out onto the floor, her fingers working frantically on the long row of buttons. As she took a step, she stopped and made a face. In minutes Henry was around the bed to reach out a supporting arm. “What’s wrong, did you step on something?”

Claire pushed the hair back from her face, forced herself to straighten. Gave him a trembling smile. Henry looked from her, back to where the stained sheet was now revealed.

Feeling a total fool for doubting her, Henry reached out to sweep her off her feet and into his arms. He sank with her cradled to him as he kissed her brow, her damp cheeks, her soft trembling lips.

“I’m sorry. I never meant to hurt you, to be such a beast. Here, just sit here. I’ll get you ready.”

Claire shook her head, smiling happily now. “Don’t be silly, it’s the way it’s supposed to be. I’ll be fine.”

But Henry ran around the room, found the washcloth he had used earlier and rinsed it out, and squeezed it dry before returning. As he knelt by her feet and raised her gown to wipe at the brown stain on her thigh, Claire shook. She put a hand on his bowed head, felt the full texture of his thick sandy locks. When he raised his face, she could have drowned in the liquid blue of his eyes. Their lips met and she knew she would never have another moment as glorious as this. She felt cherished.

<><><>

Claire had to scold Henry when he wanted to carry her. He settled for offering her his arm and she accepted, but only after he promised not to give her another pitying look. When they came down the stairs, still dressed in yesterday's clothes, they were greeted by the wedding party, now seated at two tables in the dining room, the men at one, the women and children at the other.

"There they are. Guess Banes, you and Shorty won't have to pack that bed, with them in it, after all," Phillip called.

The young couple blushed and Father raised his coffee cup in salute to the smiling couple. "Gentlemen, remember the children."

Mother called, "Good morning, come sit here. I have the coffee pot." Henry walked with Claire, helped her to be seated, and then joined the men at their table. The children and women all smiled at her as Tom McKinney bowed and said, "Good morning, Mrs. Lambton."

The other children repeated the greeting, laughing each time Claire giggled. She took the full plate of food, could hardly swallow. When she raised her head to look at Henry, he was gobbling down his full plate, his face down, but his ears red enough to tell her the men were each teasing him.

At her sly smile, Mother, then Lynne reached over to hug her. Father was explaining their change in plans. "We decided to try our luck in Montana. Phillip Gant has rented a train car so our party can travel in style on to Butte. The boys have been so upset at having to leave Shadrack and Meshack, their pet oxen, that he has agreed to take them and the loaded wagon as well as the buggy and team he had bought for Lynne. He had planned to have Shorty and Bane drive them back to the ranch."

When Lynne whispered something teasing, Claire raised her head. She smiled and teased her back about her own condition. The children were distracted, and started asking Lynne what she was going to name their first niece or nephew.

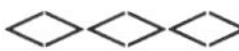

Riding the short line train to Butte, they were there in hours instead of days. Claire wondered how Phillip Gant could spend so freely. Wasn't he afraid of going broke?

If he were, he didn't act it. She whispered to Henry about it on the train, but he told her to be quiet. The man wouldn't do it if he couldn't afford it and obviously it made him happy.

Later, Claire had a chance to say something to her father. He nodded and took Phillip aside. Claire was glad when he forced the young rancher to accept some money. She was surprised to see Phillip Gant staring at her appraisingly when he walked back to join his wife. What had Lynne called him, the "Dark Prince?"

It was hard to believe Lynne's husband had been a gunfighter. According to Lynne's letter, he had killed all the men in fair fights. He had fought in the Civil war, later against the Indians, then ridden for cattlemen as a hired gun, and had later killed men defending his ranch and cattle.

The tall, handsome man was such a southern gentleman. Claire had loved how he had escorted Bonnie to the telegraph office, not hesitating to do whatever Lynne asked for her friends and family. She knew Mary Anne and the twins were already in awe and half in love with the exciting rancher. Claire let Henry make a bolster of his coat and yielded when he insisted she lean against it to get a little sleep.

The last thing she saw before her eyes closed were Mary Anne and Lynne, eyes silver with joy, talking about the ranch while the twin boys crowded against them. Claire wondered what it would be like to have such a large family. Lynne and Bonnie both had so many people to love.

As she fell asleep, she wondered what type of family Henry planned for them to have. As she looked at Lynne, she changed the thought, to wonder how many children she would want to have.

Henry stared at his sleepy bride, wondered about the whimsical smile on her face as she fell asleep. He had been surprised when she suggested they repay Phillip Gant for his hospitality. He wished he had phrased his response to it more successfully. He had seen her get her father to approach the man and offer to pay for what? The dinner, the hotel, the breakfast, the train tickets? Like Bella, he could see they would have conflicts about money.

But he was taking a young wife into an unknown country where he would have to establish a business and home. Yes, he had money. Far more than he had imagined when he left England. But he had grown up too poor to take money for granted. He had watched his father, a prosperous store owner, lose his business, his savings, and his son's future overnight in the banking crisis in England. Henry had worried that he might experience the same loss again here in America. Luckily, the Wimberley's trek west gave him an opportunity to save the money and his future.

People who had never been poor, could not understand how frightening such a loss could be. Someday, he would try to explain it to Claire. But not on this, the first day of their married life.

Lynne let the children go on with Claire's parents when the train arrived. She stood smiling at the dozing newlyweds. For a moment, she remembered their first time as man and wife. Shorty and Bane had been snow-bound with them all week, but before leaving, had prepared a steaming bath for the two and left them alone together.

After a week, she had become used to Phillip's stormy looks and moodiness. But his tenderness, his passion, she blushed remembering.

Claire woke and smiled at her blushing friend. She turned her head, stiff necked, as she stared at Henry where he leaned against her. She forgot Lynne as she studied his face, his cheek red and scrunched against her shoulder, his hair wild and disarrayed. She touched a hand to his damp cheek and brushed his fluffy little mustache. Henry grunted as he pushed her hand away, then coughed as he sat upright, embarrassed to be caught asleep by the two women.

"We're here. I wanted to show you around town, introduce you to some of my friends while Phillip and your Father take care of unloading," Lynne stood back.

Henry looked for their bags and Lynne waved her hand. "Shorty and Banes took care of them. There's a room at the end of the car if you'd like to freshen up."

CHAPTER FORTY

After touring the two boardwalk lined streets, the trio stood in front of a glass-fronted store labeled, Vandemere's Dry Goods. Across the street was another store with very similar content labeled Morrison's Market. Claire stared at Lynne.

"I want to introduce you to the Dutch couple who run this store. Ida and her husband gave us shelter when Phillip was attacked and wounded here in town. They are dear friends of ours. Phillip and the rest will join us here later."

As they entered the store, Claire was amazed at its size. She remembered the little store they had visited in Independence. When the store owner came out and bought a third of Henry's inventory to stop them selling on the street in front of the store, they had helped deliver the goods to him, entering from the back of the store. She remembered it was just one story, and had only about half as much floor space. The couple and their three children had lived at the back of the store in a single room.

Lynne left the newlyweds to look around while she walked to the back of the store calling to her friends.

Henry sniffed and Claire inhaled, then sneezed from all the dust on the open shelves. As they walked around the store, Claire was amazed at the variety and quantity of the stock. She stared up at the open area above them, surrounded by a rail. When she found the grocery area, she found the source of the smell. In a bin, there were some rotten potatoes. Henry looked at her and shook his head.

Claire tsked at him, but lifted the pan from the scale and carefully added the squishy potatoes and from the next barrel, a wrinkled apple. She found and removed a pair of sprouting onions, then handed the pan of rotten food to him. Henry raised an eyebrow, but took the gross stuff and found the back door. When he came back, with the empty pan, he wasn't surprised to see his new bride with a large smock over her best dress and a broom in hand. He put the empty pan back on the scale, then took the broom from her, making a little face.

Claire gave him a radiant smile and Henry removed his coat and hung it on the high stool behind the counter. As soon as he started sweeping, a cloud of dust motes floated above her. As though she had been placed in charge, Claire walked to the front of the store and opened the front door, propping it open with a nail keg near the front. She located a used feather duster and proceeded to dust the shelves all the way to the back, where she repeated propping open the back door with an oversized can of beans.

While Henry pushed the dirt to the back of the room, Claire stood at the front of the store, staring at the filthy windows. When she worked at Henry's shop in Boston, she had wished they had store windows so they could display his wonderful clothes to entice people into the store. She stood on the porch step, hand on hip just staring at the elaborate gold lettered store name that hid all that was inside.

Immediately Claire visualized reorganizing the entire store. Instead of randomly putting supplies on shelves, and in rows of bins, she would have a clothing store on the left side of the window with dresses and men's wear displayed on either dressmaker dummies or wire cage displays like they had used in Henry's store. On the right, she would have groceries, with the fresh produce displayed in crates on the street, calling to weary travelers to come in and restock their supplies.

Claire raised a hand to shield her eyes from the sun and stared at the store across the street. As Henry joined her, she described what she thought the Vandemeres needed to do to compete with the shop across the way. He stared at the little blonde, tilted her head back to stare in her amazing eyes and wiped a spot of dust from her nose.

"I'll stay down here. You'd better go upstairs and see what Lynne is doing. The others will be coming by for us in minutes."

Claire saw the way Henry was staring at her mouth. She was burning up in the oversized smock and her thin wool dress. Her combed and neat bun was frizzing into little curls. She was tempted to see if she stood on tiptoe if he would kiss her right on the street.

"Go on, hurry," he ordered and she handed him the feather duster and scooted past him.

At the top of the stairs, Claire took a deep breath, and removed the dusty smock. There were four doors of the gallery, one in each direction. She couldn't help but stare up at the skylight. Such an unusual feature, especially in this wilderness. Finally, she noticed there was only a path to one door, the one straight ahead and she walked up and knocked softly.

She hadn't realized she had been holding her breath, but Lynne opened the door and came out to stand beside her. "Mother and Father will be here soon. Henry and I straightened up and dusted downstairs. Did you find your friends? What's going on here?"

Lynne grabbed both of Claire's hands and moved so they were behind the railing in the shadows. "Ida's husband tried to kill himself."

"Oh, Lynne, how horrible. Is he all right? I thought you said they were good friends of yours."

"Yes, they are. I think he will be all right. The doctor has given him some Laudanum to dull the pain. Ida is staying beside him to tend him and to prevent him making another attempt. Claire, where is Henry?"

Claire pointed downstairs and Lynne and she listened as Henry talked to and finally filled a cowboy's order. He appeared half-way up the stairs. "Claire, are you ready? I can see the oxen and wagon coming down the street."

Claire started down after him and Lynne followed. "Wait, please, I want to talk to both of you."

Claire stopped when she reached Henry. Calmly, he reached up to smooth back some of her curls. Lynne stared at the newlyweds and began.

"I have no right to ask this of you. I was telling Claire how Ida's husband is in bed, with a broken arm and leg."

"How did he…" Henry began.

"He tried to kill himself, although Ida claims he fell down the stairs by accident."

"Woah," they all recognized Phillip's voice and hurried out onto the boardwalk. He had stopped the buggy, which was being driven by Mother and Mary Anne. Behind them was the covered wagon that had been home to them all this long trip. Now there was only one wagon and Claire could see that Henry's boxes and belongings had been piled into the wagon, covering the familiar mattresses that had been their beds.

Phillip rode up to the porch and stared at his beautiful wife, noted the serious pose and the way she was clutching at Claire's hand.

"It's the Vandemeres. Henrique," she shook her head, unable to continue for a minute. Phillip dismounted and tied his horse and then put the brake on the buggy and told everyone to dismount.

"Go get a piece of candy kids, then come back out and watch the wagon and buggy while we talk."

He flipped a penny at each one, and they left, looking around until Claire pointed the way to the candy on the counter at the back of the store.

"What is it darling," Mother complained.

The adults had huddled for thirty minutes before Ida Vandemere came down the stairs. "He is sleeping. Lynne, she is as pretty as you said. You are the handsome businessman she married?"

Claire immediately smiled, liking the tall, haggard woman. Henry nodded, "We're Henry and Claire Lambton."

"Henry," the woman gasped and looked like she would fall. Phillip reached out and wheeled a lidded keg over for her to plop down onto.

"Her husband is Henrique, or Henry too," Phillip said.

Claire pulled at Henry's arm and he felt the same chill. He moved his arm around her back to pull her closer.

Robert looked out at the children, who were arguing about who had bought the most candy for their penny as they climbed up and down on the wagon, buggy, and even the backs of the patient oxen. "We're losing daylight. You said it would take at least four hours to reach your place, maybe more with the oxen."

"Will you do it? Will you stay and help me run the store until Henry, until Henrique is better? I do not know you, ja, but you look like good people. I can give you room and board. I will divide the profit from all sells."

"We have a lot of items still to sell from my Boston store," Henry said.

"Ja," she said to the serious young man. "Sell them, keep all your profit. I vish I could pay you, but splitting the profit on our stock is the best I can do."

"So you're staying," Robert asked, surprised that Henry was considering it. "We had hoped Claire and you would settle next to us." He sounded so hurt, Claire moved from Henry into her Father's arms.

"I want to stay. I have a lot of ideas for the store, if Mrs. Vandemere will allow us to run things our way, then I would like to stay."

"What is your way?"

"Well, I would clean the windows and in one display the clothing. Move the groceries to the front and display them in the other window and on the street. The rest, I think we could organize into departments, so it would be easier for your customers to find things and for the clerk to wait on them more efficiently."

Henry stared at Claire as though she had grown a new head. "You want to stay?"

Mrs. Vandemere was finding her feet, her hands on her hips. "You can't just come into our business and take over running things."

Claire shook her head. "Then I'm sorry, Ida, but we can't stay. There is no way to make money with everything such a mess. You've heard my Father, he would rather we stay together."

"Ja, ja," the woman looked around frantically. "Everything is going to hell after the Morrison's built that damn place across the street. The miners are moving on. Too many thieves and killing Indians. Not enough business anymore, not for two stores here in Butte."

She turned to storm away from the travelers. "Stay, go, I have to see to my Henry," she stopped halfway up the stairs. "You look like an angel, but you are a damn, hard businesswoman, ja?"

"Ja," Claire said with a smile.

◇◇◇

Claire washed the last of the dust from the second large window. Her back ached and her arms were sore. She hated to think what the strong vinegar was doing to her hands. Phillip hadn't spoken to her. He had spent the hot afternoon carrying things up to their new bedroom, or setting them aside to display in the store while Claire finished cleaning up. At least Father, Phillip, and the boys had made quick work of unloading and moving all the belongings inside the store.

If Father hadn't been in such a rush to reach the Gant homestead before nightfall, Claire could have tried to explain again why she thought staying was the right thing.

But how did you convince so many angry people that you were doing the right thing when you couldn't convince the man who was supposed to love you? Married one day, and already Henry was probably regretting his decision.

The positive thing about the day was how busy they had been. Maybe it was seeing a pretty girl working in the store window, more likely just small town curiosity. But everyone seemed to have to stop by the Vandemeres to buy something. Henry waited on most. But Claire climbed out of the window a couple of times to greet and help the women with their shopping.

She had forgotten how much she enjoyed being a clerk. Every time she made a sale, she felt like she had won a game of checkers or dominoes. If Henry were honest, he was happier talking to customers, helping them with their purchases. At least, more than he had been since leaving Boston. Was he really excited about building a house near the Gants and becoming a rancher? Claire shook her head.

She knew she had made the right decision. Fate had taken a hand and set them down here for a reason. It wasn't just to care for the sad couple upstairs. Henry was a businessman, just like Lynne had described him. She knew if anyone could run this store at a profit, it would be her husband.

Claire tried to straighten up, arching her back to relax the muscles. When she thought of all the tearful farewells, she wanted to cry again. She had never been apart from her parents. Then saying goodbye to her friend, when she had only reunited with Lynne made her gasp. And then there were the children. She had known they would all return to live with their sister, but she hadn't realized how quiet it would be without Tom and Jim arguing or Mary Anne singing or telling her some fanciful tale from her books.

Henry came down the stairs, turning at the waist to stretch his back and shoulders. He pulled his left arm across, putting pressure on his shoulder until he felt the tightness give. He repeated it with the other arm. He paused, wondering despite himself where the other Henry had landed in his attempted plummet to death. He could understand how a man could be driven to such desperation. A man who had traveled around the world so far into the unknown, built this wonderful building, and then seen all his work and dreams vanish.

Henry stood still, watching Claire try to stretch out her aches as well. In the fading light, she was split, one side still illuminated by the evening sun, the other half black in shadow. His little virgin bride. She had worked like a slave all day, stopping only to cry or to wait on a customer.

Had he thought her fragile and helpless? He had been wrong on every count. At least no one had called her silly goose today.

Henry walked past her and moved the barrel back inside before closing and locking the front door. He wondered how long she would let him continue his charade of being angry.

As he closed and locked the back door, he turned to see her standing face to face with him. Toe to toe, she was a head shorter than him, even with the little heeled shoes and tallest mountain of blonde hair.

"Henry, I'm sorry," but she didn't get to finish since he had her in his arms, close against him, kissing her apology away. When he finished, she hung limply in his arms.

"God, you irritating woman. I wish I still had enough strength to carry you upstairs and show you what I think of taking orders from a woman. But I can't, I'm exhausted and utterly famished."

They dined on cheese from the big wedge under glass, crackers from the barrel, and wine from a big brown bottle. It was red and had a wonderful fruity taste. Ignoring her smelly hands, Claire cut another wedge for each of them, then took an apple out to polish and slice.

"I don't think I can sleep without a bath. Smell me," she held out her hand and Henry pretended to bite it. "Nope, not really a pickle, but I think I want one. You?"

Claire giggled. "Just a bite, maybe."

"There's a pump in the kitchen. I'll bring up a bucket. Don't think I have the strength to go get the pitcher, fill it, and carry it back up. Did you notice where they had the buckets?"

"In the middle, on the left side of the store, but you better take a candle or lamp to see. There's a lot of stuff in boxes along every aisle."

Henry left, and she heard him bang into at least one crate before returning with a large new bucket.

She listened to him filling the bucket with water. Remembering the couple upstairs, she found a plate and loaded it with cheese, crackers, another sliced apple. She waited until he returned and held to his shirt as she followed him back up the stairs.

Claire stopped and knocked on the door, waiting again. When Ida opened it, Claire looked inside and sighed. Someone needed to empty the slop bucket. But for now, she settled for passing the tired woman the plate of food, then handed her the half bottle of red wine.

"I will try to cook something tomorrow. But this is what we ate for supper. Do you need me to keep a tally of the things we use?"

"Na, this gude. Goodnight hard angel."

Claire managed a crooked smile and backed out as the woman closed the door.

CHAPTER FORTY-ONE

Claire woke to see Henry staring at her again. When he leaned down to kiss her he groaned and fell back. Claire started to roll over to kiss him and heard herself groan as well. Lying side by side, they both smiled. Henry lifted her hand in his and kissed it. “Maybe today will be easier.”

She could tell from Henry’s expression he didn’t believe it either. Claire forced herself to roll out of bed. She quickly pulled on the brown dress she had worn to cross the plains. Somehow, this morning, she was only sure it wouldn’t show the dirt as easily. While she sent Henry down to find the stove and get a fire started, she faced the unpleasant task of assisting Ida to clean and air out the room. At least she was used to waking before the sun.

As repulsive as the task was, she quickly took care of the worst chore, then returned to open the curtains and window and help Ida in moving her husband into a more comfortable position. While she worked, she shared Bonnie’s travails and how the hardest part came in overcoming the addiction to the doctor's prescription. Leaving the woman deep in thought, she descended to the kitchen. If he had a difficult time of lighting the stove, Henry didn't complain and for that she stopped and kissed him.

The impulsive gesture brought a smile to his face. Like her, moving about had helped to ease his stiffness. This time when he took her into his arms, the moan was in pleasure. Claire washed up at the kitchen pump, delighted to see the little store had been outfitted with the latest conveniences. It had a deep, white porcelain wash sink with indoor water and a wide white wood-burning stove. The stove had three eyes and a warming plate for the kettle. Henry explained what he had figured out about the stove. Soon she had coffee on, oats boiling, and bacon frying.

"Well, the one thing I can say about living in a store. One doesn't have to go far to find anything."

Unlike the rest of the store, the only light in the kitchen came from a small window over the sink. They sat at the tiny table across from each other and Henry smiled. "This feels like the beginning of our new life, doesn't it."

Claire stared into his eyes and wished the table wasn't between them so she could kiss him again. Instead, she blushed with pleasure as he reached across to take her hand as she reached for his. "I never knew you were so romantic, Henry."

"There's a lot we still need to learn about each other." They were both startled when a cobweb covered bell over the sink rang.

This time it was Henry who took the tray up to the sick room while Claire cleared up. She was just washing the last dish when he brought down a tray with dirty ones from upstairs. He started to apologize, but realized she was singing as she sat the whole mess into the sink, tray and all. "Look at this. It's such a pleasure, the sink is at waist height, no bending or trying to wet them with a small amount of water. And it's so deep. Look at all the suds. Feel." She grabbed and plunged his fingers beneath the water.

"Warm, how did you?"

"The well that you showed me, under the warming plate. We are finished cooking for now, so I used the hot water. Look how much cleaner the dishes are. Darling, isn't it wonderful. So civilized," she gushed and Henry swirled his bride around in the tiny kitchen.

"You, my darling, are too easily pleased. Go ahead, tell me what your plans are for today so I can get back to work."

Claire took a pad of paper and a pencil and quickly drew a grid. "What do you think? The clothing department on the right or left."

He stared at his pensive bride, noticed the curls were already escaping along her neck. This time he didn't resist temptation, but bent to kiss her there. His reward was to feel her vibrate under his lips. Smiling, he slipped his arm around her waist, "I liked the way you described it to Ida, grocery shop on the left, haberdashery on the right."

Claire leaned back to escape his roaming hands. "I love the way you say haberdashery," she said with a giggle as he repeated the word before kissing her.

For an instant Claire felt dizzily drunk. This time when the bell rang, Henry swore.

"You're right, darling. We'll have to put a stop to that or we won't be able to run the store," she said.

"Leave it to me," he said.

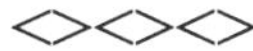

Today seemed worse than yesterday. Claire had finished all the dishes and they had barely made headway in clearing the front right corner merchandise before customers began to arrive. When an amazingly tall couple entered, they began their usual pattern of waiting on them when the woman said in a beautiful Swedish accent.

"No darling, I'd like this charming, handsome man to serve me. You can take care of Johnson's list."

Claire stared at Henry. He had discarded his coat again in the warm room and wore his white shirt with the sleeves rolled up nearly to his elbow. Claire had just been admiring the way her tanned husband looked with the neck of his shirt unbuttoned and his tie keeping company with the suit coat.

She flared red as she saw the beautiful blonde look at him with the same interest.

The tall giant beside her laughed and Claire had the good grace to smile and curtsy, turning her head to look back at them as she took the miner's shopping list.

She ground the pound of coffee for the miner as she heard his wife's silvery laughter. "Don't mind, Helga. She likes to flirt, is all. Believe me, she don't need no other man."

Claire's face turned bright red as she stared up at the tall man, his meaning evident from where he held his hand. His booming laughter made Helga stop and walk back to the other couple. Henry seized the opportunity to grab his tie and coat. By the time he had walked back to the grocery counter, he was neatly covered and proper looking.

This time, when he sent Claire with Helga, he filled the rest of Johnson's order without objection.

Claire was surprised to find she liked the big blonde. When she learned that Helga had come to try on the dress Lynne was sewing for her, she became even more excited. By the time the miner returned carrying a large tote of goods, the two women had become friends.

"I'll have to scold Lynne for not telling me she was making clothes. I have some great ideas for the latest fashions and maybe we can collaborate."

"I would love that, design one for me. I love the detail on your dress, but not the color. You are too pretty I think for such a plain dress."

Claire beamed, "Well, we only arrived in town yesterday. Taking over the store for the Vandemeres was sudden. Lynne asked us to help her friends, Ida and Henrique."

Helga motioned to Johnson. "I will go up, you want to come?"

He nodded, only setting down the tote when Henry offered to take it.

Henry rolled his eyes as the couple disappeared inside the Vandemere's room.

Claire raised a hand to smother a laugh. "What a woman," she whispered.

Henry shook his head. "And I never thought there could be a woman more endowed than Bonnie."

Without thinking Claire reached out to pinch his waist. It was what she and the girls always did to each other when one would irritate the other. Henry yelped in surprise.

"I'm shocked at you. A gentleman never notices that sort of thing."

Henry laughed, but he didn't reach for her waist to pinch. "Maybe, but a man always does."

"Well, it's not what a new husband should be noticing."

She had that delightful, dizzy sensation as she looked down to be sure she hadn't imagined his hands on her breasts. She knew she was lucky he stood between her and the window to the world.

"It is the first thing a new husband notices, believe me, when his mind is on nothing else."

To escape the torture of his hands Claire pressed flat against his chest as he held, then kissed her.

It was nearly a month later before the store was completely rearranged. Claire knew she would still be finding things to change if they stayed all year. The last of Henry's goods from Boston were now carefully shelved or displayed. In the window were three dress forms – all that Ida had in stock – each wearing a recent Boston gown. The first week, Claire had sent word to Lynne, along with an order for a bustled gown for Helga and a request for a new one for herself. Both arrived the next week with Shorty and Bane as messengers. The strange men teased each of the couple, but by now, Claire took it in stride.

Western folk seemed far less reserved. At first she had been insulted or offended whenever a stranger made a personal remark. Now she realized that most were just trying to be friendly. It was their way of getting acquainted quicker to move on to meaningful conversations when they saw so very few people.

When the-would-be miners from the wagon train finally reached town, Claire was delighted to learn that she and Henry were not the only newlyweds. George King had married Faye Brewer, the cousin he had asked her about so many months ago at the dance. Cobb and Gerald were still single. The men were polite and congratulated Henry and her on their marriage as they shopped for new denims to wear to the mine fields.

Claire waited on the cousins. After congratulating Faye, she learned James Temple had ‘paired up’ with Dorothy Brewer. It was an expression Claire didn’t like. It meant the same in the west as it did in the east and she told Dorothy she was a fool not to demand the man marry her. Dorothy, surprised Claire when she spoke behind her, “Maybe I’m the one who won’t accept him.”

Claire had been just as blunt. “Well, when you get in the family way, any husband is better than none.”

The girl had left angry, but Claire could see she was considering her options again. Leray Raglon came through the door, even though Claire could see his mother going into the Morrison’s store across the street. “Well, looks like I was right about you two,” Leray said.

His comments were offensive, but Claire was prepared to ignore them. Henry looked ready to fight the man. The other men defended her honor as well and Leray backed down and left.

Now each day, the Vandemerees came down to help in the store. Ida had taken her advice. It was difficult, but she had gradually reduced Henrique's dose to once a night. Claire had never known the little man before. With his bald head and glasses, he did not look like a husband the tall Dutch woman would have chosen. She and Henry had moved the guns to the far right corner, far away from the kitchen and into an area with no direct access. Their store had not been burglarized, but the Morrison's had been, twice. Besides all that store's money, the thieves had taken guns and ammunition.

Ida told them she always made bank deposits at the end of the day. Only a fool left the money where thieves could get it. Henry and Claire went to the bank first thing the next morning and deposited almost all of their foolish money.

Now Henrique sat behind the gun counter to dispense ammunition and demonstrate the guns. They had a special wheelchair for him and once Henry carried him down and put him in it, he did not leave it. The broken leg was elevated, the broken arm braced by a folding chair arm.

Ida took over the groceries and seemed to enjoy sitting at the front of the store, chatting with the customers. Occasionally, her Henry would yell and she would bustle over to him. Then Claire would work in the grocery section. Most of the time she preferred to work in the other sections, especially when one of the ladies would come in and she would take care of their fashion needs. Henry kept their funds from the sale of their merchandise separate from those of the general store. To date, the sales had been fairly evenly divided. When Henry complained that they would soon be out of merchandise, then their profits would be lower, Claire tried to come up with a solution.

From the first night, Claire had turned over the receipts to Ida to tally and record in her books. Claire kept a running tally of all supplies though, and as things began to dwindle, she would inform Ida and the woman would write orders to their suppliers. When Claire asked, the woman shared all the information with the young girl but looked dubious. Ida had a good head for figures and it was clear she was the one who had wanted the store. She still did not think a pretty little one like Claire could do the job.

Claire was surprised that the couple had no complaints about the way they conducted the business or by any of the changes they had made. Claire had organized the store into departments and kept both window displays up to date. There were always items of produce that would not survive the day. She used these to cook their meals, usually soup or oven roasted meals that could finish in the fancy oven while she worked.

Ida liked to bake. Now she was down, the smell of fresh bread, or if she came down early enough, hot doughnuts filled the air. Claire talked her into teaching her how to bake and to make the doughnuts in the oven. Soon she spent the early time on coming down each morning in baking the bread she had stirred up the night before. Customers loved buying the fresh bread and after she begged Ida, the fresh doughnuts.

Claire told her they should add cakes and pies too, since they sold so well.

"You bake all you want, my old feet, don't need the money so much," Ida said.

Claire did, then told Henry her new idea. "I think fresh bread every day, but maybe Cake only on Monday, Pie Tuesday, Doughnuts on Wednesday…"

"Strudel Wednesday, Crumcake Thursday, and Poffertjes Friday, you say Fritters?" she looked at the startled girl. Doughnuts Saturday, draw an even bigger crowd."

Claire laughed. "You think it's a good idea?"

"Ja, people come more that follow their stomachs, not just to see the prettiest blue-eyes out west. "Put up a sign, say -- if it ain't Dutch, it ain't much. Henry, you paint the sign."

The mousy little man in the back made a squeak. "What, what must I do now?"

Henry stopped and kissed his pretty wife. Claire wondered how much else Ida heard or saw from her high stool and blushed. Henry was driving her mad. All day he was stealing kisses or pinching her when she bent over, but at night, he went to sleep. Only on Saturday night, she blushed at the thought. But today was only Wednesday.

She saw the sparks in his eyes and knew he was having the same thoughts as she was. For a minute she wondered, Ida had said the prettiest blue eyes out west and Claire had taken it as a compliment for herself. But no man had bluer, more teasing eyes than Henry Lambton. And today, those eyes were tormenting her.

The doorbell rang and Claire stepped away from him.

Helga snapped at her husband. “Go see how little Henry is doing, I’ll check out the young one myself.”

Claire watched the big man laugh and slap his wife’s ample bottom. Today the breathtaking woman had a basket with her son inside. But when she set him down, he started crying. “He wants his Papa,” Helga said. Claire watched as the giant miner returned and carried off the basket and boy. The baby had stopped crying instantly.

Lynne was expecting. She had shown Claire the special drawstrings worked into her pretty lilac dress as she shared the news. What would her son call Phillip-- Papa, Dada, or Father? For a second, she wondered if she had a child, what would he call Henry? Lost in sweet thought, she stood at the grocery counter and sighed.

"Never mind, Henry. I'll let your pretty little wife help me today. I need some new...," she didn't finish as Henry blushed and excused himself to go back to check on the soup.

Claire looked around for Ida, saw the woman nod, and walked over to help the towering blonde. "I have a new design to show you. With your décolletage, it could be stunning."

"Fine, but what has you looking down in the mouth. Married only a month to such a handsome, attentive young man."

"What kind of undergarments did you need?" Claire asked.

Claire lifted down the box that were the first thing she had ordered from San Francisco. When she opened the box with the newest step-ins, the woman was delighted by the silk and lace garments. She especially liked the ones in colorful silk.

"Maybe these are what your Henry needs. Come on, tell Helga everything. I am an expert on men and love."

As Claire blushed again, the woman bent down and moved so she was seated in the customer's chair Henry had added the week before.

"I don't know, it must be me."

"He does seem very attentive, are you sure you're not imagining it?"

Claire looked back toward the rear of the store, watched Henry sip the hot soup from the ladle. When he saw her, he turned his back to them. "We, he, we only make love on Saturday night. I don't know if that is normal, the way it should be. I daren't ask Ida. She thinks…" Claire blushed again and knelt beside the chair, looking up at Helga's expansive assets. Henry had insisted he didn't need any more than her own bosom, but he obviously admired Helga and Bonnie more.

Helga laughed, placed a hand on the sad girl's tidy hair in its little bun, and then laughed again. "You are so precious, but your Henry is English. Tell me what you do each night, to get ready for bed."

Claire half rose out of her crouch and saw her husband had now filled a bowl and was eating soup and bread like a guilty child. "I go up, take off my clothes behind the screen, put on my gown, and get in bed. Henry comes up later, after locking up and checking everything again. He waits until he thinks I'm asleep, reading and smoking his pipe. Then he gets into bed and stares at me."

They heard Johnson's booming voice and then Henry standing, saying of course, "Join me."

Claire tried to imagine the giant fitting in the tiny space behind the Vandermere's table but couldn't.

"Quickly, if I don't get Johnson, the rest of you will have nothing to eat for lunch. Tonight, wait on him."

"He would wonder why," Claire stated.

“Fine, stop by and visit the Vandermeers, make up some excuse. Wait until you hear him go into your room.”

Claire nodded and started to protest. “I don’t want to do anything that will make him think I’m a trollop.”

Again Helga laughed. “Silly, little bride. Instead of the screen,” she rose and escorted Claire to the counter where Claire rushed to box the three pair of underwear and chemise, and wrapped them for the woman, all the time listening. “How much you will have to take off, you will find out. He is young, probably no more than a shoe or stocking. But you will stand by the fireplace.”

“We have a small black stove, but it’s not lit,” Claire protested.

“You raise your foot up, lift your skirt and petticoat out of the way like so.” She demonstrated, revealing her ankle and a glimpse of her other leg. “You struggle, you remove one shoe. He notices when you bend over?”

Claire blushed. She certainly had the little blue marks to prove it. Ever since the day she had pinched him, he had taken to surprising her with little pinches as well.

“That is it. You undress slowly, maybe ask for help with your buttons. But I seriously doubt you will get that far.”

“How, I don’t understand?”

“He is a man. When he sees you, it will raise his attention.” She raised her hand and Claire blushed even more. “Once you raise his attention, the rest will follow as the night the day.”

Claire thanked her as Helga called in a loud voice. “Johnson and Albert, time to go.”

Impulsively Claire hugged her and Helga laughed. “Men, they are all so simple. You will see.”

THE END

EPILOGUE - August, 1877

Henry complained that they couldn't leave the store, but Claire insisted. She had waited too long to visit her parents and her friends. The chance to travel on past the Gant's ranch to Fort Keogh to visit Bonnie, her brothers and husband and to see the new children she had written about was now. They needed her to help raise Bonnie's dream cabin.

All along the train ride to Butte, Claire mused on the reasons while Henry napped. Claire knew how devastated Bonnie was at losing her first child. Ever the warrior, Bonnie had written with tears on the page about this new loss. Claire could not wait to hug her again. Bonnie had claimed God must have known how empty her heart was because he had sent not one, but two beautiful boys for her to love and raise. The two were children of a woman, Stella Jamison, who had taken her own life after a brutal rape. It was such a sad story, but Claire knew the two boys could not have more loving parents to raise them.

Then there was Lynne and Phillip's new son. Claire could not wait to see and hold him. Mary Anne had insisted he was the most beautiful boy in the world. The words made her smile as she read them. She knew if she had a little boy, he would be the most handsome in Butte. That was the other reason Henry was reluctant to make the journey. Claire had reminded him how Lynne drove cattle to Ogden when she was pregnant. A woman wasn't a fragile egg.

Still, as she planned, she was glad that the train route had been extended and they would only have an hour long buggy ride to reach the Gant's ranch. Her parents would drive from Helena to the ranch and visit with all the children until they arrived. Then Phillip had sent a message by wire. They would meet them along the route and all would travel on to the Fort by train. Henry had surrendered.

The first leg of the journey had been quiet. There were only three miners sharing the car as they traveled back to the mines after a long but lucky weekend. At least from the way the men talked they were lucky. They hadn't gambled away all their pay and would have money left even after the train trip. Claire wondered if her old suitors had found any luck at mining

Claire remembered the rush to leave this morning. She had expected that Henrique would be the one to be upset, but it was Ida, who cried when they said goodbye. Claire reminded her they would only be gone one week. With luck, she hoped that it would become an annual occasion. Surely they deserved one week away from the store.

Still, until the train pulled to a halt beside the track, she couldn't hold onto her nerves. She was so anxious to see everyone. It was nearly six weeks since her parents had visited town with the children. Claire had so much to tell them. The train slowed along the flat line of track where a buggy full of people waited.

The first to rush inside the open door when the train stopped were the two boys. Tom and Jim were now taller than Claire. Twelve years old, anyone would have thought they were older. She wondered if the next time they met, they would be taller than Henry. She was amazed when Tom held out his hand and she squealed and backed into Henry.

"You brats," she protested. Jim laughed and then apologized, "It's harmless Aunt Claire. Just a horny toad. When Tom saw him beside the track, we had to catch him for you."

"For me?" she gasped, finally brave enough to lean forward. Tom held the horrible gray animal out again and it wiggled and she squealed and jumped back into Henry's arms.

"None of that boys," Henry scolded. "She's in a delicate condition."

Mary shot inside, just in time to hear Henry's announcement. She turned and yelled at the couple fussing with the small bundle. "They're going to have a baby, too."

Lynne handed the baby to Phillip as she charged inside. "You boys, I am going to pin your ears back, frightening her and…"

"Claire, I am so happy for you. When are you due, come on, sit down. Boys get rid of that nasty thing! You're going to get warts."

While Lynne rushed her friend off to a row of seats apart, Henry looked at the children, then surprised them and himself as he held his arms open wide. They all hugged and Claire looked back in amazement as she saw his damp eyes and those of the children. She smiled as she watched Tom slip the toad into her too proper husband's pocket.

Phillip came in last, helping her Father and Mother in and sending the boys back for the bags. "Did I hear you've made an announcement? It's about time, Henry."

Henry blushed, swallowing the words 'we've been trying,' but Phillip was grinning as though he had said them. Henry shook hands with his Father-in-law, who embraced him. Then Claire's Mother ignored his hand and took a big hug, reaching up to kiss him. They had been to visit twice before. But Claire's father had been busy and pushed too. He and mother had moved to Helena, where he had become indispensable to the mine owner who bought his equipment in St. Louis. It seemed the harder he worked, the happier and fitter he became. As Mother worked her way up to Claire and Lynne, Father grabbed and shook the two boys, hauling them into hugs. As soon as he released them, Mary Anne reached up to hug his neck.

“Well, this is coming at just the right time. I need to talk to you young men about an interesting proposition,” Father said.

Mary Anne joined the women and Phillip carefully handed the little girl his son and took his place with the men at the other end of the car.

Claire was so happy, she was alternating between laughing and crying. Each of the women took turns patting and hugging her and doing the same thing. Finally Lynne reached over for her son as the train lurched into motion.

“What about your buggies?” Claire asked as they moved past. The driver in the first buggy waved and Claire sat back down. Of course, Shorty and Bane were driving them home.

Lynne again smiled, for a girl they called Goose, Claire was always observing and thinking about details. Together, they had worked out a great system of making custom clothes. Judging by the sales and amount of work, they were dressing most of the women in Butte.

<><><>

The baby was asleep and Claire was trading recipes with the women when Henry yelled and stood up. Claire was drowsy but she still enjoyed his dance as much as everyone else. She was astonished when her usually reserved husband went after one boy, then the other, not stopping until he had stuffed the toad down Jim's neck.

"Hey, I didn't put it in there." Jim jumped up and straddled his giggling brother and with Henry's help, managed to stuff the frog down the front of his shirt.

It was not until the baby started crying that Phillip and Robert got the three settled down.

"Hey, if I get warts on my neck," Jim said.

"They'll be on my back," Tom said.

"You deserve them," Robert said. "You're lucky he didn't stick it down your pants."

As the boys looked in horror at each other, Phillip said, "Now get rid of that thing."

While the boys carefully carried it to the back of the car, Phillip leaned over to whisper to the other men. "They're really a lizard, not a toad."

Mother called the boys over and told them to bring her bag. All watched as each lad blushed in embarrassment, but shed their shirts so she could wash them clean with alcohol. "This may or may not work, but at least we can try," she said.

"You sure you want to go into business with those two?" Phillip asked.

"I must be crazy. But you work with them every day, what do you think?" Robert said.

Phillip made a face, "I'll miss them. They give a better day's work than most men I've met."

"Claire will love having them close again. But will Mary Anne be able to stay without them." The men looked over to where the little girl had rocked the baby back to sleep singing with her small, sweet voice.

"Lynne will never give up all three. Just be prepared for her and the girl to come for lots of visits." Phillip turned to stare at Robert. "You sure you want to start another career. A stable is a hard business to make a living at."

"Well, the mines are petering out already. My work installing equipment is past. The owner just keeps me on salary to play chess with him. Besides, I think with the boys help, designing wagons and buggies will keep us in meat and potatoes for a long time."

"We've noticed a lot less traffic. We used to have at least one wagon train a week. Then the train would bring another car full of get rich quick men," Henry said.

"Are you struggling?" Phillip asked.

"No, we've had more business each week than the one before. The new store across the street, they're closing up and planning to move. I asked the Vandermeers if they wanted to buy it, and they said certainly not." The men stared and nodded as they listened to Henry talk, but neither said anything.

"The Vandermerees even talked to me about buying their place so they can go back to San Francisco." Henry added with pride. Both men stared at him, curious if he would do it.

"Claire thinks we should seize the opportunity. She doesn't think we should buy the Morrison's store, but she has already calculated what it would cost for them to pack up their goods and ship it to Ogden where they plan to move. She made them an offer for all their stock which was only a few dollars less than that amount. They promised to give us an answer when we get back next week. Will probably take them that long to know it doesn't make sense to do all the work packing stuff to ship."

"If you do, will save you a ton on shipping as well. Increase your profits on the goods," Robert said, thoughtfully.

"She has as good a head for business as her father," Henry said. Both men sat smiling at the pretty blonde girl with pride.

Phillip laughed, "Looks like you married the goose that lays golden eggs."

Henry smiled again, "I think Claire will like that one."

<><><>

As soon as they approached the off-load ramp at the fort, they saw them. “My goodness, he is tall and good-looking, isn’t he,” Lynne said.

Claire had tried to prepare Lynne for her first meeting with Calum Douglas. It was hard to remember how they had been separated before Calum came to Boston. Lynne had arrived in this wild country first, married first, and it was not surprising that she had the first child.

Claire stared at Bonnie’s face, taking in her unique beauty. She was anxious to look into her eyes to know whether to greet her with sympathy or joy. The tall woman held a large baby in one arm who had dark skin and hair, Calum had a hand on a rambunctious little blonde boy who looked about two or three.

“Well, leave it to you, Bonnie, to get ahead of us again,” Lynne said, sailing out to the people with a smile on her face. Mother and Father kept the three children pinned as Henry helped his wife to the door. “Do you need me?” but she stepped down just as quickly as Lynne.

The two abandoned husbands stared after their wives, knowing how excited they had been about this trip and not wanting to spoil their reunion. They noticed the tall soldier now had both the squirming little boys in his arms and looked challenged to keep them from following their mother.

Both men swallowed and brushed at their own eyes as they saw the three girls embrace tearfully. Laughing and hugging like crazy fools, all three were talking at once.

"Well, he's taller than Bonnie, but do you really think he's all that good-looking," Phillip asked Henry as they descended and walked around their wives to help the Major with his charges. Henry shrugged.

The children and older couple followed next. But before the twins could unload the bags, two young privates with sparse ginger whiskers ran up to hug the three McKinney children. A year later and the boys were still below enlistment age at fifteen and seventeen.

Claire looked around, saw the platform now crowded with all the people she loved. After this baby, she definitely planned to have another three or four. Henry had argued she was an only child and they only needed one. Claire smiled, now she knew how to get around those objections.

Lynne and Bonnie were comparing children and Claire tried to answer without slighting any of them. Bonnie's two sons, Sean and Johnny of all names, were both handsome but wiggly boys. They both favored in looks, but one could see baby Johnny was part Indian. Was Bonnie naïve to think that it wouldn't matter? No, she knew Willow had never told herself stories. She always saw the truth, but bent like a willow to adjust and be happy. If it were possible to raise a half-breed son who was kind and happy, Bonnie would find a way.

Lynne's son, now he was awake, was as beautiful as Mary Anne had claimed. Claire saw he had Phillip's looks and dark wavy hair, but the child had the most amazing light gray eyes. Bonnie said, "Oh Lynne, you clever girl. You've really created a heart-breaker here."

Lynne laughed, "He is beautiful, isn't he, but so are your lads. And they're both so brawny and fit."

"I'm pregnant," Claire said, not wanting to feel left out.

Bonnie lifted her off the ground in an embrace. "Oh Claire, why didn't you write me?"

"Well, I just found out last week. I thought it would be more fun to surprise you with the news."

"With all the commotion about the toad, you forgot to tell me, when are you due?" Lynne asked.

"Next October, at least that's what the doctor thinks," Claire confessed, blushing.

"You're six months, and so tiny," Lynne said.

"And you never knew," Bonnie teased, "What a goose?"

THE END

DEAR READER

I hope you enjoy reading this book as much as I enjoyed writing it. If you like it and are so inclined, I would appreciate a kind review at

http://www.amazon.com/dp/B0122DD7LQ

If you find errors or things that I should change, please send me suggestions at biery35@gmail.com

CURRENT WORK ON AMAZON

Western Wives Series

The Milch Bride,
http://www.amazon.com/dp/B00JC6DOLK
From Darkness to Glory,
http://www.amazon.com/dp/B00LG1ZPMK
Valley of Shadows,
http://www.amazon.com/dp/B00RPTXMU4
Bright Morning Star,
http://www.amazon.com/dp/B0122DD7LQ

Myths Retold Series

Glitter of Magic,
http://www.amazon.com/dp/B00TE9P6DO
The Mermaid's Gift,
http://www.amazon.com/dp/B00W6FCTME

Mysteries

Potter's Field,
http://www.amazon.com/dp/B00KH7Q8C0

Killing the Darlings,
http://www.amazon.com/dp/B00IRRMO2A

Edge of Night,
http://www.amazon.com/dp/B00J0LLQC6

Other Novels

He's My Baby Now,
http://www.amazon.com/dp/B00N1X6ZFW

Will Henry,
http://www.amazon.com/dp/B00K5POM0O

Chimera Pass,
http://www.amazon.com/dp/B00KALJYRY

Short Stories and Novellas

Ghost Warrior,
http://www.amazon.com/dp/B00M62NBEC

Happy Girl,
http://www.amazon.com/dp/B00MHHXMEA

The Revenooer,
http://www.amazon.com/dp/B00U25K5BW